WHAT'LL I DO WITH THE Baby-o?

WHAT'LL I DO WITH THE

Baby-o?

Nursery Rhymes, Songs, and Stories for Babies

Compiled by

JANE COBB

Illustrated by

KATHRYN SHOEMAKER

Vancouver, British Columbia, Canada

Cover design by Teresa Bubela
Cover Model: Ginger Mullen and seven-month-old daughter, Brigit Warnica
Photography by David Cooper
Author photo by Myrna Cobb
Illustrations by Kathryn Shoemaker

Enclosed CD co-produced by Jane Cobb and Paul Gitlitz
Sound engineer: Paul Gitlitz
Vocals by Natasha Neufeld, Paul Gitlitz, and Jane Cobb

Printed in Winnipeg, Manitoba, Canada by Hignell Printing Ltd.

First Printing 2007

Published by Black Sheep Press

P.O. Box 2392
349 West Georgia St.
Vancouver, BC V6B 3W7
Canada

P.O. Box 2217
Point Roberts WA 98271-2217
USA

Tel: (604) 731-2653
Fax: (604) 731-2653
Email: orders@blacksheeppress.com
Web: www.blacksheeppress.com

Canadian Cataloguing in Publication Data

Cobb, Jane
What'll I do with the Baby-o? Nursery Rhymes, Songs, and Stories for Babies / compiled by Jane Cobb; illustrated by Kathryn Shoemaker.

Accompanied by a CD.
Includes bibliographical references and index.
ISBN 978-0-9698666-1-9

1. Language acquisition. 2. Language acquisition–Parent participation. 3. Early childhood education–Activity programs. 4. Children's Libraries–Activity Programs. 5. Education, Preschool–Activity programs. 6. Parent and infant. 7. Family literacy programs. 8. Infants–Development. 9. Play. I. Shoemaker, Kathryn E. II. Title.

PZ8.3.C63 2006 428.0083'2 C2006-905540-8

This book is dedicated to all my babies,
with the wish that they will grow up to be happy, and healthy, citizens of the world.

And it is dedicated to my mother, who still likes to sing with me.

—Jane

I have many people to thank for helping me with the production of this book. First of all the families who welcomed me into their lives, and taught me so many things about parenthood. Second, my friend, storyteller, mother, and program partner, Ginger Mullen, who gave me ongoing encouragement and excellent editorial advice (and skipped Brigit's precious afternoon nap the day we went to the photographer's studio). Baby Brigit, for gracing the world with her good humour and beauty. Teresa Bubela, my book designer, for leading me in the right direction. David Dunn, my computer man, for always coming to the rescue. Paul Gitlitz for helping me produce the CD. And I'd like to thank my colleagues at Vancouver Public Library for their brilliance, companionship, and support.

Table of Contents

INTRODUCTION 11

PROGRAM PLANNING 15

PRESENTATION TIPS 23

UNDERSTANDING 27

Baby Brain Development 28

Language Development and Literacy 33

The Role of Books 39

The Power of Nursery Rhymes 42

The Power of Song 45

New Parents 48

Ages and Stages 50

RHYMES 55

Introduction 56

Action Rhymes 57

Action Songs 65

Bouncing Rhymes 75

Circle Games and Dances 83

Face Rhymes 89

Finger Play and Hand Rhymes 93

French Rhymes and Songs 103

Greeting Songs 107

Goodbye Songs 111

Lullabies 115

Rhymes in Other Languages 125

Songs 129

Spanish Rhymes and Songs 137

Story Rhymes 141

Tickling Rhymes 145

Toe-Wiggling and Foot-Patting Rhymes 149

BABIES LOVE BOOKS 153
Introduction 154
Board Books for Babies 156
Board Books for Toddlers 159

SAMPLE ONE-HOUR PROGRAMS
For Parents and Babies, BIRTH TO ONE YEAR 163
Introduction 164
Week One 167
Week Two 170
Sample Questions for the Day 172

FIVE EASY STORIES TO TELL
In Parent-Infant Programs 173
The Bed Just So 174
Did You Feed My Cow? 176
A Mother Mouse and Her Children 177
The Mouse Bride 179
The Wide-Mouthed Frog 181
BIBLIOGRAPHY OF STORIES TO TELL 183

SAMPLE ONE-HOUR PROGRAMS
For Parents and Toddlers, ONE TO TWO YEARS 185
Introduction 186
Week One 189
Week Two 192

FIVE EASY STORIES TO TELL
In Parent-Toddler Programs 195
The Gunniwolf 196
Mr. Wiggle and Mr. Waggle 198
Ruth's Red Jacket 200
Stone Soup 202
The Three Billy Goats Gruff 204
BIBLIOGRAPHY OF STORIES TO TELL 206

SAMPLE HALF-HOUR PROGRAMS 207
Introduction 208

SAMPLE HALF-HOUR PROGRAMS
For Parents and Babies, BIRTH TO ONE YEAR
Week One 211
Week Two 214

SAMPLE HALF-HOUR PROGRAMS
For Parents and Toddlers, ONE TO TWO YEARS
Week One 217
Week Two 220

SPRINKLES: What to Say to Parents 223

PROGRAM RESOURCES 229
Books About Babies For Older Brothers and Sisters 230
Great Read-Alouds for Baby Programs 233
Rhyme Resources for Parents 235
Parenting Resources 237
Sample Parent Response Form 239

END NOTES
Bibliography 240
Acknowledgements 241

INDEXES
To Rhymes and Songs by **TYPE**. 243
To Rhymes and Songs by **FIRST LINE** 248
To Songs Recorded on the Enclosed CD 253

PRAISE FOR I'M A LITTLE TEAPOT! 254
ORDER FORM 255

Introduction

WHAT'LL I DO WITH THE BABY-O? has grown out of my experience delivering programs for parents and caregivers and their infants and young toddlers for the public library over the past twelve years. It has also grown out of my research and reading on infant development, early language and literacy development, and programs that best meet the needs of parents with young children. Like my first book, I'M A LITTLE TEAPOT! PRESENTING PRESCHOOL STORYTIME, which was published in 1996, it came from my desire to bring together a useful collection of material into one book so that I could pass the material on to you. The focus of this book is on material for infants, newborn to two years of age.

I hope WHAT'LL I DO WITH THE BABY-O? will be useful to many. It includes lots of rhymes and stories and booklists and program ideas for people working with parents and their infants in a variety of settings. It also includes what I hope will be useful articles on baby brain development, language and literacy development, the role of books, the power of nursery rhymes, the power of song, an introduction to working with new parents, and the ages and stages of baby development for the beginning programmer.

My goal is to help you provide programs for parents and their infants and young children whoever you are—a Children's Librarian, a Teacher, an Early Childhood Educator, an Infant Childcare Provider, a Speech Language Pathologist, a Teacher in a Parent-Child Mother Goose Program®, or a Parent, and wherever you work—in a library, community centre, preschool, daycare, home, or school, and wherever families meet to learn and have fun with language play.

I came to baby programming with fifteen years experience delivering Preschool and Toddler Programs in the library, but without a lot of experience with babies and their parents, or with library outreach programs. All I knew for sure was that programming for babies and their parents was an important part of public library service, because it brought new families into the library. Then when I started delivering outreach programs for the library, I discovered whole new communities of people who didn't know about public library services for young children.

I had lots of enthusiasm. I knew I liked to sing, I liked poetry and rhyme, and I really loved babies. But I also had lots of questions and I didn't feel adequately prepared, so I did some research to find out what would work best.

I soon learned that successful parent-child programs are aimed at the baby's parents and primary caregivers. My research on early literacy development told me that language play has to be used at home everyday between a loving caregiver and a child if it is to have any impact on a child's development, not just once a week when a family visits the library or other program. The parent's role as baby's first, and most important teacher, therefore, was a critical new piece to add to my understanding, and a critical piece to include in my programs.

Baby programs required a paradigm shift for me. I was so used to addressing the children in my preschool and toddler programs, I had to learn how to relax and address the parents, to include them, communicate with them, and show them how to play in a way that would foster their children's early language and literacy development.

I then became aware that, although I knew hundreds of rhymes, I didn't know enough rhymes that were suitable for infants, so I had to develop a repertoire. While some of the rhymes I used in my preschool programs were also suitable for babies, I needed more interactive rhymes the babies would enjoy. So I combed the resources and discovered a whole new world of rhymes, especially lullabies, that were more appropriate for them. I looked for songs that were fun for the parents to sing in a group. I looked for stories that were fun to tell, and that would introduce parents to the pleasure of listening to stories, and the pleasure of language play, so they could pass that love on to their children.

Then I found a program that provided the approach I needed. I began working in close association with the Toronto-based Parent-Child Mother Goose Program® in 1998. Through this program I learned the methods of teaching I now use in all my baby programs. The teaching in the Parent-Child Mother Goose Program® is directed to the adults who are encouraged to use the rhymes at home every day with their children. The children can be napping or nursing or crawling around during the program and this is fine because the focus is on teaching the parents, with the babies joining in the play when they are ready. This was an entirely new, different, and more relaxed approach to the babies than I had taken previously. And it was a very successful.

Once I started delivering programs using this new approach, I learned that my programs were providing much more than early literacy development for the babies. They were providing much needed support for the parents and families I serve, and were establishing a sense of community connection for those families. They were also instrumental in helping parents establish a loving bond with their children through the use of oral language. And that loving connection is the wellspring of all babies' learning.

In 2003, I became a Trainer for the Parent-Child Mother Goose Program®, and I now offer regular training workshops for people in Vancouver and throughout British Columbia. Many people—Childcare Workers, Librarians, and Health-care Professionals—take this training to learn rhymes, the method of teaching, and the philosophy of working effectively with families with young children. To find out more about this program you can visit the national website at: www.nald.ca/mothergooseprogram.

Many Children's Librarians at Vancouver Public Library, where I work, now use the Parent-Child Mother Goose Program® approach in their Babytime programs inside the library, and in their Mother Goose programs placed outside the library in community centres and health units around the city. We deliver programs for parents and their babies, birth to one year, and for parents and their young toddlers, one to two years. We also deliver the programs in several languages, and many are bilingual. The success of our outreach programs has been enormous: in reaching out to new parents who were not aware of the services of the public library, in drawing those families into the public library, in developing a sense of community for families, in introducing parents to books for babies, and in teaching the parents the skills they need to play in developmentally appropriate ways with their babies.

There are many different types of programs for families with young children, and many different ways to deliver them. This book describes what has worked best for me. Please note that it is not a description of the Parent-Child Mother Goose Program® which involves much more than I am describing here. I highly recommend this program, but I also recommend that you visit many programs to discover what would work best for you and your community.

While writing this book, I had the most fun collecting the rhymes and songs. This is an ongoing pleasure for me. With the odd exception, the rhymes are traditional, mostly British, and were found in many sources. Some I learned orally from other Storytellers, Singers, Children's Librarians, and Parents.

Along with suggestions for using the rhymes, my rhyme title notes include: sources for the rhymes I was able to trace, copyrighted songs and rhymes (used with permission, and listed at the back of the book in the Acknowledgements section), and references to popular audio resources for learning musical tunes. All of these resources should be available at your local public library.

The CD with this book includes some of my favourite songs and rhymes so that you can learn the tunes. I particularly focused on songs that would be difficult for you to find elsewhere.

Bibliographies are provided on each subject so that you can delve more deeply into subjects that interest you. The bibliographies appear after each relevant section and are not repeated at the back of the book.

I have not included many websites because, although there are many excellent resources on the web, websites tend to go in and out of date rather quickly.

Throughout this book, I have used the term early literacy. I do not mean that we are teaching the babies how to read, as the term may imply!

Early literacy is one of the terms used in the research literature to describe the skills children need to acquire, from infancy to age five, in order to be ready to learn how to read when they get to school. The other commonly used terms are: pre-literacy, emergent literacy, and reading readiness. They all have slightly different connotations but they all mean pretty much the same thing. I have chosen to use the term early literacy in order to be compatible with the language used by the Public Library Association's "Every Child Ready to Read® @ your library" initiative.

When using the term parents, I also mean to include primary caregivers.

I have alternated between the masculine and feminine pronouns (he and she) throughout the book when referring to the babies, but of course I always mean to imply both. During program delivery I am mindful to alternate between the masculine and feminine so everyone feels included.

I hope you have as much fun using this book as I have had creating it!

Program Planning

Identifying Your Audience *16*
Why Parents Attend Programs *16*
Babies' Behaviour During Programs *16*
Considering Babies' Ages *16*
Community Needs Assessment *16*
Recruitment *16*
The Purpose of Your Program *17*
Sample Goals and Objectives *17*
Using Your Strengths *18*
Flexibility *18*
Where to Place the Program *18*
Stroller Parking and Storage Space *18*
Scheduling *18*
Scheduling for Working Parents *18*
Including the Dads *19*
Multicultural Programs *19*
Registration Versus Drop-in *19*
How Many People? *19*
How Many Weeks? *19*
How Long Should Each Program Be? *20*
Providing a Snack *20*
How to Select Rhymes *20*
How to Teach a Rhyme *20*
Repetition *21*
Written Words to Rhymes *21*
More than Rhymes *21*
Basic Program Structure *21*
Using Themes *21*
Using Felt Stories and Puppets *22*
Using Recorded Music *22*
Displays *22*
Reading Aloud *22*
The Best Reward *22*

This section provides brief descriptions of topics that will likely arise as you are planning your programs. We all start out with the same questions and challenges. These are my thoughts and solutions.

IDENTIFYING YOUR AUDIENCE

Unlike preschool programs where the parents may or may not be present, and toddler programs where parents are encouraged to stay, babies will definitely be bringing their parents! Parents are key in a baby program. The babies may be sleeping or nursing or crawling around. If they are very young, they will not be able to see you. Most of the time they will not pay any attention to you at all, so it seems silly to pretend they are. This is the first reason I like to direct my attention to the parents.

The second reason is more important. All the latest research on early brain development identifies the parents' role as vital to a child's healthy development. In terms of programming, the research indicates that if the rhymes and songs we use in our programs are to have a positive impact on babies' lives, they must be used by the parent at home with the child everyday, not just once a week when the family comes to a program.

This shift in focus, the inclusion of parents that is required for a successful baby program, often confuses new programmers. If in your whole professional experience you have focused your attention on the children, it will be a paradigm shift for you to focus on the adults. But once you relax in your new role, and once the parents see how much their babies love the rhymes and songs you teach, your programs will run successfully.

WHY PARENTS ATTEND PROGRAMS

Parents like to attend programs with their infants for a variety of reasons: it gets them out of the house, it provides a way for them to meet other parents with young children, and it provides a social opportunity for both them and their children. Libraries and community centres are valuable meeting places for families. Parents also come to programs to learn some rhymes and songs, and some new ways to play with their babies. And they come to learn about early literacy and child development too.

BABIES' BEHAVIOUR DURING PROGRAMS

Babies love to socialize, and they learn a lot by watching and playing with other babies. Once they become mobile, they cannot sit still and focus for long periods of time, so we use short repetitive rhymes to play with them. Throughout the program, the babies may be sleeping, or nursing, or playing, and all this is fine, because the intention of baby programs is to have fun with language and to teach the parents some useful ways to play with their children at home.

CONSIDERING BABIES' AGES

Our audience, then, is comprised of both parents and their babies. And just as it is with any successful children's program, consideration is given during the planning stage, to the ages of the children. Baby programs are particularly demanding in this respect because the needs of children vary so much at the different ages and stages of their development, especially in the first few years.

I like to focus my programs on either: parents with young babies—birth to one, or parents with older babies—one to two. As soon as babies become mobile and start to walk, they need more movement and more stand-up rhymes. I have also found that parents of the youngest babies usually feel safer in segregated age groups where they know their new babies will be protected from the curiosity of older babies who may not have learned how to control their movements or touch gently yet. Babies are so fascinating, especially to other babies!

Mixed age groups are fine and are especially appropriate in smaller communities where there is a small population base to draw from. They are a bit more challenging to plan and manage. You have to plan a variety of activities that will capture the interest of all the ages at each program.

COMMUNITY NEEDS ASSESSMENT

If you are reading this book, you have already developed a sense of what is needed in your community. I have found it useful to go beyond my observations and gather statistics that will help me plan my programs.

I gather demographic statistics from Statistics Canada, and birth statistics from my local Health Units. I call the local schools to find out what languages are spoken in the neighbourhood.

I find out how many daycare centres there are in the community, whether babies are staying at home with their parents for the first year or two, or whether they are in daycare. I then calculate how many programs are offered in the local schools and libraries to service families' needs regarding early literacy.

These are statistics I can also present to my sponsors to justify my request for programs in my communities.

Research on early literacy has shown that the greatest impact is achieved through reaching out to the parents of the youngest children, and to parents with the least education. If you have large numbers of these parents in your community, you will want to consider outreach and use innovative methods of recruitment for your programs.

RECRUITMENT

Besides the usual avenues for advertising a program (the web page, posters, flyers, newsletters), I recruit parents for my baby programs at neighbourhood baby clinics and through referral from the local Community Health Nurses with whom I have developed a relationship. The Community Health Nurses are a great resource and often connect me with families I could not otherwise reach.

THE PURPOSE OF YOUR PROGRAM

You may want to use the program to raise the profile of your institution in the community, to entertain, to teach the parents some rhymes, or to teach the parents some early literacy skills. Whatever your purpose and goals, some thought given to this subject in the initial planning stages will give shape and definition to your program. Your objectives will determine both your content and your style of delivery.

SAMPLE GOALS AND OBJECTIVES

1. To teach parents some rhymes and songs their babies will enjoy and learn from.
2. To support parents in their role as the baby's first teacher.
3. To foster attachment between the parent and the child through the use of oral language.
4. To build a sense of community with the families served.
5. To introduce parents to books their babies will enjoy.
6. To introduce parents to the free materials and services available at the public library or community centre.

USING YOUR STRENGTHS

Are you an entertainer? Do you perform well with large groups? Or do you need a smaller group? Do you play a musical instrument? Do you speak another language? Acknowledging and using your strengths in the beginning will make your planning easier.

FLEXIBILITY

I make my initial plan based on my community needs assessment, my institution's goals, my personal strengths, and my best guess about what would work best for my community. Then if I learn that something else would work better, I change. This can be as simple as changing the program time to suit the greatest number of families in my community, or as complex as changing program structure to make the program more appealing to the people I want to attract. Perhaps I will use props and read-aloud books for one group and I will use fewer or none for another group. Sometimes I offer a healthy snack as part of my program and sometimes not. Remaining flexible is important.

WHERE TO PLACE THE PROGRAM

Choose a room, whether it is inside a library, community centre, health unit, or church that is safe, clean and comfortable for both babies and adults. I have found the ideal room to be carpeted, free of toys and books and all clutter, and big enough to hold about 20 adults comfortably seated in a circle on the floor. Parents feel most relaxed when they know their babies are safe if they happen to crawl outside the circle. This means that the children's department in a library, which is full of books that babies love to play with, is often not the ideal environment for a baby program. Best to choose a big empty room.

Once I've found the right room, I look for gym mats or carpet squares to place in a circle on the floor so parents know where to sit and are comfortable during the program.

STROLLER PARKING AND STORAGE SPACE

Babies come with equipment: strollers, car seats, diaper bags, and smallish items that need storage space. Strollers and car seats are big items that need parking space and traffic control. Give some thought to where these will be placed, near the program room, so that parents know where to put them, so strollers are safe, and so they don't block access to the program room. A table is a good place for smaller items.

SCHEDULING

Baby's nap time will determine when families can get out of the house for a program, and surprise, not all babies are the same. Not only is every baby different, but babies' sleep patterns change and evolve continuously in the first two years, so finding a time that will suit everyone is impossible. I choose a time that seems to suit the greatest number of people and then am prepared to change the time to what most of the parents say they prefer. Most of my parents have said they prefer 11:00 AM after the baby's morning nap, or 2:30 PM after the afternoon nap.

SCHEDULING FOR WORKING PARENTS

If we want to attract families who need our support, it is important for us to offer programs on weekends and in the evenings so that working parents can come. Sunday is a very popular day for working parents.

INCLUDING THE DADS

More and more fathers are taking an active role in the nurturing of their young children, including infants, and they need to be supported in their new role as caregivers. There is also new research on father involvement that demonstrates the critical role fathers play in their babies' healthy development. Working fathers come to programs when we offer them in the evenings and on the weekends.

At Vancouver Public Library, we have developing a program exclusively for dads and male caregivers and their young children. It's called Man in the Moon. We teach the dads the same rhymes and songs we teach in our other children's programs, but it's all dads, or any male caregiver, and their children. We also read and tell stories that show dads in relationships with children. The program is enormously successful. The men say they really appreciate being able to take part in a children's program exclusively for men. They also say the program helps them connect with other dads to share their experiences of fatherhood.

MULTICULTURAL PROGRAMS

We live in a diverse multicultural / multilingual society. Let's celebrate this by inviting parents to share rhymes from their countries of origin and to share rhymes in their first languages. This often generates discussion of different cultural practices around child rearing, which is a very rewarding experience for all and promotes intercultural understanding.

REGISTRATION VERSUS DROP-IN

I like to register families for my programs so I know how many people to expect. If the response is overwhelming, I try to plan another program, or take a waiting list. Registration also gives me a chance to: talk to the individual parents about the program, let the parents know what to expect, find out what language is spoken in the home, how many children will be coming, and what ages the children are. All of this information will help me plan my programs.

However, registration can be a big barrier to service. Many parents find the registration process frustrating, and some parents find it difficult to make a commitment to a weekly outing for a specified duration. Drop-in programs are great for these people. But the result is unpredictable attendance.

Your choice should reflect the goals and objectives of your institution and your program.

HOW MANY PEOPLE?

Your community needs assessment, room size, and program type will determine the size of your group. I prefer smaller groups of fifteen parents and their babies at one time. A smaller group allows me to be more observant and responsive to the individual families' needs. But many people have as many as fifty families at their drop-in programs. Your choice should be linked to your program goals and objectives.

HOW MANY WEEKS?

The number of weeks you plan will also depend on your goals and objectives. Many baby programs in the public library run for eight weeks, and some run all year long. My programs run all year in ten-week segments at a time. Remember that if you want your parents to learn the rhymes and songs, and if you want to build a sense of community, it will take some time.

HOW LONG SHOULD EACH PROGRAM BE?

The length of your program should also be based on your goals and objectives for the program. If you simply want to attract people to the public library to introduce the library's resources for families, then a half-hour program is great. If you want to offer a broader learning experience, then you will want to plan an hour-long program.

Most programs in public libraries are thirty minutes long. When a fifteen-minute social time is added to the beginning and end, the program then lasts an hour. My programs are an hour long with fifteen minutes added to the beginning and end. The program then lasts an hour and a half. You need to decide what works best for your community.

PROVIDING A SNACK

In many cultures, food is a traditional custom whenever people join together for a social activity. If your institution has the means, think about providing a light healthy snack as part of your program. No hot drinks that could spill on the baby. Another consideration is that nursing mothers need a snack if they are away from home for any length of time.

HOW TO SELECT RHYMES

Choose a variety of singing and saying rhymes, and a variety of rhymes by type: bounces, face rhymes, tickling rhymes, lullabies and so on. Select only a few to teach and repeat these each week, adding more as the weeks progress.

I select a list of rhymes I want to teach for the session, then I start with a limited number the first week. I start with anywhere from six to ten rhymes depending on my audience and my environment. Yes, that is enough.

I like to choose rhymes that have beautiful language and imagery and are easy for the parents to learn. I also choose rhymes that are good for specific activities such as diaper-changing, dressing, eating, bathing and going to sleep.

I don't usually teach rhymes I think the parents will have heard elsewhere, like "The Eensy Weensy Spider and "The Wheels on the Bus," unless the parents ask for them.

HOW TO TEACH A RHYME

1. When first introducing a rhyme or song, say or sing the rhyme or song through once so the parents can hear how it goes.
2. Repeat the rhyme line by line asking the parents to say it back to you line by line.
3. Repeat the rhyme again, slowly, all together.
4. Repeat again. Now everyone is joining in.

When teaching a song, I often separate the words from the tune. We say the words line by line, then sing la-la-la line by line for the tune. This is especially effective for more complex songs.

The parents say they really appreciate this teaching approach as it gives them a chance to learn and join in.

I also ask the parents to turn their babies around so that they can play the rhymes with their babies face to face. This way the parents get to see how much their babies are enjoying the rhyme, and the babies get to see how much their parents are enjoying the rhyme too. Face to face interaction is also how the babies learn the face muscle movements involved in producing speech sounds.

REPETITION

Babies love repetition and they need repetition to learn. There is no better way to show parents this than through demonstration.

Repetition is also the key to a successful program. Through repetition the parents can learn the rhymes and join in. I repeat the rhymes I teach three times on the spot. The first is an introduction, the second sees everyone beginning to join in and the third has parents joining in with confidence. Then I repeat the same rhymes each week, again three times on the spot, and add new ones as the weeks go by. Confidence and participation grows with repetition.

WRITTEN WORDS TO RHYMES

I teach my parents through repetition. That way, the parents can learn the rhymes and at the same time focus on their babies' responses. In the library, I often hand out rhyme sheets for parents to take home so they can learn the rhymes this way too. In my outreach programs, I hand out the rhyme sheets at the end of a ten-week program, after the parents have learned the rhymes by heart. This approach builds the parents' confidence in learning orally, the way their babies learn.

MORE THAN RHYMES

Because so many new families are isolated at this time in our social history, I like to provide more than just a rhyme time program. I like to provide a meeting place, a social group and a community of support for new parents. Parents who are new to parenting or new to the community really appreciate this aspect of the program.

BASIC PROGRAM STRUCTURE

The key to success is to plan short activities that move along seamlessly at a relaxed pace.

The opening and closing rituals should be the same each week. Parents and babies alike enjoy the predictability of a pattern.

Repeat the rhymes you have chosen each week, and add new ones as your parents gain confidence in learning and remembering the rhymes.

The stories, whether they are read-aloud books, simple felt stories, pop-ups, big books, or simply told stories, need to be short. Parents and babies alike enjoy stories that are told with lots of expression and stories that involve participation.

USING THEMES

While themes are an appropriate way to plan preschool and toddler programs, they are really inappropriate for baby programs. The focus of the baby program is the rhymes. And the objective is to teach the parents the rhymes and songs so they will enjoy playing and singing to their babies, wherever they happen to be. Sometimes I use loose thematic connections for the books I read and the stories I tell. But I repeat the rhymes and songs I teach each week, adding a new one or two in the successive weeks in response to what I observe the parents and babies love best.

USING FELT STORIES AND PUPPETS

I rarely use props in my programs for three reasons. The first is that I want the parents to know that they don't need these things in order to play happily with their babies. The second reason is that I don't want to tantalize the babies with things I don't want them to touch. Babies are naturally curious and want to touch everything they find interesting. They also can't follow directives not to touch. They simply cannot understand this concept yet. The third reason is that I want to encourage interaction between the parent and the child.

If you do use props, you should be prepared for distraction. You should also be aware that young babies can't see very far until about six months of age, so they will not be able to see them. If you choose to use props, short participation stories and songs work best. Always precede and follow with interactive play rhymes that will capture the babies' attention.

USING RECORDED MUSIC

Sometimes I use recorded music to play in the background as parents and children are assembling for a program in the library, but I never use it in the program itself. Why? Because I want the parents to know that their own voices are the best tools they can use to entertain, soothe and delight their own babies. It doesn't matter to a baby how polished it is, it is the parent's voice that is the most important sound in the baby's life. Many parents don't sing to their babies because they feel they have bad voices. They need reassurance that their voice is the baby's favourite voice, no matter what they think it sounds like.

DISPLAYS

If your program is in a library, set up displays of baby board books, baby rhyme books, recorded music, and other resources parents can borrow after the program. Parenting books are the least popular items in displays unless the parents have asked for material on a particular subject.

READING ALOUD

Choose participation stories that will get parents clapping, chanting or singing along. The babies will follow their parents' lead. Short pop-ups, lift-the-flap books, books with repetition, and books you can sing, provide this kind of activity. The key is to keep them short. The parents find them delightful.

A good story that is related to family life or the new baby, whether it is read aloud or simply told to the parents, will be relaxing and pleasurable for the adults.

Reading aloud is also a great opportunity for you to demonstrate to the parents how to talk about the pictures and concepts presented in books when they are reading aloud to their children at home.

THE BEST REWARD

This is one of the most rewarding programs you will ever do. It's lots of fun, there is a lot to learn, and the rewards are great. The best thing a mom has ever said to me which pretty well sums it up was, "Thank you for showing me how to play with my baby."

Presentation Tips

Pacing *24*
Too Fast, Too Much *24*
What to Do When Parents Chat *24*
What to Do When Babies Cry *24*
How to Use the "Disruptions" *25*
How to Respond to What You See *25*
Why Build Your Repertoire? *25*
Why Repeat So Much? *25*
Baby Food at Programs *25*
How to Teach Parents Who Speak English as a Second Language *25*
What if a Baby Doesn't Like a Particular Rhyme? *26*
Sexism, Violence and Other Complaints *26*
What to Do About Late Arrivals *26*
Have Fun! *26*

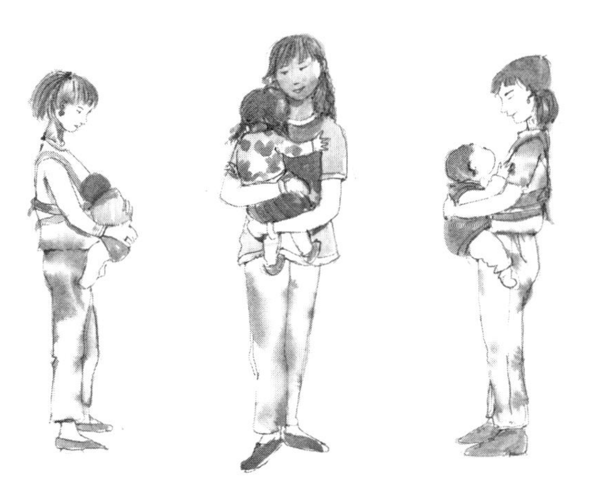

This section offers easy solutions to some of the most common problems programmers face when delivering programs for families with babies.

PACING

Keep the pace relaxed but moving along. Learn all your rhymes, songs and stories by heart, and have them all ready to roll out without pause. But do take the time to respond to what you see happening in the group. Slow down for toddlers. Slow down when you see parents struggling with rhymes they haven't learned yet.

TOO FAST, TOO MUCH

The biggest problem I see in baby programs I observe is that there are too many rhymes presented too quickly at each program. As a result, babies fuss and parents chat. The way to solve the problem is simply to slow down and repeat. A calm and focused experience is more pleasurable for all concerned.

WHAT TO DO WHEN PARENTS CHAT

The social aspect of a baby program is one of the most attractive features of the program for the adults. They love to talk with one another about all aspects of parenting and this is a great opportunity for them to meet and make new friends. For this reason, I like to make the space and myself available so that we can all chat for fifteen minutes before and fifteen minutes after the program. This gives the parents the social opportunity they need and it helps me find out what the parents are interested in, which helps me plan my programs.

During the program keep adult talk short and purposeful. Once the parents start chatting amongst themselves and the babies become restless, you've lost the group. Bring the attention back quickly with a bounce or a song.

If chatting becomes a problem during the program, I like to remind my parents that the best time for chatting is before and after the program. During the program we will focus on playing with the babies.

WHAT TO DO WHEN BABIES CRY

One of the things I love about babies is that they show their emotions without hesitation. When they are uncomfortable or unhappy, they just cry. What can the programmer do?

First we need to understand that babies have different sensitivity thresholds. Some babies will be overwhelmed in a new environment with lots of people they don't know. They will be especially sensitive to noise. Reassure the parent that the baby will settle in over time and keep your environment calm.

Some babies cry because they are over-tired or teething. The precious nap may have been missed. The baby may be colicky. We don't always know why they cry.

So when a baby cries, and this is inevitable, sing! This will usually distract and calm the baby. It will also show the parents how to use song to soothe their babies in times of distress. Being understanding, accepting, and responsive is the best approach.

If a parent wants to leave your program because the baby is inconsolable that day, make sure the parent feels welcome to come back when both parent and child are ready.

HOW TO USE THE "DISRUPTIONS"

If a baby cries, sing a lullaby. If a parent stands up to bounce or jiggle a fussy baby, ask the whole group to stand up and sing a circle song like "Shoofly" (p. 87) Work this into your program as if you'd planned it all along. Be responsive and sympathetic to the parents' needs.

If some of the babies are crawling around, let them explore their environment as long as they are safe, and reassure the parents that they will come back to play when they are ready. With a watchful eye, carry on doing the rhymes with the parents. The babies will come back!

If a book you are reading aloud or a story you are telling with the use of the felt board or any such activity loses the group's attention, cut it short and return to play rhymes.

HOW TO RESPOND TO WHAT YOU SEE

Try to be playful and responsive to the babies in your program. If you see that a baby has his socks off, play a toe-wiggling rhyme such as " This Little Piggy" (p. 152). If you see that a baby has just begun to point, play a finger pointing rhyme such as "Two Little Dicky Birds" (p. 101). Young toddlers love this simple rhyme. If someone has just learned how to clap, play "Pat-a-cake" (p. 98).

WHY BUILD YOUR REPERTOIRE?

The more songs and rhymes you know by heart, the more fun you will have and the more responsive you will be in your programs. But do control the number of rhymes you teach to the group so the parents can learn them. It's better to learn a few rhymes well than it is to hear a whole lot and not be able to remember any.

WHY REPEAT SO MUCH?

Both parents and babies love repetition and need repetition to learn. There is no better way to show this than through demonstration.

BABY FOOD AT PROGRAMS

Parents should be welcomed to breast or bottle feed their infants any time throughout the program.

Sometimes, however, parents of babies who are eating solid foods or drinking from a cup will bring these things into the program and it's disruptive for everyone. All the babies will want that cracker or that cup! So I say, "Please feel free to bring baby snacks to the program. However, we will snack before, and after the program (or during snack break). During our play time, we will put all the snacks away and play with our babies."

HOW TO TEACH PARENTS WHO SPEAK ENGLISH AS A SECOND LANGUAGE

It's a great idea to bring parents together in a multilingual community for programs and to teach some English. However, the language of intimacy between a parent and a child is going to be the parents' first language. We should, therefore, teach some rhymes in the parents' first language. If we don't know any, we can ask the parents to teach a rhyme in their own language so the whole group can learn it. I have found that most parents are shy about teaching in a group, but they will teach me privately. Then I can teach the group, giving them full credit, of course. This little strategy has worked very well for me.

Go slowly for an ESL audience. Use rhymes that have concrete language, such as

"Two Little Eyes" (p. 92), and "Head and Shoulders, Knees and Toes" (p. 76). Mix English with the parents' first language in songs like "Roly Poly" (p. 127), and "Ho, Ho, Watanay" (p. 126). And definitely give these parents written words to take home. This will help them understand what you are singing and saying. You can also ask them if they understand what the words mean, and explain if they don't understand.

I have found that after a while, once parents have become familiar with the English rhymes, they will sing in both languages to their children at home.

WHAT IF A BABY DOESN'T LIKE A PARTICULAR RHYME?

Sometimes a baby will cry when he hears a particular rhyme. A lullaby may remind him of the dreaded naptime, or a baby won't enjoy the feeling of being "dropped" through the hole at the end of "A Smooth Road" (p. 80). Delete the rhyme from your program this time, and find another one to substitute. There are hundreds of rhymes to choose from.

SEXISM, VIOLENCE AND OTHER COMPLAINTS

Sometimes parents may object to the imagery in a particular song or rhyme: the cradle falls in "Rock-a-Bye Baby" (p. 121), tails are chopped off in "Three Blind Mice," "The Old Woman Who Lived in a Shoe" whips her children, and the ladybug's children are caught at home in the fire in "Ladybug, Ladybug." You can choose not to select these rhymes or substitute words like: "she kissed them all soundly and tucked them into bed," for the "Old Woman Who Lived in a Shoe."

Complaints often provide a good opportunity for sympathetic listening, group discussion, discussion of the history of rhymes (often rooted in British political history), and the adaptability of rhymes. After listening, I suggest that parents change the words to suit their own family situations.

WHAT TO DO ABOUT LATE ARRIVALS

Parents will often arrive late for baby programs. Preparing a baby for an outing is a lot of work and the baby's nap comes first. So when parents arrive late, make them feel welcome by saying or singing hello and move along with the program. When we say hello to a latecomer, we help the parent overcome embarrassment about being late and we instantly make them feel a welcome part of the group.

If lateness becomes a problem, I find it helpful to say my programs start fifteen minutes before the formal part of the program actually begins, so parents have time to arrive, get settled and socialize before we start to sing.

HAVE FUN!

The programs we present for families of very young children are much appreciated by the parents who attend. There are not many free things they can do with their babies. And as long as we show kindness and love for those babies, we can't really go wrong.

Understanding

Baby Brain Development *28*
Language Development and Literacy *33*
The Role of Books *39*
The Power of Nursery Rhymes *42*
The Power of Song *45*
New Parents *48*
Ages and Stages *50*

This section includes brief introductions to topics that will help you better understand your audience—both the babies you work with and the people who nurture them. The more we know about these topics, the better equipped we are to help parents and caregivers observe, understand, enjoy, and interact with their babies.

Baby Brain Development

THE SCIENTIFIC RESEARCH

Baby brain development is one of the most fascinating areas of scientific research to emerge in recent history. The research was made possible when new brain imaging technologies were invented in the 1970s. These are Positron Emission Tomography (PET) and Magnetic Resonance Imaging (MRI) which are non-invasive scanning devices. These machines enabled neuroscientists to look, for the first time in history, at the structure and activity of the inside of a healthy functioning human brain. The first popular articles to appear on baby brain development as a result of new research were published in NEWSWEEK and TIME MAGAZINE in 1997. Since that time, many books and articles have been written about baby brain development and new research is emerging all the time. A brief summary of the research follows.

BEFORE BIRTH: THE FORMATION OF BRAIN CELLS

Just after conception, neurons (brain cells) are produced in a neural tube that will eventually become the baby's spinal column, and the neurons begin to journey up this tube to the various parts of the fetus's developing brain. During the nine months in the womb the fetus will develop over 100 billion neurons, almost all the neurons the baby will ever have.

The nervous system develops in a programmed sequence, from the tip of the spine up to the front of the head.

At the top of the spinal cord, the brain stem or subcortical structures of the brain develop first. Subcortical structures are primarily responsible for basic biological functions such as circulation, respiration, digestion, elimination, and for a newborn's reflex behaviors such as sucking. These subcortical structures must be fairly well developed at birth for the newborn infant to survive.

After the spinal column and the subcortical structures at the base of the brain come the cerebellum and the basal ganglia which regulate movement; the limbic system which controls emotion and memory; and finally the cerebral cortex, the part of the brain that governs thought, memory, language, mathematics, and problem solving. The cerebral cortex is the last part of the brain to develop. It is the most markedly unformed at birth, and will become the largest.

The cerebral cortex has two hemispheres. The left is primarily responsible for language, but it also predominates in any task involving sequential processing and symbol manipulation: language, mathematics, and music. The left hemisphere is generally the more analytical of the two halves. The right hemisphere processes information more holisticly, and is primarily responsible for visual-spatial skills, which are required for perceiving patterns and shapes, and for emotion. While the left hemisphere tends to dominate in most people the two hemispheres function together to give us a total experience of our world.

The cerebral hemispheres are further divided into main areas or lobes. These are: the prefrontal, frontal, parietal, temporal, and occipital lobes. Each plays a major role in various brain functions and in processing signals received from the environment. The two hemispheres are linked by a bridge called the corpus callosum.

The corpus callosum carries nerve signals so that each half of the brain knows what the other half is doing.

None of these brain centres would be able to communicate without a messenger system that conveys electrical impulses from environmental stimulation to their destination sites in the brain. Neural pathways are required.

AT BIRTH

The human baby's brain is the most undeveloped of all living mammals at birth. The growth that occurs in the first three years of life is greater than at any other time in human development. At birth, only 25% of the baby's brain is formed. By the age of three, the brain grows to about 80% of adult size, and by the age of five, to 90%.

AFTER BIRTH: THE FORMATION OF NEURAL PATHWAYS

This growth in the baby's brain is partly due to an increase in size as the baby grows, but it is mainly due to the production of miles and miles of connections, or neural pathways within the baby's brain.

Neural pathways are built in response to stimulation from the baby's environment. All the baby's five senses are involved in the creation of neural pathways: hearing, touching, seeing, smelling, and tasting. Environmental stimulation produces hundreds of trillions of connections between the neurons after birth. Neuroscientists sometimes refer to this whole busy connecting process as "getting wired."

Electrical impulses received through sensory stimulation travel along the new neural pathways on messenger links between neurons. These tube-like structures are called axons (senders) and dendrites (receivers). Each neuron in the brain has only one axon, but it has many dendrites and will generate new ones every time the baby's brain encounters a new experience.

A myelin sheath is formed around pathways that are used most frequently to strengthen and protect them. The protective sheath makes sending and receiving messages from the environment faster and more efficient as the baby develops. Of the hundreds of trillions of new connections that are made after birth, some will be strong and others will be weak; some will survive, and others won't. It is only through repeated use that new connections are strengthened and kept. Neural connections that are not used, or are used less often, will wither away and die. This withering process is called "pruning." Pruning is a natural, and essential process in healthy brain development. It helps the remaining neural connections grow bigger and stronger.

WINDOWS OF OPPORTUNITY: SENSITIVE TIME PERIODS

When neuroscientists, educators, and health care professionals talk about infant brain development, they sometimes refer to "windows of opportunity." These are the windows of time when stimulation from the outside environment must be received if the brain is to develop to its fullest potential. These windows are also sometimes called "critical periods" or "sensitive periods" in development.
The window of opportunity for the development of vision is the shortest, zero to six months. If a baby is born with cataracts, for example, these must be removed by six

months of age or the child's vision will be forever compromised.

Hearing is also critical in the first six months. Because language acquisition begins so early in life, and hearing impairment has such devastating long-term effects on cognitive development, early detection of hearing loss is critical for healthy development. Even babies who are born deaf can be taught language—sign language—if the problem is detected early enough.

The window of opportunity for language acquisition, which is the foundation for cognitive development, is from birth to two years. Babies begin to acquire language long before they can talk and the process begins with the caregiver's first communication of sounds and gestures and words that are exchanged with the baby.

The window of opportunity for emotional attachment is from birth to eighteen months. Attachment at this time is critical for the infant's developing ability to learn how to soothe herself and gain control over her own emotions. Research on child abuse and neglect reveals that infants who have not been held and touched enough at this time will develop brains that are 20 to 30% smaller in size than normal children of the same age.

The window of opportunity for the development of gross motor skills is from birth to four years. Gross motor skill development unfolds in a programmed sequence and each new skill is built upon the gains of the previous skill. First comes rolling over, then sitting up, then crawling, then standing, then walking, then running.

Research reveals that some areas of the brain are more sensitive than others to these critical time periods. Some areas are also capable of recovery and restructuring after early experiential deficits or physical damage: sometimes the brain can reorganize its functions so that intact regions assume the functions of damaged regions, and full functioning can be restored. This repairability is the result of what neuroscientists refer to as the brain's "neuroplasticity" or flexibility.

THE ELECTROCHEMICAL SYSTEM: THE INFLUENCE OF NEUROTRANSMITTERS

Along with brain cell formation and the growth of neural pathways, the baby's electrochemical system is also developing.

The axons and dendrites of the neurons send and receive messages between neurons, but they don't quite touch. The little gap that remains is called a "synapse." When an electrical impulses shoots up an axon, a neurotransmitter is released to help the impulse jump the synaptic gap to the dendrite of another neuron.

Neurotransmitters are chemicals produced in the cell body of the neurons and are used to relay, amplify and modulate electrical signals between the neurons. Scientists have now identified over 50 neurotransmitters! Some of the more popular ones you might know are: endorphins (which reduce pain and make us feel good), serotonin (which relieves depression, relaxes the body, and initiates sleep), cortisol (which governs our stress response), noradrenaline and adrenaline (which heighten awareness), and dopamine (which controls voluntary movement and emotional arousal).

The production and release of neurotransmitters is also influenced by stimulation from the baby's environment. When we caress a baby, for example, we elicit the release of transmitters that make the baby feel good. When we soothe a baby by rocking, singing, and stroking, we elicit the release of neurotransmitters that help the baby fall into sleep. When we play a game that engages the baby, we are stimulating the release of neurotransmitters that keep the baby awake and alert. Neurotransmitters work in balance to help the brain function normally in response to environmental stimulation.

Research on the production and release of neurotransmitters in the brain is the new scientific frontier and we will hear more about this in the years that lie ahead.

CONCLUSION

The research tells us that the growth that occurs in the baby's brain in the first three years of life is greater than at any other time in human development. This means that how a child thinks, how she learns, how she feels about herself and others, how she solves problems and how she responds to life's challenges, are all established before she reaches the age of three.

While many areas of a child's brain continue to grow and adapt through to adolescence, and many early deficits can be restored thanks to the brain's neuroplasticity, it is during the first three years that the foundations for thinking, language, vision, attitudes, aptitudes, and other characteristics are laid down.

Scientists now know that genetics (DNA coding) drives the creation of some of the baby's brain. Babies are born with the capacity to learn and are driven to develop the skills that will enable them to thrive in the world. But at least 50% of the baby's brain growth occurs as a result of the baby's interaction with the outside world. This means that how we respond to infants and the environments we create for them have an enormous impact on that child's development.

Research has shown that not only do babies who suffer from neglect and abuse develop brains that are actually 30% smaller than normal children of the same age, but they also have disproportionately high levels of cortisol in their brains. These children have a hard time dealing with life's challenges, reading body language cues accurately, and controlling their emotional responses. They also have a hard time paying attention and learning at school.

As early childhood educators, parents, and caregivers, our role is to foster healthy brain development with the kinds of interactions that promote healthy and happy outcomes. What can we do to create the most favourable environments for healthy brain development to occur?

We can foster attachment. Attachment to a loving caregiver in the first three years of life is critical to a baby's healthy development. Attachment provides the foundation upon which every other mental skill can flourish. Babies communicate through emotional expression, and it is through interaction that they develop the security, confidence and motivation to master the more obvious motor, verbal, and cognitive skills they need to thrive in the world. Love matters.

Parents play a vital role in their children's development. What we can do is support them in this role. Parents need a community of support so that they can give their children what they need for healthy development. What we can do is create a community of support.

Children who are damaged as a result of physical injury, neglect or abuse, can be helped if they are reached soon enough. Early diagnosis and support is critical. What we can do is notice when something is wrong and get help for the family.

Research also tells us that babies do not need expensive toys, flashcards, or video games that promise to boost their IQs for healthy development. Babies learn best through interaction with a loving adult. Just having a loving and responsive adult do lots of holding, talking, singing, reading, and playing with the baby is all babies need for optimum brain development, and the baby will do the rest of the work required herself. What we can do is create programs that support the parents, and teach them how to play with their babies in developmentally appropriate ways.

RECOMMENDED VIDEO:

Giangreco, Kathy. TEN THINGS EVERY CHILD NEEDS. Produced by WTTW/Chicago and The Chicago Production Center for Robert R. McCormick Tribune Foundation; written and produced by Kathy Giangreco. U.S.: Robert R. McCormick Tribune Foundation, 1997. (one hour)
This excellent video describes exactly what every child needs for optimal brain development. The ten things are: interaction; touch; a stable relationship with a loving adult; a safe, healthy environment; self-esteem; quality child care; communication; play; music; and reading. Each need is expressed clearly by scientists, doctors, and early child development specialists while showing parents interacting with their children in appropriate ways.

BIBLIOGRAPHY

Eliot, Lise. WHAT'S GOING ON IN THERE? HOW THE BRAIN AND MIND DEVELOP IN THE FIRST FIVE YEARS OF LIFE. New York: Bantam Books, 1999.
An expert on the brain reviews current knowledge on brain and behavioral development for sensory and motor functions, language, and intelligence. Look here for maps and diagrams.

Golinkoff, Roberta, Andrew Meltzoff, and Patricia Kuhl. THE SCIENTIST IN THE CRIB. New York: Morrow, 1999.
Three authors discuss development of the brain, visual perception, categorizing, social skills, and language in infants up to age four. Suitable for parents.

Nash, J. Madeleine. "Fertile Minds," TIME, vol. 149, issue 5, p48, Feb. 3, 1997.
This popular article contains clear descriptions of the biology of baby brain development.

Silberg, Jack. BRAIN GAMES FOR BABIES, TODDLERS AND TWOS. London: Hamlyn; New York: Sterling, 2002.
A great book to recommend to parents. Lots of good bits of information on baby brain development, photographs of parents and babies playing together and fun things to do to foster development.

Teicher, Martin H. "Scars that Won't Heal: the Neurobiology of Child Abuse." SCIENTIFIC AMERICAN: Mar 2002, Vol. 286, Issue 3, p68-75.
This article reports the findings of a study that examined the enduring negative effects of maltreatment at an early age on a child's brain development and function.

"Your Child From Birth to Three." NEWSWEEK. Special Edition. Spring/Summer 1997.
Contains useful information on the biology of baby brain development.

Language Development and Literacy

WHAT IS LITERACY?

The popular view of literacy throughout most of our history was that it was an ability to decode (read) and encode (write) letter symbols, and that the process for learning how to do this began when a child got to school at the age of six. The scientific research of the last decade, however, reveals a deeper truth. We now know that literacy is built upon a previously learned set of skills with language and communication; that it begins with the oral communication between a parent and a child; and it begins at the beginning of life. Everything a child learns about language and communication in the first few years of life will determine the difficulty or ease with which he later learns to read and write at school. The parents' role in this daily process, how they communicate, and how much they communicate with their children, is critical to the process.

The following summary of infant language development in the first two years shows how babies begin to develop the communication skills they need to bring to the process of learning literacy and why parents and caregivers are the key figures in this process.

BEFORE BIRTH

The budding of the first skill for later understanding language happens in the baby's sixth month in the womb. Hearing is the first of the baby's five senses to develop. At six months, the fetus's auditory nerves are in place and he will listen and respond to all the sounds in his environment: the rush of blood coursing through the mother's veins, the mother's heart beat, and the sound of the mother's voice. This is why babies prefer and respond the most to the speech sounds of the mother after birth. These are sounds the baby recognizes. The sounds are not as loud as they were in the womb, but they are familiar. The baby will also respond to the familiar sound of the father's voice.

BIRTH THROUGH YEAR ONE

At birth, a baby can show he is ready for his first attempts to communicate. If you stick out your tongue a few times slowly and repeatedly, then wait, the baby will respond by sticking out his little tongue too. If you open your mouth wide, the baby will open his mouth wide. He may not be able to smile yet, because he doesn't have enough strength in his cheek muscles, but he will be delighted with this little game that shows him you know he can communicate with you.

The baby's journey of language learning is dependent upon his interaction with the people in his world. Heredity (genetic makeup) plays some part in how he will learn language. Babies are "wired for language" and are driven to learn, but at least

50% of his achievements will come from his interactions with his environment. This means that his parents, and especially his primary caregiver, will have an incredible impact on how he develops. Fostering this early language development is easy. All parents need to do is talk, talk, talk, and the baby will do the rest of the work required.

PARENTESE

When parents speak to their babies they use a special language that is reserved just for babies. This is a high-pitched, sing-songy, repetitive pattern of speech that is called "baby talk," or "parentese," or "motherese." Even adults who don't have children of their own know instinctively how to do this. The parent's use of exaggerated inflections and animated facial expressions helps the baby tune in to the speech patterns of the language. Babies respond to this by making faces, wiggling their bodies, kicking their feet, and showing excitement. They like it! When they have had enough stimulation and need a rest, they will look, or turn away, move less, frown, arch their backs or look worried.

Babies enjoy imitation. They try to match our sounds and gestures, and they like it when we match our sounds and gestures to theirs.

LEARNING A SECOND LANGUAGE

All babies are born with the capacity to learn language—whatever language in the world that is spoken to them the most. A baby's sensitivity to speech sounds is so great, he can distinguish between all the different sounds of all the different languages spoken in the world. This is a skill that will be lost by the time he reaches adulthood. The latest research reveals that the window of opportunity for learning a second language begins to close between nine months and the baby's first birthday. After the age of eight, learning a second language becomes much more difficult, as all adults who have tried will know. This is why researchers say the optimum time for children to learn a second language is in the first eight years of life.

VISUAL CONNECTIONS

A baby's vision is blurry at first and he can't see in the distance, so the parents have to move in very close to the baby's face, about one foot, so that the baby can see them. It is important for parents to look at the baby when they talk to him because this helps the baby see them, and see the connection between the speech sounds they are making and the corresponding face muscle movements that go with them. The baby is absorbing all this knowledge, he is watching intently, and he will later use this knowledge to generate his own speech sounds in the months that lie ahead.

COOING

The first sounds the baby can make are soft cooing sounds. These are long vowel sounds like "oo," "aa," and "ee." Babies start to do this at about two months of age. And they love it when parents coo back to them.

TURN TAKING

By about six weeks, the baby will enjoy a rhythmic conversation with the parent. The baby will respond to the parent's sounds with intent gazes, jerky gestures, sometimes grunting. He will try to initiate a conversation with these gestures and he will look expectantly to the parent for a response. At two months he will add cooing to his repertoire. The conversational game that evolves will look something like this: mother talks, pauses, then baby smiles; father touches, pauses, then baby waves her little arms; mother asks a question, waits, and the baby coos.

This rudimentary conversation with sounds and gestures eliciting responses is a simple game of turn-taking. This is the model of turn-taking that provides the basis for the conversation with words that will take place a bit later on. The rhythmic dance of action and response back and forth between the baby and the parent is the beginning of the baby's ability to have a conversation. A child who is engaged in this way is a child who will eventually become an excellent conversationalist as an adult, one who can talk and also listen.

Babies are born wanting to communicate, and will show frustration and disappointment when their attempts to make it happen are ignored. Their disappointment is expressed in fussing and in disorganized responses.

FIRST WORDS

The first word the baby will consistently recognize and understand is his own name. This is because it is the word most often repeated to him in a cheerful manner. He knows his name, and he knows it refers to him by the time he is about four and a half months old. (Babies don't connect what "mommy" and "daddy" mean until about six or seven months. A happy moment for parents!)

At around six months, the baby will start to use consonant sounds and will start to say sounds like "ba-ba-ba," or "da-da-da." At around seven or eight months, most babies will start to "babble." Babbling is not random; it is conscious, controlled practice with the sounds of the native language the baby has heard from his parents.

At around nine or ten months, most babies can show they understand: the names of family members; the words for familiar things, like shoe, juice, teddy; and some events in their lives, like bath time, walk, bedtime, peek-a-boo. The baby is only beginning to make word sounds, and so he may have some trouble making his meaning clear when he tries to speak, but he can understand a lot more than he can say. Comprehension always precedes and exceeds expression.

Research indicates that by nine or ten months of age, on average, a baby can understand the meaning of about 40 words. The number of words he knows is governed by the amount of speech he has heard from his parents. Now he begins to pick up language from everyone in his environment. Research indicates, however, that the speech has to be directed to the baby in order to be meaningful to him. An adult conversation that takes place while he is in the vicinity will be boring and meaningless to him. This is why little children become so restless when adults talk to one another for any length of time. They can't understand the language yet.

VOCABULARY

Research indicates that vocabulary is a fundamental building block for language, and the measurement of infant vocabulary is one of the greatest predictors of the child's later success at learning how to read. This is why it is so important to talk to the baby. Children need to know many words, and the meaning of those words, long before they come to print-based language to be able to learn how to read.

Research shows, too, that an infant's language development depends a great deal not only on how often the baby is spoken to (quantity), but on the tone in which the talk is delivered (quality). Infants who are spoken to often, and are spoken to in a positive way with lots of encouraging words, have much better outcomes than children who do not. And these outcomes last for a lifetime.

Most babies will say their first meaningful word at about one year of age.

After the baby's first birthday he learns language at an astounding rate, and research shows here, too, that the style the parent or caregiver uses in communication with the child has a huge impact on how this language development will take shape.

YEAR TWO

In the twelve to twenty-four month period, the baby will begin to say more words that actually mean something. The sounds may not be exact , but the meaning is clear. Again, these words are always things that are meaningful—to him: bedtime, bathtime, familiar objects, people, and animals.

At this point, most parents replace "parentese" by something called "infant-directed speech." Infant-directed speech means using simple and short phrases, and expanding on the baby's new words by putting them into short sentences and repeating the words, fully pronounced, back to the baby. An example is this: the baby says, "ju," and the parent asks, "More juice? Would you like more juice?" Again, this talk needs to be a description of the baby's actions if it is to be interesting or useful to him. The habit parents have of using infant-directed speech to help the baby learn will continue beyond the baby's second year. Here too, the tone of delivery makes all the difference, not only to the baby's developing language and cognitive skills, but also to his developing sense of self-esteem.

At first, from twelve to eighteen months, the baby's words will appear very slowly and will be formed with great effort. The baby is focusing intently on how to produce speech sounds that make his meaning clear. Then around eighteen months there is a vocabulary explosion. By the age of six years, researchers estimate that the average child will know the meaning of about 13,000 words. The time required to develop this amount of vocabulary indicates how much time and attention children need to practice making speech sounds before they get to school.

Two-word sentence phrases, like "Mommy come", will appear in the eighteen to twenty-four month period. The time period is general. Not all babies will develop at exactly the same time. But while time periods vary from child to child, the sequence of learning does not. First comes sound, then comes meaningful sound, then words, then phrases, then sentences.

There are many more words, or speech sounds, for the baby to learn before he can master communication, and many more ways to combine those word sounds into phrases and then sentences so he can make himself perfectly understood. But he is on his way. His understanding of language sounds and how they go together to form meaning is the foundation he needs.

In the years that follow, a baby's language will become much more complex. He will build his comprehension skills. He will learn about semantics (word meaning) and syntax (grammar and word order). He will learn how to make inferences and predictions. He will learn ordering and sequencing skills. And he will increase his vocabulary dramatically. He will need all of these skills before he can successfully learn how to read. He learns all these things just by talking with the people in his world.

Fortunately, much of the communication is instinctive—both for the baby and for the parents. But knowing how and why babies respond, and knowing what we as parents and caregivers can do to provide the optimum environments for speech/language development is very helpful to the baby.

These are a baby's first steps toward literacy.

WHAT PROGRAMMERS CAN DO

1. Make programs and materials easily accessible for parents.
2. Include and address the parents in programs.
3. Encourage and support the parents in their role as their babies' first teachers.
4. Teach parents rhymes and songs to play with the baby at home.
5. Demonstrate effective methods of communication through role modeling.
6. Tell parents why we are teaching these things so they understand how they are helping their babies take their first steps toward literacy.

WHAT PARENTS & CAREGIVERS CAN DO

1. Talk to your baby about what you are doing and about what the baby is doing.
2. Play with your baby.
3. Be responsive to your baby's cues.
4. Repeat words and word sounds. Babies need repetition to learn.
5. Give positive feedback. Encourage your baby's attempts to speak.
6. Use expressive vocabulary (say sandals, boots, and slippers, not just shoes).
7. Make connections between your baby and the world around him.
8. Follow your baby's lead. Show interest in the things that interest him.
9. Read aloud and share board books with your baby.

10. Give your toddler a crayon to practise drawing so he can develop the fine motor control he will need to learn how to write.

BIBLIOGRAPHY

Bernier, Tamara. THE BABY HUMAN. Richmond Hill, ON: BFS Entertainment and Multimedia Ltd, 2004. (DVD, approx. 150 mins.)
This excellent resource includes three useful episodes: To Walk, To Think, and To Talk. It covers the baby's challenges in the first two years in learning how to do these things from the baby's point of view. Suitable for parents.

Dickinson, David K. and Patton O. Tabors editors. BEGINNING LITERACY WITH LANGUAGE. Baltimore: Paul H. Brookes Publishing, 2001.
A report on how everyday interactions with young children form their abilities to achieve literacy when they get to school. Chapters written by many different researchers.

Golinkoff, Roberta Michnick and Kathy Hirsh-Pasek. HOW BABIES TALK: THE MAGIC AND MYSTERY OF LANGUAGE IN THE FIRST THREE YEARS OF LIFE. New York: Dutton, 1999.
A guide to language development in the first three years. Suitable for parents.

Golinkoff, Roberta, Andrew Meltzoff, and Patricia Kuhl. SCIENTIST IN THE CRIB. New York: Morrow, 1999.
Discusses development of the brain, visual perception, categorizing, social skills, and language in infants up to age four. Suitable for parents.

Hart, Betty and Todd R. Risley. MEANINGFUL DIFFERENCES IN THE EVERYDAY EXPERIENCE OF YOUNG AMERICAN CHILDREN. Baltimore: Paul H. Brookes, 1995.
This book reports the results of a research study into the effects of poverty on language development, which found substantial differences in both the quantity and quality of language spoken to children that affected child development. Academic.

McGuinness, Diane. GROWING A READER FROM BIRTH: YOUR CHILD'S PATH FROM LANGUAGE TO LITERACY. New York: W. W. Norton, 2004.
This highly recommended book covers ages zero to five. McGuinness, a cognitive developmental psychologist, links new research on language development to a child's later ability to master reading, and tells parent what they can do to promote healthy language development with their children. Suitable for parents.

The Role of Books

Babies who are introduced to age-appropriate books from infancy on will grow up loving books. It's that simple. It is never too early to start. When books are introduced throughout the first year of a baby's life by a warm and loving adult, in the ways that are consistent with the baby's development, the rewards for both parent and child will last a lifetime. What is sharing books with infants all about?

In essence, a book is a presentation of someone's ideas, encoded in pictures (in the case of children's first books) or in words (in the case of adult's books), and sometimes both (in both adults' and children's books). And why do we read them? We read to find things out—about the world and about ourselves. It is no different for babies when age-appropriate books are introduced in ways that correspond to the baby's stage of development.

When a parent reads aloud, even before the baby is born, the baby is treated to a glorious feast of sound patterns that the baby will recognize and be comforted by after birth. This is the perfect time to indulge in wonderful children's picture books. The language in children's picture books is much more sophisticated, poetic, and rhythmic, than conversational speech and will give the baby an aural treat.

When a parent introduces board books and demonstrates the mechanics of page turning, the baby sees how books work. When a parent talks about what is going on in the pictures, the baby learns that this toy (the book) is well worth looking at because it triggers lots of talk, which interests him and soothes him. And this experience is especially valuable when the parent uses this first reading opportunity to increase the baby's vocabulary and make connections between the book's world and the baby's world.

The first thing a baby will do with a book is put it in his mouth. This is perfectly predictable. This is how the baby explores his world. Everything of interest goes in the mouth. The next thing to happen is that the baby will use his fingers to try to grasp the book and open it. Board books were created with this kind of use in mind: they are small enough for a baby to hold, the sturdy pages stand up to oral exploration, they don't rip like paper pages, and they are easy for little hands to manipulate.

The first books babies are interested in looking at are books of baby faces, like the wonderful series by Margaret Miller called "Baby Faces." These books present the opportunity for parents to point to the book baby's eyes, say "baby's eyes", then point to their own child's eyes and say "Aiden's eyes," and so forth naming all the facial features on both babies. The parent can also talk about the feelings the baby in the picture is showing, and ask Aiden if he sometimes feels that way too. Simple emotions like happy, sad, frustrated, angry, and sleepy, are all shown in the pictures of baby's first books. This talking experience is like the conversations parents have with their babies. The talk is still in "parentese." The only difference is that the conversation is inspired by the book.

When the baby starts pointing to things in the pictures and the parent talks about what the baby is showing interest in, the parent can follow the baby's lead and make connections between the pictures in the book and the people, objects, animals and events in the baby's own world. What a wonderful way to name things! Building the baby's vocabulary is what this is all about. And the conversation is all based on what the baby is showing curiosity about.

Later, as baby's language develops and he begins to say a few words, parents can use books to extend their baby's vocabulary. Now the dog isn't just a dog, the dog says "whoof, whoof!", and it is a big black lab like the neighbour's dog. When the baby is able to take a book and choose for himself what he wants to have read to him, parents can find out all kinds of things their baby is interested in, and read that book over and over again for just as long as the baby finds it fascinating.

A book that is inappropriate for the baby's age (fuzzy, tiny, or cluttered illustrations), a book with pages that tear easily, a book used when the baby is in a bad mood, or a book left lying on the floor will not do any good at all in starting the baby on his first steps toward reading. An appropriate book has to be used interactively with a loving adult when the baby is in a receptive mood. When used in this way, as an activity that is based on the child's interests, encompassed by the parent's warmth and affection, the baby will always associate reading with a warm and loving experience. This is how a lifelong love of books and reading begins.

When children who have been exposed to books in this way get to school they already know many things about how books work and what they are for. They are motivated to read because they want to hear what the author has to say. They know that books have a front and a back, that they have an upside down and a right side up. They know how to turn pages from right to left, and they know books have stories that have a beginning, a middle and an end.

Parents can help build their children's comprehension skills by talking to their children about what they are reading and seeing in the pictures. Comprehension skills are a very important aspect of learning to read and many children have problems with this.

Children who are familiar with books by the time they get to school will also know that print symbols represent words, and that the print symbols move across the page from left to right in our culture. Parents can help their children understand this concept by tracking their fingers under the text when they are reading to their children in their preschool years. This develops the child's curiosity about text.

Only the child who has been talked to and read to regularly will be ready for the next level of complexity, which is the mechanics of learning how to read print symbols. When the mechanics of reading are introduced, generally around the age of six, the child will use all her skill and understanding in speech and sound production, and apply what she has learned to a new thing, which is interpreting written symbols.

Learning the sound/symbol correspondence between oral and written language is hard work for some children. They need a firm grasp of the sounds of language, the sounds that letters make, a wide range of vocabulary, and familiarity with books in order to be ready to learn to do it successfully.

Again, the parents' and caregivers' role, as the baby's first and most important teachers, is critical, and what they do to prepare their children for reading success, right from the start, makes a world of difference.

You will find more information about this topic in the BABIES LOVE BOOKS section of this book.

WHAT PROGRAMMERS CAN DO

1. Search for and provide books that are appropriate for babies.
2. Show parents and caregivers what kinds of books will appeal to their babies.
3. Talk to parents and caregivers about why reading books with their babies is important and what babies learn from the experience.
4. Demonstrate what to say when we talk about the pictures in books.

WHAT PARENTS & CAREGIVERS CAN DO

1. Read aloud to your baby.
2. Choose books that are appropriate for your baby's age.
3. Ask a librarian if you need help with book selection.
4. Read books when your baby is in a good mood so that reading is a positive experience.
5. Talk to your baby about what you see in the pictures. Talk about what he is looking at too! Children often notice things in the pictures that adults don't.
6. Make reading fun.

RECOMMENDED VIDEO

WHAT CHILDREN NEED IN ORDER TO READ: PREPARING YOUNG CHILDREN FOR READING SUCCESS. Produced by Susan DeBeck. Vancouver: DeBeck Educational Video, 1998.
This video focuses on preschool children rather than babies, but it describes very well the processes involved in learning how to read.

BIBLIOGRAPHY

McGuinness, Diane. GROWING A READER FROM BIRTH: YOUR CHILD'S PATH FROM LANGUAGE TO LITERACY. New York: W. W. Norton, 2004.
This highly recommended book covers ages zero to five. McGuinness, a cognitive developmental psychologist, links new research on language development to a child's later ability to master reading, and tells parent what they can do to promote healthy language development with their children. Suitable for parents.

McGuinness, Diane. WHY OUR CHILDREN CAN'T READ: AND WHAT WE CAN DO ABOUT IT. New York: Simon and Schuster, 1997.
This is a well-researched critical book for teachers and everyone who is interested in an analysis of historical methods used in teaching children how to read. It includes a critique of: "whole language," "phonics," and other methods that have failed for many, and describes a system that McGuinness says works for all children.

The Power of Nursery Rhymes

INTRODUCTION

For centuries, caregivers around the world in all cultures, and in all languages, have used rhythmic patterns of speech, sound, and movement to delight, soothe, and communicate with their babies. Some cultures call these activities croons or ditties or love songs. In English-speaking cultures, we call them nursery rhymes.

Most of our nursery rhymes come from a very long history of British folk tradition, and have been passed down orally from one caregiver to another over many generations. Original authors and sources are unknown. The first printed versions in English were published by John Newbery in about 1695. These traditional nursery rhymes have been honed and refined and adapted and used over time until they are the perfect little gems they are today.

Modern poets and songwriters continue to add original compositions to our collections. These often become absorbed over time into the folk tradition, passing orally from one caregiver to another, until the original authors become unknown.

"Twinkle, Twinkle, Little Star" is a good example of evolution in the folk tradition. The original melody for this popular song was written in the early eighteenth century by a French compose, now unknown, as a song called "Ah! vous dirai-je, Maman." It was not originally a children's song. Mozart wrote many variations of the melody which is why he is sometimes credited as the original composer. The words, almost as we know them today, were written as a poem called "The Star" by Jane Taylor, and were published for the first time in England in 1806. Originally, there were five verses, but now only the first is commonly known.

So nursery rhymes are a "living" art form that is constantly changing and evolving. They are chosen and adapted to reflect the habits and traditions of the people who use them.

Babies love nursery rhymes and they respond instinctively to them. But what is it that they like about them and why is it so important that we use them in play with babies?

NURSERY RHYMES FOSTER ATTACHMENT

Nursery rhymes give parents and caregivers something to say to their babies. They give them a language and a repertoire for play. And the repertoire is something the parent and child can share and enjoy for as long as they enjoy doing these things together for the rest of their lives.

When parents hold, rock, and touch their babies as they say the rhymes, the close physical contact establishes an emotional bond between them. Babies enjoy being held and touched and parents enjoy seeing their babies happy and engaged with them.

Nursery rhymes express emotion. A quiet face-touching rhyme, like "The Moon Is Round," can be used to share a quiet moment. A lullaby can be used to soothe both parent and child in times of distress. A bouncing or galloping rhyme, like "Ten Galloping Horses," can be used to connect with a rambunctious child.

Sharing the kind of rhyme that reflects the baby's feelings helps the baby feel understood, which is a powerful feeling at any age. The selection of the right rhyme at the right time then becomes a powerful communication tool for the parent.

The many different emotions expressed in nursery rhymes also offer parents a vehicle for talking about feelings. The ability to identify and talk about feelings is fundamental to a child's social and emotional well-being.

NURSERY RHYMES FOSTER BRAIN DEVELOPMENT

The close physical contact, the face-to-face interaction, and the eye contact between the parent and the child all stimulate the firing of synapses in the baby's brain that build neural connections.

Through the repetition of a familiar rhyme babies soon perceive pattern and sequence in events, and they learn to anticipate—the little drop through the knees at the end of a bouncing rhyme like "A Smooth Road," for example, or the tickle that comes at the end of a tickling rhyme. This helps babies develop prediction skills which are a part of cognitive development.

NURSERY RHYMES FOSTER LANGUAGE DEVELOPMENT

Through face-to-face play with the parent, the baby learns the cheek, lip and tongue muscle movements required for making speech sounds.

The strong rhythm and beat of nursery rhymes when accompanied by a parent's rhythmic body movement, helps the baby absorb the patterns and rhythms of language with her whole body. Bouncing rhymes, or lap rhymes, especially, are enormously powerful in teaching the beat of language. Long before they can speak, infants can move their bodies in response to familiar patterns of sound and movement. When they are more mobile, they will climb up on a parent's lap for a familiar rhyme, initiating play with the parent through gesture and body movement.

The rhyme and alliteration in nursery rhymes helps the baby tune in to the smaller units of sound in language. The smallest units of sound, like the "b" sound in "Baa Baa Black Sheep," are called phonemes. Phoneme imitation helps the baby learn to speak. Later this same skill will be required for learning how to read. A child's ability to play with the sounds of language, and to hear and say phonemes by the age of six is a predictor of reading success.

The expressive and often humourous vocabulary of nursery rhymes teaches babies many new words. Face rhymes introduce the names of facial features. Many action rhymes name the different body parts. Children are exposed to wonderful expressions like "cobbler, cobbler, mend my shoe" and "hickory dickory dock." This vocabulary often becomes a part of a child's repertoire for communication. A sizable vocabulary is another predictor of reading success.

Many nursery rhymes have little stories in them. They are little stories for little people. They have a beginning, a middle, and an end. Children who become familiar with this pattern develop an understanding of basic story structure. This is a narrative skill that will be required for reading and reading comprehension. The same narrative skill helps children construct stories about their own experiences, and helps them learn to communicate in words with the people around them. A child's ability to describe people, places and events is a predictor of reading success.

Hearing stories without seeing illustrations helps babies develop the ability to create pictures in their minds out of the words they hear. This is the beginning of vocabulary formation and story making, and helps foster imagination.

Often nursery rhymes have memorable little characters in them. These rhymes introduce babies to the stock characters of our culture: Old Mother Hubbard, the Old Woman Who Lived in a Shoe, and Humpty Dumpty, will all reappear in stories children read when they get to school. The recognition of these characters helps children understand the stories in which these stock characters appear.

ADDITIONAL BENEFITS

Nursery rhymes can be played anywhere anytime: in a grocery store line-up, at the doctor's office, on the change table, in the middle of the night, or on a car ride.

No expensive toys are required. Babies learn best through playful interaction with their loving caregivers.

On top of all this, the rhymes are just fun to do!

WHAT PROGRAMMERS CAN DO

1. Use nursery rhymes in your programs.
2. Teach parents the rhymes.
3. Suggest practical times, such as diaper-changing and hand-washing, when parents can use the rhymes.
4. Introduce resources where parents can find more rhymes. (There is a bibliography of Rhyme Resources for Parents in the Program Resources section of this book.)

WHAT PARENTS & CAREGIVERS CAN DO

1. Say nursery rhymes in play with your baby. You probably know a few, but you can learn more by attending baby programs and by borrowing collections of nursery rhymes from the public library. Many of these are beautifully illustrated too.
2. Use rhythm and beat when you say the rhymes in play with your baby.
3. Repeat the rhymes your baby likes best. Pretty soon, your baby will be saying them back to you.

The Power of Song

INTRODUCTION

Singing to babies fosters the same kinds of development as the nursery rhymes we say, and has additional benefits.

The singing voice will capture a baby's attention. Whether it's a room full of fifty babies at a gathering or just one unhappy baby on the change table, all the babies will stop what they are doing, and listen when you sing. They love the singing voice. But what is it they like about it, and why is it so important that we sing to babies?

SINGING FOSTERS ATTACHMENT

The singing voice offers caregivers a powerful tool for connecting in loving ways with babies.

The singing voice will alter a baby's state of emotional arousal. When we sing a lullaby we calm and relax a baby into sleep. When we sing a bouncing, dancing or clapping song we keep the baby alert and engaged in play. A song can be used at any time of the day or night to calm a fussy baby.

When we sing at predictably stressful times —during daily care routines, such as face and hand-washing, diaper-changing, dressing and undressing, naptime, and bedtime— we distract the baby and help her get through the experience with delight rather than frustration.

Singing also relaxes the adult in stressful situations, and provides an outlet for adult frustration.

When we sing during transitional times— such as preparing to eat, cleaning up, getting ready to go out—we help young children prepare emotionally for the next activity so they can move happily through the transition.

Matching the mood of the song to the baby's mood helps the baby feel understood.

When we sing to babies at stressful times rather than using less desirable means of control, we show empathy, support, and respect for the baby's feelings. This helps us build a relationship of trust and maintain a close emotional bond with the baby.

In all these circumstances, we are teaching and modelling for the baby how to soothe himself. In time, children will sing to calm, comfort, and delight themselves. Many children who are sung to regularly eventually sing themselves to sleep.

Like poetry, singing expresses emotions that are difficult to convey through any other vehicle in our language. Giving babies this tool for expressing their emotions, right from the start will help them get in touch with their feelings and help them develop into expressive communicators.

SINGING FOSTERS LANGUAGE DEVELOPMENT

Singing raises the pitch of our voices and elongates the vowel sounds, just like "parentese," which is the language that babies love and understand best. These are the easiest sounds for them to hear and imitate. Babies start cooing in vowel sounds at about two months so singing is a natural language for them.

Songs have a stronger rhythm and beat than conversational language. This inspires body movement. The rhythmic movements we use when we sing—such as swaying, rocking, bouncing, clapping or dancing—help the baby absorb the sound patterns of language with her whole body. Feeling the timing, tempo and beat of language helps the baby learn to speak and will support her later introduction to literacy.

Songs break words into syllables. Often there is a different note used to sing the different syllable sounds. Playing with the smaller units of sound in words also helps the baby learn to speak and will support her later introduction to literacy.

Like the nursery rhymes we say, songs are full of rhyme and repetition, but in songs these sounds are even more pronounced.

Babies can sing melodies and they can do the motions to action songs long before they can speak. The encouragement and practice with vocalizing helps babies develop their vocal cords for singing and speaking. The exchange of sound and movement with the caregiver also helps the baby learn how to communicate and take turns in a back and forth rhythm.

Songs introduce unique vocabulary. What a wonderful way for children to hear about twinkling stars, and babushkas, and silver moons sailing o'er the sky!

SINGING FOSTERS BRAIN DEVELOPMENT

When we learn songs, the words are stored in the left hemisphere of the brain while the melodies are stored in the right. Singing helps young children integrate the two halves of brain function.

Singing builds memory skills. The repetition of songs helps babies build the brain capacity for memory in general. Alphabet songs and counting songs, like "This Old Man," help children remember the sequence of letters and numbers.

Basic concepts babies need to learn, like fast/slow, high/low, soft/loud, up/down and many more are experienced through singing. Even a simple song like "Roly Poly" teaches these concepts.

Singing inspires creativity. When children remember the tune and forget the words, they will often make up their own words. Sometimes these are better, or at least more interesting, than the original words.

Research indicates that singing also develops spatial-temporal skills in young children, that is, being able to perceive patterns and put the pieces of a puzzle together without visual representation. This helps the baby develop problem-solving skills.

SINGING FOSTERS MOTOR SKILL DEVELOPMENT

Singing inspires rhythmic body movements like rowing, bouncing, dancing, and clapping, and the movements help babies develop body awareness and the muscle and motor skills required for movement.

SINGING FOSTERS SOCIAL SKILL DEVELOPMENT

Babies love to sing and dance with us. Toddlers especially love to play circle games like "Ring around the Rosie" with us. This experience helps children develop cooperation and social skills. Learning to play together prepares a child for a lifetime of social success at school and in life.

ADDITIONAL BENEFITS

When we sing songs from our family's cultural heritage, such as an African-American spiritual, a Yiddish or Irish lullaby, a Mexican folk song, etc., we introduce the baby to the family's cultural heritage and help the baby feel connected to his cultural roots, right from the start.

Singing in a group has a magical appeal all its own. When used in a group setting, singing creates bonds between the participants who enjoy singing together.

WHAT PROGRAMMERS CAN DO

1. Sing songs in your programs. You don't have to be a great singer. In fact, your parents will appreciate your voice more if it isn't perfect.
2. Teach parents your songs.
3. Talk briefly about the benefits babies derive from singing.
4. Encourage parents to sing to their babies. Many parents don't sing because they think their voices aren't good enough. Tell them it doesn't matter to the baby what they think it sounds like, that their voice is the voice their baby loves and needs the most.
5. Encourage parents who speak English as a second language, to sing songs they know in their first language. Musical tones and rhythms vary across cultures. These tones and rhythms reinforce whatever language the baby is learning, and expose them to the family's cultural traditions. Children have the capacity to absorb them all!

WHAT PARENTS & CAREGIVERS CAN DO

1. Sing to your baby. While it is fun to use children's songs, any song you know will do.
2. Remember, your voice is the most important sound in your baby's life. Your voice is the voice your baby loves best. It doesn't matter how polished you think it is.
3. Use beat and rhythmic movement in play with your baby.
4. Play with simple musical instruments like rattles for shaking, pots and pans and spoons for clanging and drumming. This is lots of fun and will encourage your baby to develop an appreciation for the music of sound beyond the human voice.
5. Listening to recorded music is an enjoyable experience for you and your baby but it does not inspire the same kinds of development as interactive singing unless you sing, clap and dance along to the music in play with your baby as you both listen to it together.

New Parents

Since our audience is comprised of both parents and babies, it is helpful to consider the parents' needs as well as the babies' needs and developmental stages.

Family structures and dynamics have changed enormously in the past century and are constantly changing and evolving. Today, more mothers are working. Often both parents work. More young children and infants are in group day care. More fathers take an active role in the nurturing of their young children. There are more single parents. Grandparents live farther away. An increase in immigration has brought many different approaches and cultural practices to child-rearing in North America.

So what is life like for today's parents?

Being a new parent is a very demanding job. It means being on call and in demand twenty-four hours a day.

Nothing really prepares new parents for the way they're going to feel when the baby arrives. This is a unique, personal, and deeply moving experience.

Besides the great joy that parents feel when the baby arrives, they can also feel overwhelmed with the enormity of the task that lies before them. Being responsible for the life of a helpless little human being can be scary.

The many changes that the baby brings to parents lives are not always expected. This is a time of transition, and transitions are not always easy.

Parents are bombarded with conflicting advice—from professionals and non-professionals alike—about how to raise their children. Often the advice conflicts with the parent's instincts about what is best for their baby. This can make decision-making a challenge.

Every baby is born with a unique temperament. It is the parent's job to learn to recognize their own baby's traits, characteristics, and temperament, and respond in appropriate ways. This can be difficult work, especially if the baby's temperament is different from the parent's. Time and effort is required for the parent and infant to develop synchronized interactions.

New mothers who are breast feeding are tired. Sleep is a big issue, not only for the baby but also for the mom and dad. Most new babies feed several times during the night, especially in the first few months. Many babies have a hard time learning how to go to sleep and go back to sleep when they wake up during the night. Babies have their own sleep schedules and may sleep all day then stay awake all night. It takes time for babies to adjust to the family's sleep patterns. And just when parents think a healthy sleep pattern has been established, the baby changes! All this means that the mother is not getting enough sleep to feel good. Dad may be sleeping on the couch so he can get enough sleep to get up and go to work the next day, and he is tired too.

Many parents are isolated at this time in our social history. Grandparents and other family members who could offer support often live far away. Family traditions are not being transmitted through the grandparents as they once were.

Many more mothers than is commonly realized suffer from post-partum depression.

Some signs you may notice might include what looks like shyness, quietness, or a reluctance to participate. Your kindness and gentle support will help her through this time. Post-partum depression can be debilitating for the mother, and it can also have a damaging affect on the infant. A depressed mother may be emotionally unavailable and therefore unresponsive to her new infant. The sociability and support from other adults at parent-child programs can be of enormous assistance at this time.

Many new parents simply don't know any other parents with babies the same age, people they could share experiences with and get advice from. The best programs for parents therefore include social time, a time to connect and make friends with other new parents.

Many parents don't know any rhymes, or songs, or games to play with their babies that would enhance their relationship with the baby and help the baby develop. For this reason, it's a good idea to teach the rhymes. This way parents can remember them and use them at home.

Many first time parents have unrealistic expectations of their babies. It is helpful for them to be brought together with other families with babies the same age so they can develop an understanding of what is "normal" for their own babies. Being more realistic brings more patience.

Returning to work is a big issue for many parents. A parent may be torn between wanting to stay home to continue the care and nurturing of the baby, and at the same time, want to return to work, either to earn a living, or to maintain a career. A parent may also feel guilty about wanting a break from the baby. Once again, this is a difficult decision and a time of transition.

Other social and cultural factors that influence parenting styles that you may notice in your programs may include socio-economic status, educational levels, or cultural and linguistic backgrounds. All of these factors influence the way people parent. All of these factors also influence what the programmer observes about the practices and patterns of parent-infant interactions at programs.

Everyone who works with parents and their infants should keep in mind that all parents want what is best for their children. We can offer encouragement and support; we can teach a variety of ways to play with the baby; and we can make books, videos and other information available. But we do need to keep in mind that while some parents may need or want our help in solving problems, in the end, it is the parent's role to determine what is best for his or her own child.

WHAT PROGRAMMERS CAN DO

1. Empathize with parents, understand the stresses of parenthood, and show support.
2. Offer a social outlet for information sharing and companionship.
3. Teach parents the rhymes so they can remember them when they get home.

WHAT PARENTS & CAREGIVERS CAN DO

1. Take care of yourself. Good nutrition and exercise will help you feel batter. Rest when your baby rests.
2. Find social supports for yourself.
3. Reach out to friends and make new friends. Public libraries, community centres, and baby clinics are good places to find information and make new friends.
4. Tell friends how they can help. Often people want to help but they don't know what you need.
5. Remember that no one is perfect!

Ages and Stages

This quick reference list was created to help you get ready to respond to the developmental milestones you might observe with the babies in your groups. It is not meant as a definitive or exclusive list, but rather as a helpful list of things to watch for. Detailed accounts of milestones and developmental stages can be found in the bibliography at the end of this section and in the Parenting Resources bibliography in the PROGRAM RESOURCES section of this book.

Please note: the age limits are only approximations. What is more important than the timing for us, as programmers, is that we observe the developments and respond when we see an achievement. Babies are generally so delighted with their own developing abilities it is difficult not to notice!

IMPORTANT THINGS TO REMEMBER

1. Every baby develops at his or her own pace in his or her own unique way. No two babies are exactly alike.

2. Every baby is born with a unique temperament. Some babies are more sensitive and fussy than others.

3. Many parents have unrealistic expectations of their babies, and do not know a lot about child development, especially when they are first-time parents. When reassuring parents that their babies are "normal," I find it helpful when I know a little bit about this topic myself. With this information, I can help them better understand and empathize with their babies.

4. If a question comes up about baby's development, I always refer parents to other parents or to the Community Health Nurse. I am not an expert in child development!

THE MILESTONES

SMILING

Most babies cannot smile when they are newborn. They lack the control in their cheek and face muscles. The first 'smiles' may be grimaces. Most babies will be able to produce a genuine smile somewhere between six weeks and three months.

TONGUE AND MOUTH MOVEMENT

Babies have control over their tongues at birth. If you stick out your tongue a bit and wait for the baby to respond, she will stick out her little tongue back to you, just to let you know she understands the game. I think babies enjoy the song, "Mmm-Ah, Went the Little Green Frog" (p. 68), for its fun tongue movement. Babies can also open their mouths wide. If you open your mouth wide and wait, the baby will open his mouth wide back to you.

LITTLE HANDS

Babies keep their fingers curled in a little fist after birth. This is why toe-wiggling and foot-patting rhymes were invented! The baby will soon be able to unclasp his tiny hand but will not be able to participate in simple finger play rhymes, like "Two Little Dicky Birds" (p. 101), until he has developed more manual dexterity (or fine motor skills) at about one year of age.

VISION

Vision is not very well developed at birth. Newborns can see objects that are held up to about twelve inches from their faces and they have no peripheral vision.

Newborns can see black and white clearly, but they can't see colours well until they are about four months old.

Vision improves gradually. Peripheral vision starts to develop around three months of age. Binocular vision, required to see in three dimensions and for depth perception, occurs around seven months.

By nine months a baby's vision is fully developed.

Babies enjoy looking at bright lights, strong patterns, and slowly moving objects. Most of all, babies like to look at faces. Encourage parents to get up close to their baby's face with face-touching rhymes, like "The Moon Is Round" (p. 91).

ROLLING OVER

This is a terrific milestone in baby's development. It will likely happen (back to front, and front to back) around six months. It signals a huge gain in gross motor skill development. Celebrate the moment with applause and with rolling over games like "Leg Over Leg" (p. 59) Extra caution is now needed on the change table at home.

SITTING UP

Babies are generally able to sit up without support by about seven months. Being able to pull up to a sitting position takes longer and happens at around eleven months when the baby has developed enough strength in his upper body and enough balance to do it. Lap games like "Row Your Boat" (p. 70), and other rowing games can help babies learn how to do this.

TEETHING

Teething can be very painful for babies and can happen any time during the first year, from three to twelve months. Signs are usually fussiness and drooling. Sympathy and understanding are the best responses. Soothing and distracting rhymes will help.

SOLID FOODS

Solid foods are usually introduced around six months. This is when parents start to bring little food containers and various baby snacks to programs. I don't allow any eating during my programs, except nursing of course, because I find it removes the parent and baby from the interactive play which is the purpose of the program. If a baby is hungry for a snack, we all stop and have a snack. If snack is a part of your program and time is made for this, then this is the time for snacking, not during the play part of the program. Then you can make a rhyme like "Here's a Cup" (p. 97), part of your snack ritual.

COOING AND BABBLING

Babies will coo and gaa when parents talk to them anywhere between six weeks to six months. Babbling, that is practising recognizable speech sounds, will start to happen in earnest around seven or eight months. Look for rhymes that correspond to babies' speech sounds. Baa, baa, baa can be extended with "Baa, Baa Black Sheep," for example.

CLAPPING

The ability to bring hands together in a clapping motion is also a terrific milestone. It happens about the age of eight months. This means the baby has gained a lot of strength and control in her arms and hands, and it means she is developing hand-eye coordination. Celebrate and encourage this development with clapping games like "Pat-a-Cake" (p. 98).

POINTING

This stage signals the beginning of the development of fine muscle control in the fingers. It is also a huge milestone in baby's communication. Now he can point to things he wants and point to things he is interested in. Now is the time for naming and talking about what the baby is pointing to so he can develop vocabulary. When I see this, I introduce the simplest finger rhymes. Rhymes like "There Was a Little Mouse" (p. 99), and "Come a'Look a'See" (p. 94) are very popular at this time.

CRAWLING

At about eight to nine months most (not all) babies will begin to crawl. This action signals a huge advance in baby brain development. And, of course, mobility. Now it's fun to play "chase" with little games like "Slowly, Slowly" (p. 148).

STANDING UP

From a very early age, babies will push their feet against stationary objects, including parents' bodies, to strengthen their leg muscles. Before a baby can stand, she needs to have developed strong leg muscles and a good sense of balance. Most babies will try to pull themselves up on furniture like the coffee table, between nine and ten months. Extra caution needs to be taken in the program room now. Babies can bang their heads when they pull themselves up under a table. A baby can usually stand alone, without support, at about thirteen months. She needs a lot of practise getting her balance and will fall down a lot. A song like "Boom, Boom, Baby Goes Boom, Boom" (p. 131), will take the shock out of falling.

WALKING

At about thirteen to fourteen months most babies will take their first tentative steps. How different the world looks now! And the baby loves it so much he will want to do it all the time! An obviously dramatic milestone, signalling many changes at home, and in programs. Celebrate baby's accomplishment with simple circle games that the babies can participate in, such as "Ring around the Rosie" (p. 86). Babies who have just learned how to walk love to play falling down games and they never seem to tire of this. Throughout the second year, circle games are a wonderful way for baby, now a young toddler, to practise his new walking skills.

SLEEP

Every baby is unique, but all babies need to learn how to put themselves to sleep and get back to sleep by themselves when they wake up during the night, and this can take a long time. Some babies might sleep through six to eight hours a night somewhere between six and eight months, but others will take much longer. Relaxation and a regular routine before bedtime helps babies learn to sleep. Teach the parents some lullabies. Lullabies will help both the parent and the baby make it through the long nights.

CRYING AND ATTACHMENT

Crying is a big topic of conversation with new parents. They will often ask, for example, "How long should I let my baby cry when I'm teaching him to go to sleep?" The Community Health Nurses I work with say: "Never let a baby under six months cry." Here are the reasons: Crying is the way a baby communicates his discomfort, or hunger, or fatigue, or fear, or boredom. He has no other way of showing how he feels. When a parent does not respond in a loving way by picking him up, soothing him, feeding him, or addressing his needs, the baby learns he can't trust the parent to support him and comfort him when he needs it the most. The trust that babies develop with their parents is critical to the baby's social/emotional health. The pattern of responsiveness that is established in the first year, in the baby's first and most important relationship, is the pattern that will form the basis for all the baby's future relationships with people. It will also determine how he ends up feeling about himself.

Interpreting baby's cries, listening for the pitch and tone of the sound, and watching for signs in the baby's body language, are all parents' work, and interpretation can be a difficult task sometimes.

In programs where a baby cries, and this certainly will happen, show the parents how to respond by having the whole group sing a lullaby. This soothes the baby without fail, especially if it's the baby's favourite comforting song. It makes the parent feel better too.

BIBLIOGRAPHY

Allen, K. Eileen and Lynn Marotz. DEVELOPMENTAL PROFILES: PRE-BIRTH THROUGH EIGHT. Second Edition. Albany, NY: Delmar Publishers Inc, 1994.

Kopp, Claire B. BABY STEPS: A GUIDE TO YOUR CHILD'S SOCIAL, PHYSICAL, MENTAL, AND EMOTIONAL DEVELOPMENT IN THE FIRST TWO YEARS. New York: Henry Holt, 2003.

Leach, Penelope. BABYHOOD: STAGE BY STAGE, FROM BIRTH TO AGE TWO: HOW YOUR BABY DEVELOPS PHYSICALLY, EMOTIONALLY, MENTALLY. New York: Knopf: Distributed by Random House, 1983.

Leach, Penelope. THE FIRST SIX MONTHS: GETTING TOGETHER WITH YOUR BABY. Photographs by John Campbell. London: Fontana/Collins, 1986.

Leach, Penelope. YOUR BABY AND CHILD: FROM BIRTH TO AGE FIVE. Photographs by Jenny Matthews. New York: Alfred A. Knopf, 1997.

VIDEOS AND DVDS

AMAZING BABIES: MOVING IN THE FIRST YEAR WITH BEVERLY STOKES. Toronto, ON: Amazing Babies Videos, 1995. (1 videocassette (VHS) 47 minutes.)
This is a wonderful video on baby development that will keep all members of the family fascinated as they realize the amazing intelligence of their new baby.

A BABY'S WORLD: A WHOLE NEW WORLD: AGES NEWBORN TO 1 YEAR. *Produced by David Hickman. The Learning Channel.* Bethesda, MD: Discovery Enterprises Group; Montreal: Distributed by Alliance Video, 1994. (60 minutes.)
Shows how babies motivate others to care for them and gradually make sense of the world, and how babies conquer movement, from sitting, crawling, standing to finally walking.

Bernier, Tamara. The BABY HUMAN. Richmond Hill, ON: BFS Entertainment and Multimedia Ltd, 2004.
(DVD, approx. 150 minutes.)
This excellent resource includes three useful episodes: To Walk, To Think, and To Talk. It covers the baby's challenges in the first two years in learning how to do these things from the baby's point of view.

A SIMPLE GIFT: COMFORTING YOUR BABY. Infant Mental Health Promotion Project, Department of Psychiatry, the Hospital for Sick Children; [produced by] Dreams and Realities. Van Nuys, CA: Child Development Media, 1998. (10 minutes.)
Based on the ideas of attachment theory, this video discusses the development and importance of an infant's attachment relationship with parents in the first year of life and shows specifically how and why parents should respond when their baby cries.

Rhymes

Introduction *56*
Action Rhymes *57*
Action Songs *65*
Bouncing Rhymes *75*
Circle Games and Dances *83*
Face Rhymes *89*
Finger Play and Hand Rhymes *93*
French Rhymes *103*
Greeting Songs *107*
Goodbye Songs *111*
Lullabies *115*
Rhymes in Other Languages *125*
Songs *129*
Spanish Rhymes *137*
Story Rhymes *141*
Tickling Rhymes *145*
Toe-Wiggling and Foot-Patting Rhymes *149*

This section includes rhymes for any and all occasions for parents with infants, and for parents with young toddlers to play together. The age focus is birth to two years. The rhymes are divided into the above categories to make finding appropriate rhymes easy and fun. They are all rhymes I have used successfully in my programs. The rhymes within each category are listed alphabetically by first line.

Introduction

The rhymes have been organized into categories to make them more manageable and accessible. Of course there is no one right way to play a rhyme. Any rhyme with a strong beat can be played as a bouncing rhyme. Any slow song will do as a lullaby. Finger plays can be played on little toes. Finger plays can also be played using one hand, the other hand, one foot, the other foot and the head, which makes five! Some finger rhymes work very well for young toddlers as circle games. Once you teach parents the words and give them some ideas about how to hold and touch their babies while saying them, they will invent methods of their own. The "right way" is the way the parent and child enjoy doing the rhyme together the most.

All the rhymes can be used with all ages and are enjoyable to children from infancy into the primary grades. The words remain the same, we just change the actions to suit the child's level of development and ability. For example, you can use a rhyme like "Round and Round the Haystack" (p. 147) as a tickling rhyme with an infant, then as a circle game with a toddler, and again as a tickling rhyme with a preschooler who will find it very amusing and can say it himself. "Jelly in the Bowl" (p. 59), is fun to play with an infant, and preschoolers love to stand up and act it out themselves. The lullabies and comforting songs children hear in infancy continue to comfort them for the rest of their lives.

Most of the rhymes are from the folk tradition. The exceptions have copyright notes under the titles.

Feel free to adapt the rhymes and use family names in them. For example, say the baby's name instead of Sally in "Clap Your Hands, Little Sally" (p. 66).

Rhyme titles, on each section's table of contents, are ordered by title, along with page numbers for quick access. The rhymes within each section are ordered alphabetically by first line.

Action Rhymes

Acka Backa Soda Cracker *58*
The Bear and the Bees (Wiggle Waggle) *63*
Chop Chop Choppity Chop *58*
Criss Cross Applesauce *58*
Hickory Dickory Dock *58*
I Saw a Snake Go By One Day *58*
I'm Toast in the Toaster *59*
Jack in the Box *59*
Jelly in the Bowl *59*
Leg over Leg *59*
The Little Boy Goes in the Tunnel *59*
Little Man in a Coal Pit *60*
Marching in Our Wellingtons *60*
Mix and Stir *60*
The North Wind Shall Blow *60*
Pat Your Head *60*
Popcorn! *60*
Slice Slice *61*
There Was a Little Man *61*
These Are Baby's Fingers *61*
This Is the Key to the Kingdom *61*
Tony Chestnut *62*
The Turtle Went up the Hill *62*
Up, Up the Candlestick *62*
Way Up High in the Banana Tree *63*
You Be the Ice Cream *63*

These rhymes have a lovely lilt to the language. The actions that accompany them reinforce the rhythm, rhyme and repetition of the language.

Acka Backa Soda Cracker

Bounce baby side to side, lift up on "up goes you," and hug on "I love you!"

Acka backa soda cracker
Acka backa boo;
Acka backa soda cracker
Up goes you.
Acka backa soda cracker
Acka backa boo;
Acka backa soda cracker
I love you!

Chop Chop Choppity Chop

Take baby's hands and make a chopping scissor motion, down at the feet and up over the head. The tummy is the pot. Older children like to act it out standing up: they chop at ankle level, then at head level, then jump into an imaginary pot. It's fun to say in the kitchen as you chop the vegetables for supper, letting the baby know that supper is coming.

Chop chop choppity chop,
Cut off the bottoms,
And cut off the tops.
What there is left,
We will put in the pot,
So chop chop choppity chop.

Criss Cross, Applesauce

This is a nice little drawing game to play on a baby's back or tummy. It's also fun for older children to play on their parents, or on each other in pairs.

Criss, cross,
Draw an X on baby's back.
Applesauce.
Pat baby's shoulders in rhythm to the beat.
Spiders crawling up your back,
Walk fingers in a tickly fashion up your baby's back.
Crawling here,
Lightly tickle one shoulder.
Crawling there,
Lightly tickle the other shoulder.
Spiders crawling in your hair.
Tickle baby's scalp.
Tight squeeze,
Give a little hug.
Cool breeze,
Blow gently on baby's neck.
And now you've got the shivers!
Tickle baby all over.

Hickory Dickory Dock

Hickory dickory dock,
The mouse ran up the clock.
Walk two fingers up baby's arm like a pair of legs.
The clock struck one,
Give baby a little kiss on the nose.
The mouse ran down,
Hickory dickory dock.
Run fingers back down the same arm.

I Saw a Snake Go By One Day

© Lois Simmie. This poem is much-loved by parents and toddlers alike. Improvise actions with a baby.

I saw a snake go by one day,
Make an eye-spy motion, then make a snake motion with one hand.
Riding in his Chevrolet.
Pretend you're at the steering wheel.
He was long
Stretch your arms out to the side as wide as they can go.
And he was thin
Now extend your arms to the front and hold them straight out together.
And he didn't have a chin.
Point to your chin.
He had no chin,
Point to your chin again.

But what the heck
Shrug.
He had lots and lots and lots of neck.
Roll your hands around themselves just under your chin.

I'm Toast in the Toaster

This is a fun rhyme to do, with baby on your lap facing you, or on your hip as you're standing in a grocery store line-up.

I'm toast in the toaster
I'm getting very hot
Gently bounce.
Tick, tock, tick, tock
Sway side to side.
Up I pop!
Toss baby up in the air.

Jack in the Box

This can be a hand rhyme where you hide your thumb in your fist and the child places her hand on top for the lid. Or it is fun for toddlers to play standing up and crouching down, sitting still, still, still, then jumping up.

Jack in the Box
Jack in the Box
Sit so still
Will you come out?
Yes, I will!

Jelly in the Bowl

This is a great lap rhyme. Older children like to stand up and act it out.

Jelly in the bowl
Jelly in the bowl
Wibble wobble, wibble wobble
Jelly in the bowl.
Rock baby back and forth on your knee.

Candles on the cake
Candles on the cake
Blow 'em out, blow 'em out
Candles on the cake.
Hold fingers (candles) up. As you blow them out, curl them into your fist.

Biscuits in the tin
Biscuits in the tin
Shake 'em up, shake 'em up
Biscuits in the tin.
Bounce baby on your knee.

Leg Over Leg

Here is a great diaper-changing rhyme. Take baby's feet in your hands and cross her legs back and forth, over and over, until you lift up on "whoops," to slip the diaper under. It's also fun to play as a game to teach baby how to roll over. (A stile is a little step up over a fence or wall.)

Leg over leg,
The dog went to Dover,
When he came to a stile,
Whoops!
He went over.

The Little Boy (or Girl) Goes in the Tunnel

Here is a game to make pulling a shirt over baby's head a little more fun for both parent and child. Arms in sleeves first, then gently knock three times on baby's head, then pull the shirt up and over.

The little boy goes in the tunnel
Begin to put shirt over head.
Knock, knock, knock
Tap lightly on top of head.
Up he comes, and up he comes
Out the top!
Quickly pull shirt down. All done!

Little Man in a Coal Pit

Here is a variation for pulling a shirt over baby's head, for those who like the imagery of the coal pit. It's dark in there from the baby's point of view!

Little man in a coal pit
Goes knock, knock, knock.
Up he comes,
Up he comes,
Out at the top.

Marching in our Wellingtons

We like to use this one as a stand-up rhyme for toddlers on a rainy day. It's fun for a parent to say to get a dawdling toddler to walk along.

Marching in our wellingtons
Tramp, tramp, tramp
Marching in our wellingtons
We won't get damp.

Splashing through the puddles
In the rain, rain, rain
Splashing through the puddles
And splash home again.

Mix and Stir

Babies who love face rhymes love this rhyme. Older children like to stand up and act it out themselves.

Mix and stir and pat in the pan
Take baby's hands and make stirring motion, then pat baby's tummy.
I'm going to make a gingerbread man
Trace outline of baby's shape on head and shoulders with index fingers.
With a nose so neat
Touch baby's nose.
And a smile so sweet
Trace a smile on baby's mouth.
And gingerbread shoes on his gingerbread feet.
Pat baby's feet.

The North Wind Shall Blow

Toddlers love to act this out. It's especially nice to do on a cold winter day.

The north wind shall blow
Cup hand and blow.
And we shall have snow
Flutter fingers down from the sky.
And what will poor robin do then,
Poor thing?
Hands up, "I don't know."
He'll sit in the barn,
Crouch down.
And keep himself warm,
With his head tucked under his wing,
Poor thing!
Tuck head under arm.

Pat Your Head

This one is fun for little toddlers to act out themselves.

Pat your head
And rub your tummy
Tickle your toes
And hug your mummy.

Popcorn!

This rhyme is fun to play sitting down or standing up with baby on your hip.

Pop, pop, pop,
You put the corn in the pot.
Bounce baby to the beat.
Pop, pop, pop,
Bounce.
You shake it till it's hot.
Jostle side to side.
Pop, pop, pop,
Bounce.
Lift the lid and what have you got?
Pretend to lift lid from baby's head.
Pop, pop, pop,
Bounce.
Popcorn!
Swing baby up in the air.

Slice Slice

This is an indispensable rhyme for quieting a fussy child.

Slice, slice, bread looks nice.
Spread the palm of your hand down one side of the baby, then the other, very slowly. This is very calming.
Spread, spread, butter on the bread.
Now slowly spread the palm of your hand down baby's front, first with one hand then the other.
Some jam on top to make it sweet,
Touch the top of baby's head.
And now it's good enough to eat!
Trace a circle around baby's mouth.

There Was a Little Man

This is a fun rhyme to say any time, but especially as you clean up after a meal.

There was a little man,
Use your pointer finger.
Who had a little crumb,
Point to an imaginary crumb on your baby's cheek.
And over the mountain he did run,
Run fingers up over baby's head.
With a belly full of fat,
Pat baby's tummy.
And a tall black hat,
Pat the top of baby's head.
And a pancake stuck to his bum, bum, bum!
Pat baby on his little bottom.

These Are Baby's Fingers

Use your own baby's name for "baby."

These are baby's fingers,
These are baby's toes,
This is baby's belly button,
Round and round it goes!

This Is the Key to the Kingdom

This lovely story rhyme is easier than it looks. Toddlers love to act it out imitating their parents' actions.

This is the key to the kingdom.
Hold up your thumb for the key, then palms wide apart for the kingdom.
And in the kingdom, there is a town,
Bring palms closer, about a foot apart.
And in the town, there is a hill,
Bring your fingertips together and make a hill with your forearms.
And on the hill, there is a street,
Hold arms straight out in front of you, parallel to one another.
And on the street, there is a house,
Bring fingertips together again, and form a pitched roof.
And in the house, there is a room,
Make a floor with thumbs touching and parallel palms up for the walls.
And in the room, there is a bed,
Make a headboard with one hand up and the other palm flat for the bed.
And on the bed, there is a basket,
Cup your hands for the basket.
And in the basket, there is a blanket,
Fold one palm down on the other.
And under the blanket, there is a BABY!
Open your hands as if you have a precious jewel hidden inside.

Now do the whole thing backwards.

Baby under the blanket,
Palms together.
Blanket in the basket,
Cupped hands.

Basket on the bed,
Headboard and frame.
Bed in the room,
Thumbs together, walls up.
Room in the house,
Pitched roof.
House on the street,
Parallel arms.
Street on the hill,
Curved forearms, fingertips touching.
Hill in the town,
Parallel palms held about a foot apart.
Town in the kingdom,
Now stretch your arms out wide.
And THIS is the key to the kingdom.
And hold up your thumb.

Tony Chestnut

Parents find the puns in this rhyme amusing. Say or sing slowly to the tune of "Frère Jacques."

Tony Chestnut
Touch toe, then knee, then chest, then head.
Knows I love you
Touch nose, eye, heart, then child.
Tony knows, Tony knows.
Toe, knee, nose. Toe knee, nose.
Tony Chestnut
Toe, knee, chest, head.
Knows I love you
Nose, eye, heart, child.
That's what Tony knows.
Toe, knee, nose.

The Turtle Went Up the Hill

Walk your fingers up baby's body or arm. Toddlers like to act this one out themselves.

The turtle went up the hill,
Creepy, creepy, creepy.
Creep fingers slowly up baby's body.
The snake went up the hill,
Slither, slither, slither.
Make a snake hand slither up baby's body.
The rabbit went up the hill,
Boing, boing, boing.
Hold up two fingers, and bounce up baby's body.
The elephant went up the hill,
Thud, thud, thud.
Make the side of your fist thud up baby's body.
And a great big rock came down the hill,
Bumpity, bumpity, bumpity, bumpity, CRASH!
Take baby's hands and roll roly-poly style, from up high to down low, then thump the floor for the crash.

Up Up The Candlestick

For a baby, pretend the baby's body is the candlestick and walk your fingers up her body, then nibble at her fingers, call for grandma, and take her hands and roll roly-poly style at the end. Actions for toddlers are below.

Up up the candlestick
Hold up your forearm to make a candlestick. Walk the fingers of your other hand up the candlestick.
Went little Mousie Brown.
He took a bite of candle
Nibble at your fingertips.
Then he couldn't get back down.
Shake head, no.
He called for his Grandma,
"Grandma! Grandma!"
Cup hands to your mouth to call for grandma.
But Grandma was in town.
Wave hands toward "town" behind you.
So he curled himself into a ball
Huddle over your hands.
And rolled himself back down.
Roll hands down to the ground.

Way Up High In The Banana Tree

This is a rhyme in sign language that parents and toddlers love to do. You can say it again using any kind of fruit you like.

Way up high
Hold hand up high in the air.
in the banana
Pretend to peel a banana, using your index finger as the banana.
tree,
Make a tree by waving your hand in the air supported at the elbow with your other hand.
I saw
Point to yourself, then point to your eyes.
a banana
Pretend to peel that banana again.
looking at me.
Point to your eyes, then to yourself.
I shook that tree as hard as I could,
Shake two fists.
And down came the banana
Point your index finger (the banana) down.
Mmmm, mmmm, good!
Rub your tummy.

The Bear and the Bees (Wiggle Waggle)

© Dennis Lee. This is an indispensable diaper changing rhyme. With baby lying on his back facing you, take his feet, and say ...

Wiggle waggle went the bear,
Catching bees in his underwear!
Press one knee to tummy, then the other knee, back and forth in rhythm to the beat.
One bee out, and one bee in,
Legs spread apart, then legs together.
And one bee bit him on his big bare skin!
Then zero in for a playful pinch on baby's bottom.

You Be the Ice Cream

What love this little rhyme expresses!

You be the ice cream
Touch baby's cheek, then lick your finger, mmmm.
And I'll be the freezer.
Give baby a shivery hug.
You be the lemon
Touch baby's cheek again, then lick finger and made a sour face.
And I'll be the squeezer.
Give baby a little squeeze.

You be the hot dog
Squirt some mustard on.
And I'll be the bun.
Enfold baby in a cozy hug.
You be the baby
Give a little bounce.
And we'll have some fun!
Give a hug and a tickle.

Action Songs

Baby Put Your Pants On *66*
Big Blue Boat *66*
Clap Your Hands, Little Sally *66*
Come Along and Sing with Me *66*
The Cuckoo Clock *72*
Dirty Bill *71*
The Eensy Weensy Spider *66*
Everybody Knows I Love Your Toes *67*
The Grandfather Clock *67*
Grandma Mose *67*
Head and Shoulders *67*
I Love Bubble Gum *69*
I'm a Little Teapot *68*
Jeremiah *68*
Let's Clap Our Hands Together *68*
Mmm-Ah Went the Little Green Frog *68*
Obidayah *69*
On My Foot There Is a Flea *69*
Peek-a-Boo *69*
Rain Is Falling Down *70*
Roly Poly *70*
Round and Round the Garden *70*
Row Your Boat *70*
A Rum Sum Sum *71*
She Didn't Dance *72*
Teddy Bear, Teddy Bear *72*
These Are the Toes of My Baby *72*
Tick Tock, Tick Tock *72*
Tommy Thumbs *73*
Up Down, Turn Around *73*
The Wheels on the Bus *73*
When the Rain Comes Down *74*
Zoom Zoom Zoom *74*

All the rhymes in this section have actions as well as little tunes that go with them. Traditional tunes you likely know are provided in the notes for some. Tunes you might not know and can learn from sound recordings, including the enclosed CD, are also included in the notes.

Baby Put Your Pants On

This is a wonderful song to use when dressing and undressing a wriggly child. The tune is "Mama's Little Baby Loves Shortnin' Bread." The tune is on the enclosed CD.

Baby put your pants on, pants on, pants on,
Baby put your pants on, 1 2 3.

Baby put your shirt on, shirt on, shirt on,
Baby put your pants on, 1 2 3.

Baby put your socks on …
Baby put your shoes on …
Baby put your hat on …

Now that you're all dressed, all dressed, all dressed,
Now that you're all dressed, let's go play!

Now sing it all again in reverse order.

Baby take your hat off, hat off, hat off
Baby take your hat off, 1 2 3.

etc., then:

Now that you're all naked, all naked, all naked,
Now that you're all naked
Let's take a bath!

Clap Your Hands, Little Sally

With babies, clap hands, roll hands around each other, touch knees, toes, and other parts of the body as you sing. Toddlers love to stand up and act this out. You will find the tune on The Baby Record *(CD) by Bob McGrath and Katharine Smithrim.*

Clap your hands, little Sally,
Clap your hands, little Sally Brown,
Clap your hands, little Sally,
Clap 'em, Sally Brown.

Turn around, little Sally …
Bend your knees, little Sally …
Touch your toes, little Sally …

Come Along and Sing with Me

This is a nice opening song, sung to the tune of "Mary Had a Little Lamb."

Come along and sing with me, sing with me, sing with me,
Come along and sing with me, on a sunny Tuesday.

Take baby's hands and clap.
Come along and clap with me, clap with me, clap with me,
Come along and clap with me, on a sunny Tuesday.

Come along and roll with me …
Come along and stretch with me …

The Eensy, Weensy Spider

This is one everyone seems to know, so it's great to use when everything else is new. Follow with the great big spider if you like.

The eensy weensy spider
Climbed up the water spout;
Thumbs and pointer fingers climb up each other.
Down came the rain,
Raise hands and lower them, wriggling fingers.
And washed the spider out;
Sweep arms out to the side.
Out came the sunshine,
Raise hands above head and form circle.
And dried up all the rain;
And the eensy weensy spider
Climbed up the spout again.
Repeat climbing motion.

Everybody Knows I Love Your Toes

Touch all the baby's body parts you love as you sing this song.

Everybody knows I love your toes,
Everybody knows I love your toes,
I love your feet, your hands, your mouth and your nose,
And everybody knows I love your toes.

Now make up other verses about all the little things you love about the baby's body.

The Grandfather Clock

I like this little rhyme because it uses the word "stop" at the end in a playful way. Toddlers like to stand up and sway back and forth like the pendulum of a grandfather clock swaying faster and faster until "stop!"

The grandfather clock goes
Tick tock, tick tock, tick tock, tick tock,
Sway baby slowly from side to side.
The kitchen clock goes
Tick tock, tick tock, tick tock, tick tock,
Sway a little faster.
And Mommy's little watch goes
Tick-tick-tick-tick-tick-tick.
Jiggle or tickle.
Stop!
Use the sign language signal for stop: left palm held flat, right palm perpendicular on top. Stop, go still, and wait a bit before you do it again.

Grandma Mose

This one makes a great call and response rhyme. Call out a line, then the parents call out the line back to you and follow your actions.

Grandma Mose was sick in bed
Lay head down on hands, palms together.
She called for the doctor
And the doctor said,
Thumb and pinky finger make a telephone. Hold your thumb to your ear, and your pinky finger to your mouth.
Grandma Mose, you ain't sick
Wave your finger in "tut tut" fashion.
All you need is a peppermint stick.
Get up, shake, shake, shake, shake,
Shake hands up high four times.
Get down, shake, shake, shake, shake,
Shake hands down low four times.
Turn around, shake, shake, shake, shake,
If standing, turn around and shake hands four times on the beat. If sitting, just roll hands then shake four times.
Get out of town, shake, shake, shake, shake,
Shake right hand over right shoulder twice, then shake left hand over left shoulder twice.

Head and Shoulders

Don't forget this old favourite. Simply point to the various body parts mentioned as you sing.

Head and shoulders
Knees and toes
Knees and toes
Knees and toes
Head and shoulders
Knees and toes
Eyes, ears, mouth, and nose.

Big Blue Boat

Hold your baby on your lap facing you (toddlers like to hold your hands), and row back and forth. On the second verse, you can raise your arms up and wave from side to side. The tune is on the enclosed CD.

I love to row in my big blue boat,
My big blue boat, my big blue boat;
I love to row in my big blue boat,
Out on the deep blue sea.

My big blue boat has two red sails,
Two red sails, two red sails;
My big blue boat has two red sails,
Two red sails.

So come for a ride in my big blue boat,
My big blue boat, my big blue boat;
So come for a ride in my big blue boat,
Out on the deep blue sea.

I'm a Little Teapot

Here's one for the toddlers, sitting or standing. I like to follow this one by drinking up the tea with "Here's a Cup" *(p. 97)**.*

I'm a little teapot, short and stout,
Sit or stand straight with arms as sides.
Here is my handle, and here is my spout.
Place one hand on hip for handle, and hold up the other arm to form the spout.
When I get all steamed up, hear me shout,
Show excitement on face and get ready.
"Tip me over, and pour me out."
Both adult and child bend over at the waist as if pouring tea.

I'm a special teapot, yes it's true,
Here, let me show you what I can do.
I can change my handle and my spout.
Tip me over and pour me out.

Jeremiah

This is a great rhyme to use at diaper-changing time. Blow gently, then blow a big raspberry on baby's tummy. There is a little tune on Kathy Reid-Naiman's CD Say Hello to the Morning.

Jeremiah, blow the fire
Puff puff puff.
First you blow it gently,
Then you blow it ROUGH!

Let's Clap Our Hands Together

Suit actions to words. Make up your own verses. You will find the tune on The Baby Record *CD by Bob McGrath and Katharine Smithrim.*

Let's clap our hands together,
Let's clap our hands together,
Let's clap our hands together,
Because it's fun to do.

Let's tap our legs together ...
Let's roll our hands together ...
Let's touch our noses together ...
Let's blink our eyes together ...
Let's all stand up together ...
Let's turn around together ...
Let's all sit down together ...

Mmm-Ah Went the Little Green Frog

Say "mmm" then say "ahh" sticking out your tongue. Babies love this song.

Mmm-ahh went the little green frog one day,
Mmm-ahh went the little green frog.
Mmm-ahh went the little green frog one day,
And they all went mmm-mmm-ahh.
But ... we know frogs go
(clap) sha-na-na-na-na.
(clap) sha-na-na-na-na.
(clap) sha-na-na-na-na.
We know frogs go
(clap) sha-na-na-na-na.
They don't go mmm-mmm-ahh.

I Love Bubble Gum

This silly song has actions for the bubble gum part only. Draw your hands out in waves as if you are handling an ever bigger bubble on "ballupe, ballupe, ballupe," then clap hands on "bupp." Make up your own silly rhymes using pesos or lira, or other foreign currencies and rhyme the words with different foods.

My mother gave me a nickel
To go and buy a pickle.
I didn't buy a pickle,
I bought bubble gum!

Ballupe, ballupe, ballupe, bupp!
Ballupe, ballupe, ballupe, bupp!
Ballupe, ballupe, ballupe, bupp!
I love bubble gum!

My mother gave me a dime
To go and buy a lime.
I didn't buy a lime,
I bought bubble gum!

Ballupe, ballupe, ballupe, bupp!
Ballupe, ballupe, ballupe, bupp!
Ballupe, ballupe, ballupe, bupp!
I love bubble gum!

Obidayah

This is a lovely swinging song. You can listen to the tune on the enclosed CD.

Swing me just a little bit higher,
Obidayah do,
Swing me just a little bit higher,
I love you.
Swing me over the garden wall,
But swing me gently so I don't fall,
Just a little higher,
Obidayah do!

On My Foot There Is A Flea

Creep your fingers (flea) up from baby's foot to the top of his head and back down again, touching the baby's various body parts as you go, then pat the soles of his feet at the end. Simply sing up the scale and back down again as you go. Listen to the tune on Kathy Reid-Naiman's More Tickles & Tunes *CD.*

On my foot there is a flea
Now he's climbing up on me
Past my belly
Past my nose
On my head where my hair grows
On my head there is a flea
Now he's climbing down on me
Past my belly
Past my knee
On my foot
Take that, you flea!

Peek-a-Boo

The tune is "Frère Jacques." You can listen to the tune on the enclosed CD.

Peek-a-boo, peek-a-boo
I see you, I see you.
Peek, then point to baby.
I see your button nose
Touch baby's nose.
I see your tiny toes
Touch baby's toes.
Peek-a-boo,
I see you.
Point to baby.

Rain Is Falling Down

Second verse shared by Sally Jaeger. You can hear the tune on The Baby Record *CD by Bob McGrath and Katharine Smithrim. It is also on the enclosed CD.*

Rain is falling down. Splash!
Rain is falling down. Splash!
Flutter fingers down baby's body, and clap on "splash."
Pitter-patter, pitter-patter,
For little babies, pitter-patter fingertips down baby's body. For older babies and toddlers, clap hands in rhythm to the beat. Two beats for "pitter", two beats for "patter."
Rain is falling down. Splash!
Flutter fingers down baby's body again, and clap on "splash."
Sun is peeking out. Peek!
Cover your face with your hands, and peek out one side on "peek."
Sun is peeking out. Peek!
Cover your face with your hands again, and peek out on the other side.
Peeking here, peeking there,
Peek out from behind your hands again, one side and then the other.
Sun is peeking out. Peek!
Peek again!

Roly Poly

Sing to the tune of "Frère Jacques." Take baby's hands in your own. Any concept opposites are fun to do.

Roly poly, roly poly
Up, up, up ... up, up, up,
Roll baby's hands around each other, then stretch up and up and up.
Roly poly poly, roly poly poly,
Down, down down ... down, down, down.
Roll baby's hands, then stretch down and down and down.
Roly poly, roly poly
Out, out, out ... out, out, out,
Roll baby's hands, then stretch apart for "out."
Roly poly poly, roly poly poly,
In, in, in ... in, in, in.
Roll baby's hands, then pull together for "in."

More verses:
Roly poly ... front, and back.
Roly poly ... left, and right.
Roly poly ... fast and slow.

Round and Round the Garden

Say or sing this little favourite. It's fun to play on a bare tummy at diaper-changing time, or on a little palm when hands are big enough.

Round and round the garden
Like a teddy bear.
Draw a circle on baby's tummy.
One step, two step,
Tickle you under there!
Walk fingers up for a tickle under baby's arm.

Row Your Boat

Rock infant back and forth. Infants love the "aaahh" part as it's the first sound they can make. Take hands with toddlers and row. This is also a lovely song to sing as a round.

Row, row, row your boat,
Gently down the stream.
Merrily, merrily, merrily, merrily,
Life is but a dream.

Row, row, row your boat,
Gently down the stream.
If you see a crocodile,
Don't forget to scream, aaahh!

A Rum Sum Sum

This song has many variations. It can be "Ram Sam Sam" too. It's complete nonsense and fun to do. Toddlers love to act it out.

A rum sum sum
A rum sum sum
Roll hands.
Gooley, gooley gooley, gooley gooley
Pretend your fingers are playing with sticky gum.
Rum sum sum.
Roll hands again.

A rum sum sum
A rum sum sum
Gooley, gooley gooley, gooley gooley
Rum sum sum.
Repeat actions.

A raffi, a raffi!
Stretch arms up in celebration!
Gooley, gooley gooley, gooley gooley
Pull as if pulling on sticky gum caught in your fingers.
Rum sum sum.
Roll hands again.

A raffi, a raffi!
Gooley, gooley gooley, gooley gooley
Rum sum sum.
Repeat actions.

Dirty Bill

© Aubrey Davis. Parents and babies love this bathtime song. Listen to the tune on Kathy Reid-Naiman's CD More Tickles & Tunes.

Chorus:
Scrub, scrub, splash, splash, splash.
Scrub, scrub, splash, splash, splash.
Pretend to scrub one arm, then the other, then pretend to splash water.
I'm Dirty Bill from Vinegar Hill,
Point to self or baby with your thumb.
I never had a bath and I never will.
Wag your finger.
I'm Dirty Bill from Vinegar Hill,
I never had a bath and I never will!
Repeat actions.

1. Catch him,
Grab baby's arms.
Snatch him,
Pull baby close.
Put him in the tub,
Pretend to place in tub.
Pour on the water
Pretend to pour water over head.
And scrub, scrub,scrub!
Scrub.

Repeat chorus.

2. Put him in the bathtub, put him in the sink,
Wash away the dirt and the stink, stink, stink. (x 2)

Repeat chorus.

3. We're going to wash him up, wash him down,
Wash him around and around and around. (x 2)

Scrub, scrub, splash, splash, splash.
Scrub, scrub, glub, glub, glub.

She Didn't Dance

Parents clap hands or bounce baby in time to the music, then lift baby in the air to dance her up to the sky. Sing it a second time for the boys, saying, "He didn't dance," and "He is like a gentleman, he is like a king." The tune is on Kathy Reid-Naiman's CD, A Smooth Road to London Town.

She didn't dance, dance, dance,
She didn't dance at all today
She didn't dance, dance, dance,
No, nor yesterday.
So dance her up and up and up and up
Dance her up in the sky
Dance her up and up and up and up
And she'll be down by and by.

She is like a lady, she is like a queen
She is like a lady, off to the fair at Lynn.
So dance her up and up and up and up
Dance her up in the sky
Dance her up and up and up and up
And she'll be down by and by.

Teddy Bear, Teddy Bear

This is an acting out rhyme for parents and toddlers to do together with the parent helping. Go slowly for young toddlers. The tune is "Bluebird, Bluebird, Through My Window."

Teddy Bear, Teddy Bear, turn around.
Teddy Bear, Teddy Bear, touch the ground.
Teddy Bear, Teddy Bear, show your shoe.
Teddy Bear, Teddy Bear, I love you.
Give baby a little hug.
Teddy Bear, Teddy Bear, go upstairs.
Teddy Bear, Teddy Bear, say your prayers.
Teddy Bear, Teddy Bear, turn out the light.
Teddy Bear, Teddy Bear, say good night.
Lay your head on your hands.

These Are the Toes of My Baby

Sing to the tune of "Take Me Out to the Ball Game." Substitute your own baby's name for "baby."

These are the toes of my baby.
Touch baby's toes.
These are the toes of my (gal/guy),
These are his feet and his tiny knees—
Touch his feet, then his knees.
I can't help it, I'll give them a squeeze.
Give knees a little squeeze.
And he's got two arms just for hugging,
Hug baby.
And hands that clap and wave.
Clap baby's hands and wave.
But it's his eye, nose, ears, and his chin
Touch facial feature.
That really draw me in!
Tickle under baby's chin.

Tick Tock, Tick Tock

This is fun as a lap rhyme, for little babies or as a stand-up rhyme for young toddlers. Sway back and forth, then freeze on "stop."

Tick tock, tick tock,
Listen to the little clock.
Tick tock, tick tock,
Now it's time for us to stop!

The Cuckoo Clock

Hold baby in the air and sway her back and forth like a pendulum until you toss her into the air or lift on "cuckoo!" Or, simply sway her on your knee and lift up at "cuckoo."

Tick tock, tick tock,
I'm a little cuckoo clock.
Tick tock, tick tock,
Now the time is one o'clock.
Cuckoo!
Lift once.

Tick tock, tick tock,
I'm a little cuckoo clock.
Tick tock, tick tock,
Now the time is two o'clock.
Cuckoo! Cuckoo!
Lift twice.

Tick tock, tick tock,
I'm a little cuckoo clock.
Tick tock, tick tock,
Now the time is three o'clock.
Cuckoo! Cuckoo! Cuckoo!
Lift three times.

Tommy Thumbs

This is a popular rhyme with older babies and toddlers. Hold up two thumbs, then two index fingers, and so on. You can hear the tune on Kathy Reid-Naiman's CD Tickles and Tunes.

Tommy Thumbs are up and
Tommy Thumb are down
Tommy Thumbs are dancing
All around the town.
Dance 'em on your shoulders,
Dance 'em on your head,.
Dance 'em on your knees and
Tuck them into bed.

... Peter Pointer, Toby Tall, Ruby Ring, Paula Pink, and Finger Family.

Up Down, Turn Around

This is a great opener for a program. Follow by waving and singing hello to everyone. Toddlers love to do this standing up so they can turn their whole bodies around for the turn around part. You can listen to the tune on the enclosed CD.

Up, down,
Hold baby's hands up in the air, then down to the floor.
Turn around,
Roll baby's hands.
Touch the sky,
Hands up in the air again.
And touch the ground,
Hands down to the floor again.
Wiggle fingers,
Touch baby's fingers.
Wiggle toes,
Touch baby's toes.
Wiggle shoulders,
Touch baby's shoulders.
Say hello.
Wave hands.

The Wheels on the Bus

Take baby's feet and cycle legs for the wheel going round, and act out the rest. We like to sing this until we run out of bus riding ideas.

The wheels on the bus go round and round,
Round and round, round and round.
The wheels on the bus go round and round
All around the town.

The people on the bus go up and down,
Up and down, up and down.
The people on the bus go up and down,
All around the town.

Additional verses:

The wipers on the bus go swish, swish, swish...
The horn on the bus goes beep, beep, beep...
The money on the bus goes plink, plink, plink...
The lights on the bus go on, off, on...
The babies on the bus go, "Waa, waa, waa," ...
The mothers on the bus go, "Shh, shh, shh," ...
The driver on the bus says, "Move on back," ...
The driver on the bus says, "Move up front," ...
The doors on the bus go open and shut ...
The wheels on the bus...

When the Rain Comes Down

© 1986 Bob Devlin. This is a lovely and soothing song, especially nice with sign language actions. You can learn motions to signs on the web by looking up "American Sign language" in a Google search. Listen to the tune on Kathy Reid-Naiman's CD Tickles and Tunes.

1. When the rain comes down, it comes down on everyone.
When the rain comes down, it comes down on everyone.

Flutter fingers down for rain. For "everyone," move palms up and out.

Chorus:
No matter if you're rich or poor,

Flap fingertips of both hands together for "no matter." "Rich" is taking money from your palm, "poor" is indicating a hole in your sleeve at the elbow.

No matter if you're great or small,

Flap fingertips for "no matter" again. "Great" is your hand held high up, "small" is your hand held near the ground.

When the rain comes down, it comes down on us all.

2. When the sun shines down, it shines down on everyone.
When the sun shines down, it shines down on everyone.

For the sunshine sign, hold hand up, fingertips touching, then fingertips open to make the rays shine down. Do this twice, then make the sign for everyone.

Chorus:
No matter if you're rich or poor,
No matter if you're great or small,
When the sun shines down, it shines down on us all.

3. When a robin sings, he's singing for everyone. (2x)

Make a bird beak open and shut with thumb and index finger.

Sing chorus, ending with the robin singing.

4. When a flower blooms, it's blooming for everyone. (2x)

Cover the fingertips of one hand with your other hand then push your fingertips up and through the other hand while opening your fingers for the flower's bloom.

Sing chorus, ending with the flower blooming.

5. When a baby smiles, she's smiling for everyone. (2x)

A simple rocking motion, then draw a smile on baby's face.

Sing chorus, ending with the baby smiling.

6. When the rain comes down, it comes down on everyone. (2x)

Sing chorus with the rain falling down again.

Now make up your own verses!

Zoom, Zoom, Zoom

Listen to this tune on Kathy Reid-Naiman's CD Say Hello to the Morning.

Zoom, zoom, zoom,
We're going to the moon.
Zoom, zoom, zoom,
We're going to the moon.

Take baby's hands (or arms) and slide back and forth.

If you'd like to take a trip,
Climb aboard my rocket ship,

Walk fingertips up baby's arm.

Zoom, zoom, zoom,
We're going to the moon.

Slide hands back and forth again.

5, 4, 3, 2, 1,

Count down on baby's fingers using a suspenseful voice.

Blastoff!

Gently lift baby in the air for a little thrill.

Bouncing Rhymes

Baby, Baby Dumpling *76*
Bangor Boats *76*
Bouncy Bouncy Baby *76*
Cha-Cha-Chabogin *76*
Dickery Dean *82*
Doctor Foster *76*
From Wibbleton to Wobbleton *76*
Giddyap, Horsie, to the Fair *77*
The Grand Old Duke of York *77*
Here We Go, Up, Up, Up *77*
Humpty Dumpty *77*
I Want Someone to Buy Me a Pony *77*
Mother and Father and Uncle John *78*
Och a Na Nee *78*
One, Two, Three *78*
Our Dear Friend Mother Goose *78*
Pace Goes the Lady *78*
Pony Girl *78*
Rickety, Rickety Rocking Horse *79*
Ride a Cock Horse *79*
Ride Baby Ride *79*
A Robin and a Robin's Son *79*
See-saw, Margery Daw *79*
She Fell into the Bathtub *79*
A Smooth Road *80*
A Smooth Road to London Town *80*
Ten Galloping Horses *80*
This Is The Way the Farmer Rides *80*
This Is the Way the Ladies Ride *81*
To Market, To Market *81*
Tommy O'Flynn *81*
Trit, Trot to Boston *82*
Trot, Trot, Trot *82*

Bounces can be played with the baby sitting on your lap while you are sitting on the floor, or sitting on a chair, or they can be played with toddlers as ankle-riding games. Hold new babies on your arm, supporting the spine and the head, as you bounce gently to the beat. Older babies and toddlers love a more vigourous bounce. Always hold the baby facing you so you can see how much the baby likes it, whether you are going too fast or too slow, and so the baby can see that you are enjoying the rhyme too.

Baby, Baby Dumpling

Yes, this is "Davy Davy Dumpling" for babies.

Baby, baby dumpling
Put him in the pot,
Sugar him and butter him
And eat him while he's hot!

Bangor Boats

A bouncing and rowing rhyme.

Bangor boats away,
We have no time to stay
Bounce.
So row your boats, row your boats
Make rowing motion.
Bangor boats awaaay!
Bounce again, then lean baby way back on your knee.

Bouncy Bouncy Baby

Babies love this bounce and the parents love the nonsense words. The tune is on the enclosed CD.

Bouncy bouncy baby
Thribbidee-obidee-oopsee-day,
Bouncy bouncy baby, this is the way we play.

I'm smart, so smart,
Because I knew just how to do it from the start.
It's spring
That counts,
And when daddy gets home
I'll show him how to
Bounce, bounce, bounce, bounce!

Bouncy bouncy baby
Thribbidee-obidee-oopsee-day,
Bouncy bouncy baby
This is the way we play.

Cha-Cha-Chabogin

Bounce, then gently let baby fall through your knees, then fall off to the side at the end.

Cha-cha-chabogin
Cha-cha-chabin
Look out little baby
You might fall in!

Cha-cha-chabogin
Cha-cha-chabout
Look out little baby
You might fall out!

Doctor Foster

This little story rhyme is fun to play as a knee bounce with infants, and as a marching rhyme with toddlers, especially on a rainy day.

Doctor Foster went to Gloucester
In a shower of rain.
Bounce or march to the beat.
He stepped in a puddle
Right up to his middle
Let baby fall between your knees. Toddlers like to jump right into the puddle.
And never went there again!
Shake head.

From Wibbleton to Wobbleton

Jostle baby from side to side. One side is Wibbleton, one side is Wobbleton, and fifteen miles is in the middle. Make up your own verses with the names of towns in your area.

From Wibbleton to Wobbleton is fifteen miles.
From Wobbleton to Wibbleton is fifteen miles.
From Wibbleton to Wobbleton
From Wobbleton to Wibbleton
From Wibbleton to Wobbleton is fifteen miles!

Giddyap, Horsie, to the Fair

Giddyap, horsie, to the fair.
What'll we buy when we get there?
A penny apple and a penny pear.
Giddyap, horsie, to the fair.

The Grand Old Duke Of York

This popular preschool action rhyme makes a wonderful bounce for babies. Raise and lower knees to give baby a ride as you go up and down the hill, then sway from side to side to go left to right. Gently drop baby down between your knees on "out of sight."

Oh, the grand old Duke of York,
He had ten thousand men,
He marched them up to the top of the hill
And he marched them down again.
And when they were up they were up,
And when they were down they were down,
And when they were only half way up
They were neither up nor down.
Oh he marched them to the left,
He marched them to the right,
He marched them round and round and round,
And he marched them out of sight!

Here We Go, Up, Up, Up

A foot-riding bounce. Sit on a chair with your legs crossed. Set your baby on your foot and hold her hands.

Here we go, up, up, up.
Raise your foot up in three stages.
Here we go, down, down, down.
Lower your foot in three stages.
Here we go, backward and forward.
Move your foot in and out.
And here we go, round and round.
Rotate your foot in a circle.

Humpty Dumpty

This is one of several traditional nursery rhymes excellent for bouncing. This one has a natural "fall" between the knees.

Humpty Dumpty sat on a wall.
Knees up, bounce baby on top.
Humpty Dumpty had a great fall.
Knees down, or spread knees apart so baby falls.
All the king's horses, and all the king's men,
Pull baby up on your knees again and bounce away.
Couldn't put Humpty together again.

I Want Someone to Buy Me a Pony

Bounce sedately until you get to the jig-jog part, pause, then jostle. Listen to the tune on Kathy Reid-Naiman's CD Say Hello to the Morning.

I want someone to buy me a pony,
Jig-jog, jig-jog, jigga jog gee.
Not too fat and not too bony,
Jig-jog, jig-jog, jigga jog gee.
For I want to go for a ride,
All around the countryside
With a ... jig-jog, jig-jog, jig-jog, jig-jog, jig-jog, jigga jog gee.
With a ... jig-jog, jig-jog, jig-jog, jig-jog, jig-jog, jigga jog gee.

Mother and Father and Uncle John

Jog along until you get to the falling off parts. Mother falls off to one side, father to the other, and Uncle John goes on faster and forever.

Mother and Father and Uncle John
Went to the market, one by one.
Mother fell off!
Father fell off!
But Uncle John went on, and on,
And on, and on, and on!

And here's a variation for the grandmothers in the crowd:

Grandma and Ma and a horse named Tom
Went to market one by one.
Grandma fell off!
And Ma fell off!
But the horse named Tom went on and on
And on and on!

Och a Na Nee

I like to use this gentle Scottish knee bounce especially when I have grandparents visiting a program.

Och a na nee, when I was wee,
I used to sit on grandma's knee.
Her apron tore, and I fell on the floor!
Let baby fall through your knees.
Och a na nee na nee.
Pull baby back up on your knee.

One, Two, Three

A simple bounce with a lift at the end.

One, two, three.
Stella's on my knee,
Rooster crows,
And away she goes.

Our Dear Friend, Mother Goose

New words to the tune of "The Grand Old Duke of York" capturing a spirit of cooperation. Use the same actions.

Oh, our dear friend, Mother Goose,
She had ten thousand friends,
They all marched up to the top of the hill
And they all marched down again.
And when they were up they were up,
And when they were down they were down,
And when they were only half way up
They were neither up nor down.
Oh they all marched to the left,
They all marched to the right,
They all marched round and round and round,
And they all marched out of sight!

Pace Goes the Lady

Older babies and toddlers love this one.

Pace goes the lady, the lady, the lady,
Pace goes the lady, the lady,
Whoa!
Bounce gently, stop on "Whoa," and pause before you start again.
Canter goes the gentleman, the gentleman, the gentleman,
Canter goes the gentleman, the gentleman,
Whoa!
Bounce more vigourously and pause again on "Whoa."
Gallop goes the huntsman, the huntsman, the huntsman,
Gallop goes the huntsman
Bounce very vigourously.
And tumbles in the ditch!
Let baby fall between your knees.

Pony Girl (or Pony Boy)

Play with this rhyme as a knee bounce, or as a foot-riding bounce.

Pony girl, pony girl,
Won't you be my pony girl?
Giddy-up!, giddy-up!, giddy-up!,
WHEE!
My pony girl.

Rickety, Rickety Rocking Horse

Rickety, rickety rocking horse,
Over the fields we go,
Rickety, rickety rocking horse,
Giddy-up! Giddy-up! Whoa!

Ride a Cock Horse

There is a nice little tune to this bouncing rhyme on the CD that comes with This Little Piggy *by Jane Yolen.*

Ride a cock horse to Banbury Cross,
To see a fine lady upon a white horse.
With rings on her fingers,
And bells on her toes,
She shall have music
Wherever she goes!

Ride, Baby, Ride

© Louise Cullen. This is a simple bounce with cute sound effects. I learned it from The Baby Record *by Bob McGrath and Katharine Smithrim.*

Ride, baby (baby's name), ride,
Che, che-che, che-che, che.
Ride, baby, ride,
Che, che-che, che-che, che.
Ride, baby, ride,
Che, che-che, che-che, che.
Ride, my baby, ride,
Che, che-che, che-che, che.

A Robin and a Robin's Son

A robin and a robin's son
Went to town to buy a bun
Bounce slowly.
They couldn't decide on plum or plain
Touch one of the baby's cheeks on "plum," and the other one on "plain."
And so they went back home again.
Bounce more quickly.

See-saw, Margery Daw

Rock baby back and forth on your knee.

See-saw, Margery Daw,
Johnny shall have a new master,
He shall have but a penny a day,
Because he can't work any faster.

See-saw, sacradown.
Which is the way to London Town?
One foot up and the other foot down,
That is the way to London Town.

See-saw, Jack in the hedge,
Which is the way to London Bridge?
Put on your shoes, and away you trudge,
That is the way to London Bridge.

She Fell into the Bathtub

Hold your baby on your knee facing you.

She fell into the bathtub,
She fell into the sink,
Lean baby to one side then the other.
She fell into the raspberry jam,
Let her fall between your knees.
And came out pink!
Lift her up again.
We put her in the backyard
And left her in the rain.
Flutter your fingers down baby's body for the rain.
By half past suppertime,
Rock back and forth.
It washed her clean again!
Give baby a big hug.

A Smooth Road

Bounces are best face to face, so with your baby on your lap facing you, say …

A smooth road, a smooth road
A smooth road, a smooth road.
Gently rock baby side to side.
A bumpy road, a bumpy road
A bumpy road, a bumpy road.
Start bouncing.
A rough road, a rough road
A rough road, a rough road.
Bounce vigourously.
A hole!
Spread your knees and let baby drop down through the hole.

In my groups we like to add "a windy road," and "a jiggly road" too. Think of some others!

A Smooth Road to London Town

Here's a longer version. Listen to the tune on Kathy Reid-Naiman's A Smooth Road to London Town.

A smooth road to London town
A smooth road to London town
Gently bounce baby on your knee.
The road goes up and the road goes down
Raise and lower your knees.
A smooth road to London town.

But … by and by we come to a dell
There the roads are not so swell
A bumpy road, a bumpy road, a bumpy road to London town.
Bounce more vigourously for this part.

A smooth road to London town
A smooth road to London town
Return to a gently bounce.
The road goes up and the road goes down
Raise and lower knees again.
A smooth road to London town.

But … by and by we come to a wood
There the roads are not so good
A rough road, a rough road, a rough road to London town.
Bounce more vigourously.

Ten Galloping Horses

With baby on your lap facing you, take baby's hands and ride.

Ten galloping horses rode through the town.
Five were white and five were brown.
Five rode up and five rode down.
Pull your knees up to ride high, then lower them again.
Ten galloping horses rode through the town!

This Is the Way the Farmer Rides

There are many versions of this rhyme. Choose one you like the sound of. This first one is the American version.

This is the way the farmer rides,
The farmer rides, the farmer rides.
This is the way the farmers rides,
So early in the morning.

This is the way the lady rides,
The lady rides, the lady rides,
This is the way the lady rides,
So early in the morning.

This is the way the gentleman rides,
The gentleman rides, the gentleman rides
This is the way the gentleman rides,
So early in the morning.

This is the way the baby rides,
The baby rides, the baby rides,
This is the way the baby rides,
So early in the morning.

This is the way the farmer rides,
The farmer rides, the farmer rides.
This is the way the farmers rides,
So early in the morning.
So early in the morning.

This Is the Way the Ladies Ride

This one is the British version. Start with a little bounce, and bounce more and more vigourously as you get to the hunter.

This is the way the ladies ride,
Nim, nim, nim.
This is the way the gentlemen ride,
Trim, trim, trim.
This is the way the farmers ride,
Tur-rot, tur-rot, tur-rot.
And this is the way the hunters ride,
Gallopa-gallopa-gallopa-gallop!

This Is the Way the Ladies Ride

Another British version.

This is the way the ladies ride,
Nimble-nim, nimble-nim.

This is the way the gentlemen ride,
Gallop-a-trot, gallop-a-trot.

This is the way the farmers ride,
Jiggety-jog, jiggety-jog.

This is the way the delivery boy rides,
Tripperty-trot, tripperty-trot,

Till he falls in a ditch with a flipperty,
Flipperty, flop, flop, FLOP!

This Is the Way the Ladies Ride

And another British version!

This is the way the ladies ride,
Pace, pace, pace, pace, pace.

This is the way the gentlemen ride,
Gallop-a-trot, gallop-a-trot, gallop-a-trot.

This is the way the farmer men ride,
Hobble-de-hoy, hobble-de-hoy, hobble-de-hoy.

To Market, To Market

Jog along with your baby on your knee, then lift her up in the air on the last line.

To market, to market, to buy a fat pig,
Home again, home again, jiggety jig.
To market, to market, to buy a fat hog,
Home again, home again, jiggety jog.
To market, to market, to buy a plum bun,
Home again, home again, market is done.
To market, to market, to buy a pound of butter,
Home again, home again, throw it in the gutter!

Tommy O'Flynn

You can sing this one for Tommy or Sally O'Flynn, depending on the sex of your baby. The tune is "Mulberry Bush."

Tommy O'Flynn and his old grey mare,
Went off to see the country fair.
Bounce along.
The bridge fell down and the bridge fell in
Drop your knees down, then spread knees to let baby fall in.
And that was the end of Tommy O'Flynn,
O'Flynn, O'Flynn.
Bring baby back up on your knees and bounce again.

Trit, Trot To Boston

It's fun to say the last verse when you're going to stop bouncing because you're all played out.

Trit, trot to Boston.
Trit, trot to Lynn.
Watch out little baby
Or you might fall in!

Trit, trot to Boston
Trit, trot to Dover
Watch out little baby
Or you might fall over!

Trit, trot to Boston,
To buy a loaf of bread.
Trit, trot home again.
The old trot's dead.

Trot, Trot, Trot

Trot, trot, trot.
Go and never stop.
Trudge along, my little pony,
Where it's rough and where it's stony.
Go and never stop.
Trot, trot, trot, trot, trot!

Dickery Dean

© Dennis Lee. This bouncy rhyme with a strong beat is fun to play with an agitator motion.

"What is the matter with Dickery Dean?
Bounce.
He jumped right in to the washing machine!"
Let child fall between your knees.
Chug, chug, chug, chug,
Chug, chug, chug, chug,
Agitator motion.
"Nothing's the matter with Dickery Dean
Bounce.
He dove in dirty, and he jumped out clean!"
Lift baby down and up.

Circle Games and Dances

The Baby Bear Waltz *84*
Can You Point Your Fingers and Do the Twist? *84*
Creeping, Creeping, Creeping *84*
Here is a Beehive *84*
Mama's Little Baby Loves Dancing Dancing *85*
Nelly Go 'Cross the Ocean *85*
The Ponies Are Walking *85*
Rig a Jig Jig *86*
Ring Around the Rosie *86*
Round and Round the Cobbler's Bench *86*
Round and Round the Haystack *87*
Sally Go Round the Sun *87*
See the Sleeping Bunnies *87*
See the Ponies *87*
Shoofly *88*

Circle dances are wonderful to play with groups of parents and babies. They get everybody up and moving around; they're a good way to encourage socializing; and they're a good thing to do when you need to stand up and play when a baby needs a jiggle. They are also wonderful for parents and babies to play together at home. Toddlers especially love circle games, and the simpler they are, the better for them.

The Baby Bear Waltz

© Sally Jaeger and Kathy Reid-Naiman. Listen to the tune of this lovely waltz on Kathy Reid-Naiman's CD Say Hello To The Morning. *Parents stand up and waltz round the room with their babes in arms.*

123, 123 waltzing with bears.
123, 123 dance round the chairs,
123, 123 that's what we'll do.
123, 123 waltzing with you.

123, 123 waltz round the room,
123, 123 dance round the moon.
123, 123 glide past the stars.
123, 123 waltzing to Mars.

Can You Point Your Fingers and Do the Twist?

Here's a dancing song for toddlers I learned from Helen Moore at Richmond Public Library.

Can you point your fingers and do the twist?
Can you point your fingers and do the twist?
We're gonna go up
And down,
Go back up
And turn around.
Can you point your fingers and do the twist?

Can you stand on one leg and shake your hands?
Can you stand on one leg and shake your hands?
We're gonna go up
And down,
Go back up
And turn around.
Can you stand on one leg and shake your hands?

Now add your own verses.

Creeping, Creeping, Creeping

You can play this little finger rhyme as a simple circle game with toddlers. They may not be able to jump yet, but they like to try.

Creeping, creeping, creeping,
Comes the little cat;
Creep fingers up baby's arm.
But bunny with his long ears
Hops like that!

Here Is A Beehive

Toddlers love to play this favourite finger rhyme as a circle game. Parents stand in a circle holding their arms up to make a roof for the hive. Children stand in the middle and run out of the hive on the count at the end. Parents grab and tickle as the little bees are caught.

Here is a beehive,
But where are all the bees?
They're hidden away where nobody sees.
Can you count them,
As they come out of the hive?
One, two, three, four, five! Bzzzzzzz.

Mama's Little Baby Loves Dancing Dancing

Here's another song I learned from Helen Moore at Richmond Public Library. Sing to the tune of "Mama's Little Baby Loves Shortnin' Bread."

Mama's little baby loves dancing, dancing,
Mama's little baby loves turning round.
Mama's little baby loves dancing, dancing,
Mama's little baby loves to boogie on down.
Lean to the left,
Lean to the right,
Hug that baby nice and tight!
Lean to the left,
Lean to the right,
Hug that baby nice and tight!
Mama's little baby loves dancing, dancing,
Mama's little baby loves turning round.
Mama's little baby loves dancing, dancing,
Mama's little baby loves to boogie on down.

Nelly Go 'Cross the Ocean

© Kathy Reid-Naiman. This circle game is fund to play when the babies need an energetic bounce. Listen to the tune on Kathy's CD More Tickles & Tunes.

Circle left, then face the centre of the circle.
Nelly go cross the ocean,
Nelly go cross the sea,
Nelly go cross the mountain top,
But then come back to me.

Circle right, then face the centre of the circle.
Nelly go cross the prairies,
Nelly go cross the plains,
Nelly go cross the desert sands
And then come back again.

Jump up and down facing the centre of the circle.
Nelly jump up and down now,
Nelly jump up and down,
Nelly turn round and round and round,
And round and round and round.

The Ponies Are Walking

© Kathy Reid-Naiman 1998. Listen to the tune on Kathy's CD Say Hello to the Morning. *This song is fun as a knee bounce; and it's fun to play in a circle. I especially like it because it teaches young children how to control their speed.*

The ponies are walking, they're walking along,
Walking along, walking along,
The ponies are walking, they're walking along,
Whoa! Whoa! Whoa!

The ponies are trotting, they're trotting along,
Trotting along, trotting along,
The ponies are trotting, they're trotting along,
Whoa! Whoa! Whoa!

The ponies are walking, they're walking along,
Walking along, walking along,
The ponies are walking, they're walking along,
Whoa! Whoa! Whoa!

The ponies are galloping, they're galloping along,
Galloping along, galloping along,
The ponies are galloping, they're galloping along,
Whoa! Whoa! Whoa!

The ponies are walking, they're walking back home,
Walking back home, walking back home,
The ponies are walking, they're walking back home,
Whoa! Whoa! Whoa!

Rig a Jig Jig

Hold baby facing out and start by walking in a circle to the left. You will find the tune on Kathy Reid-Naiman's CD A Smooth Road to London Town.

Circle to the left:
As I was walking down the street,
Down the street, down the street,
As I was walking down the street,
Heigh ho, heigh ho, heigh ho!

Circle to the right:
A mom and babe I chanced to meet,
Chanced to meet, chanced to meet,
A mom and babe I chanced to meet,
Heigh ho, heigh ho, heigh ho!

Walk in to the middle of the circle:
A rig a jig jig and away we go,
Away we go, away we go,

Walk back out to the circle:
A rig a jig jig and away we go,
Heigh ho, heigh ho, heigh ho!

Sing again for a dad and babe, a big black dog, or any other people or animals you're likely to meet.

Ring Around the Rosie

This is the best loved circle game of all time. All stand in a circle holding hands. Fall down, and get up again, then do it all again as many times as you like. There are many versions of the second verses. This is one I put together from various sources.

Ring around the rosie
Pocket full of posies.
Husha, Husha,
We all fall down!
Join hands and circle left. All fall down at the end.
The cows are in the meadow
Eating buttercups.
Thunder, lightning,
We all stand up!
Pretend to pick buttercups, drum the floor for thunder, and all jump up.

Do it all again circling to the right.

Round and Round the Cobbler's Bench

This rhyme is fun to say while walking along the street. To play at the program, parents stand in a circle holding babies in front or in back piggy-back style. Step in time to the beat.

Circle to the left.
Round and round the cobbler's bench,
The monkey chased the weasel.
The monkey thought t'was all in fun,
Pop! goes the weasel.
Jump on "pop."

Circle to the right.
A penny for a spool of thread,
A penny for a needle.
That's the way the money goes,
Pop! goes the weasel.
Jump again on "pop."

Then do it all again.

Round and Round the Haystack

This little tickling rhyme can be played as a circle game with young toddlers. Walk sideways, the way little ones do when they learn to walk by moving around the coffee table. All stand in a circle holding hands to start.

Round and round the haystack
Went the little mousie,
Step sideways to the left in rhythm to beat.
One step, two step,
Step into the circle.
Into his wee housie!
All raise arms up together to form house. Then play again moving to the right.

Sally Go Round the Sun

This little circle rhyme provides endless fun for toddlers. Join hands, walk in a circle, and fall down at the end. You can listen to the tune on Kathy Reid-Naiman's CD Tickles and Tunes.

Sally go round the sun,
Sally go round the moon,
Sally go round the chimney top
Every afternoon.
Boom!

See the Sleeping Bunnies

Toddlers and preschoolers love this circle game. Parents stand in a circle and sing while children lie down on the floor in the middle of the circle and pretend to be sleeping bunnies. Parents clap in rhythm as they sing "wake up...", and children hop toward them. This is a nice game to use to get all standing in a circle for another circle game, like Ring around the Rosie. Listen to the tune on Kathy Reid-Naiman's CD A Smooth Road to London Town.

See the little bunnies sleeping till it's nearly noon,
Shall we wake them with a merry tune?
Oh so still ... are they ill ...?
Wake up soon. *(Pause.)*

Wake up, wake up, wake up little bunnies,
Wake up, wake up, wake up little bunnies,
Hop little bunnies, hop, hop, hop,
Stop little bunnies, stop, stop, stop.

See the Ponies

Young toddlers and their parents can manage this one quite easily. Listen to the tune on Kathy Reid-Naiman's CD Tickles and Tunes.

See the ponies walking, walking,
Down the country lane. (x 2)

See the ponies trotting, trotting,
Down the country lane. (x 2)

See the ponies galloping, galloping,
Down the country lane. (x 2)

See the ponies coming home,
All tired out, all tired out, all tired out. (x 2)

Shoofly

> *Listen to the tune of this popular circle game and dance on the enclosed CD. All stand in a circle to start. Parents with young infants hold them facing out so they can experience the thrill of meeting other babies face to face in the middle of the circle for that part of the dance. This one is also a fun dance to play at home in front of a mirror. Give toddlers time to learn how to walk backwards.*

Circle to the left and sing:

Shoofly, don't bother me,
Shoofly, don't bother me,
Shoofly, don't bother me,
'Cause I belong to somebody.

Then circle to the right and sing:

Shoofly, don't bother me,
Shoofly, don't bother me,
Shoofly, don't bother me,
'Cause I belong to somebody.

Now walk in to the circle, facing baby out toward other babies, and sing:

I feel, I feel, I feel like a morning star.
Walk in to the circle:
I feel, I feel, I feel like a morning star.
Back out of the circle:
I feel, I feel, I feel like a morning star.
Walk in to the circle:
I feel, I feel, I feel like a morning star.
Back out of the circle:

Circle to left and right again as you repeat the Shoofly verse. Repeat as many times as you like.

Face Rhymes

Brow Bender, Eye Peeper *90*
A Butterfly Kiss *90*
Chop-a-Nose Day *91*
Earkin, Hearkin *90*
Eye Winker, Tom Tinker *90*
Eyes, Nose, Cheeky Cheeky Chin *90*
Hana, Hana, Hana *90*
Head Bumper *91*
Here Sits Farmer Giles *91*
Here Sits the Lord Mayor *91*
Knock at the Door *91*
The Moon Is Round *91*
Ring the Bell *92*
Two Little Eyes *92*

Most babies love to have their faces touched, and they enjoy the predictability of face rhymes. They like the touch, and they like the anticipation as you start at the top of the head and work your way down to the chin for the gentle tickle at the end. It's a good way for babies to learn the names of their facial features too. In time, the baby will be touching the parent's face and tickling under the parent's chin. Face rhymes are also the perfect way to calm a baby when you have a wash cloth in your hand.

Brow Bender, Eye Peeper

Brow Bender, ... *forehead*
Eye Peeper, ... *eyes*
Nose Dropper, ... *nose*
Mouth Eater, ... *mouth*
Chin Chopper, ... *chin*
Knock at the door, ... *tickle baby's chin.*
Ring the bell, ... *pull lightly on one ear.*
Lift the latch, ... *raise baby's nose lightly.*
Walk in, ... *pop a forefinger in baby's mouth.*
Take a chair, ... *tickle cheek.*
Sit by there, ... *tickle other cheek.*
And how do you do this morning?

A Butterfly Kiss

© Felicity Williams, Pocket Full of Stars, *Annick Press, 1997.*

A butterfly kiss
Goes like this ...
Flutter your eyelashes against baby's cheek.
An ice cream kiss
Goes like this ...
Place a licky kiss on baby's cheek.
A Wee Willie Winkie kiss
Goes like this ...
Kiss your fingertips then delicately run them around baby's face.
But a big bass drum kiss
Goes like THIS!
Blow a big raspberry kiss on baby's tummy or neck.

Earkin, Hearkin

Adapted from Yiddish.

Earkin, hearkin
Wiggle the lobe of each ear.
Eyekin, spykin
Touch the corner of each eye.
Cheeky, chucky
Touch each cheek.
Chin, chin, chin
Pat under chin.
And down the hatch.
Run fingers down to baby's tummy and tickle.

Eye Winker, Tom Tinker

Eye winker,
Gently touch the corner of one eye.
Tom Tinker,
Then touch the other eye.
Nose smeller,
Touch the nose.
Mouth eater,
Touch the mouth.
Chin chopper,
Touch under chin.
Guzzle whopper!
Tickle belly.

Eyes, Nose, Cheeky Cheeky Chin

Touch baby's facial features as you sing to the tune of "Someone's in the Kitchen with Dinah."

Eyes, nose, cheeky cheeky chin,
Eyes, nose, cheeky cheeky chin,
Eyes, nose, cheeky cheeky chin,
Cheeky cheeky chin, nose, eyes.

Hana, Hana, Hana

This is a fun little Japanese face rhyme.

Hana, hana, hana.
Touch nose.
Kuchi, kuchi, kuchi.
Touch mouth.
Mimi, mimi, mimi.
Touch ears.
Mei.
Touch at the corner of the eyes.

Head Bumper

Head bumper,
Eye winker,
Nose dropper,
Mouth eater,
Chin chopper,
Gully, gully, gully!

Here Sits Farmer Giles

Here sits Farmer Giles.
Touch baby's forehead.
Here sit his two men.
Touch over two eyes.
Here sits the cockadoodle.
Touch the nose.
Here sits the hen.
Touch the mouth.
Here sit the little chickens.
Touch the teeth.
Here they run in.
Touch baby's lips.
Chin chopper,
Chin chopper,
Chin, chin, chin.
Tickle baby's chin.

Here Sits the Lord Mayor

Here sits the Lord Mayor.
Touch baby's forehead.
Here sit his men.
Eyes.
Here sits the cockadoodle.
One cheek.
Here sits the hen.
The other cheek.
Here sit the little chickens,
Nose.
Here they run in.
Mouth.
Chin chopper, Chin chopper,
Chin, chin, chin.
Tickle chin.

Knock at the Door

A shorter version of "Ring the Bell."

Knock at the door.
Gently "knock" on baby's forehead.
Peep in.
Gently lift baby's eyebrow.
Lift up the latch.
Gently press up on baby's nose.
Walk in!
Put a finger in baby's mouth.

The Moon Is Round

This is a beautiful rhyme to say as you caress baby's face. It's also a fun thing to say to distract baby as you do the actions with a washcloth in hand at face-washing time.

The moon is round
As round can be.
Trace a circle around baby's face.
Two eyes,
A nose,
And a mouth,
Then point to baby's eyes, nose, and mouth.
Like me!
Then give a little kiss or hug.

Chop-a-Nose Day

Toddlers especially love this one.

My mother and your mother
Point to yourself, then to the baby.
Went over the way.
Run your fingers over your baby's head.
Said my mother to your mother,
Point to baby, then to self.
"It's chop-a-nose day!"
Pretend to steal baby's nose. Touch her nose with your index and middle fingers, then take your hand away showing her your thumb poking through where her nose once was.

Ring the Bell

Ring the bell.
Gently tug on a lock of hair, or on baby's ear.
Knock at the door.
Tap gently on baby's forehead.
Peep in.
Gently lift an eyebrow.
Lift the latch.
Gently press up on baby's nose.
And walk right in.
Put a finger in baby's mouth.
Let's go down cellar and eat apples!
Run your fingers down to baby's tummy for a tickle.

Two Little Eyes

This is a fun rhyme to use any time, and especially at mealtimes. It's also nice to use with the strokes of an infant face massage. Touch the baby's facial features as you say the rhyme.

Two little eyes to look around.
Two little ears to hear each sound.
One little nose to smell what's sweet.
And one little mouth that likes to eat.

Finger Play and Hand Rhymes

Baby's Nap *99*
Bunnies' Bedtime *98*
Chicken in the Barnyard *94*
Cobbler, Cobbler *94*
Come A 'Look A' See *94*
Creeping, Creeping, Creeping *94*
The Dog Says, "Bow Wow" *94*
Foxy's Hole *98*
Here Are My Lady's Knives and Forks *94*
Here Is a Beehive *95*
Here Is a Bunny *95*
Here Is a Nest for a Bluebird *95*
Here Is a Tree *95*
Here Is the Church *95*
Here's a Ball for Baby (3 versions) *96*
Here's a Cup *97*
Here's a Leaf *97*
Here's a Little Boy *97*
Let's Go to Sleep *97*
Mix the Bannock *97*
Once I Caught a Fish Alive *98*
Pat It *98*
Pat-a-Cake *98*
See My Ten Fingers Dance and Play *99*
Soft Kitty *99*
There Was a Little Mouse *99*
These Are Baby's Fingers *99*
This Is My Mother *99*
This Is the Boat, the Golden Boat *100*
This Little Cow *100*
This Little Girl Found an Egg *100*
This Little Train *100*
Tommy Thumbs *101*
Two Little Bluebirds *101*
Two Little Dicky Birds *101*
Under the Darkness *101*
What Do You Suppose? *102*
Where Is Thumbkin? *102*
Whoops! Johnny *102*
Wind the Bobbin Up *102*

Babies become fascinated with their own hands—as soon as they discover them! Finger rhymes reinforce this fascination, and develop manual dexterity in toddlers. Keep them slow and simple for young toddlers so they can join in.

Chicken in the Barnyard

Toddlers love this kind of simple finger rhyme.

Chicken in the barnyard
Staying out of trouble.
Draw a little circle in baby's palm.
Along came a turkey
Slowly creep fingers up baby's arm.
And ... "Gobble, gobble, gobble!"
Tickle baby's underarm, or move in for a gobble on baby's neck.

Cobbler, Cobbler

A good one for young toddlers.

Cobbler, cobbler, fix my shoe,
Get it done by half-past two,
Pound fists together.
Now my toe is peeping through,
Poke index finger through fingers of other hand.
Cobbler, cobbler, mend my shoe.
Pound fists together again.

Come A'Look A' See

© Louise Cullen. This is a lovely song to sing any time. It's also great to use while washing a reluctant toddler's little hands. Listen to the tune on The Baby Record *(CD), by Bob McGrath and Katharine Smithrim, or on Kathy Reid-Naiman's CD* A Smooth Road to London Town.

Come a'look a'see,
Here's my mama.
Point to thumb.
Come a'look a'see,
Here's my papa.
Point to index finger.
Come a'look a'see,
My brother tall,
Point to tall finger.
Sister, baby,
Point to ring finger, then baby finger.
(Kiss sound.)
Kiss baby's fingers.
I love them all!

Creeping, Creeping, Creeping

This little rhyme is fun as a tickle rhyme for infants, and it's a fun finger rhyme for toddlers to do themselves. It's also a simple circle game to play with toddlers.

Creeping, creeping, creeping,
Comes the little cat;
Creep fingers up baby's arm.
But bunny with his long ears
Hops like that!

The Dog Says, "Bow Wow"

Beginning with the thumb for the dog, each finger represents one of the animals. On the little finger, say the cat says "Meee-," then nip the little finger lightly as you say "OW!"

The dog says, "Bow wow."
The cow says, "Moo, moo."
The lamb says, "Baa, baa."
The duck says, "Quack, quack."
And the kitty cat says, "Meee–OW!"

Here Are My Lady's Knives and Forks

Here are my lady's knives and forks,
Lock fingers, knuckle to knuckle, then invert pointing fingers upward.
Here is my lady's table,
Invert so fingers are facing down.
Here is my lady's looking glass,
Face knuckles toward you.
And here is the baby's cradle.
Face knuckles up again, straighten index fingers and pinkies, and move hands in a rocking motion.

Here Is a Beehive

Make a fist and say the rhyme, then unfold your fingers one at a time, and buzz in for a little tickle. You can also play this on baby's little fist, unwrapping the fingers one at a time.

Here is a beehive,
But where are the bees?
Hidden away where nobody sees.
Here they come creeping out of the hive.
One, two, three, four, five!
Bzzzzzzz.

Here Is a Beehive

This is a wonderful variation from Sally Jaeger. The added "sh" between the lines helps toddlers learn to aspirate when they are having difficulty with this as they learn how to speak.

Here is a beehive.
Make a fist.
Shhh.
But where are the bees?
Shhh.
Hidden away where nobody sees.
Shhh.
Here they come creeping out of the hive.
One, two, three, four, five!
Unfold one finger at a time.
Buzzzz.
Tickle.

Here Is a Bunny

With babies: touch ears, then form a circle with your arms, touch ears again, and end with a hug. Toddlers like to play the bunny ears part and the parent's hand can make the hole.

Here is a bunny with ears so funny,
And here is his hole in the ground.
At the first sound he hears,
He pricks up his ears,
And jumps in his hole in the ground.

Here Is a Nest for a Bluebird

Toddlers love to imitate the actions as parents say this rhyme.

Here is a nest for a bluebird,
Cup hands.
And here is a hive for a bee,
Fold hands together in a ball.
Here is a hole for a bunny,
Form circle with fingertips and thumbs touching.
And here is a house for me.
Make a peaked roof and hold over baby's head.

Here Is a Tree

You can sing this little rhyme to the tune of "Rock-a-Bye Baby."

Here is a tree with its leaves so green,
Hold up one arm. Your wiggly fingers are the leaves.
Here are the apples that hang between,
Make two fists.
When the wind blows, the apples will fall,
Drop fists down to the ground.
And here is a basket to gather them all
Lace fingers of both hands together, palms up.

Here Is the Church

Here is the church,
Lock fingers, knuckle to knuckle.
And here is the steeple,
Place pinkies together in an arch.
Open the door
Open thumbs wide pointing upward.
And see all the people.
Waggle fingers.

Here's a Ball for Baby

Here's a ball for baby,
Big and soft and round.
Hold up two hands touching fingertips to form ball.
Here is baby's hammer,
Make a fist.
See how he can pound.
Pound fist on palm of other hand.
Here is baby's music,
Clapping, clapping so.
Clap hands.
Here are baby's soldiers,
Standing in a row.
Hold ten fingers erect.
Here is baby's trumpet,
Toot, toot, toot, toot, toot.
Hold one fist in front of other at mouth.
Here's the way that baby,
Plays at peek-a-boo.
Spread fingers in front of eyes.
Here's a big umbrella,
To keep my baby dry.
Hold index finger of right hand erect. Place palm of left hand on top of finger.
And here is baby's cradle,
Make cradle of interlocked fingers, knuckles up, erect index and pinky fingers.
To rock-a-baby bye.
Rock hands.

Here's a Ball for Baby
Here is a shorter version.

Here's a ball for baby,
Big and soft and round.
Fingertips form a ball.
Here is baby's hammer,
See how he can pound.
Pound a fist on palm of other hand.
Here are baby's soldiers,
Standing in a row.
Hold ten fingers erect.
Here is baby's music,
Clapping, clapping so.
Clap hands.

Here's a Ball for Baby
And here is another variation. When children are familiar with a rhyme, it fills them with delight when we change it a little for a surprise. Then it becomes a brand new game.

Here's a ball for baby,
Big and soft and round.
Hold up two hands touching fingertips to form ball.
Here is baby's hammer,
Make a fist.
See how he can pound.
Pound fist on palm of other hand.
Here is baby's trumpet,
Tootle-tootle-too.
Hold one fist in front of other at mouth.
Here is baby's favourite game
Cover your eyes.
It's called Peek-a-Boo!
Peek!

Here's a Cup

This is a favourite before snack time.

Here's a cup,
Make a fist with one hand.
And here's a cup,
Make a fist with your other hand.
And here's a pot of tea.
Now stick your thumb up from one fist.
Pour a cup,
"Pour" into one cup (fist).
And pour a cup,
Reverse teapot and "pour" into other cup (fist).
And drink it up with me!
Pretend to sip from a cup.

Here's a Leaf

I use this rhyme every year to celebrate the arrival of spring. We always smell one another's flowers at the end.

Here's a leaf,
Hold up one hand, palm flat.
And here's a leaf,
Hold up other hand, palm flat.
And that, you see, makes two.
Put wrists together as two leaves growing on a stem.
Here's a bud, that makes a flower,
Fold hands into one big fist.
Watch it bloom for you!
Now slowly open your fingers keeping wrists together to make the bloom.

Here's a Little Boy

Say this one at least twice, once for little boys and once for little girls.

Here's a little boy (girl),
Hold up one index finger.
And here is his bed.
The other flat palm is the bed.
Here is his pillow,
This is the thumb of the palm hand.
Where he lays down his head.
Lay your index finger in your open palm.
Here are his covers,
Wiggle the fingers of palm hand.
Let's pull them up tight.
Close "blanket" fingers over "little boy."
Sing him a lullaby,
Rock the "baby."
And kiss him good night.
Bring your hands to your lips and kiss your fingertip.

Let's Go to Sleep

"Let's go to sleep," the little caterpillars said
Hold out one hand and wiggle your fingers.
As they curled themselves up in their little beds.
Curl your fingers into a fist, palm up.
"We shall awaken by and by,
Uncurl your fingers.
And when we do, we'll be beautiful butterflies."
Hook your thumbs together and fly your butterfly up in the air.

Mix the Bannock

Bannock, first brought to Canada from Scotland, is a kind of bread eaten by Coastal and Northern First Nations. It is cooked in the oven or in a frying pan. Act this out by mixing, stirring, pouring and baking, then spread child's hand with "jam" and nibble.

Mix the bannock,
Stir the bannock,
Pour it in the pan.
Bake the bannock,
Taste the bannock,
Covered with strawberry jam!

Bunnies' Bedtime

"My bunnies now must go to bed,"
The little mother rabbit said.
"But I will count them first to see
If they have all come back to me.
One bunny, two bunnies, three bunnies dear,
Four bunnies, five bunnies, yes, you're all here.
You are the prettiest things alive,
My bunnies, one, two, three, four, five."

Once I Caught a Fish Alive

Count baby's fingers up to ten, nibble baby's little finger, and give it a big kiss.

One, two, three, four, five,
Once I caught a fish alive,
Six, seven, eight, nine, ten,
Then I let him go again.
Why did I let him go?
Because he bit my finger so.
Which one did he bite?
This little finger on the right.

Pat It

This is a sweet rhyme for a hurt little hand.

Pat it,
Kiss it,
Stroke it,
Bless it;
Three days sunshine,
Three days rain,
Little hand
All well again.

Pat-a-Cake

This British rhyme is so much fun to play when babies discover clapping. As with all rhymes, use your own baby's name for "baby," and the first letter in his or her name for the "B." There is a nice tune on the CD with This Little Piggy *by Jane Yolen.*

Pat-a-cake, pat-a-cake, baker's man,
Bake me a cake as fast as you can.
Take your baby on your knee facing you, then take baby's hands and clap.
Roll it, and pat it, and mark it with a B,
Roll baby's hands, pat baby's palm, draw a B.
And put it in the oven for Baby and me.
Turn palms up and gently poke into baby's tummy, or pat baby's tummy.

Foxy's Hole

This game is fun to play with older babies and toddlers.

Put your finger in Foxy's hole.
Hold up a fist so baby can poke her finger into the "hole."
Foxy's not at home.
Shake your head.
Foxy's at the back door,
Picking on a bone.
Gently "nip" baby's finger with your pinky finger.

See My Ten Fingers

This game is fun to play while baby is lying on the change table.

See my ten fingers dance and play.
Ten fingers dance for me today.
Wiggle baby's fingers.
See my ten toes dance and play.
Ten toes dance for me today.
Wiggle baby's toes.

Soft Kitty

This is a great rhyme to use to teach babies how to touch gently. Stroke baby's hand as if stroking a cat.

Soft kitty, warm kitty,
Little ball of fur;
Lazy kitty, pretty kitty,
Purr, purr, purr.

There Was a Little Mouse

Toddlers love this rhyme. It will likely spring to mind at mealtimes when babies want to share, and at pretend tea times too.

There was a little mouse
Run your fingers down baby's arm to his hand.
Who found a piece of cheese
Scratch away at the cheese.
He gave this one a piece
Offer cheese to baby, then to self, then to anyone else.
He gave this one a piece
He gave this one a piece
He gave this one a piece
Then he ran up into his house
And went to sleep!
Run fingers back up and under baby's arm for a sleep.

These Are Baby's Fingers

Gently touch baby's fingers, then toes, then circle baby's belly button for a little tickle. Again, substitute your own baby's name for "baby."

These are baby's fingers.
These are baby's toes.
This is baby's belly button.
Round and round it goes.

Baby's Nap

This is a shorter version of "Here is a Little Boy."

This is baby ready for a nap.
Hold out your index finger.
Lay him down in a loving lap.
Lay finger down in baby's palm.
Cover him up so he won't peep.
Wrap baby's fingers around your index finger.
And rock him till he's fast asleep.
Rock finger back and forth.

This Is My Mother

Wiggle fingers one at a time.

This is my mother.
Thumb.
This is my father.
Index finger.
This is my brother tall.
Tall finger.
This is my sister.
Ring finger.
This is the baby.
Baby finger.
Oh, how I love them all!
Kiss fingertips.

This Is the Boat, the Golden Boat

All the parents in my groups have loved to say and play with this rhyme. The imagery is so beautiful. Older children love it too.

This is the boat, the golden boat,
That sails the silver sea.

Make a boat by placing one hand on top of the other, palms down.

And these are the oars, the ivory oars,
That lift and dip, that lift and dip.

Now stick out your thumbs on either side of your palms, and move them in a rowing motion.

These are the ten little fairy folk,
Running along, running along,

Hold up ten fingers and dance them in the air.

To take the oars, the ivory oars,
That lift and dip, that lift and dip,

Now return to the boat and take up the oars (thumbs out), and lift up and down.

And carry the boat, the golden boat,
Over the silver sea.

This Little Cow

Start with the pinky finger and work your way up all the fingers until at the end you "pounce" on the baby's thumb, then tickle up her arm as you "chase her away."

This little cow eats grass,
This little cow eats hay.
This little cow drinks water,
And this little cow runs away.
And this BIG cow does nothing at all
But lie in the fields all day!
Let's chase her and chase her and chase her away!

This Little Girl Found an Egg

This is a translation of a Spanish rhyme. Start with either the thumb or the baby finger and end with an affectionate gobble.

This little girl found an egg,
This little girl cooked it,
This little girl peeled it,
This little girl salted it,
And this little girl ran all the way home
And ate it!

This Little Train

This little train ran up the track.
It went, "Toot, toot,"
And then came back.

Run fingers up one arm and back down again.

This little train went up the track.
It went, "Toot, toot,"
And then came back.

Repeat actions with the other arm.

Tommy Thumbs

Toddlers love to do this rhyme using just thumbs and pointer fingers.

Tommy Thumbs up and
Thumbs up, both hands.

Tommy Thumbs down,
Thumbs down.

Tommy Thumbs dancing
Thumbs up and bounce to the right.

All around the town.
Bounce to the left in front of you.

Dance 'em on your shoulders,
Bounce them on your shoulders.

Dance 'em on your head,
Bounce them on your head.

Dance 'em on your knees and
Bounce them on your knees.

Tuck them into bed.
Fold arms hiding hands.

Peter Pointer up and Peter Pointer down ...
Repeat using index finger.

Toby Tall up and Toby Tall down ...
Repeat using tall finger, and so on.

Ring Man up and Ring Man down ...
Baby Finger up and Baby Finger down ...
Finger Family up and Finger Family down ...

Two Little Bluebirds

This utterly simple rhyme with easy finger actions provides endless amusement for young toddlers who want to do it themselves. I love to play it when I see toddlers pointing for the first time.

Two little blue birds
Sitting on a hill,
Hold up both index fingers.
One named Jack,
The other named Jill.
Hold up one then the other.
Fly away, Jack,
Fly away, Jill,
First one, then the other of the "little birdies" flies behind your back.
Come back, Jack,
Come back, Jill.
Back to starting position.

Two Little Dicky Birds

Here is a variation for those who love to say "dicky birds."

Two little dicky birds
Sitting on a wall,
Hold up both index fingers.
One named Peter,
One named Paul.
Hold up one then the other.
Fly away, Peter!
Fly away, Paul!
First one, then the other of the "little birdies" flies behind your back.
Come back, Peter,
Come back, Paul.
Back to starting position.

Under the Darkness

Under the darkness
Fingers touching, arch arms to form sky.
There are stars.
Index fingers point up to indicate stars.
Under the stars, there's a tree.
Form the sign for tree by holding up one forearm and wiggle fingers for branches of the tree.
Under the tree, there's a blanket.
Rest one palm on back of other hand.
And under the blanket, there's me!
Open palms.

What Do You Suppose?

This is a wonderfully silly rhyme that's fun to say when babies start to point.

Bzzzzzz.
Use index finger to fly around baby.
What do you suppose?
A bee sat on my nose!
Land that finger on baby's nose.
Then what do you think?
He gave me a great big wink,
Wink.
And said, "I beg your pardon,
I thought you were the garden!"

Where Is Thumbkin

Sing to the tune of "Frère Jacques." Hide hands behind your back to start, or simply hold up two fists with thumbs hidden inside.

Where is thumbkin ?
Where is thumbkin?
Here I am!
Pop one thumb out.
Here I am!
Pop the other thumb out.
How are you today, sir?
Nod one thumb.
Very well, I thank you.
Nod the other thumb.
Run away, run away,
Tuck one thumb away into your fist.
Run away and hide.
Now tuck the other thumb away into your other fist. Hide hands behind your back if you wish.

Repeat with "pointer" finger. These are all the fingers of the "Thumbkin" rhyme that young infants and toddlers can manage.

Whoops! Johnny

Young toddlers love this rhyme. It helps them develop manual dexterity and hand-eye coordination. Start with the baby's pinky finger and name all the fingers Johnny. The "whoops" is the slide between the thumb and the index finger. Then do it again and substitute Johnny with your own child's name.

Johnny, Johnny, Johnny, Johnny,
Whoops! Johnny,
Whoops! Johnny,
Johnny, Johnny, Johnny.

Wind the Bobbin Up

Musical notation is in This Little Puffin *by Elizabeth Matterson, revised edition, 1991. Roll hands, pull apart, then follow directions.*

Wind the bobbin up, wind the bobbin up,
Pull, pull, clap, clap, clap.
Point to the ceiling, point to the floor,
Point to the window, point to the door.
Clap your hands together, one, two, three,
Put your hands upon your knee.

French Rhymes
Comptines et Chansons

Alouette, gentille alouette *104*
Au clair de la lune *104*
Bateau sur l'eau *104*
C'est le temps *104*
Do, do, l'enfant do *105*
Fais dodo *105*
Frère Jacques *105*
Il pleut, il mouille *105*
Maman, papa, et oncle Simon *105*
Les marionnettes *104*
Le petit coupeur de paille *105*
Les petits poissons *105*
Sur le pont d'Avignon *106*
Tape, tape, tape *106*
Trotte, trotte *106*
Vent frais *106*

Here are a few French rhymes for those who speak French. There is a bibliography of resources where you can find more rhymes and songs in French at the end of this section.

Les marionnettes

Jeux de mains.

Ainsi font, font, font
Les petites marionnettes
Agitez les mains en l'air en tournant les poignets.
Ainsi font, font, font
Trois petits tours et puis s'en vont.
Un, deux, trois… parties!
Cachez les mains derrière le dos.
Les mains aux côtés, sautez, sautez marionnettes
Les mains aux côtés,
marionnettes recommencez.

Alouette, gentille alouette

Refrain:
Alouette, gentille alouette
Alouette, je te plumerai.

Je te plumerai la tête (bis) - head
Et la tête (bis)
Alouette (bis)
Oooh!

Refrain

Je te plumerai le bec (bis) - beak
Et le bec (bis)
Et la tête (bis) …

Je te plumerai les yeux (bis) - eyes
Je te plumerai le cou (bis) - neck
Je te plumerai les ailes (bis) - wing
Je te plumerai les pattes (bis) - leg
Je te plumerai la queue (bis) - tail

Au clair de la lune

Au clair de la lune,
Mon ami Pierrot.
Prête-moi ta plume,
Pour écrire un mot.
Ma chandelle est morte,
Je n'ai plus de feu.
Ouvre-moi ta porte pour l'amour de Dieu.

Au clair de la lune
Pierrot répondit:
Je n'ai pas de plume,
Je suis dans mon lit.
Va chez la voisine,
Je crois qu'elle y est,
Car, dans sa cuisine,
On bat le briquet.

Bateau sur l'eau

Bateau sur l'eau
La rivière, la rivière
Bateau sur l'eau
La rivière au bord de l'eau.
Le bateau a chaviré
Tous les enfants sont tombés
Dans l'eau. PLOUF!

C'est le temps

Sur l'air de Old MacDonald.

C'est le temps de se laver,
i-a-i-a-o.
Avec un peu de savon,
i-a-i-a-o.
Du savon par-ci,
Du savon par-là.
Youpi! Youpi! Ça sent bon.

Amusez-vous à composer vos propres paroles à partir de situations vecues: C'est le temps de changer de couche, de s'attacher, d'aller se promener, de bien ranger, etc.

Do, do, l'enfant do

Do, do, l'enfant do,
L'enfant dormira bien vite;
Do, do, l'enfant do,
L'enfant dormira bientôt.

Fais dodo

Refrain:
Fais dodo, Colas mon p'tit frère
Fais dodo, t'auras du lolo

Maman est en haut
Qui fait des gateaux
Papa est en bas
Qui fait du chocolat

Fais dodo, Colas mon p'tit frère
Fais dodo, t'auras du lolo.

On fait la bouillie
Pour l'enfant qui crie:
Et tant qu'il criera,
Il n'en aura pas.

Fais dodo, Colas mon p'tit frère
Fais dodo, t'auras du lolo.

Frère Jacques

Frère Jacques, Frère Jacques,
Dormez-vous? Dormez-vous?
Sonnez les matines, sonnez les matines,
Din, dan, don. Din, dan don.

Il pleut, il mouille

Il pleut, il mouille,
C'est la fête à la grenouille.
La grenouille a fait son nid,
Dessous un grand parapluie.

Maman, papa, et oncle Simon

Maman, papa, et oncle Simon
Allaient au marché un par un
Maman tombait, papa tombait
Mais oncle Simon galopait, galopait, galopait!

Le petit coupeur de paille

Le petit coupeur de paille
Le petit coupeur de blé
Le petit coupeur de paille
Le petit coupeur de blé

Non jamais je n'oublierai
Le petit coupeur de paille
Non jamais je n'oublierai
Le petit coupeur de blé.

Les petits poissons

Les petits poissons
Dans l'eau
Nagent, nagent, nagent, nagent, nagent.
Les petits poissons
Dans l'eau
Nagent aussi bien que les gros.
Les petits, les gros,
Nagent comme il faut
Les gros, les petits,
Nagent bien aussi.

Sur le pont d'Avignon

Sur le pont d'Avignon
On y danse, on y danse
Sur le pont d'Avignon
On y danse tout en rond

Les éléphants font comme ça ...
Les lions font comme ça ...
Les souris font comme ça .... .

Tape, tape, tape

Tape, tape, tape les petites mains, mains, mains
Tourne, tourne, tourne, joli moulin, lin, lin
Vole, vole, vole, petit oiseau, zo, zo
Nage, nage, nage poisson dans l'eau, lo, lo.

Trotte, trotte

Trotte, trotte, cheval blanc
Trotte, trotte, dans le vent
Trotte, trotte, cheval noir
Trotte, trotte, tous les soirs
Trotte, trotte, cheval gris
Trotte, trotte, toute la nuit
Trotte, trotte, cheval beige
Trotte, trotte, dans la neige.

Vent frais

Vent frais,
Vent du matin,
Vent qui souffle
Au sommet des grands pins,
Joie du vent qui souffle,
Allons dans le grand
Vent frais, vent du matin.... .

BIBLIOGRAPHY

COMPTINES ET CHANSONS: COLLECTION DU PROGRAMME LA MÈRE L'OIE POUR ENFANT ET PARENT. Textes choisis par Megan Williams. Toronto, Ontario: Parent-Child Mother Goose Program, 2000.
Programme la Mère l'Oie pour Enfant et Parent, 720 Bathurst St., Ste. 500A, Toronto, ON M5S 2R4. Email: mgoose@web.net

COMPTINES À CHANTER, Volume 1. Toulouse, France. Éditions Milan, 2002.
Éditions Milan, 300, rue Léon-Joulin, 31101 Toulouse Cedex 9, France. 27 comptines sur un CD.

COMPTINES À CHANTER, Volume 2. Toulouse, France. Éditions Milan, 2002.
Éditions Milan, 300, rue Léon-Joulin, 31101 Toulouse Cedex 9, France. 27 comptines sur un CD.

PETITES CHANSONS POUR TOUS LES JOURS. Paris, France: Éditions Nathan, 1996.
30 comptines sur un CD.

Greeting Songs

Bell Horses *108*
Come A'Look A'See *108*
Come Along and Sing with Me *108*
Hello Everyone *108*
Hello, My Friends, Hello *109*
Here Are *109*
Hickety Pickety Bumblebee *109*
I'm in the Mood *110*
Let's Clap Our Hands Together *110*
The More We Get Together *110*
Up Down, Turn Around *110*

Using the same greeting song at the beginning of the program each week calls everyone's attention and signals that it's time to start. Start by singing, and everyone will join in. At home, greeting songs are nice to sing when a baby wakes up from a nap.

Bell Horses

This is a lovely little tune to sing on its own, or with bells or a tambourine, and it's a good companion to the same song used as a good-bye song without the last verse. The tune is on The Baby Record *(CD) by Bob McGrath and Katharine Smithrim.*

Bell horses,
Bell horses,
What's the time of day?
One o'clock,
Two o'clock,
Time to go away…

Little Bell,
Little Bell,
Where are you?
Here I am!
Here I am!
How do you do?

Come A'Look A' See

© Louise Cullen. The tune is on The Baby Record *(CD) by Bob McGrath and Katharine Smithrim, and on Kathy Reid-Naiman's CD* A Smooth Road to London Town. *Sit down and start to sing. The parents and children will soon join you.*

Come a'look a'see,
Here's my mama.
Point to thumb.
Come a'look a'see,
Here's my papa.
Point to index finger.
Come a'look a'see,
My brother tall,
Point to tall finger.
Sister, baby,
Point to ring then baby fingers.
(Kiss sound.)
Kiss the fingertips of your finger family.
I love them all.

Come Along and Sing with Me

This is a nice opening song, sung to the tune of "Mary Had a Little Lamb."

Come along and sing with me, sing with me, sing with me,
Come along and sing with me, on a sunny Tuesday.

Take baby's hands and clap.
Come along and clap with me, clap with me, clap with me,
Come along and clap with me, on a sunny Tuesday.

Come along and roll with me …
Come along and stretch with me … .

Hello Everyone

The tune is "Good Night Ladies."

Hello everyone, hello everyone,
Hello everyone, it's nice to see you here,

Proceed around the circle having parents fill in their names and their baby's names: parent, then baby, then next parent, "It's nice to see you here." Then next baby, and next parent, keeping the parent-child pattern as you go around the circle.

Hello "_____" *(parent says name),*
Hello "_____" *(parent says baby's name)*
Hello"_____" *(next parent says name),*
It's nice to see you here.

Hello "_____" *(next baby's name),*
Hello "_____" *(next parent says name),*
Hello "_____" *(next baby's name),*
It's nice to see you here.

End with:
Hello everyone, hello everyone,
Hello everyone, it's nice to see you here.

Hello, My Friends, Hello

Here is a greeting song to go with "Goodbye, My Friends, Goodbye." Ask your audience for more ways to say hello in other languages.

Hello, my friends, hello,
Hello, my friends, hello,
Hello, my friends, hello, hello, my friends,
Hello, my friends.

in Coast Salish:
Ee ch aw' y al', my friends, ee ch aw' y al' …

in Cantonese:
Nay ho ma, my friends, nay ho ma …

in French:
Bonjour, mes amies, bonjour …

in German:
Guten tag, my friends, guten tag …

in Hindi:
Namustay, meri dost, namustay …

in Japanese:
Kanishiwa, my friends, kanishiwa …

in Korean:
Yo bo say yo, my friends, yo bo say yo …

in Punjabi:
Sat sri akal, meri dost, sat sri akal …

in Spanish:
Ola, mis amigos, ola …

in Swahili:
Jambo, my friends, jambo …

in Tagalog:
Komasta, my friends, komasta …

in Ukrainian:
Yukshamia, my friends, yukshamia …

Here Are

This is a nice song to use with a smaller group. It is especially helpful in learning participants' names. The parent says her name and the baby's name on the first line, then the rest of the group repeats their names twice. The tune is "One Little Two Little Three Little Indians."

Here are, here are, (*parent's name*) and (*baby's name*).
Here are, here are, (*parent's name*) and (*baby's name*). *Group joins in.*
Here are, here are, (*parent's name*) and (*baby's name*). *Group repeats.*
Here we are together.

Repeat for every parent and child.

Hickety Pickety Bumblebee

This is also a nice hello song to use with a small group. Sing a verse for each parent and each child.

Hickety pickety bumblebee,
Won't you say your name for me,
"_____" (*parent says name*)
"_____" (*group repeats name, echo fashion*)
That's a very nice name.

Repeat for all the parents and babies.

I'm in the Mood

© Raffi. This song makes a lovely and gentle opener for a program, and it's also nice for parents to sing with their children at home. The tune is on Raffi's Rise and Shine *CD. Words and music are in* The Second Raffi Songbook.

I'm in the mood for singing.
Hey, how about you?
I'm in the mood for singing.
Hey, how about you?
I'm in the mood for singing,
Singing along with you.
Hey, hey, what do you say?
I'm in the mood for that today.
Hey, hey, what do you say?
I'm in the mood for that.

I'm in the mood for clapping ...

My additional verse:
I'm in the mood for stories ...

I'm in the mood
If you're in the mood,
Then we're in the mood for that.

Let's Clap Our Hands Together

This is a nice opener for young toddlers who can join in with the actions with their parents help. Sing to the tune of "The Farmer in the Dell."

Let's clap our hands together,
Let's clap our hands together,
Let's clap our hands together,
Because it's fun to do.

Let's tap our legs together ...
Let's roll our hands together ...
Let's stomp our feet together ...
Let's blink our eyes together ...
Let's hit the ground together ....

The More We Get Together

The more we get together, together, together,
The more we get together, the happier we'll be.
For your friends are my friends,
And my friends are your friends.
The more we get together, the happier we'll be.

The more we play together ...
The more we sing together ....
The more we read together ...

Repeat first verse.

Up Down, Turn Around

This is a great opener for a program. Follow by waving and singing hello to everyone. Toddlers love to do this standing up, and then they turn their whole bodies around for the turn around part. The tune is on the enclosed CD.

Up, down,
Hold baby's hands up in the air, then down to the floor.
Turn around,
Roll baby's hands.
Touch the sky,
Hands up in the air again.
And touch the ground,
Hands down to the floor again.
Wiggle fingers,
Touch baby's fingers.
Wiggle toes,
Touch baby's toes.
Wiggle shoulders,
Touch baby's shoulders.
Say hello.
Wave hands.

Goodbye Songs

Bell Horses *112*
Down By the Station *112*
Goodbye Everyone (two versions) *112*
Goodbye, My Friends, Goodbye *112*
The Goodbye Train *113*
It's Time to Say Goodbye to Our Friends *113*
Now It's Time to Say Goodbye *113*
So Long *113*
Up Down, Turn Around *114*

The same goodbye song sung at the end of a program each week provides a warm goodbye to your guests and signals that the program is over and it's time to go. Parents can use goodbye songs at home as they prepare baby for an outing. Toddlers especially love to say goodbye. Lullabies are also a good way to end if your program is in the evening.

Bell Horses

This is a lovely little song to sing at the end of a program, especially when it is also used at the beginning. It's also lovely with bells or a tambourine, or car keys!

Bell horses,
Bell horses,
What's the time of day?
One o'clock,
Two o'clock,
Time to go away....

Down By the Station

This is a nice goodbye for toddlers.

Down by the station
Early in the morning
See the little puffer bellies
All in a row.
See the station master
Pull the little handle
Chug, chug, toot, toot,
And off we go.

Goodbye Everyone

The tune is "Good Night Ladies."

Goodbye everyone, goodbye everyone,
Goodbye everyone, we'll see you again next week.

Wave goodbye.

Merrily we roll along, roll along, roll along,
Merrily we roll along, we'll see you again next week.

Roll hands.

Sweet dreams everyone, sweet dreams everyone,
Sweet dreams everyone, we'll see you again next week.

Lay your head down on your hands.

Goodbye Everyone

You can also use this song to sing goodbye to each participant by name.

Goodbye everyone, goodbye everyone,
Goodbye everyone, I'll see you again next week.

Goodbye Michael, goodbye Sammy, goodbye Angela, we'll see you again next week.

Continue around the circle until you've said goodbye to everyone.

Goodbye, My Friends, Goodbye

Here is a closing song to go with "Hello, My Friends." Ask your audience for more ways to say goodbye in other languages.

Goodbye, my friends, goodbye,
Goodbye, my friends, goodbye,
Goodbye, my friends, goodbye, my friends,
Goodbye, my friends.

in Coast Salish:
Ee tsun, my friends, ee tsun ...

in Cantonese:
Joy-guin, my friends, joy-guin ...

in French:
Au revoir, mes amies, au revoir,

in German:
Auf wiedersehn, my friends, auf wiedersehn ...

in Hindi:
Namustay, meri dost, namustay ...

in Japanese:
Sayonora, my friends, Sayonora ...

in Korean:
An yiung, my friends, an yiung ...

in Punjabi:
Sat siri akal, meri dost, sat siri akal …

in Spanish:
Adios, mis amigos, adios …

in Swahili:
Kwahiri, my friends, kwahiri …

in Tagalog:
Pa-a-lam, my friends, pa-a-lam …

in Ukrainian:
Yukshamia, my friends, yukshamia …

The Goodbye Train

The tune is "She'll Be Comin' Round the Mountain." Toddlers like to join in on the toot-toot part.

Oh the goodbye train is leaving, see you soon,
Toot toot!
Oh the goodbye train is leaving, see you soon,
Toot toot!
Oh the goodbye train is leaving, see you soon,
Toot toot!

Oh we'll say goodbye to Lisa, see you soon,
Toot toot!
Oh we'll say goodbye to Sasha, see you soon,
Toot toot!
Oh we'll say goodbye to Michael, we will say good bye to Nico, we will say goodbye to Lily, see you soon,
Toot toot!

It's Time to Say Goodbye to Our Friends

The tune is "She'll Be Comin' Round the Mountain."

Well it's time to say goodbye to our friends,
Oh it's time to say goodbye to our friends,
Well it's time to say goodbye, wave our hands and give a smile,
Oh it's time to say goodbye to our friends.

Now It's Time to Say Goodbye

Sing to the tune of "London Bridge."

Now it's time to say goodbye,
Say goodbye, say goodbye,
Now it's time to say goodbye,
I'll see you all next week.

Say goodbye to all the children by name, then repeat the chorus.

So Long

Parent and children join hands and sway to the music.

So long, it's been good to see you,
So long, it's been good to see you,
So long, it's been good to see you,
So long, and I'll see you next week.

Up Down, Turn Around

This is a nice companion piece to the same song used as an introduction. Toddlers may want to do this standing up, and then they turn their whole bodies around for the turn around part. The tune is on the enclosed CD.

Up, down,
Hold baby's hands up in the air, then down to the floor.
Turn around,
Roll baby's hands.
Touch the sky,
Hands up in the air again.
And touch the ground,
Hands down to the floor again.
Jiggle tummy,
Touch baby's tummy.
Blink your eyes,
Touch above baby's eyes. Toddlers can blink.
Blow a kiss,
Blow baby a kiss. Toddlers like to do this themselves.
And say good-bye.
Wave hands.

Lullabies

All Little Ones Are Sleeping *116*
All the Pretty Little Horses (Hush-a-Bye) *118*
Autumn Lullaby (Bye, Baby, Bye) *117*
Babushka Baio *117*
Baby's Boat *116*
Brahms' Lullaby (Lullaby, and Good Night) *119*
Bye O Baby, Bye *117*
Canadian Lullaby (Bed Is Too Small) *116*
Close Your Eyes *120*
Douglas Mountain *122*
Fuzzy Wuzzy Caterpillar *117*
Ho, Ho, Watanay *118*
Hush, Little Baby *118*
I See the Moon *118*
I'll Love You Forever *116*
Kum ba yah *119*
Listen to the Tree Bear *119*
Lou, Lou, Lou, Pretty Baby *119*
Lullaby, Lullaby *120*
Mister Moon / The Cuckoo *120*
The Moment I Saw You *120*
Once: a Lullaby *121*
Prairie Lullaby *124*
Raisins and Almonds *123*
Rock-a-Bye, Baby *121*
Rock-a-Bye You *121*
Rock Me Easy *121*
Rose, Rose, Rose, Red *122*
Sailing *122*
Sleep, Baby, Sleep *122*
Star Light, Star Bright *122*
Tall Trees *123*
Twinkle, Twinkle Little Star *123*
Watch the Stars *124*
Yo Te Amo *124*

A lullaby is a great way to connect with a child at any time of the day or night. I like to teach my parents a variety of lullabies so they can choose the one or ones they like the best, and make them a part of their family's tradition. Listening resources to most tunes are provided in the title notes.

All Little Ones Are Sleeping

© 1968 Jean Ritchie, Geordie Music Publishing Co. Listen to the tune on the enclosed CD.

Chorus:
All through the night,
All through the night,
All little ones are sleeping.
All through the night,
All through the night,
All little ones are sleeping.

In a hole down under ground
(I say "burrow" underground.)
Little bunnies can be found.

Repeat chorus.

Sparrow sleeps up in a tree,
My warm bed is best for me.

Repeat chorus.

God bless babes and beasts and birds,
All small things that have no words.

Repeat chorus.

I'll Love You Forever

A mother from Bountiful, BC, taught me this beautiful song. Someday I will record the tune. Meanwhile, you can invent your own.

Another day's passed
You're growing so fast
Soon you'll be walking, I know.
I'll hold your hand
And I'll help you stand,
Till one day you'll walk on your own.

And I'll love you forever,
Forever and ever my baby you'll be,
Yes, I'll love you forever
Forever and ever my baby you'll be,
Forever and always my baby you'll be.

I want you to know,
Wherever you go
Should life find us miles apart.
I'll always care,
And always be there,
As mother's love lives in the heart.

And I'll love you forever,
Forever my baby you'll be
Yes I'll love you forever,
Forever and ever my baby you'll be
Forever and always my baby you'll be.

Canadian Lullaby (Bed Is Too Small)

Listen to the tune on the enclosed CD.

Bed is too small for my tired head,
Give me a hilltop with trees,
Tuck a cloud up under my chin,
Lord, blow the moon out ... please.
Take a moment and blow softly.

Rock me to sleep in a cradle of leaves,
Sing me a lullaby of dreaming,
Tuck a cloud up under my chin,
Lord, blow the moon out ... please.
Blow softly.

Baby's Boat

Alice C.D. Riley and Jessie L. Gaynor 1898. Listen to the tune on the enclosed CD.

Baby's boat's a silver moon
Sailing o'er the sky.
Sailing o'er a sea of sleep
While the stars go by.

Chorus:
Sail, baby, sail. Far across the sea.
Only don't forget to sail back again to me.

Baby's fishing for a dream
Fishing near and far.
Her line, a silver moonbeam is,
Her bait, a silver star.

Chorus:
Sail, baby, sail. Far across the sea.
Only don't forget to sail back again to me.

Autumn Lullaby (Bye, Baby, Bye)

Listen to the tune on Kathy Reid-Naiman's CD On My Way to Dreamland.

The sun has gone from the shining sky,
Bye, baby, bye.
The dandelions have closed their eyes,
Bye, baby, bye
The stars are lighting their lamps to see,
If babes and squirrels and birds and bees,
Are fast asleep as they ought to be,
Bye, baby, bye.

The squirrel keeps warm in his furs of gray,
Bye, baby, bye.
'Neath feathers, birdies are tucked away,
Bye, baby, bye.
In yellow jackets, the bees sleep tight
And cuddle close through the chilly night,
My baby's snug in her gown of white,
Bye, baby, bye.

The squirrel nests in a big oak tree,
Bye, baby, bye.
He finds a hole in the trunk, you see,
Bye, baby, bye.
The robin's home is a nest o'erhead,
The bees, they nest in a hive instead,
My baby's nest is her little bed,
Bye, baby, bye.

Bye O Baby, Bye

You can listen to the tune of this lovely simple lullaby on Kathy Reid-Naiman's CD On My Way to Dreamland

Bye o baby bye, bye o baby bye.
Mama's gone to the mail boat,
Mama's gone to the mail boat, bye.

Bye o baby bye, bye o baby bye.
Papa's gone to the mail boat,
Papa's gone to the mail boat, bye.

Fuzzy Wuzzy Caterpillar

A mother whose son has cerebral palsy taught me this one. It is her son's favourite song. Listen to the tune on the enclosed CD.

Fuzzy wuzzy caterpillar
Crawling on the ground.
Crawl up child's arm with your caterpillar finger.
Fuzzy wuzzy caterpillar
Never makes a sound.
Shhh.
Soon you will be sleeping
Softly lullaby
Lay head down on your hands.
Then when you awaken you will be a butterfly.
Hook thumbs together and make your hand a butterfly.

Babushka Baio

You will find musical notation to this Russian lullaby in Your Baby Needs Music *by Barbara Cass-Beggs. Listen to the tune on the enclosed CD.*

Go to sleep my darling baby,
Babushka baio.
See the moon is shining on you,
Babushka baio.

I will tell you many stories,
If you close your eyes.
Go to sleep my darling baby,
Babushka baio.

Ho, Ho, Watanay

Iroquois, collected by Alan Mills, English words by Alan Mills, French words by Evy Paraskevopoulos, Mandarin words by Sanya Sladojevic. This is a beautiful song that translates well into other languages. Listen to the tune on the enclosed CD.

Ho, ho, watanay,
Ho, ho, watanay,
Ho, ho, watanay,
Kiokina, kiokina.

Do, do, mon petit
Do, do, mon petit
Do, do, mon petit
Et bonne nuit, et bonne nuit.

Sleep, sleep, little one,
Sleep, sleep, little one,
Sleep, sleep, little one,
Now go to sleep, now go to sleep.

Schway baa siao bough bough,
Schway baa siao bough bough,
Schway baa siao bough bough,
Zuo ge how mung, zuo ge how mung.

All the Pretty Little Horses (Hush-a-Bye)

This lullaby is from the American south. The story has it that a black woman sang this to her master's child while her own baby lay unattended.

Hush-a-bye, don't you cry
Go to sleepy little baby.
When you wake, you shall have cake,
And all the pretty little horses.

Blacks and bays, dapple and grays,
Coach and six little horses.
Hush-a-bye, don't you cry
Go to sleepy little baby.
When you wake, you shall have cake,
And all the pretty little horses.

Way down yonder, down in the meadow,
There's a poor wee little lamby.
The bees and butterflies pickin' at its eyes,
The poor wee thing is cryin' Mammy.

Hush-a-bye, don't you cry
Go to sleepy little baby.
When you wake, you shall have cake,
And all the pretty little horses.

Hush, Little Baby

Sing either Mama or Papa, or alternate. Listen to the tune on Kathy Reid-Naiman's A Smooth Road to London Town.

Hush little baby, don't say a word,
Mama's gonna buy you a mocking bird,
And if that mocking bird don't sing,
Mama's gonna buy you a diamond ring,
And if that diamond ring turns brass,
Mama's gonna buy you a looking glass,
And if that looking glass gets broke,
Mama's gonna buy you a billy goat,
And if that billy goat won't pull,
Mama's gonna buy you a cart and bull,
And if that cart and bull turn over,
Mama's gonna buy you a dog named Rover,
And if that dog named Rover won't bark,
Mama's gonna buy you a horse and cart,
And if that horse and cart fall down,
You'll still be the sweetest little baby in town.

I See the Moon

Meredith Willson © Frank Music Corp. Listen to the tune on the enclosed CD.

I see the moon, and the moon sees me,
Down through the leaves of the old oak tree.
Please let the moon that shines on me,
Shine on the ones I love.
Over the mountains, over the sea,
Back where my heart is longing to be.
Please let the moon that shines on me,
Shine on the ones I love.

I hear a lark, and he calls to me,
Singing a song with a memory.
Please send the song he sings to me
Back to the ones I love.
Over the mountains, over the sea,
Back where my heart is longing to be.
Please take the song he sings to me,
Back to the ones I love.

Kum Ba Yah

This African-American spiritual is variously spelled Kumbaya, and Cum By Yah. It means "Come by here." It was popularized in the 1960s by Joan Baez.

Kum ba yah, my Lord, kum ba yah.
Kum ba yah, my Lord, kum ba yah.
Kum ba yah, my Lord, kum ba yah.
Yah yah, kum ba yah.
Yah yah, kum ba yah.

Someone's sleepin', my Lord,
Kum ba yah.
Someone's sleepin', my Lord,
Kum ba yah.
Someone's sleepin', my Lord,
Kum ba yah.
Yah yah, kum ba yah.
Yah yah, kum ba yah.

Someone's cryin', my Lord
Kum ba yah...

Someone's singin', my Lord
Kum ba yah...

Kum ba yah, my Lord....

Listen to the Tree Bear

This little poem sounds nice to the tune of a rocking "Down by the Station."

Listen to the tree bear,
Crying in the night,
Crying for his mammy
In the pale moonlight.
What will his mammy do
When she hears him cry?
She'll tuck him in a coco pod
And sing a lullaby.
She'll tuck him in a coco pod
And sing a lullaby.

Lou, Lou, Lou, Pretty Baby

Listen to the tune on the enclosed CD.

Lou, lou, lou, pretty baby,
Close your eyes.
Lou, lou, lou, pretty baby,
Dream of paradise.
Mother is here by you,
Father is nearby too,
Lou, lou, lou, pretty baby,
Close your eyes.

Brahms' Lullaby (Lullaby, and Good Night)

You can hear the tune to this lullaby on the web; type the title in a Google search.

Lullaby, and good night, with roses bedight,
With lilies o'er spread, is baby's wee bed.
Lay thee down now and rest,
May thy slumber be blest.
Lay thee down now and rest,
May thy slumber be blest.

Lullaby, and good night, thy mother's delight,
Bright angels beside, my darling abide.
They will guard thee at rest,
Thou shalt wake on my breast.
They will guard thee at rest,
Thou shalt wake on my breast.

Lullaby, Lullaby

© Connie Kaldor Word of Mouth. Listen to the tune on Kathy Reid-Naiman's CD A Smooth Road to London Town.

Lullaby, lullaby, baby fuss and baby cry
You'll be sleeping by and by
Sleepy little baby.

Things go right, things go wrong
Hearts may break but not for long
You will grow up big and strong
Sleepy little baby.

Lullaby, lullaby, little baby close your eyes
You'll be sleeping by and by
Sleepy little baby.

Things go right, things go wrong
Hearts may break but not for long
You will grow up big and strong
Sleepy little baby.

Lullaby, lullaby, baby fuss and baby cry
You'll be sleeping by and by
Sleepy little baby.

Mister Moon

Mister Moon and the Cuckoo are partner songs that can be sung together or separately. They make a nice round together. Listen to the tune on the enclosed CD.

Mr. Moon Mr. Moon
You're out too soon
The sun is still in the sky.
Go back into your bed
And cover up your head
Until the day goes by.

The Cuckoo

'Twas on a summer's evening
I walked the forest through.
When suddenly I heard it
A soft and sweet cuckoo,
Cuckoo, cuckoo, cuckoo, cuckoo, cuckoo,
Cuckoo, cuckoo, cuckoo, cuckoo, cuckoo.

The Moment I Saw You

Traditional tune—words by Graham Nash. © Nash Notes. This is another beautiful lullaby from the woman in Bountiful, BC. The tune is on the enclosed CD.

The moment I saw you
I wanted to hold you,
And keep you warm
On that cold grey morn.
The moment I held you,
I wanted to kiss you,
And welcome you here
On the day you were born.

Close Your Eyes

You will find the tune to this lovely song on Joanie Bartels' Lullaby Magic. *You can listen to an MP3 of the tune on the web too.*

Now it's time to say good night,
Good night, sleep tight.
Now the sun turns out its light,
Good night, sleep tight.
Dream sweet dreams for me.
Dream sweet dreams for you

Close your eyes and I'll close mine.
Good night, sleep tight.
Now the moon begins to shine,
Good night, sleep tight.
Dream sweet dreams for me.
Dream sweet dreams for you.

Close your eyes and I'll close mine.
Good night, sleep tight.
Dream sweet dreams for me.
Dream sweet dreams for you.

Once: a Lullaby

This poem by B.P. Nichol makes a lovely lullaby sung to the tune of "The Muffin Man." It's also lovely to use asking your audience to supply the various animals and animal sounds as you go along. Toddlers love it.

Once I was a little lamb,
A baby lamb, a little lamb,
Once I was a little lamb,
Baaa, I fell asleep.

Once I was a little calf,
A baby calf, a little calf,
Once I was a little calf,
Mooo, I fell asleep.

Once I was a little girl (or boy)
A baby girl, little girl,
Once I was a little girl,
Now I'm asleep.

Rock Me Easy

These words are from Jelly Belly *by Dennis Lee (Macmillan of Canada 1983 Key Porter) © 1983. The tune is traditional. Elvis Presley used the tune in "Love Me Tender." Listen to the tune on Kathy Reid-Naiman's CD* A Smooth Road to London Town.

Rock me easy, rock me slow,
Rock me where the robins go.
Rock the branch and rock the bough,
Rock the baby robins now.
Rock me up and rock me down,
Rock me off to sleepy town,
Rock me gently up the stairs,
To snuggle with my teddy bears.
Rock me easy, rock me slow,
Rock me where the robins go.

Rock-a-Bye, Baby

Perhaps the most popular lullaby of our time. Most people only know the first verse.

Rock-a-bye, baby, on the treetop,
When the wind blows the cradle will rock,
When the bough breaks the cradle will fall,
And down will come baby, cradle and all.

Rock-a-bye, baby, thy cradle is green,
Father's a nobleman, mother's a queen,
Sister's a lady, and wears a gold ring,
And brother's a drummer, and drums for the king.

Rock-a-bye, baby, way up on high,
Never mind, baby, mother is nigh,
Up to the ceiling, down to the ground,
Rock-a-bye, baby, up hill and down.

Rock-a-Bye, Baby

Here is another version.

Rock-a-bye, baby,
Daddy's away,
Brothers and sisters
Have gone out to play;
But here by your cradle,
Dear baby, I'll keep,
To guard you from danger,
And sing you to sleep.

Rock-a-Bye You

© Theresa Mckay. Listen to the tune to this beautiful lullaby on Kathy Reid-Naiman's CD A Smooth Road to London Town.

Rock-a-bye you high, rock-a-bye you low,
Rock-a-bye you close, rock-a bye you slow.
Rock-a-bye you high, rock-a bye you low,
Rock-a-bye you everywhere we go.

Rock-a-bye the sun, rock-a bye the moon,
Rock-a-bye the sweet flowers growing in June.
Rock-a-bye you love, my turtle dove,
Rock-a-bye you everywhere we go.

Rose, Rose, Rose, Red

This mournful song has a medieval quality, and it sounds like cathedral bells when you sing it as a round with a group of parents.

Rose, Rose, Rose, Red,
Will I ever see thee wed,
I will marry at thy will, sire,
At thy will.

Ding-dong, ding-dong,
Wedding bells on a May morn,
Carve my name in a mossy stone,
In a mossy stone.

Ding-dong, ding-dong,
Funeral bells on a September morn,
My Rose Red is dead and gone,
She's dead and gone.

Sailing

This is a nice rocking song, and a good song to use to call your group back to the circle after some other activity. It's also wonderful to sing as a round. Listen to the tune on Kathy Reid-Naiman's CD A Smooth Road to London Town.

Sailing, sailing, over the water
Sailing, sailing, over the sea
Sailing, sailing over the ocean
Sail back home to me.

Sleep, Baby, Sleep

Listen to the tune on Kathy Reid-Naiman's CD A Smooth Road to London Town. *I have added verses from many different sources.*

Sleep, baby, sleep,
The big stars are the sheep;
The little stars are the lambs, I guess,
The big white moon is the shepherdess,
Sleep, baby, sleep.
Sleep, baby, sleep.

Sleep, baby, sleep,
Thy father guards the sheep;
Thy mother shakes the dreamland tree,
Down fall the little dreams on thee,
Sleep, baby, sleep.
Sleep, baby, sleep.

Sleep, baby, sleep,
Our cottage vale is deep;
The little lamb is on the green,
With woolly fleece so soft and clean,
Sleep, baby, sleep.
Sleep, baby, sleep.

Sleep, baby, sleep,
Down where the woodbines creep;
Be always like the lamb so mild,
A kind and sweet and gentle child,
Sleep, baby, sleep.
Sleep, baby, sleep.

Star Light, Star Bright

There is a very nice tune to this on The Baby Record *by Bob McGrath and Katharine Smithrim.*

Star light, star bright,
First star I see tonight,
I wish I may, I wish I might,
Have this wish I wish tonight.

Douglas Mountain

Arnold Sundgaard / Alec Wilder, Ludlow Music Inc. Additional verses by Kathy Reid-Naiman. Listen to the tune on Kathy's CD, On My Way to Dreamland.

Snow is falling on Douglas Mountain,
Snow is falling so deep.
Snow is falling on Douglas Mountain,
Putting the bears to sleep, to sleep,
Putting the bears to sleep.

Snow is falling on Douglas Mountain,
Snow is falling all around,
Snow is falling on Douglas Mountain,
Covering up the ground, the ground,
Covering up the ground.

Snow is falling on Douglas Mountain,
Snow is falling so white,
Snow is falling on Douglas Mountain,
Kissing the trees good night, good night
Kissing the trees good night.

Raisins and Almonds

You will find the musical notation to this beautiful Yiddish lullaby, popularized in the 50s and 60s by Joan Baez, in Jane Yolen's The Lullaby Songbook.

To my little one's cradle in the night
Comes a little goat snowy and white;
The goat will trot to the market,
While mother her watch does keep,
Bringing back raisins and almonds.
Sleep my little one, sleep.

Tall Trees

This song came to me through storytelling circles all the way from an Aboriginal child in Australia, or so the story goes. I always sing this before I tell a story. It calms everyone. It sounds beautiful as an echo song too. Listen to the tune on the enclosed CD.

Tall trees,
Arms up.
Warm fire,
Arms crossed over your chest.
Strong wind,
Arms wave in front.
Rushing water;
Arms wave down low.
I feel it in my body,
Touch your body, or your child's body, toes to head.
I feel it in my soul.
Arms up again.

Twinkle, Twinkle, Little Star

A French song, adapted by Mozart, words by Jane Taylor.

Twinkle, twinkle, little star
How I wonder what you are!
Up above the world so high,
Like a diamond in the sky
Twinkle, twinkle, little star
How I wonder what you are.

Additional verses:

When the blazing sun is gone,
When he nothing shines upon,
Then you show your little light,
Twinkle, twinkle, all the night.
Twinkle, twinkle, little star
How I wonder what you are.

Then the traveller in the dark
Thanks you for your tiny spark.
He could not tell which way to go,
If you did not twinkle so.
Twinkle, twinkle, little star
How I wonder what you are.

In the dark blue sky you keep,
And often through my curtains peep,
For you never shut your eye,
'Til the sun is in the sky.
Twinkle, twinkle, little star
How I wonder what you are.

As your bright and tiny spark,
Lights the traveller in the dark,
Though I know not what you are,
Twinkle, twinkle, little star.
Twinkle, twinkle, little star
How I wonder what you are.

Watch the Stars

Traditional. Adapted and arranged by Kathy Reid-Naiman and Ken Whiteley. Listen to the tune on Kathy Reid-Naiman's CD A Smooth Road to London Town.

Watch the stars, see how they run,
Oh, watch the stars, see how they run,
Oh, the stars run down
At the setting of the sun,
Oh, watch the stars, see how they run.

Watch the moon, see how it glows,
Watch the moon, see how it glows,
The moon glows white
In the middle of the night,
Oh, watch the moon, see how it glows.

Watch the wind, see how it blows,
Watch the wind, see how it blows,
Oh, the wind blows strong
The whole night long,
Oh, watch the wind, see how it blows.

Now make up your own verses.

Prairie Lullaby

© Connie Kaldor Word of Mouth. Listen to the tune on Connie Kaldor's CD Lullaby Berceuse, *or on Kathy Reid-Naiman's CD* A Smooth Road to London Town. *(A coulee is a ravine and a slough is a creek.)*

When the sun on the prairie is going to bed
You can see it turn golden and red in the west
There's the barest of breeze in the shelter belt trees
Singing each baby to rest.

Chorus:
They sing lullaby, lullaby, coulees and sloughs
Lullaby, lullaby, coulees and sloughs.
The wind in the willows whispers to you
Lullaby, lullaby, coulees and sloughs.

When the baby meadowlark is fussy and tired
Her mama will cradle her under her wing
She'll call to the winds that blow in from the west
And this is the song she will sing.

Chorus:
They sing lullaby, lullaby, coulees and sloughs
Lullaby, lullaby, coulees and sloughs.
The wind in the willows whispers to you
Lullaby, lullaby, coulees and sloughs.

Yo Te Amo

This little lullaby is in Spanish and in English. Yo te amo means I love you. Look for other languages in the next section. The tune is on the enclosed CD.

Yo te amo
Yo te amo,
All day long I sing this little song to you,
Yo te amo
Yo te amo,
Darling I love you.

Rhymes in Other Languages

Cho Chi *126*
Das Ist Der Daumen *126*
Deem Chung Chung *126*
Frère Jacques *126*
Hana, Hana, Hana *126*
Ho, Ho, Watanay *126*
Liang Zhe Lao Hu *127*
De Maan Is Rond *127*
Norwegian Lullaby *128*
Roly Poly (Cantonese) *127*
Roly Poly (Mandarin) *127*
Tortillitas *128*
Yo Te Amo *128*

Here are a few rhymes in other languages that are easy to do even when you don't speak the language. I have spelled them the way they sound. Parents are delighted when we show them that we are making an effort to learn something in their first language. Invite them to share more.

Cho Chi

This is a Japanese play rhyme. The words are just sounds and have no particular meaning.

Cho chi, cho chi
Clap hands.
A waa waa,
Open palm taps mouth.
Kai kulu, kai kulu,
Roll hands.
Otzumu ten, ten, ten.
Tap head.

Das Ist Der Daumen

A German finger rhyme.

Das ist der daumen
Der schuttelt die pflaumen
Der lezt sie auf
Der tragt sie nach hause
Und der kleine schell est sie alle alle auf.

Translation:
This is the thumb
He shakes down the plums
He gathers them up
He carries them home
And this little fellow eats them all all up.

Deem Chung Chung

A Mandarin finger rhyme. Thank you to Claire Chiang for the complete verse.

Deem chung chung,
Tap index fingers together.
Chung chung fey!
Fly your fingers away on "fey."
Fey hu lai chee gey.
Waft hands in a flying motion.
Lai chee shuk,
Just say this.
Mo deng bop?
Palms up.
Faye hui bay bee
Fly to baby's toes.
Ge gurk zee-may.
Tickle!

Translation:
Two little bugs meet,
And then they fly away.
They fly to the lai-chee tree.
The fruit ripens.
Now where to hide?
Fly to baby's little toe and hide there.

Frère Jacques

A French classic. Used as the base tune for many rhymes.

Frère Jacques, Frère Jacques,
Dormez-vous? Dormez-vous?
Sonnez les matines, sonnez les matines,
Din, dan, don. Din, dan, don.

Hana, Hana, Hana

A Japanese face rhyme.

Hana, hana, hana, hana.
Touch nose.
Kuchi, kuchi, kuchi, kuchi.
Touch mouth.
Mimi, mimi, mimi, mimi.
Touch ears.
Mei.
Eyes.

Ho, Ho, Watanay

Iroquois, collected by Alan Mills, English words by Alan Mills, French words by Evy Paraskevopoulos, Mandarin words by Sanya Sladojevic. Added languages are spelled phonetically. You can listen to the tune on the enclosed CD.

Ho, ho, watanay, (x3) *(Iroquois)*
Kiokina, kiokina.

Do, do, mon petit (x3) *(French—boy)*
Do, do, ma petite (x3) *(French—girl)*
Et bonne nuit, et bonne nuit.

Sleep, sleep, little one, (x3) *(English)*
Now go to sleep, now go to sleep.

Schway, baa, siao bough bough, (x3) *(Mandarin)*
Zuo ge how mung, zuo ge how mung.

Nan ne te, ses key, (x3) *(Carrier)*
Go nan ne te, go nan ne te. (glottal stop G)

Schlaf, schlaf, kindlein klein, (x3) *(German)*
Jetzt schlafe ein, jetzt schlafe ein.

Dorme, dorme, mis bimbo, (x3) *(Italian—boy)*
Dorme dorme mis bimba, *(Italian—girl)*
E sogni d'odra, e sogni d'ora.

Be_khob, koochakam, (x3) *(Persian)*
Va ght - khobe, va ght - khobe.

Soja, nikke kake, (x3) *(Punjabi)*
Hun to soja, hun tu soja.

Duerme, duerme, mi bebé (x3) *(Spanish)*
A la cama, a la cama.

Nemure, akachan (x3) *(Japanese)*
Saa nemure, saa nemure.

Liang Zhe Lao Hu

This Mandarin rhyme about two tigers can be sung to the tune of "Frère Jacques."

Liang zhe lao hu, liang zhe lao hu
(Two tigers, two tigers.) Hold up two fingers.
Pao de quai, pao de quai,
Running fast, running fast.
Yi zhe mei you yenjin,
(One has no eyes.) Point to baby's eyes.
Yi zhe mei you weiba,
(One has no tail.) Point to baby's bottom.
Zhen qui quai, zhen qui quai.
(How strange, how strange.)

De Maan Is Rond

A Dutch "Moon is Round."

De maan is rond
De maan is rond
Twee ogen, een neus, en een mond.

Roly Poly (Cantonese)

Sing the the tune of "Frère Jacques."

Roly poly, roly poly,
Siong, siong siong, (up, up, up)
Siong, siong siong,
Roly roly poly, roly roly poly,
Ha, ha, ha, (down, down, down)
Ha, ha, ha.

Roly poly, roly poly,
Chud, chud, chud, (out, out, out)
Chud, chud, chud.
Roly roly poly, roly roly poly,
Yap, yap, yap, (in, in, in)
Yap, yap, yap.

Roly poly, roly poly,
Zuo, zuo, zuo, (left, left, left)
Zuo, zuo, zuo.
Roly roly poly, roly roly poly,
Yau, yau, yau, (right, right, right)
Yau, yau, yau.

Roly Poly (Mandarin)

Sing the the tune of "Frère Jacques."

Roly poly, roly poly
Shang, shang, shang, (up, up, up)
Shang, shang, shang.
Roly roly poly, roly roly poly,
Xia, xia, xia, (down, down, down)
Xia, xia, xia.

Roly poly, roly poly
Chu, chu, chu, (out, out, out)
Chu, chu, chu.
Roly roly poly, roly roly poly,
Ru, ru, ru, (in, in, in)
Ru, ru, ru.

Roly poly, roly poly
Zuo, zuo, zuo, (left, left, left)
Zuo, zuo, zuo.
Roly roly poly, roly roly poly,
You, you, you, (right, right, right)
You, you, you.

Tortillitas

A Spanish hand rhyme. Tortillitas are little tortillas.

Tortillitas para Mama
Tortillitas para Papa
Clap hands flipping them over as if you're flipping a tortilla.
Las quemaditas para Mama
The burnt ones for mama!
Las mas bonitas para Papa.
The best ones for papa.

Translation:
Little tortillas for Mama,
Little tortillas for Papa,
The burnt ones for Mama,
The good ones for Papa.

Norwegian Lullaby

The tune to this hypnotic lullaby is on the enclosed CD.

Tra la la, La la la, La la la lie,
Tra la la, La la la, La la la lie,

Na skal fingrene sove
(Now shall your fingers sleep.)
Na skal fingrene sove.

Tra la la, La la la, La la la lie,
Tra la la, La la la, La la la lie,
Na skal fottene sove
(Now shall your feet sleep.)
Na skal fottene sove.

Tra la la, La la la, La la la lie,
Tra la la, La la la, La la la lie,
Na skal moonen sove
(Now shall your mouth sleep.)
Na skal moonen sove.

Tra la la, La la la, La la la lie,
Tra la la, La la la, La la la lie,
Na skal nesen sove
(Now shall your nose sleep.)
Na skal nesen sove.

Tra la la, La la la, La la la lie,
Tra la la, La la la, La la la lie,
Na skal oyene sove
(Now shall your eyes sleep.)
Na skal oyene sove.

Tra la la, La la la, La la la lie,
Tra la la, La la la, La la la lie,
Na skal babyen sove
(Now shall baby sleep.)
Na skal babyen sove.

Yo Te Amo

The tune to this song is on the enclosed CD.

Yo te amo,
Yo te amo,
All day long I sing this little song to you,
Yo te amo
Yo te amo,
Darling I love you.
(I love you in Spanish.)

Ich liebe dich,
Ich liebe dich,
All day long I sing this little song to you,
Ich liebe dich,
Ich liebe dich,
Darling I love you.
(I love you in German.)

Wo I knee,
(I love you in Mandarin, the way I spell it!)

Je t'aime.
(I love you in French.)

Ti amo.
(I love you in Italian.)

Songs

Ally Bally (Coulter's Candy) *130*
As I Was Walking to Town One Day *130*
Baby Put Your Pants On *130*
Boom, Boom, Baby Goes Boom Boom *131*
Circle of the Sun *131*
Dance to your Daddy *131*
Down By the Bay *131*
Horsey, Horsey *132*
Hungry, Hungry *132*
Hurry, Hurry *133*
I Had a Rooster *133*
It's Time to Put Away *134*
Land of the Silver Birch *134*
Let's All Clean Up Together *134*
Lightly Row *134*
May There Always Be Sunshine *134*
My Dog Rags *134*
My Paddle *135*
Pick It Up (Dropped My Hat) *133*
Pretty Painted Butterfly *135*
Put Your Shoes On Lucy *135*
Simple Gifts *136*
Sittin' in a Highchair *135*
What'll I do with the Baby-o? *136*
Wiggly Woo *136*
Wobbidobs *132*
You Are My Sunshine *136*

These are songs to sing for the simple pleasure of singing. They are lovely to sing to a baby any time, and they are lovely to sing with a chorus of parents and babies together. Singing together in a group not only teaches parents pretty songs to sing at home, it boosts parents' confidence, ability, and desire to sing at home. You can invent little actions to go with them if you like to use actions. Resources where you can listen to the tunes are listed in the title notes.

Ally Bally (Coulter's Candy)

This is an old Scottish lullaby. Coulter's Candy was a brand of candy that was popular when it was written. The tune is on Kathy Reid-Naiman's CD A Smooth Road to London Town, and also Tickles and Tunes.

Chorus:
Ally Bally, Ally Bally Bee,
Sittin' on yer mammy's knee
Greetin' for a wee penny
To buy some Coulter's candy.

Ally Bally's gettin' mighty thin
A bag of bones covered over with skin
Soon he'll be gettin' a real double chin
From suckin' Coulter's candy.

Repeat chorus.

Ally Bally's got a tummy ache
It isn't the tatties and it isn't the cake
But what it is, for goodness sake
It's too much Coulter's candy.

Repeat chorus.

Go to sleep now my little one
Seven o'clock and the playing's done
But when you wake with the morning sun
You'll get some Coulter's candy.

Repeat chorus.

Alley Bally, Ally Bally Bee
When you grow up you'll go to sea
Making pennies for your daddy and me
To buy some Coulter's candy.

As I Was Walking to Town One Day

This is a great audience participation song. Parents suggest various animals to meet, then children join in as they learn how to say animal names and noises. Listen to the tune on The Baby Record *by Bob McGrath and Katharine Smithrim.*

As I was walking to town one day,
I met a dog upon the way,
And what do you think that dog did say?
... woof, woof, woof, woof!

As I was walking to town one day,
I met a cat upon the way,
And what do you think that cat did say?
... meow, meow, meow, meow

Now add your own verses.

Baby Put Your Pants On

A dressing song. Sing to the tune of "Mama's Little Baby Loves Shortnin' Bread." The tune is on the enclosed CD.

Baby put your pants on, pants on, pants on
Baby put your pants on, 1 2 3.

Baby put your shirt on, shirt on, shirt on,
Baby put your shirt on, 1 2 3.

Baby put your socks on ...
Baby put your shoes on ... *etc.*

Now that you're all dressed, all dressed
all dressed
Now that you're all dressed, let's go play!

(Now sing in reverse order for undressing.)

Baby take your shoes off, shoes off, shoes off
Baby take your shoes off, 1 2 3 *etc.*

Now that you're all naked, all naked, all naked
Now that you're all naked
Let's take a bath!

Boom, Boom, Baby Goes Boom Boom

© Ferron. This is a lovely song to sing as a round and it's great to sing when a baby falls down. It really takes the shock out of falling, and that means no tears. The tune is on the enclosed CD.

Boom, boom, baby goes boom boom,
Baby goes boom boom down.
You might cry, but everybody does it,
Everybody boom booms down.

Circle of the Sun

© 1980 Sally Rogers P. Thrushwood Press Publishing. This one is a lovely cuddling song, or you can act it out as the words suggest. Listen to the tune on Kathy Reid-Naiman's CD A Smooth Road to London Town.

Babies are born in the circle of the sun,
Circle of the sun on the birthing day.
Babies are born in the circle of the sun,
Circle of the sun on the birthing day.

Chorus:
Clouds to the north, clouds to the south,
Wind and rain to the east and the west,
Babies are born in the circle of the sun
Circle of the sun on the birthing day.

Babies learn to walk …
Babies learn to talk …
Babies learn to laugh ….

Dance to your Daddy

This is a Gaelic song popular on the East Coast. The tune is on the enclosed CD.

Dance to your daddy,
My little laddie,
Dance to your daddy,
My little lamb.
You shall have a fishy
In a little dishy,
You shall have a haddock
When the boat comes in.

Dance to your daddy,
My little lassie,
Dance to your daddy,
My little lamb.
You shall have an apple,
You shall have a plum,
You shall have an apple
When your dad comes home.

Dance to your daddy,
My little laddie,
Dance to your daddy,
My little lamb.
You shall have a fishy
In a little dishy,
You shall have a haddock
When the boat comes in.
You shall have a haddock
When the boat comes in.

Down By the Bay

This is a fun song to sing in a group. After parents have learned the verses, they will make up their own rhymes. Raffi sings this traditional song on Singable Songs for the Very Young.

Down by the bay
Where the watermelon grows,
Back to my home,
I dare not go,
For if I do,
My mother will say,
"Did you ever see a goose kissing a moose?"
Down by the bay!

Repeat verse adding in new rhymes …

"Did you ever see a whale with a polka dot tail?"
"Did you ever see a fly wearing a tie?"
"Did you ever see a bear combing his hair?"
"Did you ever see llamas eating their pajamas?"
"Did you ever have a time when you couldn't make a rhyme?"

Now make up your own rhymes.

Wobbidobs

© Tom Pease, Tomorrow River Music, 1993. This song is more complex than the rest, but well worth the effort of learning it. Start with the baby toe and tickle your way across to the great big wobbidob. You will find the tune on Kathy Reid-Naiman's CD More Tickles & Tunes.

Down at the bottom, where you reach the ground,
When you look down they're prob'ly wiggling around.
Some call them piggies and some call them toes
But over at our house, this is how it goes;

Chorus:
Little pede, Pede ludy, Ludy whistle, Whistle nozzle,
Great, Big, Wobbidob.
Little pede, Pede ludy, Ludy whistle, Whistle nozzle, Great, Big, Wobbidob.

I'm on a mission, I've taken the job,
To tell the whole world about their wobbidobs.
Imagine the whole world your mom and your pop,
Scrubbing and singing the wobbi-do-wop.

Little pede, Pede ludy, Ludy whistle, Whistle nozzle,
Great, Big, Wobbidob.
Little pede, Pede ludy, Ludy whistle, Whistle nozzle, Great, Big, Wobbidob.

Start with the little,
Move to the middle,
And don't forget to scrub in between.
I'll bet you a nickel,
It's gonna tickle,
But you can sing this song until they're all clean.

Little pede, Pede ludy, Ludy whistle, Whistle nozzle,
Great, Big, Wobbidob.
Little pede, Pede ludy, Ludy whistle, Whistle nozzle, Great, Big, Wobbidob.

Horsey, Horsey

This is a fun bounce or walk along song. Listen to the tune on Kathy Reid-Naiman's CD A Smooth Road to London Town.

Horsey, horsey, on your way,
We've been together for many a day,
So let your tail go swish,
And your wheels go round,
Giddyup we're homeward bound!
I like to take my horse and buggy,
And go riding through the town,
I like to hear old Dobbin's clip clop,
I like to see the wheels go round.
Clip clop, clip clop, clip clop, clip clop,

Horsey, horsey, on your way,
We've been together for many a day,
So let your tail go swish,
And your wheels go round,
Giddyup we're homeward bound!

Hungry, Hungry

Here is one that's fun to sing before snack time. Pound your hands on the floor in a quick drumming style. Sing to the tune of "One Little, Two Little, Three Little Indians."

Hungry, hungry, I am hungry
Table, table, here I come.
I could eat a moose goose burger
Sixteen pickles and a purple plum!

Hurry, Hurry

This one is fun to act out with young toddlers. Sing to the tune of "One Little, Two Little, Three Little Indians," and add your own verses.

Hurry, hurry, where's the fire?
Hurry, hurry, where's the fire?
Hurry, hurry, where's the fire?
Ding Ding Ding Ding Ding.

Hurry, hurry, drive the fire truck …
Hurry, hurry, spray the water …
Hurry, hurry, climb the ladder …
Hurry, hurry, save the children …
Hurry, hurry, go back home …
Hurry, hurry, go to sleep ….

Pick It Up (Dropped My Hat)

Woody Guthrie © Folkways Music Publishers, Inc. This song is really fun to sing when babies start experimenting with gravity and the release reflex by dropping things. Listen to the tune on Kathy Reid-Naiman's CD A Smooth Road to London Town. *On this CD the song is called "Dropped My Hat."*

Verse:
I dropped my thumb, pick it up, pick it up;
I dropped my thumb, pick it up, pick it up;
I dropped my thumb, pick it up, pick it up
And put it back with my fingers.

Pick, pick, pick it,
Pick it up, pick it up.
Pick, pick, pick it,
Pick it up, pick it up.
Picka, picka, picky,
Pick it up, pick it up
Pick it up, pick it up.

I dropped my toys, …
And put 'em back in their places.

I dropped my candy…
And throw it away in the garbage.

I dropped my apple…
And wash it clean in the water.

I dropped my dolly…
And lay her back in the cradle.

I dropped my shoe…
And put it with my other shoe.

I dropped my head…
And put it back on my shoulders.

My verses:

I dropped my hat…
And I put it back on my head.

I dropped my shoe…
And I put it on my foot.

I dropped my book…
And I put it back in my mouth!

I Had a Rooster

This is a cumulative folk song that toddlers love.

I had a rooster
And the rooster pleased me
I fed my rooster on the green berry tree
My little rooster went
Cock-a-doodle-doo
A-doodely, doodely, doodely doo.

I had a cat and the cat pleased me
I fed my cat on the green berry tree
My little cat went,
Meow, meow, meow,
And my little rooster went,
Cock-a-doodle doo
A-doodley, doodely, doodely doo.

I had a cow ….

Add any animals you like and keep the list growing.

It's Time to Put Away

This is an extremely useful song! Sing to the tune of "The Farmer in the Dell."

It's time to put away,
It's time to put away,
It's time to put away our toys,
It's time to put away.

Add verses to put away anything!

Land of the Silver Birch

Canadian children sing this song at Guides, Scouts, and campfires. It makes a wonderful burping song for babies.

Land of the silver birch, home of the beaver,
Where still the mighty moose wanders at will,
Blue lake and rocky shore
I will return once more.

Chorus:
Boom de de boom boom,
Boom de de boom boom,
Boom de de boom boom,
Bo-o-o-o-m.

Down in the forest, deep in the lowlands,
My heart cries out for thee, hills of the north,
Blue lake and rocky shore
I will return once more.

High on a rocky ledge, I'll build my wigwam,
Close by the water's edge, silent and still,
Blue lake and rocky shore
I will return once more.

Land of the silver birch, home of the beaver,
Where still the mighty moose wanders at will,
Blue lake and rocky shore
I will return once more.

Let's All Clean Up Together

An essential clean up song! Sing to the tune of "The Farmer in the Dell." Add your own verses.

Let's all clean up together,
Let's all clean up together,
Let's all clean up together,
Because it's fun to do.

Lightly Row

The tune to this song is on the enclosed CD. Parent and baby face one another and gently row back and forth.

Lightly row,
Lightly row,
Over the deep blue sea we go,
Smoothly glide,
Smoothly glide,
On the gentle tide.

Let the wind and waters be,
Mingled with our rhyme of glee,
Sing and float,
Sing and float,
In our rowing boat.

May There Always Be Sunshine

Charlotte Diamond sings this song on Blue Carrot Diamond. *It's lovely with sign language. You can add your own verses too. You can see authentic hand motions for signs on the web. Search Google for "American Sign Language."*

May there always be sunshine
May there always be blue skies
May there always be Mama (Papa)
May there always be me.

Signs:
always = point index finger of right hand and move it in circles at shoulder level.

sunshine = start with both hands in front of your chest then raise them up overhead and bring them down and apart in a large arc.

blue skies = start with both hands, palms up, at belly level, then lift them up and apart in a big circle, ending with fingertips touching above your head.

mama = with right hand open, touch thumb twice to the side of your chin.

papa = make motion of tipping your hat.

me = point to yourself with the index finger of your right hand.

My Dog Rags

Elizabeth Deutsch and Evelyn Atwater © 1959 Sing'n Do Co. Inc. Listen to the tune on Kathy Reid-Naiman's CD A Smooth Road to London Town.

I have a dog and his name is Rags,
He eats so much that his tummy sags,
His ears flip flop and his tail wig wags,
And when he walks he goes, zig zag.

Chorus:
He goes flip flop, wiggle waggle, zig zag,
He goes flip flop, wiggle waggle, zig zag,
He goes flip flop, wiggle waggle, zig zag,
I love Rags, and he loves me.

My dog Rags he likes to play,
He rolls around in the mud all day,
I whistle *(pause)*, but he won't obey,
He always runs the other way.

Repeat chorus.

My Paddle

Many Canadians learn this song, attributed to Pauline Johnson, in elementary school. It's lovely as a round. The tune is on the enclosed CD.

My paddle's keen and bright,
Flashing with silver,
Follow the wild goose flight,
Dip, dip, and swing.
Dip, dip, and swing.

Dip, dip and swing her back,
Flashing with silver,
Follow the wild goose track,
Dip, dip, and swing.
Dip, dip, and swing.

Pretty Painted Butterfly

A traditional Caribbean song. Listen to the tune on Kathy Reid-Naiman's CD A Smooth Road to London Town.

Pretty painted butterfly,
What will you do all day?
I'll roam about the sunny skies,
Nothing to do but play.
Nothing to do but play,
All the live long day.
So fly, butterfly, so fly, butterfly,
Don't waste your time away.
So fly, butterfly, so fly, butterfly,
Don't waste your time away.

Put Your Shoes On, Lucy

By Hank Fort © Copyright 1947 by Bourne Co. Listen to the tune on Kathy Reid-Naiman's CD A Smooth Road to London Town. *This is a fun song to sing or say while putting on baby's little shoes.*

Put your shoes on, Lucy,
Don't you know you're in the city?
Put your shoes on, Lucy,
It's really such a pity,
That Lucy can't go barefoot
Wherever she goes
Because she loves to feel the wiggle of her toes,
She loves to feel the wiggle of her toes.

Sittin' in a High Chair

Words by Martha Cheney and Hap Palmer ©Hap-Pal Music, Inc. Music: Traditional. The tune is "Mama's Little Baby Loves Shortnin' Bread." Add any kind of food your baby likes!

Chorus:
Sittin' in a high chair, big chair, my chair
Sittin' in a high chair, bangin' my spoon!
Sittin' in a high chair, big chair, my chair
Sittin' in a high chair, feed me soon!

Bring on a plate, bring on a cup,
Papa's gonna fill this baby up.

Bring on bananas, bring on the bread,
Mama's gonna get this baby fed.

Repeat Chorus

Bring on the carrots, bring on the peas,
Mama come serve this baby please.
Bring on the pancakes stacked in a pile,
Papa's gonna make this baby smile.

Repeat Chorus
Bring on a napkin, bring on a sponge,
Clean me up 'cause I'm all done.

Wiggly Woo

A dad in one of my programs recalled this song from his childhood in England. He used it to change his wiggly baby's diaper. Musical notation is in This Little Puffin *by Elizabeth Matterson, revised edition, 1991.*

There's a worm at the bottom of my garden.
And his name is Wiggly Woo.
There's a worm at the bottom of my garden
And all that he can do,
Is wiggle all night,
And wiggle all day,
Whatever else the people do say;
There's a worm at the bottom of my garden,
And his name is Wiggly, Wig-Wig-Wiggly,
Wig-Wig-Wiggly Woo-oo!

Simple Gifts

A traditional Shaker hymn. Listen to the tune on Kathy Reid-Naiman's CD A Smooth Road to London Town.

'Tis the gift to be simple, 'tis the gift to be free,
'Tis the gift to come down where we ought to be,
And when we find ourselves in the place just right,
It will be in the valley of love and delight.
When true simplicity is gained,
To bow and to bend we will not be ashamed,
To turn, to turn will be our delight,
Till by turning, turning we come round right.

What'll I do with the Baby-o?

© 1964, 1971, Jean Ritchie Geordie Music Publishing Co. Clap or bounce to this wonderful Appalachian song. Alternate pronouns he and she when you sing in a group. The tune is on the enclosed CD.

Chorus:
What'll I do with the baby-o?
What'll I do with the baby-o?
What'll I do with the baby-o?
If she won't go to sleepy-o?

1. I'll dress him up in calico (3x)
   Send him to his daddy-o.
   Calico is a brightly coloured cloth.
2. I'll wrap her up in a tablecloth (3x)
   Throw her up in the old hay-loft.
3. I'll dance him east I'll dance him west (3x)
   Dance with the one that I love best.
4. I'll dance her up I'll dance her down (3x)
   Dance her all around the town.
5. I'll pull his nose and tickle his chin (3x)
   Wrap him up in a counterpin.
   A counterpin is a bedspread.
6. I'll dance her north I'll dance her south (3x)
   Pour a little moonshine in her mouth!
7. I'll tell your daddy when he comes home (3x)
   And I'll give Old Blue your chicken bone.
   (Teething babies used to get a leg-bone to gnaw while others were eating.)

You Are My Sunshine

Don't forget to sing this old favourite. Older children just love to pretend to be sad.

Chorus:
You are my sunshine, my only sunshine,
You make me happy when skies are grey,
You'll never know, dear, how much I love you,
Please don't take my sunshine away.

The other night, dear, as I lay sleeping,
I dreamed I held you in my arms,
But when I woke, dear, I was mistaken,
And I hung my head and I cried.

Spanish Rhymes
Canciones de Mamá Ganzo

Hola a todos *138*
Arrullo *138*
Caballito blanco *138*
Canción de despedida *138*
Cinco calabacitas *138*
Cinco pollitos *138*
Hallando un huevo *138*
Las lechusas *139*
Mi carita *139*
Mis cinco sentidos *139*
Mis manos amistosas *139*
La manzana *139*
Palmas, palmitas *139*
Los pollitos *139*
¡Que linda manita! *140*
¡Que llueva! *140*
La señora gorda *140*
Tortillitas para mamá *140*
Tres pecesitos *140*

Here are a few Spanish rhymes and songs. There is a bibliography of resources where you can find more rhymes and songs in Spanish at the end of this section.

Hola a todos

Es una canción para abrir el círculo. Se puede in cluir los nombres de las personas presentes. Cante a la melodía de "Good Night Ladies."

Hola a todos *(repítelo tres veces)*
Nos vamos a divertir!

Canción de despedida

Es una canción para despedir a todos. Se puede incluir los nombres en vez de "todos." Cante a la melodía de "Good Night Ladies."

Adiós a todos *(repítelo tres veces)*
Nos tenemos que despedir.

Arrullo

Arrulle al niño para que se duerma. Se puede sustituir niño por niña.

Duérmete mi niña,
Duérmete mi sol,
Duérmete pedazo
De mi corazón.

Caballito blanco

Esta canción cuenta de la nostalgia.

Caballito blanco, sácame de aquí.
Llévame a mi pueblo, donde yo nací.
Tengo, tengo, tengo
Tu no tienes nada.
Tengo tres ovejas en una cabaña.
Una me de leche.
Otra me da lana,
Y otra mantequilla para la semana.

Cinco calabacitas

Cinco calabacitas sentadas en un portón;
La primera dijo: "Se está haciendo tarde."
Apunte al dedo pequeño.
La segunda dijo: "Hay brujas en el aire."
Apunte al segundo dedo.
La tercera dijo: "No se hace."
Apunte al tercer dedo.
La cuarta dijo: "Es una noche de espanto."
Apunte al cuarto dedo.
La quinta dijo: "Corremos, corremos."
Apunte al pulgar.
"U-u-u-u," hizo el viento,
Y se apagaron las luces
Aplauden una vez recio.
Las cinco calabacitas
Corrieron a esconderse.
Corren los dedos hacia detrás de su espalda.

Cinco pollitos

Juegue con los deditos de su bebé.

Cinco pollitos
Tiene mi tía;
Uno le canta
La sinfonía.
Éste toca el tambor,
pom, pom!
Éste la guitarra,
rom, rom!
Éste los platillos,
chin, chin!
Y éste la campanita,
tilín, tilín!

Hallando un huevo

Cuente con los dedos para cada "éste." Busque agua primero en el codo, después al hombro. Termine haciendo cosquillas en la axila.

Éste niño halló un huevo,
Éste lo coció,
Éste lo peló,
Éste le hechó la sal,
Y éste gordo chaparrito se lo comió.

Le dió sed,
Y se fué a buscar agua …
Buscó y buscó …
¡Y aquí halló!
Y tomó y tomó y tomó ….

Las lechusas

Se usa la melodía de "Frère Jacques." Esta canción calma a los niños.

Las lechusas, las lechusas,
Hacen "shhh," hacen "shhh,"
Todos calladitos,
Todos tranquilitos,
Hacen "shhh," hacen "shhh."

Mi carita

Se canta con la melodía de "Clementine." Toque las partes de la cara.

Mi carita, redondita, tiene ojos y nariz.
Y tambien una boquita para cantar y reír.
Con mis ojos, veo todo,
Con mis nariz, hago "¡achiss!"
Con mi boca, como ricas palomitas de maíz.

Mis cinco sentidos

Toque las partes del cuerpo cuando se las menciona.

Una boquita para comer,
Señale la boca.
Mi naricita para oler,
Señale la nariz.
Mis dos ojitos para ver,
Señale los ojos.
Mis dos orejitas para oir,
Señale las orejas.
Mis dos manitas para tocar,
Señale las manos.
¿Y mi cabecita?
Descanse la cabeza sobre las manos, como si se fuera a dormir.

Mis manos amistosas

Una rima linda que enseña el movimiento de manos.

Yo tengo dos manos,
Y son unas manos muy especiales.
Ellas juntas pueden aplaudir,
Aplauda.
Ellas pueden girar al mismo tiempo,
Gire las manos.
Ellas pueden frotarse,
Frote una mano con la otra.
Ellas pueden abrazarse,
Agárrese las manos y aprételos.
Como dos amigas.

La manzana

Se cantan esta canción en varios países, usando frutas diferentes.

La manzana se pasea
De la sala al comedór.
No me piques con cuchillo,
Pícame con tenedor.
Al picar una manzana,
Un dedito me corté.
Mi mamá me dió un besito
Y un pedazo de pastel.

Palmas, palmitas

Se puede empezar una conversación, ¿qúe va a traer Papá?"

Palmas, palmitas
que viene papá.
Viene de lejos,
¿Qúe me traerá?

Los pollitos

Esta canción da al niño un sentido del amor del cantante.

Los pollitos dicen, "pió, pió, pió,"
Cuando tienen hambre,
Toque el estómago.
Cuando tienen frío.
Haga ademán de tener frío.
La mamá les busca el maíz y el trigo,
Les da la comida,
Toque la boca.
Y les presta abrigo.
Póngalos debajo de los brazos para protegerlos.
Bajo las dos alas, acurrucaditos,
Duermen los pollitos hasta el otro día.
Haga ademán de dormir.

¡Que linda manita!

Cuando se canta esta canción, toque la palma, juegue con los deditos, y muestre al bebé cómo se mueve la muñeca.

Que linda manita
Que tiene el bebé,
Que linda, que mona,
Que bonita es.
Pequeños deditos
Rayitos de sol,
Que gire, que gire
Como un girasol.

¡Que llueva!

Cuando se habla de la lluvia, se puede pasar las manos delicadamente de la cabeza a los pies del bebé.

Que llueva, que llueva,
La vieja está en la cueva.
Los pajaritos cantan,
Las nubes se levantan.
¡Que sí! ¡que no!
¡Que caiga un chaparrón!

La señora gorda

Esta canción cuenta una historia. A los niños les gusta mucho cuando se usa voces diferentes.

La señora gorda fue de paseo.
Rompió *a un farola con su sombrero.*
Al golpe de cristal,
Aplaude una vez recio.
Salió el gobernados.
"Que bién ha sido elatrevido
Que ha roto a mi fasola?"
"Perdone, caballero, que yo no he sido.
Ha sido mi sombrero por atrevido!"
"Si ha sido su sombrero, lo voy a castigar
Para que otro día, ya sabe respetar!"

Tortillitas para mamá

Esta rima es muy tradicional. Se puede cambiar mamá y papá, y sustituir el bebé, para que toda la famila tiene las tortillitas más bonitas a veces.

Tortillitas para mamá.
Tortillitas para papá.
Las quemaditas para mamá,
Las más bonitas para papá.

Tres pecesitos

Es muy divertido usar una voz profunda para la parte del tiburón, y una voz alta para la parte del pecesito pequeño.

Tres pecesitos se fueron a nadar,
El más pequeño se fue al fondo del mar.
Vino un tiburón y le dijo "¡ven acá!"
"No no no no no, porque se enoja mi mamá."

BIBLIOGRAPHY:

Ada, Alma Flor and Isabel Campoy. MAMÁ GOOSE: A LATINO NURSERY TREASURY/ UN TESORO DE RIMAS INFANTILES. New York: Hyperion, 2004.

Ada, Alma Flor and Isabel Campoy. PIO PEEP!: TRADITIONAL SPANISH NURSERY RHYMES. New York: HarperCollins, 2003.

Griego, Margo et al. TORTILLITAS PARA MAMA AND OTHER NURSERY RHYMES. New York: Henry Holt, 1981.

Hall, Nancy Abraham and Jill Syverson-Stork. LOS POLLITOS DICEN / THE BABY CHICKS SING. New York: Little Brown, 1994.

Hinojosa, Tish. CADA NINO / EVERY CHILD. Cambridge, MA: Rounder, 1996.

Story Rhymes

As I Was Going Down the Stair *142*
As I Was Standing in the Street *142*
Catch Her Crow *142*
Diddle, Diddle, Dumpling *142*
Grandma Mose *142*
Gregory Griggs *142*
Grey Goose and Gander *142*
Hannah Bantry in the Pantry *142*
Here Am I (Little Jumping Joan) *143*
Hippity Hop *143*
How Many Miles to Babylon? *143*
Ladybug, Ladybug *143*
Let's Go to Bed *143*
The Man in the Moon *143*
My Old Friend Jake *143*
Old John Muddlecombe *143*
On Saturday Night I Lost My Wife *143*
One Misty Moisty Morning *144*
There Was a Man Named Michael Finnegan *144*
There Was a Young Farmer from Leeds *144*
There Was an Old Woman Lived Under the Stairs *144*
There Was an Old Woman Tossed Up in a Basket *144*

These are rhymes for the simple pleasure of saying and imagining. I like to sprinkle my programs with rhymes that have beautiful sounds and imagery to contemplate. Applicable situations will arise, and it's always nice to know a rhyme for the occasion. The parents and children love them. Many have a strong beat that you can bounce to.

As I Was Going Down the Stair

A nice rhyme to say as you're going up and down stairs with toddlers.

As I was going down the stair
I met a man who wasn't there.
He wasn't there again today,
I wish, I wish he'd stay away.

As I Was Standing in the Street

As I was standing in the street
As quiet as could be,
A great big ugly man came up
And tied his horse to me.

Catch Her Crow

Catch her crow,
Carry her kite,
Take her away
Till the apples are ripe.
When they are ripe
And ready to fall
Down will come baby
Apples and all.

Diddle, Diddle Dumpling

This is a fun rhyme to say at bedtime as you remove baby's shoes and socks.

Diddle, diddle, dumpling, my son John
Went to bed with his trousers on
One shoe off, and one shoe on,
Diddle, diddle, dumpling, my son John.

Grandma Mose

Grandma Mose was sick in bed.
She called for the doctor
And the doctor said,
"Grandma Mose, you ain't sick,
All you need is a peppermint stick.
Get up, get down, get outa town!"

Gregory Griggs

Gregory Griggs, Gregory Griggs,
Had twenty-seven different wigs.
He wore them up, he wore them down,
To please the people of the town.
He wore them east, he wore them west,
But he never could tell
Which he liked best.

Grey Goose and Gander

The one-strand river is the sea.

Grey goose and gander
Waft your wings together
And carry the good king's daughter
Over the one-strand river.

Hannah Bantry in the Pantry

A rhyme to say when all your dinner guests are gone!

Hannah Bantry in the pantry
Gnawing on a mutton bone.
How she gnawed it,
How she clawed it,
When she thought she was alone.

Here Am I (Little Jumping Joan)

Jump like jumping beans.

Here am I
Little Jumping Joan
When nobody's with me
I'm all alone.

Hippity Hop

Say this one while on your way to the store to get a dawdling toddler moving along.

Hippity hop
To the barber shop
To buy a stick of candy.
One for you,
And one for me,
And one for Jack-a-Dandy.

How Many Miles to Babylon?

Say this on those late night car rides.

How many miles to Babylon?
Three score and ten.
Can I get there by candlelight?
Yes, and back again.
If your heels are nimble and light,
You can get there by candlelight.

Ladybug, Ladybug

This is a nice rhyme to say as you prepare children to go home after a long day in child care.

Ladybug, ladybug, fly away do,
Fly to the mountain and feed upon dew.
Feed upon dew and sleep on a rug,
Then fly away home like a good little bug.

Let's Go to Bed

"Let's go to bed," said Sleepy Head
"Tarry a while," said Slow
"Put on the pot," said Greedy-gut
"We'll sup before we go."

Man in the Moon

Say this one at bedtime.

The man in the moon,
Looked out of the moon,
Looked out of the moon and said,
I think it's time for all good children
To think about going to bed!

My Old Friend Jake

I always think of this rhyme on a windy day.

My old friend Jake
Was thin as a snake,
And light as a drip of rain.
One windy day Jake blew away,
And never was seen again.

Old John Muddlecombe

Say this one while searching for your child's hat.

Old John Muddlecombe
Lost his cap.
He couldn't find it anywhere,
Poor old chap.
He walked down the high street,
And everybody said,
"Silly John Muddlecombe,
You've got it on your head!"

On Saturday Night I Lost My Wife

On Saturday night I lost my wife
And where do you think I found her?
Up in the moon,
Singing a tune,
With all the stars around her.

One Misty Moisty Morning

A great rhyme for a rainy day.

One misty moisty morning,
When cloudy was the weather,
I chanced to meet an old man,
Clothed all in leather.
He began to compliment,
And I began to grin,
How do you do?
And how do you do?
And how do you do again?

There Was a Man Named Michael Finnegan

Children love this one as it reminds them of daddy's prickly whiskers.

There was a man named Michael Finnegan.
He had whiskers on his chin-a-gin.
He shaved them off but they grew in-a-gin,
Poor old Michael Finnegan begin-a-gin.

There Was a Young Farmer from Leeds

There was a young farmer from Leeds,
Who swallowed a packet of seeds.
It soon came to pass,
He was covered in grass,
And couldn't sit down for the weeds!

There Was an Old Woman Lived Under the Stairs

There was an old woman
Lived under the stairs.
She sold apples and she sold pears.
If you asked her for one,
She'd give you two.
A nicer old woman I never knew.

There Was an Old Woman Tossed Up in a Basket

There was an old woman
Tossed up in a basket,
Seventeen times as high as the moon!
And where she was going,
I could not but ask it,
For under her arm she carried a broom.
"Old woman, old woman, old woman," quoth I,
"Oh whither, oh whither, oh whither so high?"
"To sweep the cobwebs out of the sky."
"Can I go with you?"
"Aye, by and by."

Tickling Rhymes

Bumblebee, Bumblebee *146*
A Butterfly Kiss *146*
Chicken in the Barnyard *146*
Creepy Mouse *146*
Here is a Beehive *146*
I'm Going to Bore a Hole *146*
Jeremiah *146*
The Little Mice Go Creeping *147*
Pussy Cat, Pussy Cat *147*
Round About, Round About *147*
Round and Round the Garden *147*
Round and Round the Haystack *147*
Round the World *147*
See the Little Mousie *148*
Slowly, Slowly *148*
Teddy Bear, Teddy Bear *148*
There Was a Little Mouse *148*
Three Tickles (Pizza Pickle) *147*
What Shall We Do with a Lazy Katie? *148*

Babies differ in their responses to tickling, but most babies enjoy light intermittent tickling. Each baby will also have a favourite ticklish spot, which is for the parents to discover through experimentation. These nursery rhymes are great fun because of the anticipated little tickle at the end.

Bumblebee, Bumblebee

Speak in a droning voice as you draw circles in the air in front or the baby, then dart in for a tickle at the end.

Bumblebee, bumblebee
Come out of the barn
With a bag of honey
Under each arm
Bzzzzzzzzzzz!

A Butterfly Kiss

© *Felicity Williams,* Pocket Full of Stars, *Annick Press, 1997.*

A butterfly kiss
Goes like this …
Bat eyelashes against baby's cheek.
An ice cream kiss
Goes like this …
Pretend to lick baby's cheek.
A wee Willie Winkie kiss
Goes like this …
Kiss your fingertips and gently run them over baby's face.
But the big bass drum kiss
Goes like THIS!
Blow a raspberry on baby's neck.

Chicken in the Barnyard

Chicken in the barnyard
Staying out of trouble.
Draw a little circle in baby's palm.
Along came a turkey
Slowly creep fingers up baby's arm.
And … "Gobble, gobble, gobble!"
Tickle baby's underarm, or move in for a gobble on baby's neck.

Creepy Mouse

Creep fingers up baby's arm as you say this in a suspenseful voice, then tickle his neck.

Creepy mouse,
Creepy mouse,
All the way up
To Baby's house!

Here Is A Beehive

Make a fist and say the rhyme, then unfold your fingers one at a time, and buzz in for a little tickle. You can also play this on baby's little fist, unwrapping the fingers one at a time.

Here is a beehive,
Where are the bees?
Hidden away where nobody sees.
Here they come creeping out of the hive,
One, two, three, four, five!
Bzzzzzzz.

I'm Going to Bore a Hole

Index finger draws ever smaller circles in the air above baby then zooms in for a gentle tickle on baby's tummy.

I'm going to bore a hole,
And I don't know where.
I think I'll bore a hole right …
THERE!

Jeremiah

Great at diaper-changing time. Blow gently, then blow a big raspberry on baby's tummy. There is a little tune on Kathy Reid-Naiman's CD Say Hello to the Morning.

Jeremiah, blow the fire
Puff, puff, puff.
First you blow it gently,
Then you blow it ROUGH!

The Little Mice Go Creeping

Make up a suspenseful little tune. Go faster toward the end.

The little mice go creeping, creeping, creeping,
The little mice go creeping all through the house.

The big black cat goes stalking, stalking, stalking,
The big black cat goes stalking all through the house.

The little mice go scampering, scampering, scampering,
The little mice go scampering all through the house.

Three Tickles (Pizza Pickle)

© Dennis Lee. Clap baby's hands in rhythm to the beat, then tickle nose, toes and tummy.

Pizza, pickle pumpernickel
My little guy shall have a tickle.
One for his nose,
And one for his toes,
And one for his tummy,
Where the hot dog goes!

We make up our own lines at the end, and say:

And one for his tummy,
Where the tofu goes!

And one for his tummy,
Where the apple sauce goes!

Pussy Cat, Pussy Cat

Draw a circle on baby's palm, then walk fingers up to the armpit for a tickle.

Pussy cat, pussy cat,
Where have you been?
I've been to London
To visit the queen.

Pussy cat, pussy cat,
What did you there?
I chased a little mouse
Under her chair!

Round About, Round About

Index finger draws circles in the air above baby then zooms in for a gentle tickle on baby's favourite spot.

Round about, round about,
Went the wee mouse.
Up a bit, up a bit,
In his wee house.

Round and Round the Garden

Draw a circle on baby's palm (or tummy), then walk fingers up to a favourite spot for a tickle.

Round and round the garden
Like a teddy bear.
One step, two step,
Tickle you under there!

Round and Round the Haystack

A variation on "Round and Round the Garden."

Round and round the haystack
Goes the little mousie
One step, two step
Up into her housie.

Round the World

Draw a big circle in the air around the baby, then zoom in for a tickle.

Round the world!
Round the world!
Catch a big bear.
Where are we going to catch him?
Right in THERE!

See the Little Mousie

See the little mousie
Creeping up the stairs
Looking for a warm nest
There, oh there!

Slowly, Slowly, Very Slowly

This is a little tickle to play on baby's arm or leg. It's also fun to act out with toddlers in a game of chase.

Slowly, slowly, very slowly
Creeps the garden snail.
Slowly, slowly, very slowly
Up the garden rail.
Slowly creep fingers up baby's arm or leg.

Quickly, quickly, very quickly
Runs the little mouse.
Quickly, quickly, very quickly
Up into his house!
Quickly run fingers around baby's tummy and up to his underarm or some other ticklish spot.

Teddy Bear, Teddy Bear

A tickle variation on this well known rhyme. It can be sung to the tune of "Bluebird, Bluebird, Through My Window."

Teddy bear, teddy bear,
Touch the ground,
Take baby's hands and touch the floor.
Teddy bear, teddy bear,
Turn around,
Turn baby's hands in a circular motion.
Teddy bear, teddy bear,
Walk down the street,
Walk fingers down baby's legs.
Teddy bear, teddy bear,
Tickle those feet!
Tickle those little bare feet.

There Was a Little Mouse

There was a little mouse,
And he lived just there.
Touch a spot on baby's body.
And when anybody came,
He ran right up there!
Run fingers up arm or leg for a tickle.

What Shall We Do with a Lazy Katie?

Sing to the tune of "What Shall We Do with a Drunken Sailor."

What shall we do with a lazy Katie?
What shall we do with a lazy Katie?
What shall we do with a lazy Katie?
Early in the morning.

Roll her around and tickle her all over,
Roll her around and tickle her all over,
Roll her around and tickle her all over,
Early in the morning.

Heave ho and up she rises,
Heave ho and up she rises,
Heave ho and up she rises,
Early in the morning.

Toe-Wiggling and Foot-Patting Rhymes

Cobbler, Cobbler (two versions) *150*
Cock-a-Doodle-Doo *150*
Diddle, Diddle Dumpling *150*
Hob, Shoe, Hob *150*
Hugh, Hugh at the Age of Two *150*
Let's Go to the Woods Today *151*
Pitty, Patty, Polt *151*
Put Your Shoes on, Lucy *151*
See-saw, Margery Daw *151*
See-saw, Sacradown *151*
Shoe the Colt *151*
Shoe the Little Horse *152*
There Is a Cobbler on Our Street *152*
This Little Cow *152*
This Little Pig Had a Rub-a-Dub-Dub *152*
This Little Piggy Went to Market *152*
Wee Wiggy, Poke Piggy *152*

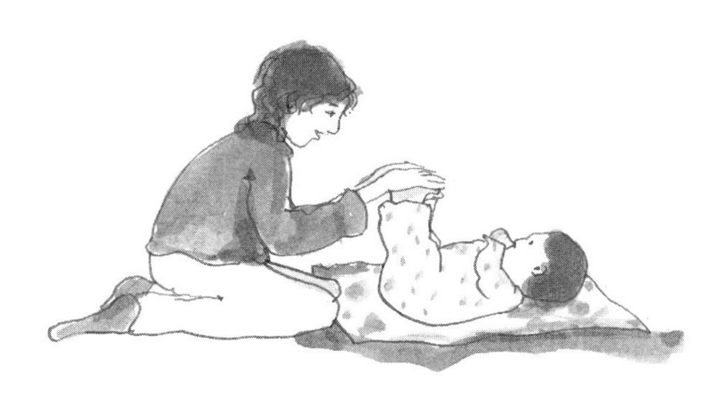

Babies' tiny hands are clenched in a fist when they are newborn, and so it's nice to play rhymes on little toes. This helps the baby develop body awareness. Of course, any rhyme you can play on fingers is also fun to play on little toes.

Cobbler, Cobbler

This is a great rhyme for putting on shoes. Older children who know the rhyme will want to act it out themselves.

Cobbler, cobbler,
Mend my shoe.
Pat baby's foot.
My big toe
Is poking through.
Wiggle big toe.
Stitch it up,
And stitch it down,
Walk fingers up and down baby's foot.
And I will give you
Half a crown.
Pretend to hand over a coin.
Cobbler, Cobbler,
Mend my shoe
Pat foot again.
Get it done by half past two.
Half past two is much too late,
Get it done by half past eight!
Tap your watch or your wrist.

Cobbler, Cobbler

Here is a shorter version without the crown.

Cobbler, cobbler, mend my shoe.
Have it done by half past two;
Stitch it up, and stitch it down.
Make the very best in town.

Cock-a-Doodle-Doo

This little rhyme is fun to say while patting the soles of baby's shoeless feet. I always think of it when a baby crawls off without a shoe.

Cock-a-doodle-doo,
My dame has lost her shoe.
My master's lost his fiddling stick,
And knows not what to do.

Cock-a-doodle-doo,
What is my dame to do?
'Til master finds his fiddling stick,
She'll dance without a shoe.

Cock-a-doodle-doo,
My dame has found her shoe.
And master's found his fiddling stick,
Sing doodle, doodle, doo.

Diddle, Diddle Dumpling, My Son John

This is a fun rhyme to say at bedtime as you remove baby's shoes and socks.

Diddle, diddle, dumpling, my son John
Went to bed with his trousers on
One shoe off, and one shoe on,
Diddle, diddle, dumpling, my son John.

Hob, Shoe, Hob

Pat soles of baby's feet.

Hob, shoe, hob
Hob, shoe, hob
Here a nail,
And there a nail,
And that's well shod.

Hugh, Hugh

© Dennis Lee. Pat soles of baby's feet and tickle at the end.

Hugh, Hugh,
At the age of two,
Built his home in a big brown shoe.
Hugh, Hugh,
What'll you do?
There's holes in the soles
And the rain comes through!

Let's Go to the Woods Today

"Let's go to the woods today," says this little pig.
"What to do there?" says that little pig.
"Look for our baby," says this little pig.
"What to do when with her?" says that little pig.
"Tickle her and tickle her and tickle her!" says this little pig.

Let's Go to the Woods Today

A variation.

"Let's go to the woods today," says this little pig.
"What to do there?" says that little pig.
"Look for our mother," says this little pig.
"What to do when with her?" says that little pig.
"Kiss her and kiss her and kiss her!" says this little pig.

Kiss those tiny toes!

Pitty, Patty, Polt

Pat soles of baby's feet in rhythm with the beat.

Pitty, patty, polt.
Shoe the wild colt.
Here's a nail.
There's a nail.
Pitty, patty polt.

Put Your Shoes on, Lucy

Hank B. Fort Jr. © Bourne Canada. This is a jazzy song to say or sing as you put on baby's shoes. Bounce, then end in a foot tickle. Listen to the tune on Kathy Reid-Naiman's CD A Smooth Road to London Town.

Put your shoes on, Lucy
Don't you know you're in the city?
Put your shoes on, Lucy,
It's really such a pity,
That Lucy can't go barefoot
Wherever she goes
Because she loves to feel the wiggle
Of her toes.
She loves to feel the wiggle of her toes.

See-saw, Margery Daw

This is a leg-cycling rhyme. More verses on *p. 79.*

See-saw, Margery Daw
Johnny shall have a new master.
He shall have but a penny a day,
Because he can't work any faster.

See-saw, Sacradown

This is a variation.

See-saw, sacradown,
This is the way to London Town.
One foot up
The other foot down.
And that is the way to London Town.

Shoe the Colt

A great diaper-changer. Pat the soles of baby's feet.

Shoe the colt,
Shoe the colt,
Shoe the wild mare,
Here a nail,
There a nail,
Yet she goes bare.

Shoe The Little Horse

Pat soles of baby's feet in rhythm to the beat.

Shoe the little horse,
Shoe the little mare,
But let the little colty
Go bare, bare, bare.

There Is A Cobbler

Pat soles of baby's feet. Toddlers like to pound their fists together in rhythm to the bang, bang, bang part.

There is a cobbler on our street,
Mending shoes for little feet,
With a bang and a bang and a bang, bang, bang,
With a bang and a bang and a bang, bang, bang.

Mending shoes the whole day long,
Mending shoes to make them strong.
With a bang and a bang and a bang, bang, bang,
With a bang and a bang and a bang, bang, bang.

Fix the heels and fix the toes,
Fix the holes in case it snows.
With a bang and a bang and a bang, bang, bang,
With a bang and a bang and a bang, bang, bang.

This Little Cow

The big cow is the big toe!

This little cow eats grass,
This little cow eats hay.
This little cow drinks water,
And this little cow runs away.
And this BIG cow does nothing at all
But lie in the fields all day!
Let's chase her and chase her and chase her away!

This Little Pig Had a Rub-a-Dub-Dub

Start with the little toe.

This little pig had a rub-a-dub-dub,
And this little pig had a scrub-a-dub-dub,
This little pig-a-wig ran upstairs,
And this little pig-a wig cried out "BEARS!"
Down came the jar with a big slam bam!
Pat baby's foot.
And this little pig had all the jam.

This Little Piggy Went To Market

Start by wiggling the baby's big toe and end with the little toe. A perfect rhyme for the change table or after a bath.

This little piggy went to market.
This little piggy stayed home.
This little piggy had roast beef.
This little piggy had none.
And this little piggy cried,
"Wee! wee! wee! wee!"
All the way home.

Wee Wiggy, Poke Piggy

Name baby's toes, starting with the little toe, then pretend to gobble up the big toe.

Wee Wiggy,
Poke Piggy,
Tom Whistle,
John Gristle,
And old big
GOBBLE, gobble, gobble!

Wobbidobs

Don't forget this wonderful song! It's in the Songs section, p. 132.

Babies Love Books!

Introduction:

When is the best time to start reading to a child? *154*
What do babies learn from books? *154*
What books appeal to babies? *154*
Why does my baby put the books in his mouth? *155*
Characteristics of the Best Board Books for Babies *155*
Characteristics of the Best Board Books for Toddlers *155*

Books:

Board Books for Babies (Birth to One Year) *156*
Board Books for Toddlers (One to Two Years) *159*

Introducing books to babies is an easy and pleasurable activity for both parent and child. Babies love books when they are the right books, offered at the right time. When babies are introduced to books at birth, they grow up loving books and wanting to learn how to read when they get to school.

Introduction

WHEN IS THE BEST TIME TO START READING TO A CHILD?

When they are babies! It's never too early to start. Babies can hear their parents' voices in about the sixth month of development in the womb, and will recognize the sound patterns of books read to them in the womb after they are born, so before birth is a wonderful time to start.

After birth is a wonderful time too, because then you can see the baby's response which is really fun to watch.

In the first three months of life, babies' vision is blurry at a distance, so parents need to hold the book about twelve inches from the baby's face so she can see it. There are many physical positions to assume that work: parent and baby can lie down on the floor on their tummies together, and look at a book that way, (this activity also helps the baby practice holding her heavy head up), or the parent can hold the book in the air as they both lie on the floor on their backs, or the parent can share a book with the baby cradled in his arms. The baby will love to hear the sound patterns of the language in longer books, and she will love to look at the pictures too, if they are not too small and cluttered. At about three months of age, the baby will be grasping for the book. By about six months, she will be sitting up, so the parents can have the baby sitting on their laps, and look at the book together that way. Suggest these little ways to parents.

WHAT DO BABIES LEARN FROM BOOKS?

When we share books with babies we are showing them many important concepts they will need to know in order to learn how to read when they go to school. We are showing them that books are interesting toys, and that books are about people, like them! We are showing them that books have a front and back (cover), an upside down, and right side up, and we are showing them how to turn pages.

When books are introduced so effortlessly in infancy, reading becomes an accessible and enjoyable activity.

Later, as older preschoolers become interested in the text, we can show them that print moves across the page from left to right, and we start reading text from the top left corner of the page. Parents can show this to their children by tracking their fingers under the text as they read aloud. These experiences develop a child's curiosity about text, sound and meaning, and about how these things are related.

WHAT BOOKS APPEAL TO BABIES?

The very first books that have unfailing appeal to babies are those without words that simply show photographs of real baby faces, like the series of BABY FACE books by Margaret Miller, or the series of BABY-FACES by Roberta Intrater. Along with these, the simple black and white illustrations of Tana Hoban's board books, BLACK ON WHITE, WHITE ON BLACK, and so on, will have enormous appeal. These are simple, bold, black and white images and patterns surrounded with lots of white space. These books provide endless opportunities for parent talk and baby fascination with pictures. When the baby has developed enough fine muscle control to be able to point to details that interest him (about six months), parents should follow the baby's lead and talk and ask him questions about what he is pointing to. In this way, a "conversation" is born. The baby learns the tone and intonation of questions and answers, and will imitate these with his own sounds. This activity increases baby's interest and comprehension.

WHY DOES MY BABY PUT THE BOOKS IN HIS MOUTH?

Parents are often afraid to give their babies a book because the baby "only puts it in his mouth." Every baby will put the book in his or her mouth. You can count on it! The mouth is the baby's primary sense organ, and so everything of interest goes into the mouth to be tasted and felt and tested. This is normal and expected behaviour. Parents need to be reassured about this. Board books for babies are designed with this kind of use in mind and the heavy cardboard pages are sturdy enough to stand up to this kind of exploration. If there is concern about the baby actually eating the cardboard, which might happen if the baby is left unattended with the book, suggest to parents that they give their baby some other object, like a favourite stuffed toy, to hold in their hand while they look at the book.

CHARACTERISTICS OF THE BEST BOARD BOOKS FOR BABIES

— A small format appropriately sized for babies' hands.
— Rounded edges so that babies won't poke or otherwise injure themselves as they learn how to handle books.
— Clear, bright images. (Bright primary colours, or black and white images for first books.)
— Colourful and uncluttered illustrations so babies can identify objects on the page. (One object per page for very young babies.)
— One or two, if any, words per page.
— Photographs depicting human baby faces are sure winners.

CHARACTERISTICS OF THE BEST BOARD BOOKS FOR TODDLERS

— Books about babies' daily life experiences (animals, dressing, etc.).
— Tactile experience, or the "Touch and Feel" books.
— Rhyming board books.
— "Point and Say" books identifying familiar objects.
— Stories with repeated phrases.
— Stories that have simple, predictable plots, with a strong beginning, middle and end.
— Books with animal sounds.
— Very simple concept books: shapes, colours, counting to five or ten.

The best contain some element of joy or humour or some little surprise that will delight the parent as much as the baby.

A word of caution: Watch out for board books that are simply popular picture books for older children (32 pages of story) remade into board books (14 to 18 pages). The majority of board books published fall into this category. While these may be sought after by older siblings who like this format, they are developmentally inappropriate for babies.

Another word of caution: Baby board books go out of print very quickly, so the ones I am recommending may no longer be available for purchase by the time you want to buy them. The following lists are IN PRINT as of July 2006.

Board Books For Babies

Acredolo, Linda. Photographs by Penny Gentieu. New York: Harper Collins, 2003.

BABY SIGNS FOR BEDTIME
BABY SIGNS FOR MEALTIME
MY FIRST BABY SIGNS

Lovely! Colour photographs of babies doing the signs, one sign per page, with the object or activity depicted on the facing page. Simple instructions for the signs. There are more books in this series. Multicultural.

Bailey, Debbie. Photos by Susan Huszar. TALK-ABOUT BOOKS series. Toronto: Annick, 1991.

MY DAD

This is the only baby book I know that includes a First Nations dad with his children. We need more books that show dads with their children, and we need more First Nations books for babies. There are eighteen books in this series. Colour photographs set in a bright yellow border. Multicultural.

D K Publishing. BABY'S WORLD series. New York: Dorling Kindersley, 2005.

BABY COLORS (2003)
BABY ANIMALS (2004)
COUNT WITH ME (2003)
GOOD NIGHT (2002)
GOOD MORNING (2002)
PLAYTIME (2002)
THINGS THAT GO (2003)

For older babies. Colour photographs of babies and their toys and activities. A few lines of descriptive text per page. Multicultural.

D K Publishing. FIRST LIFT-THE-FLAP BOOK FOR BABIES series. New York: Dorling Kindersley, 2005.

BABY TALK
NOISY FARM

Large cardboard flaps, bright primary colours, one baby or animal per page on a white background. Baby's first words. Very appealing.

D K Publishing. TOUCH-AND-FEEL AND LIFT-THE-FLAP series. New York: Dorling Kindersley, 2005.

BABY SAYS PEEKABOO! (2006)
BATHTIME PEEKABOO! (2005)
BEDTIME PEEKABOO! (2006)
PLAYTIME PEEKABOO! (2005)

Colour photographs of babies and baby toys on a white background. Large heavy card flaps are easy for babies to lift. Text is a question and answer conversation. Very engaging. Multicultural.

Dodd, Emma. AMAZING BABY series. San Diego, CA: Silver Dolphin, 2006.

CLEVER COLOR!

Tiny format. Beautiful shapes and colours.

Grover, Lorie Ann. New York: Little Simon, 2005.

WHEN DADDY COMES HOME

Colourful illustrations with not-so-sturdy flaps show babies' excitement when daddy comes come. Recommended for daddy appeal.

Harwood, Beth. AMAZING BABY series. San Diego, CA: Silver Dolphin, 2006.

BABY BOO!
TWINKLE, TWINKLE!

Beautiful shapes and colours. Very engaging. A few words per page.

Hoban, Tana. New York: Greenwillow, 1993.

WHITE ON BLACK (1993)
BLACK ON WHITE (1993)
WHAT IS THAT? (1994)
WHO ARE THEY? (1994)

These books with white objects on a black background, or black objects on a white background—really grab young babies' attention. No words, one or two objects per page.

Hudson, Cheryl Willis. Colour illustrations by George Ford. WHAT-A-BABY series. New York: Scholastic, 1997.

GOOD NIGHT BABY.
LET'S COUNT BABY.

Colour illustrations show African American babies and toddlers at play. Short text is perfect for reading aloud to babies.

Intrater, Roberta Grobel. BABY FACES series. New York: Scholastic, Cartwheel Books.

EAT (2002)
HUGS & KISSES (2002)
PEEK-A-BOO! (1997)
SLEEP (2002)
SMILE! (1997)
SPLASH! (2002)

Ideal first books, highly recommended. Each page features a colour photograph of an expressive baby face on a black background. A couple of words per page describe the emotions depicted or tell a little story in rhyme. Multicultural.

Katz, Karen. New York: Little Simon, 2003.

DADDY AND ME

Colourful illustrations with not-so-sturdy flaps show dad and baby building a dog house. Recommended for its daddy appeal.

Kenyon, Tony. Cambridge, MS: Candlewick, 1998.

PAT-A-CAKE

Colour illustrations on a white background depict a toddler and a baker acting out the rhyme.

Laden, Nina. San Francisco: Chronicle Books, 2000.

READY, SET, GO!
PEEK-A-WHO?

Fun illustrations and cut out peek holes, fun little text. Perfect little toys.

MacKinnon, Debbie. Photographs by Anthea Sieveking. MY FIRST LIFT-THE-FLAP BOOK series. London: Frances Lincoln, 2005.

FIND KITTY!
FIND MY BOOTS!
FIND MY DUCK!
FIND MY SPADE!

Uncluttered colour photographs of one baby, and one or two toys per page, on a white background. Each book has a little story to read aloud. Older babies love the photographs and they love lifting the heavy card flaps to see what's underneath.

Miller, Margaret. LOOK BABY! BOOKS series. New York: Little Simon, 1998.

BABY FACES (1998)
BABY FOOD (2000)
BABY PETS (2003)
I LOVE COLORS (1999)
PEEKABOO BABY (2001)
WHAT'S ON MY HEAD? (1998)

Ideal first books, highly recommended. Big colourful photographs of baby faces on a white background on each right page, bright colours on the page opposite, one or two words per photograph. Multicultural.

Murphy, Mary. Candlewick, 2005.

I KISSED THE BABY!

An ideal first book. Black or white animals on a black or white background, all bragging about kissing and feeding and tickling the new baby duck. A great read-aloud for programs too.

Oxenbury, Helen. Cambridge, MS: Candlewick, 1995.

I CAN.
I HEAR
I SEE
I TOUCH

Classic Oxenbury illustrations perfectly capture a baby's world. One baby or one object per page on a white background. One word per page.

Porter-Gaylord, Laurel. Pictures by Ashley Wolff.

I LOVE MY DADDY BECAUSE...

Colour illustrations show animal dads with their young and a human dad and baby at the end. The text recounts all the reasons to love a daddy. Recommended for its daddy appeal.

Sterling Publishers, 2004.

FARM BABIES

Each double page spread has a bright colour on the left with a few words of colourful text naming animals and animal sounds. The opposite page shows a full colour photograph of the animal in its natural setting.

Taylor, Ann. Illustrations by Marjorie van Heerden. New York: HarperCollins, 1999.

BABY DANCE

Colour illustrations show a dad dancing with his baby girl while mom rests. African American. Lovely.

Board Books For Toddlers

When babies reach about the one-year mark, they they are ready for vocabulary, pictures that label things in their expanding world, first concept books, and sturdy lift-the-flap books they can manipulate and that have little surprises underneath.

Abrams, Pam. Photographs by Bruce Wolf. New York: Scholastic, Cartwheel, 2004.

NOW I EAT MY ABC'S

Eye-catching photographs of food illustrate the letters of the alphabet.

Asim, Jabari. Illustrations by LeUyen Pham. New York: Little Brown, 2006.

WHOSE KNEES ARE THESE?
WHOSE TOES ARE THOSE?

Lovely stories in rhyme about a brown baby's knees and toes. Highly recommended.

Barron's Educational Series, 2004.

BANG, BANG!
KNOCK, KNOCK!
MUNCH, MUNCH!
TAP, TAP!
THIS LITTLE BUNNY
THIS LITTLE DOGGY
THIS LITTLE LAMB
THIS LITTLE FISH

These tiny board books have board sliders young toddlers love to play with. A few words per page.

Battaglia, Aurelius. New York: Random House, 2005.

ANIMAL SOUNDS

A tall format board book that is pleasing. Simple colour illustrations, simple text.

Beaumont, Susanna. BABY SENSES series. Berkhamsted, Herts, UK: Make Believe Ideas, 2005.

SIGHT

This is a wonderful book portraying simple emotions and what the facial expressions that go with them look like. Each page shows children making the facial expression and has a circle cut out showing a mirror on the last page so children can practise making the faces. Highly recommended for identifying and talking about feelings. There are seven books in this series: Taste, Smell, Hearing, Sight, Touch, Speech, Record Book. Multicultural.

Black, Michel. EASY-OPEN series. Cambridge, MS: Candlewick Press, 2005.

OFF TO BED
OUT TO PLAY

These uniquely designed books have board pages of different widths for easy opening by little hands. Black and white photographs of children and their clothes and toys have a colour on the object represented accompanied by one-word descriptions.

Boynton, Sandra. New York: Simon and Schuster, 1995.

BLUE HAT, GREEN HAT
MOO BAA LA LA LA
OPPOSITES

Humourous little first concept books. Colour illustrations. There are eight titles in this series.

Campbell, Rod. New York: Little Simon.

DEAR ZOO (1999)
FARM BABIES (2003)
I WON'T BITE (London, Macmillan, 2005)

Board book editions of these classics are ideal for toddlers. Dear Zoo has lift-the-flaps, I Won't Bite has a pop-up on the last page.

Cousins, Lucy. Cambridge, MS: Candlewick Press, 1999.

COUNT WITH MAISY
MAISY'S COLORS
WHERE IS MAISY?
WHERE IS MAISY'S PANDA?

Engaging first books about Maisy mouse. The last two titles have lift-the-flaps.

DK Publishing. New York: Dorling Kindersley, 2005.

BABY'S BUSY WORLD

Large format, adorable photographs of babies and their things, great for vocabulary building.

DK Publishing. BABY GENIUS series. New York: Dorling Kindersley, 2003.

ANIMAL COUNTING
COLORS
FIRST WORDS
ZOO ANIMALS

Large format board books, great photographs, good for vocabulary building.

DK Publishing. MY FIRST BOARD BOOKS series. New York: Dorling Kindersley.

MY FIRST COLORS BOARD BOOK (2004)
MY FIRST TRUCK BOARD BOOK (2006)
MY FIRST TRUCK BOARD BOOK (2004)
MY FIRST OPPOSITES BOARD BOOK (2006)

First concepts beautifully introduced. Great for vocabulary building. There are fourteen books in this series.

DK Publishing. MY FIRST TOUCH AND FEEL series. New York: Dorling Kindersley, 2003.

MY FIRST BABY ANIMALS TOUCH AND FEEL
MY FIRST KITTEN TOUCH AND FEEL
MY FIRST PUPPY TOUCH AND FEEL

Large format board, large uncluttered photographs, lots to talk about. Animal lovers will love these.

DK Publishing. LET'S LOOK series. New York: Dorling Kindersley, 2006.

FARM

For older toddlers. Colour photographs of farm scenes, and more text than usual for a board book, describe the vocabulary of the farm. Perhaps there will be more in this series.

DK Publishing. New York: Dorling Kindersley, 2005.

WORDS IN MY WORLD

Small format, full-page board flaps, great for vocabulary building. Guaranteed to intrigue toddlers.

Ernst, Lisa Campbell, illustrator. Maplewood, NJ: Blue Apple Books, 2006.

BREAKFAST TIME!
GOOD MORNING, SUN!

Soft pastel illustrations tell little stories about a bunny toddler. A few words per page.

Fernandes, Kim, illustrator. Toronto: Kids Can Press, 2006.

Burton, Katherine. ONE GRAY MOUSE
Fernandes, Eugenie. BUSY LITTLE MOUSE

Cute plasticine illustrations that parents will enjoy as much as the toddlers.

Horacek, Petr. Cambridge, MS: Candlewick, 2001.

WHAT IS BLACK AND WHITE?

An ingeniously designed board book. Highly recommended. Different page sizes are easy for little fingers to turn and they become a zebra in the end.

Kubler, Annie. Child's Play, 2003.

HEAD, SHOULDERS, KNEES AND TOES…

Illustrates toddlers having fun acting out the rhyme. One toddler per page. Multicultural.

Marzollo, Jean. Photographs by Walter Wick. New York: Scholastic, Cartwheel.

I SPY LITTLE ANIMALS (1998)
I SPY LITTLE BUNNIES (2006)
I SPY LITTLE WHEELS (1998)

These are wonderful little eye spy books for toddlers. Rhyming text on the left page shows the object to find. Simple full colour illustrations on the right page show the object hidden.

Murphy, Mary. New York: Harcourt, Red Wagon, 2002.

I LIKE IT WHEN…

This is a board book edition of the classic story about the love shared between a penguin parent and child.

Oxenbury, Helen. New York: Simon & Schuster, Little Simon,1999.

ALL FALL DOWN
CLAP HANDS
TICKLE, TICKLE

Classic Oxenbury illustrations of toddlers at play with little stories in rhyme. Large format. Multicultural.

Priddy, Roger. BRIGHT BABY series. New York: Priddy Books, St. Martin's Press, 2002.

ANIMALS
COLORS
FIRST WORDS
TRUCKS

Very simple. One uncluttered colour photograph of the object on a white background accompanied by (usually) one word per page.

Priddy, Roger. New York: Priddy Books, St. Martin's Press, 2002.

HAPPY BABY THINGS THAT GO

Lots of colour photographs of machines certain to please young truck lovers. A few words of text describe the vehicles.

Priddy, Roger. New York: Priddy Books, St. Martin's Press, 2004.

MY BIG ANIMAL BOOK
MY BIG TRUCK BOOK
MY LITTLE WORD BOOK

Large format board, lots of objects named, engaging, great for vocabulary building. Text in the first two titles asks little questions for toddlers to answer. Toddlers love these.

Sami. FLIP-A-SHAPE series. Maplewood, NJ: Blue Apple Books, 2006.

GO!
YUM!

Colourful first shapes with cut out boards to feel the shapes. Great for toddlers and special needs. Multicultural.

Santoro, Christopher. New York: Random House, 1993.

OPEN THE BARN DOOR...

A tiny board book with sturdy little flaps introducing animal sounds. Toddlers love it.

MY WORLD series. Markham, ON, Canada: Scholastic, 2003.

MY FIRST CANADIAN BODIES
MY FIRST CANADIAN COLOURS
MY FIRST CANADIAN OPPOSITES
MY FIRST CANADIAN TRUCKS

I don't see what makes these books "Canadian" except for the titles and the spelling of the word"colour." They are simply excellent first books for building vocabulary whether they are being read in Ottawa or in Dallas. Multicultural.

Shannon, David. DIAPER DAVID series. Scholastic, Blue Sky Press, 2005.

DAVID SMELLS!
OH, DAVID!
OOPS!

These board books about bad David provide a humourous view of life with a toddler, and are a refreshing break from the other sweet books on this list. Highly recommended.

Stanley, Mandy. New York: HarperCollins, 2006.

HOW DO YOU FEEL?

Lively colour illustrations of animals show the emotions described. A great vehicle for inspiring talk about emotions. Also in this series: WHAT DO YOU SAY? *and* WHAT DO YOU DO?

Sample One-Hour Programs
for Parents and Babies, Birth to One Year

Introduction *164*

Week One: Hello Everyone *167*
Week Two: Welcome Back *170*

Sample Questions for the Day *172*

Programmers often feel more comfortable getting started with a new approach when they have sample templates to work from. These samples include both my Plan (the list of things I intend to do), and my Program (the delivery, which sometimes requires changes). I have included both to show you how easy it is to change things in your delivery in response to what you observe. I have also included a Talk heading to show you how easy it is to incorporate communication with the parents in your delivery.

Introduction to One-Hour Programs for Parents and Babies, Birth to One Year

MY PROGRAM MODEL

My one-hour programs for parents and their babies are based on the Parent-Child Mother Goose Program®. The program structure and teaching methods of this model form the basis of all the early literacy programs I deliver for parents and their young children both in the library and out in the community.

Please note: There is much more to a Parent-Child Mother Goose Program® than I am describing here. For information about that program visit the Canadian national website at: www.nald.ca/mothergooseprogram.

The Parent-Child Mother Goose Program® requires two trained teachers who share equally in the role of teaching and in leading the group's activities. In my outreach programs, I partner with other community agencies who can help me deliver my programs in a way that suits the community. My partners also help me reach my target audience. I have written the following sample programs as if I were delivering a program alone so you can see how this approach can be used when the program is delivered by one person.

The teaching in the Parent-Child Mother Goose Program® is aimed at the adults, who are encouraged to learn the rhymes and songs and to use them at home with their babies. The babies can be joining in, crawling around, napping or nursing. We all sit in a circle on the floor.

Each program lasts an hour and a half. Fifteen minutes in the beginning allows parents to arrive and get settled before we start to sing and fifteen minutes at the end allows them time to pack up and say goodbye to their new friends. The formal part of the program lasts one hour. The pace is relaxed.

MY GOALS

1. To foster attachment between the parent and the child through the use of oral language.
2. To teach parents some rhymes and songs their babies will enjoy and learn from.
3. To support parents in their role as the baby's first teacher.
4. To build a sense of community with the families I serve.
5. To introduce parents to books their babies will enjoy.
6. To introduce parents to the free materials and services available at the public library.

NUMBERS

I register fifteen families for my infant programs and hope that ten to thirteen families will come each week. I limit the group size to fifteen so that I can pay attention to the needs of the individual families each time we meet. Any more than this and I can't give families the attention they need.

I don't take in new families part way through the program because this really upsets the group dynamic and group bonding that takes place over a ten-week session.

DURATION

My programs are ten weeks long and run three times a year. Parents get to come for three ten-week sessions. This is the amount of time required to accomplish the goals of the program.

PHONE CALLS

I phone the parents every week on the evening before the program: to build a relationship with each family, to have a private moment, and to remind them of the program the next day. Parents who are often sleep deprived or feeling isolated say they really appreciate the connection and the reminder.

SOCIAL TIME

I stay and talk to the parents and their babies throughout the social time so that I can help them feel relaxed and comfortable with me and with the setting, and so I can help them make connections with one another and answer any questions. This time also provides me with valuable insights into the families' needs which I can incorporate into my program.

SNACK TIME

I offer a healthy snack half way through the program. This is another opportunity for parents and children's social interactions. My snacks are always raw fresh fruits and vegetables (like apples, grapes, carrot sticks and broccoli), cheese and crackers, juice and water.

PROPS

This is an oral program, so I don't use any props. Babies learn best through playful interaction with a loving adult. This method also conveys the message that parents don't need toys in order to play happily and beneficially with their babies.

MY TEACHING METHODS

When I introduce a rhyme for the first time, I say it through once, then I ask the parents to repeat the lines back to me line by line. Then we all say it a second and third time together. When the parents know the rhymes, all of us, babies and parents alike, enjoy repeating the rhymes three times each time we do them.

When I teach a song, I use this same method. I also often separate the tune from the words. We sing la-la-la through the tune, then we sing the lines one line at a time, then we all sing it again with everybody joining in.

The parents say they really appreciate this way of learning.

QUESTION FOR THE DAY

In an hour-long infant program, with fifteen families, I often include an open-ended question to pass around the circle. This facilitates information sharing amongst the parents, and storytelling in an informal way. To avoid too much adult talk, I say: "Three responses, then we'll have another rhyme." A list of sample questions I have used is included on page 172.

MY FORMULA

Greeting song
Name song
One or two rhymes
Question for the day
Five or six rhymes
Snack break
Repeat one or two rhymes
Lullaby
Story
Goodbye song

RHYME SELECTION

I choose my selection of rhymes by type. I always include at least one bouncing rhyme, a face rhyme, a tickling rhyme, a song and a lullaby. I also alternate between saying and singing rhymes. This lends a very nice rhythm to the overall pattern of the program.

GETTING STARTED

I start my ten-week programs with only six or seven rhymes besides the opening and closing songs. I then add one or two each week as the weeks unfold and the parents gain confidence in learning and remembering the rhymes. Yes, six or seven rhymes are enough to start. At the end of a ten-week program the parents know about twenty rhymes they like to use on a daily basis with their babies.

STORYTELLING

At the end of my hour-long programs, I tell a short story for the parents' listening pleasure. I tell them that the rhymes are little stories for their little babies and that the longer stories are bigger stories for them. My parents find the storytelling immensely pleasurable. The babies like it too.

I tell folktales from around the world. I try to find stories from my families' countries of origin. Often the stories will lead to interesting discussions about the different sense of humour, beliefs and customs of different cultures and at different times in history.

There is something about telling a story face to face, from my mouth to your ear, that makes it more intimate and more personal than reading a story from a book. It also shows parents and children that you can have stories in your head, that you can think of them and use them over and over again whenever you like and wherever you are. And they can find more stories in books.

Five stories that have worked well for me in parent-infant programs are in FIVE EASY STORIES TO TELL IN PARENT-INFANT PROGRAMS. These stories will get you started. It's perfectly all right to repeat stories more than once in a ten-week session. Everybody enjoys hearing a good story more than once. The bibliography at the end of that section will lead you to more.

Storytelling in a Toddler Program is a little different. I discuss the difference in that section of the book.

RECORD KEEPING

I keep a record of my activities, making a note of what worked and what didn't, and anything special I want to do the next week. I also note participant responses, and any questions or comments they had. These things often lead to follow-up in the weeks ahead and help me plan the program so that it is responsive to parents' and babies' needs. And, of course, I keep attendance statistics.

HAVE FUN!

My samples are meant to assist you in planning whatever program model you use. Please use these as a starting point and substitute your own ideas and the rhymes, songs, and stories that you love best.

Sample One-Hour Program for Parents and Babies, Birth to One Year
Week One: Welcome Everyone!

THE PLAN

1. Welcome Song: Come Along and Sing with Me
2. Introductions
3. Hello Song: Hello Everyone
4. Question for the Day: What is your name and your baby's name and age?
5. Bounce: A Smooth Road
6. Song: Rain is Falling Down
7. Rhyme: Leg Over Leg
8. Rhyme: The Moon is Round
9. Lullaby: Ho, Ho, Watanay
10. Snack Break
11. Repeat Song: Rain is Falling Down
12. Repeat Rhyme: The Moon is Round
13. Repeat Lullaby: Ho, Ho, Watanay
14. Song: Tall Trees
15. Story: A Mother Mouse
16. Goodbye Song: Goodbye Everyone

SETTING

The plan is ready and the snack has been prepared. The room has been cleared of all clutter and mats have been placed in a circle on the floor. A box of age-appropriate board books has been placed nearby. I welcome everyone individually as they come in the door.

SOCIAL TIME

The parents sit and chat and the babies play as the group assembles. Everyone is curious about everyone else and about what will happen. I join the parents by sitting on the floor and taking part in their conversations.

THE PROGRAM

1. Welcome Song: Come Along and Sing with Me

2. Talk: (Introductions)
Welcome to the first week of our Parent-Child Mother Goose Program. My name is _____ and I'm going to be leading you in the program. Each week I will teach you some rhymes your baby will love and we'll repeat the rhymes every week so you will get a chance to learn them. I won't be handing out written words to the rhymes until the end of the ten-week program, but don't worry, you will all know them by heart by then so you won't need the written words. You'll learn the way your babies learn, through repetition. Everybody needs lots of repetition to learn new things.

The program will last for an hour and a half, and each week we'll do the same thing. We'll play with our babies using rhymes for half an hour, then we'll have a little snack break, then we'll sing a lullaby, and then I'll tell you a story at the end. The story is for your listening pleasure.

Let's start by singing a hello song so that we can begin to get to know one another and remember everyone's names. We'll sing this song each week. This is how it goes. Say your name and then your baby's name as we go around the circle.

3. Hello Song: Hello Everyone

Talk:
Since we are all getting to know one another, let's go around the circle again and say your

names again, and your baby's names and ages. We will have three responses, then a play rhyme.

4. Question for the Day: What is your name and your baby's name and age?

Three responses to the question.

Talk:
Each week I will teach you some new rhymes to play with your baby and we'll repeat them from week to week so that you will get to know them by heart and so you can play them often with your baby at home. Baby's love interactive rhymes and they love repetition.

This first rhyme is a bouncing rhyme called "A Smooth Road." Take your baby on your knee facing you so that you can see how much your baby likes the rhyme, and so that she can see how much you are enjoying the rhyme too. If your baby is very small bounce gently to the beat of the rhyme. If your baby is sitting up already she will like a more vigourous bounce.

5. Bouncing Rhyme: A Smooth Road
(Repeat three times.)

Three more responses to the question.

Talk:
Now lay your baby down on her back and we'll sing a nice little peek-a-boo song. First we flutter our fingers down the baby's body to imitate the rain and then we'll let the sun peek out.

6. Song: Rain is Falling Down
(Repeat three times.)

Three more responses to the question.

Talk:
Rhymes can soothe and distract babies at fussy times. Diaper changing can be a fussy time. Here is a rhyme to say as you change baby's diaper. Lay your baby down on his back and we'll pretend we're changing the baby. By the way, a stile is a little step up over a stone fence. In England where they have lots of stone fences, stiles were built to let people go up and over the fence.

7. Rhyme: Leg Over Leg
(Repeat three times.)

Three more responses to the question.

Talk:
Most babies love to have their faces touched. Here is a face rhyme I love.

8. Rhyme: The Moon is Round
(Repeat three times.)

(In the weeks to come, I will suggest that parents use this rhyme when they have to wash the baby's face and we will practise as if we were holding a washcloth. Babies don't like having their faces washed and this rhyme will turn a fussy moment into a moment of pleasure for both parent and child.)

Three more responses to the question.

Talk:
I'm going to teach you a lullaby now. Every baby needs a lullaby. A lullaby can be used at any time of the night or day to soothe your baby. This one is in Iroquois, then French, then English.

9. Lullaby: Ho, Ho, Watanay
(Repeat each verse a couple of times.)

Three more responses to the question.

10. Snack Break (Ten Minutes)

(During the snack break, I notice which families are isolated and I talk to them. I help them to feel a part of the group. I call attention back to the program by sitting down and singing.)

11. Repeat Song: Rain is Falling Down
12. Repeat Rhyme: The Moon is Round
13. Repeat Lullaby: Ho, Ho, Watanay

Talk:
Each week I will tell you a story. I hope you will enjoy hearing them as much as I enjoy telling them. Let's sing one more lullaby before the story.

14. Song: Tall Trees

15. Story: A Mother Mouse and Her Children

(This story is accompanied by sign language and it's short. A very nice introduction to oral storytelling for parents who may be new to the experience of listening to a story. At story's end, I always say, "Snip, snap, snout, this tale's told out" to release parents from listening. This little tradition comes from "The Three Billy Goats Gruff" story.)

Talk:
Next week we will repeat the same rhymes so don't worry if you can't remember them yet. Within a few weeks you will come to know the rhymes by heart.

I have brought a box of age-appropriate baby books for you to borrow after the program. Babies love books. The first books babies love are books of baby faces, like these ones. Take a couple home after the program to share with your baby and see what happens. Oh, babies like to explore books by tasting them. This is fine. The board book pages are sturdy and will stand up to this kind of use. Let your baby taste the books! And now it's time to say goodbye.

16. Goodbye Song: Goodbye Everyone

SOCIAL TIME

My parents have now been exposed to eight new songs. I reassure them that they will learn the rhymes as the weeks unfold, and I tell them I look forward to seeing them again next week.

RECORD KEEPING

In week one I usually notice the parents are a little shy, and that a few parents stand up to jiggle fussy babies. Next week I plan to add a stand-up song "Shoofly," before the snack break. This will give parents a fun way to stand up and jiggle without being self-conscious about a fussy baby, and it will help the group become more sociable. The babies will love it too.

Sample One-Hour Program for Parents and Babies, Birth to One Year
Week Two: Welcome Back!

THE PLAN

1. Welcome Song: Come Along and Sing with Me
2. Repeat introductions for parents who missed the first week.
3. Hello Song: Hello Everyone
4. Bounce: A Smooth Road
5. Question for the Day: Where did baby's name come from?
(This question often reveals cultural and family backgrounds and often family dynamics. It's a great one for helping families get to know one another quickly.)
6. Song: Rain is Falling Down
7. Rhyme: Leg Over Leg
8. Rhyme: The Moon is Round
9. New Song: Shoofly
10. Snack Break
11. Repeat Song: Rain is Falling Down
12. Repeat Rhyme: The Moon is Round
13. Lullaby: Ho, Ho, Watanay
14. Song: Tall Trees
15. Story: The Wide-Mouthed Frog
16. Goodbye Song: Goodbye Everyone

SETTING

The room is set up. The snack is ready. The baby books are ready. In week two, everyone is beginning to feel more relaxed and comfortable with the routine. Babies too.

SOCIAL TIME

The parents tell me they didn't remember any of the rhymes, or only one, and could I sing them again. Or, they might tell me their baby loved a particular rhyme and could I sing it again. In any case, I reassure them that they will learn the rhymes, and that we will repeat all the rhymes from Week One.

THE PROGRAM

1. Welcome song: Come Along and Sing with Me

2. Talk:
(Introductions repeated: program duration, program schedule, learning through repetition. We don't use props or toys during the program because we don't need these things to play happily with our babies.)

3. Hello song: Hello Everyone

Talk:
We are going to repeat the rhymes so don't worry if they haven't remembered them yet. And now you understand how many repetitions your babies need in order to understand something!

Take your baby on your knee facing you and we will play our bouncing rhyme. Face to face contact is very important for the baby.

4. Bounce: A Smooth Road
(Repeat three times.)

5. Question for the Day: Tell us the story of your baby's name. Where did your baby's name come from?

Three responses to the question.

6. Song: Rain is Falling Down
(Repeat three times.)

Talk:
It's important to get up close to the baby because baby's vision is blurry at first, and you have to move in to about twelve inches away so your baby can see you. Watching you make the sounds when you talk and

sing will help your baby see the connection between the sounds you make and the corresponding face muscle movements that go with them. This will help him learn how to speak. Your baby is very busy watching you to see how you do that. Your baby is very keen to communicate with you. And, of course, your baby just loves your face.

Three more responses to the question.

7. Rhyme: Leg Over Leg
(Repeat three times.)

Three more responses to the question.

8. Rhyme: The Moon is Round
(Repeat three times.)

Three more responses to the question.

Talk:
Now we're going to stand up and dance in a circle. Hold your baby facing out so she can feel what it's like to move through space this way. She'll get a delightful surprise too. We'll walk in a circle to the left, then to the right, then into the middle and back out again. The babies will love this. It's also fun to play at home in front of a mirror. The baby doesn't know yet that the baby she sees in the mirror is herself!

9. New Song: Shoofly

10. Snack Break

11. If time, repeat rhyme: Rain is Falling Down and/or The Moon is Round

13. Lullaby: Ho, Ho, Watanay

Talk:
Now let's sing "Tall Trees" before our story.

14. Song: Tall Trees

Talk:
This is a fun story you can tell your baby to get him to open his mouth wide at nursing time or mealtime.

15. Story: The Wide-Mouthed Frog
"Snip, snap, snout, this tale's told out."

Talk:
I hope you enjoyed sharing the board books with your baby. Babies also love books with bold black and white patterns like these ones by Tana Hoban. Talk to your baby about all the different things you see in the pictures. Oh, and let the baby taste and feel the books. All babies like to put books in their mouths. Board books are created for babies with this kind of use in mind.

This week you will remember more of the rhymes. Next week we'll say them again and add a new one. But now it's time to say goodbye.

16. Goodbye Song: Goodbye Everyone

SOCIAL TIME

Make sure you talk to everyone, not just the families you seem to feel most comfortable with. Make everyone feel welcome.

RECORD KEEPING

One of the parents asked for a waking-up song. I will teach "When Cows Get Up in the Morning" next week.

Soon I will also ask the local Community Health Nurse to visit so she can join in our singing and playing and talk to the parents about sleep. That week I will ask the question, "What rituals do you use before bedtime to help your baby get to sleep?"

Sample Questions for the Day
in Parent-Infant Programs

1. Please say your name and your baby's name and age. (This way parents get to know one another. Usually asked in Week One.)

2. Where did your baby's name come from? (This will be endlessly fascinating to the baby as he/she grows up. It can also be a parent's introduction to family storytelling. Remind parents this is an important story to tell their children.)

3. What do you like to do with your baby on a rainy day? (Gives parents ideas.)

4. What are your holiday plans?

5. How do you know when your baby likes (doesn't like) a rhyme? (Helps parents learn how to read baby's body language.)

6. Who played rhymes with you when you were a child, if anyone? (This question evokes warm memories and helps parents realize the important gift they are giving their child in playing the rhymes with them. It's okay if they can't remember or if no one did. In the weeks that follow parents will often remember.)

7. Doing the same thing before bedtime every night can help your baby settle down for a sleep. What bedtime rituals do you like to use to help your baby get off to sleep?

8. Teething can be a difficult and painful experience for your baby. What are some things you have tried to ease your baby's pain?

9. Every baby is born with a unique temperament. Some babies are more sensitive to sights and sounds than others, some are easy going, some are fussy. Often the baby's temperament is different from the parent's and it can be challenging sometimes to understand a baby's temperament. What is your baby's temperament?

10. Parenting is a very demanding job that lasts all day and all night too. What do you like to do for yourself to take a break from your full time job of nurturing your baby?

11. Who provides support for you in your very important role as your baby's nurturer?

12. What is the best thing about being a parent?

13. What is your baby's favourite rhyme? (Ask this about week five or six, after the parents have learned the rhymes.)

14. What do you enjoy the most about the program?

15. What will you miss when the program is not running? (Use this one before a break in sessions, and before you ask parents to fill in evaluation forms. It gives them ideas. Ask parents if they want to be on an email list to keep in touch.)

Invite parents to suggest questions they would like to ask of the group. Some questions that have come up for me are: "Where is the nearest foodbank?" "Where can I get inexpensive clothes for my baby?" "When should I introduce solid food for my baby?" "My baby is a fussy eater, he makes such a mess. What should I do?" I always ask the other parents for their input, whether I know the answers or not.

Five Easy Stories to Tell
in Parent-Infant Programs

The Bed Just So *174*
Did You Feed My Cow? *176*
A Mother Mouse and Her Children *177*
The Mouse Bride *179*
The Wide-Mouthed Frog *181*

Bibliography of Stories to Tell *183*

Story selection is pleasant but time-consuming work. You will read many before you find the one that appeals to you for telling. In the context of parent-child programs, especially when the parents are not used to listening to stories, the stories need to be short. Here are some of my favourites to get you started on your search. You will find lots more good stories to tell in the collections listed in the bibliography and you will find more stories in folktale collections in your local public library. They are shelved by country (or geographic region) in the 398.2 section in both the children's and adults' collections.

The Bed Just So

Once there was a tailor who fell asleep over his work all day. He fell asleep all day, because he couldn't get any sleep at night. Every night, when he began to fall asleep, thought he heard someone—or something—grumbling and complaining and stomping around his room. Then suddenly, Swoosh! his covers would be torn off his bed. And he would shiver and shake all night long. the "This can't go on," the tailor said. And he went to see the Wise Woman in the village.

"I must be witched," he told her. "Every night, when I go to bed, I hear someone—or something—grumbling and complaining and stomping around the room. Then suddenly—Swoosh!—the covers are torn off my bed and I shiver and shake all night long."

"No," the Wise Woman said. "If you were witched, your feet would be on backwards. And your hair would be growing upside down. No. Your trouble is that a hudgin has moved in with you."

"A hudgin!" said the tailor. "What should I do?"

"Make a bed for him," the Wise Woman said. "Then he will have his own bed and he will leave your bed alone."

So the tailor bought a bed for the hudgin. It was a big, high bed made of oak wood just like his own.

"Now," said the tailor, "you have your bed and I have mine. Let's both have a good night's sleep."

But as soon as the tailor began to fall asleep, he heard a voice grumbling and complaining:

> Too high and too hard!
> Too high and too hard!

Every day the tailor made a new bed for the hudgin, and every night the voice woke him up, grumbling and complaining.

The next night, the tailor made a little low bed of feathers and ferns. But as soon as he began to fall asleep, a voice woke him up:

> Too soft and too tickly!
> Too soft and too tickly!

The next day, the tailor found a match box in a kitchen drawer, and he thought, why not? It looks sort of like a little bed. And he put the matchbox in a cupboard in his bedroom and closed the door. That night the voice complained:

> Too dark and too stuffy!
> Too dark and too stuffy!

Next he tried a hammock. But the voice said:

> Too long and too loose!
> Too long and too loose!

The tailor built a cradle. Why hadn't he thought of that before! It would be perfect. But that night, the little voice complained:

> Too teeter and too totter!
> Too teeter and too totter!

The poor tailor could not find a bed to please the hudgin. "I will never get a good night's sleep," thought the tailor. He was very very tired.

But that night he cracked open a walnut to eat after dinner. He looked at the half walnut shell, and it looked to him like a tiny bed. "Why not?" the tailor thought. "I have tried everything else."

So he lined the walnut shell with cotton and peach down. He put a maple leaf on for a cover. And he put it on the window sill in his bedroom.

Just then, he heard a happy humming sound. The tailor looked in the walnut shell. There he saw a tiny dot, no bigger than a mustard seed!

"Ah, that must be the hudgin," said the tailor. He shut his eyes tight to listen. And he heard a contented little voice sighing:

> Just so. Just so.
> I like a bed made, just so.

And at last, both the tailor and the hudgin got a good night's sleep.

Notes:
By Jeanne Hardendorff © 1975. I learned this story from another storyteller. Sadly, the only print version is now out of print. The hudgin comes from British folklore. It is a little elf-like creature who is angry for having been driven out of his comfortable home and is looking for a good place to sleep.

Did You Feed My Cow?

Did you feed my cow? ... Yes Ma'am.
Can you tell me how? ... Yes Ma'am.

What did you feed her? ... Corn and hay.
What did you feed her? ... Corn and hay.

Did you milk her good? ... Yes Ma'am.
You milk her like you should? ... Yes Ma'am.

How did you milk her? ... Squish, squish, squish.
How did you milk her? ... Squish, squish, squish.
Hand motions—milking.

Did my cow give milk? ... Yes Ma'am.
Was it smooth as silk? ... Yes Ma'am.

How did it taste? ... Mmm Mmm good!
How did it taste? ... Mmm Mmm good!
Rub your tummy.

Did my cow like to play? ... Yes Ma'am.
Did my cow run away? ... Yes Ma'am.

How did she run? ... Clop, clop, clop.
How did she run? ... Clop, clop, clop.
Clop hands on your lap.

Did my cow get sick? ... Yes Ma'am.
Was she covered in tick? ... Yes Ma'am.

How did she die? ... Ugh, ugh, ugh!
I said, how did she die? ... Ugh, ugh, ugh!
Hands at your throat in a choking motion.

Did the buzzards come? ... Yes Ma'am.
To pick her bones? ... Yes Ma'am.
Picking motion.

How did they come? ... Flap, flap, flap.
I said, how did they come? ... Flap, flap, flap.
Flap arms.

How did they come? ... Flap, flap, flap.
How did they come? ... Flap, flap, flap.
Repeat softly.

How did they come? ... Flap, flap, flap.
How did they come? ... Flap, flap, flap.
More softly.

... and that was the end of the poor old cow!

Notes:
This is a call and response chant made popular by Ella Jenkins. It shows parents how rhythmic and fun language can be. It's also very short, and so you can use it when you are short of time.

You can ask the audience to clap along with you to begin, if you like, to establish a rhythm. The storyteller leads and the audience replies, "Yes Ma'am," or as directed. The audience will also follow the storyteller's actions. I usually repeat it at least twice. The parents find it very amusing, and older kids do too. They like the death part the best!

A Mother Mouse and Her Children

One day, a mother mouse and her children went for a walk. They came to a corner. Around the corner there was a great big enormous cat! The mother mouse was scared. Her children were scared. They ran around behind the mother mouse. They were all scared, but the mother mouse was brave. She looked that cat right in the eyes and she said, "Woof, woof, woof woof woof woof!"

"Help me, help me," she said to her children. So they all went, "Woof, woof, woof woof woof woof!" And that great big enormous cat ran away!

The mother mouse looked at her children and said. "Listen my children, there is something to learn here. Never, never, never underestimate the value of a second language!"

THE SIGNS:

ONE: hold up one finger.

DAY: hold one arm parallel to your chest. Place the elbow of your other arm on the back of your hand and lower your hand to lay your arm down on the other arm. Your hand makes an arc to indicate the sun crossing the sky.

MOTHER: the thumb of the open hand moves away from the side of the chin.

MOUSE: brush your index finger across the tip of your nose.

CHILDREN: hold out two palms down and move them down in a stepping motion to indicate many children in a large family in descending order.

WALK: walk fingers down your forearm into your palm.

CORNER: place fingertips together pointing away from your body.

GREAT BIG ENORMOUS: Hold palms parallel in front of you and move them away from each other by degrees as you say the words.

CAT: indicate a cat's whiskers by placing your thumbs and index fingers in a diamond at your nose, and move your hands out to a point at the side of your face.

Repeat these actions every time you say the words.

SCARED: hold palms facing your chest and shiver in fright.

BRAVE: box your fists straight up in the air in front of your chest.

WOOF: one hand makes a barking dog mouth motion.

HELP ME: Place the fist of one hand, thumb pointing up, in the palm of the other hand and thrust both hands in an upward motion.

LISTEN: Make an "L" with thumb and pointer and put your thumb close to your ear.

LEARN: pretend to pick something out of your palm and put it in your head.

NEVER: wag your index finger.

SECOND: hold up two fingers.

LANGUAGE: Form two "Ls" with your thumbs and index fingers held in front of you and wiggle them away from each other.

Notes:
This funny short story is made wonderful for telling by using a few gestures from sign language. Audiences love it. I came across it as a little anecdote when I was studying teaching ESL at university. I learned the sign language gestures years later, from Beth Hutchinson, who works in the Parent-Child Mother Goose Program®. If you would like to see the hand motions for the signs using the web, type "American Sign Language" into a Google search, and you will find excellent resources there for learning signs.

The Mouse Bride

There once was a little mouse who decided she wanted to get married. And so she looked around at all the other mice and decided she didn't want to marry the mouse next door. She wanted to marry someone everybody knew, someone who was very powerful. She was thinking about this one day when she went outside, and she felt the warm sun on her fur, and she had an idea. She walked out into the middle of the field, and looked up at the sun and she said,

"Excuse me! Excuse me! Mr. Sun, Mr. Sun, it's me, Little Mouse, and I was wondering if you would be my ... spouse?"

Well the sun had never been asked to be anyone's husband before. So he boasted and puffed out his chest and sent out his warm rays and agreed that he would marry Little Mouse. As he was boasting about how he could cast his light out all over the sky, along came a big cloud and covered up the sun. And Little Mouse looked. She didn't want to marry the sun any more because the cloud was much stronger than the sun if he could cover him up, and so she said to Mr. Cloud,

"Excuse me! Excuse me! Mr. Cloud, Mr. Cloud, it's me, Little Mouse, and I was wondering if you would be my spouse?"

Well, the cloud was very flattered. He puffed himself up until he was as large and puffy as he could be, and he said,

"Why sure, I'll marry you, Little Mouse." And as he was puffing himself up, along came the wind and blew him right out of the sky. Huh, thought Little Mouse. She didn't want to marry the cloud who was much weaker than the wind. She wanted to marry the wind. So she said,

"Excuse me! Excuse me! Mr. Wind, Mr. Wind, it's me, Little Mouse, and I was wondering if you would be my spouse?"

And the wind, well, he was most flattered indeed. He blew somersaults in the air, he blew the leaves off the trees, and he blew and he blew until he came to something he couldn't blow through. It was a tall stone wall, standing in the middle of a field. And he tried and he tried, but no matter how hard he blew, he could not blow through that wall. And so the mouse was not so impressed with the wind any more and she looked at that wall and she said,

"Excuse me! Excuse me! Mr. Wall, Mr. Wall, it's me, Little Mouse, and I was wondering if you would be my spouse?"

And the wall, well, no one had ever asked for his hand in marriage before, so he stood up as tall and straight as he could, and said he would marry Little Mouse. She looked him up and down. After all, he was going to be her new husband, so she was looking him up and down to see what she was in for, and then she noticed at the bottom there was a little hole right through that wall. Whereas the wind couldn't get through the wall, there was something that could. And so she went right through that little hole and on the other side she met another mouse. Obviously there was someone who was stronger than the wall, stronger than the wind, stronger than the cloud, and stronger than the sun, and so she decided she wanted to marry the little mouse.

"Excuse me! Excuse me! Mr. Mouse, Mr. Mouse, it's me, Little Mouse. I was wondering if you would be my spouse?"

And the little mouse said yes, and they got married and they had many, many beautiful babies.

Notes:
Retold by Ginger Mullen. This amusing story is told in Africa, Asia and in Central America. Sometimes the parents search for the appropriate husband for Little Mouse, and sometimes it is Little Mouse herself who does the searching and asking. There are many picture book versions: The Mouse Bride: A Chinese Folktale, *retold by Monica Chang. Flagstaff, AZ: Northland Pub, 1992;* The Mouse Bride *by Joy Cowley, New York: Scholastic, 1995; and* The Rat's Daughter *by Joel Cook, Honesdale, PA: Boyds Mills Press, 1993, to mention a few.*

The Wide-Mouthed Frog

Once there was a wide-mouthed frog who lived down in a swamp. She was very excited because she had just given birth to some brand new babies! Well, she thought her babies were just the most wonderful babies in the world. Her babies were much too special to eat the flies and mosquitoes that other frog babies ate. Her babies needed something better. But she didn't know what. So she went on a journey to find out what other mothers fed their hungry babies.

And so she went on her journey, and as she hopped along, she sang,

"I'M A WIDE-MOUTHED FROG,
I'M A WIDE-MOUTHED FROG!"

Hop, hop, hop.

Soon she came to a turtle.

"Oh Ms. Turtle, Ms. Turtle, excuse me. What do you feed your hungry babies?"

Ms. Turtle replied, "Why I feed my babies on these tender mushrooms."

"Well," said the wide-mouthed frog, "those mushrooms smell a little earthy to me. Thank you, I'll keep looking."

And so she carried on along her journey, and as she hopped she sang,

"I'M A WIDE-MOUTHED FROG,
I'M A WIDE-MOUTHED FROG!"

Hop, hop, hop.

Soon she came to a deer grazing in some bushes.

"Oh Ms. Deer, Ms. Deer, excuse me. What do you feed your hungry babies?"

Ms. Deer replied, "Why, I feed my babies on the tender new shoots at the tops of these little trees."

"Oh, well I could never climb a tree to reach that food for my babies. Thank you, I'll keep looking."

And so she carried on along her journey, and as she hopped she sang,

"I'M A WIDE-MOUTHED FROG,
I'M A WIDE-MOUTHED FROG!"

Hop, hop, hop.

Soon she came to an owl, high up in a tree.

"Oh Ms. Owl, Ms. Owl, excuse me. What do you feed your hungry babies?"

Ms. Owl hooted and replied, "Why, I feed my babies on fine, fresh mice."

"Eew, a live mouse! Well anyway, I could never catch a mouse for my babies. Thank you, I'll keep looking."

And so she carried on along her journey, and as she hopped she sang,

"I'M A WIDE-MOUTHED FROG,
I'M A WIDE-MOUTHED FROG!"

Hop, hop, hop.

Soon she came to the edge of a wide, wide river. There, swimming toward her was a … large crocodile. Loudly, she called out to the crocodile,

"Oh Ms. Crocodile, Ms. Crocodile, excuse me. What do you feed your hungry babies?"

Still swimming toward her, Ms. Crocodile called out, "Why, I feed my babies on … wide … mouthed … frogs!"

"Oh. Well. Thank you very much," said the narrow-mouthed frog. *(Purse your lips!)* And she hopped away as quickly as ever she could. Hop! Hop! Hop!

In disgust, the crocodile turned around and swam away.

And as the wide-mouthed frog hopped quickly home, she decided to feed her hungry babies on delicious flies and mosquitoes, just like the other frog moms. They were the perfect food for wide-mouthed frogs.

Notes:
I like to tell this story using a southern accent. You can make it local by using animals that live in your area. You can also expand and contract the story by adding more animals for Ms. Frog to visit. It's a great story for parents to tell their babies to get them to open their mouths wide at mealtimes. There are a few slightly different picture book versions including the pop-up by Keith Faulkner and illustrated by Jonathan Lambert (New York: Dial Books for Young Readers, 1996). I like this version the best because it's about a parent and child. Dad could also be the one looking for food for his hungry baby.

When my friend Ginger Mullen tells this story to her baby, Brigit, she has Ms. Frog hop up the streets to their house meeting all their animal friends along the way, and she ends it like this: Baby Brigit, what do you eat? And baby Brigit said, "When I open my mouth WIDE, I get lots of milk. But when I don't, I get nothin'!"

Bibliography of Stories to Tell
in Parent-Infant Programs

When stories are told in parent-infant programs, the stories are for the listening pleasure of the adults. Since many parents are being introduced to the pleasure of listening to stories, and may not be used to it at first, the stories need to be short. In time, parents learn that storytelling is a wonderful activity they can share with their children at home.

FOLKTALE COLLECTIONS

Briggs, Katharine. BRITISH FOLK TALES AND LEGENDS: A SAMPLER . New York: Routledge, 1997, 2002. My favourite is "The Two Pickpockets."

Cole, Joanna. BEST LOVED FOLK-TALES OF THE WORLD. Garden City, New York: Doubleday, 1982. There are dozens of great stories to tell in this large collection. My favourites are: "It Could Always Be Worse," and "The Seal's Skin."

Danziger, Ruth, editor. GRANDMOTHER SPIDER AND OTHER FOLKTALES TO TELL, Toronto: Parent-Child Mother Goose Program, 2004. My favourites are: "Anansi Gets Some Common Sense," "The Mirror of Matsuyama," and "The Proud Rooster."

Lottridge, Celia Barker. YOU CAN TELL A STORY: A HANDBOOK FOR NEW STORYTELLERS WITH SEVEN STORIES TO TELL. Toronto: Parent-Child Mother Goose Program, 2002. My favourites are: "Eat Coat Eat," "Four Grains of Rice," "Just Enough," and "The Lion's Whisker."

Minard, Rosemary, editor. WOMENFOLK AND FAIRYTALES. Boston: Houghton Mifflin, 1975. "The Woman Who Flummoxed the Fairies."

Pellowski, Anne. HIDDEN STORIES IN PLANTS: UNUSUAL AND EASY-TO-TELL STORIES FROM AROUND THE WORLD, TOGETHER WITH CREATIVE THINGS TO DO WHILE TELLING THEM. New York: Macmillan, 1990. "The Wise Woman of the Birch Wood" is enchanting.

RAW HEAD, BLOODY BONES: AFRICAN-AMERICAN TALES OF THE SUPERNATURAL. Selected by Mary E. Lyons. New York: Maxwell Macmillan International, 1991. "Dead Aaron" is a great story to tell for Halloween. It's also available in picture book format as THE DANCING SKELETON by Cynthia C. DeFelice (New York: Macmillan, 1989).

Schimmel, Nancy. JUST ENOUGH TO MAKE A STORY: A SOURCEBOOK FOR STORYTELLING. Berkeley, CA: Sisters' Choice Press, 1978. This collection is well known for the story of "The Tailor." There are lots of good bibliographies here too.

Sierra, Judy. MULTICULTURAL FOLKTALES: STORIES TO TELL YOUNG CHILDREN. Phoenix: Oryx, 1991. I like to tell: "Drake's Tale," "The Elegant Rooster," and "The Teeny Tiny Woman."

Sierra, Judy and Robert Kaminski. TWICE UPON A TIME. New York: Wilson, 1989. I love the story of "The Nungwama."

Wolkstein, Diane. THE MAGIC ORANGE TREE, AND OTHER HAITIAN FOLKTALES. New York: Schocken Books, 1980, c1978. Two of these tales are my favourites: "I'm Tipingee, She's Tipingee," and "Owl."

Yolen, Jane, editor. FAVORITE FOLKTALES FROM AROUND THE WORLD. New York: Pantheon, 1986. There are dozens more great stories to tell in this large collection. My particular favourites are: "The Hodja and the Cauldron," "Lazy Jack," and "The Old Man and the Old Woman who Switched Jobs."

PICTURE BOOKS

Asbjornsen, P. C. and J. E. Moe. THE MAN WHO KEPT HOUSE. New York: Margaret McElderry, 1992.

Batt, Tanya Robyn. THE FAERIE'S GIFT. Illustrated by Nicoletta Ceccoli. Cambridge, MA: Barefoot Books, 2003.

DeFelice, Cynthia C. THE DANCING SKELETON. Illustrated by Robert Andrew Parker. New York: Macmillan, 1989. This story is great for Halloween. You will also find it in RAW HEAD, BLOODY BONES: AFRICAN-AMERICAN TALES OF THE SUPERNATURAL, selected by Mary E. Lyons (Maxwell Macmillan, 1991). The version there is called "Dead Aaron."

Zemach, Margot. THE THREE WISHES: AN OLD STORY. New York: Farrar, Straus & Giroux, 1986.

… and many more

Sample One-Hour Programs
for Parents and Toddlers, One to Two Years

Introduction *186*

Week One: Hello Everyone *189*
Week Two: Welcome Back *192*

Toddlers experience an explosion of brain activity as they explore their world, and they show daily advances in speech/language, social, emotional, cognitive, and motor skill development. And so they need programs that reinforce this new growth. These sample programs for toddlers and their parents again include both my Plan (the list of things I intend to do), and my Program (the delivery, which sometimes requires changes). I have included both to show you how easy it is to change things in your delivery in response to what you observe with the toddlers. I have also included a Talk heading to show you how easy it is to incorporate communication with the parents in your delivery.

Introduction to One-Hour Program for Parents and Toddlers, One to Two Years

MY PROGRAM MODEL

My programs for parents and their toddlers are based on the Parent-Child Mother Goose Program® model. They are structured similarly to my programs for parents and infants under one. Again, the teaching is aimed at the parents with the children joining in as they are ready. The programs can be delivered in the library or out in the community.

MY PROGRAM MODEL GOALS

1. To foster attachment between the parent and the child through the use of oral language.
2. To teach parents some rhymes and songs they and their young toddlers will enjoy using together.
3. To support parents in their role as the baby's first teacher.
4. To build a sense of community with the families I serve.
5. To introduce parents to books their young toddlers will enjoy.
6. To introduce parents to the free materials and services available at the public library.

SIMILARITIES TO INFANT PROGRAMS

Much of the format of the program remains the same as it is in the parent-infant programs. The teaching is aimed at the adults, with the toddlers joining in as they are ready.

The duration is ten weeks, and parents are encouraged to attend three ten-week sessions.

The programs generally last for an hour and a half, with social time for the parents and the babies built in.

Phone call reminders are still used to remind the families of the program the next day and keep them connected to the group.

My teaching methods are the same as they are for the infant programs. I teach the rhymes line by line. I hand out the words at the end of a ten-week session after the parents have learned the rhymes by heart. We repeat the rhymes three times each time we do them. The instruction is still oral and it is still aimed at the parents who are encouraged to use the rhymes and songs at home with their children.

Lullabies and calming rhymes are still used to calm both children and parents.

I still encourage the use of age-appropriate board books for the toddlers at home.

I don't use props at all in my young toddler programs. Toddlers find these things fascinating and naturally want to touch them, so I leave them behind and we just play with language using our voices and our bodies. I want to show the parents that they don't need "things" to engage their children's attention and play happily with them. All little children really want is their parents' loving attention.

DIFFERENCES FROM INFANT PROGRAMS

The babies, now young toddlers, are walking and are very active. They are also beginning to talk. I make changes to the program structure in response to the children's ages and stages of development, and to what I observe they are learning to do.

I use rhymes that the toddlers can participate in themselves, simple finger rhymes, standing-up rhymes, and rhymes we can play in a circle. We stand up to play with rhymes whenever the toddlers need to stand up.

The snack is also for the children now, so we cut the fruit in small pieces for them and make a ritual of washing hands and serving it with them.

Storytelling is still a big part of the program, but now the stories are favourite children's folktales, especially the tales that involve participation. This keeps the toddlers' attention.

IMPORTANT: I don't pass a question around the circle. Too much adult talk is not interesting to toddlers of this age.

IMPORTANT: It will take toddlers a few weeks to settle in to the program. Until they feel comfortable with the people, the environment, and the program structure, they may wander away from the circle and seem restless. This may seem like a chaotic time, but toddlers need this time to adjust. They will settle in within a few weeks. Keep the pace slow and relaxed.

IMPORTANT: Storytelling at the end of the parent-toddler program is a little different from storytelling in a parent-infant program. Now the story is suitable for toddlers who enjoy listening and participating along with their parents.Longer story rhymes, such as "This is the Key to the Kingdom" are also great to tell as little stories.

NUMBERS

I register twelve to thirteen families for my toddler programs and hope that ten will come each week. The groups need to be small for toddlers who need a lot of individual attention, and often feel overwhelmed in larger groups. I don't take new families into the program as the weeks unfold because I want to nurture the growing relationships of trust within the group.

PROGRAM PLANNING

I choose my selection of rhymes for the series based on what I know the toddlers will love to do. They love to play with fingers, they love to "do" the rhymes on their parents, they love stand-up rhymes, and they love rhymes they can learn to say themselves. I keep them simple and I slow down. Toddlers need time to listen and think about how they are going to respond. I give them the time they need. I teach roughly twenty songs total in the ten-week program. I tell a story each week, repeating the ones they love best, and teaching the story to the parents so they can retell the stories at home.

GREETING SONG

Rituals are extremely important for young toddlers. They will settle in quickly once they become familiar with a pattern. I like to use "Up Down, Turn Around" for my toddler programs because it is a rhyme that the toddlers can do standing up or sitting down and it is a gentle invitation to play.

HELLO SONG

Toddlers are very interested in hearing their own names, so I like to use a song that repeats their names and encourages them to say them. A song like "Hickety Pickety Bumble Bee" is good for this.

GOODBYE SONG

Toddlers enjoy learning the names for things including the names of their new friends, so we name each parent and child in a goodbye song at the end as well as the hello song in the beginning.

MY FORMULA

Greeting song
Name song
One or two bounces
Two or three lap rhymes
One or two stand-up rhymes
A circle game
Snack break
Repeat rhymes
Lullaby
Story
Goodbye song

RHYME SELECTION

As in the infant programs, I use a variety of rhymes, at least two bounces, action rhymes parents and toddlers can do together and simple fingerplays that the toddlers can manage themselves. I include stand-up rhymes and am ready to play these when I see that the toddlers are standing up and need a stretch. I include a song that is just fun to sing in a group, like "My Dog Rags." I also include a soothing lullaby and I am ready to sing it any time, especially when a toddler cries. I alternate between saying and singing rhymes. In toddler programs I try to be very flexible and respond to the toddlers basing the rhyme sequence on what I observe they need moment by moment. This shows the parents how they can use the rhymes to respond to their children at home.

STORYTELLING

Storytelling at the end of the parent-toddler program introduces parents to the kinds of stories their toddlers will enjoy. These are usually simple folktales or story rhymes. Toddlers love stories with lots of repetition and lots of opportunity for participation.

I repeat stories in a ten-week session so parents can learn them, and I encourage my parents to retell the stories to their children at home. Children love the same story over and over again. The beauty of a told story is that you can use it whenever you like. You can tell a story when you're lying in the dark, taking a walk, or riding on the bus. Parents can find more stories their children will like in books. And they can tell stories they make up themselves.

Children love to hear personal stories about the every day events in their lives. Hearing these stories gives shape and order to their experiences. It strengthens the emotional bonds between the parent and child. It also helps children learn to use narrative structure as they learn how to express themselves. Soon they will become little storytellers themselves.

At some point in the ten-week session, I tell my parents how important storytelling is for the development of their children's narrative skills. Children learn about the pattern and sequence of events through listening to stories, and this familiarity helps children gain access to the world of stories when they learn how to read.

RECORD KEEPING

I keep a record of my activities, and of what worked and what didn't, making a note of anything special I want to do at the next session. I make a note of participant responses, and of any questions or comments they had so I will remember to follow up the next week. I pay particular attention to the responses of the toddlers and will find rhymes that match their level of motor skill and language development. And, of course, I keep attendance statistics.

HAVE FUN!

My samples are meant to assist you in planning. Please substitute the rhymes and stories that you love best for your own programs.

Sample One-Hour Program for Parents and Toddlers, One to Two Years
Week One: Welcome Everyone!

THE PLAN

1. Welcome Song: Up Down Turn Around
2. Introductions
3. Hello Song: Hickety Pickety Bumble Bee
4. Bounce: Rickety Rickety Rocking Horse
5. Rowing Song: My Big Blue Boat
6. Rhyme: Chicken in the Barnyard
7. Rhyme: Whoops Johnny
8. Stand-up Rhyme: Tick Tock
9. Circle Game: The Ponies Are Walking
10. Circle Game: Ring Around the Rosie
11. Rhyme: Here's a Cup
12. Snack Break
13. Clean-up Song: Let's all Clean up Together
14. Repeat rhyme: Tick Tock
15. Lullaby: Bed Is Too Small
16. Story: Mr. Wiggle and Mr. Waggle
17. Goodbye Song: Goodbye Everyone

SETTING

The plan is ready and the snack has been prepared. The fruit has been cut into small toddler-sized pieces, and paper plates are ready. All clutter and toys have been removed or hidden so the toddlers can stay focused on the program. Mats have been placed in a circle on the floor so parents know where to sit. A box of age-appropriate board books is ready. I welcome everyone by name as they come in the door.

SOCIAL TIME

Now that the toddlers are eating on their own, we make a big ritual of snack time. First the toddlers wash their hands, then they sit down, then they are given a paper plate to put their food on. Toddlers are slow eaters! Parents chat, snack, and help their children with their food. In the end we all clean up together, toddlers too, and we sing a clean up song like "We All Clean Up Together." Toddlers love helping.

THE PROGRAM

1. Welcome Song: Up Down, Turn Around

2. Introductions:
Welcome to the first week of our Parent-Child Mother Goose Program. My name is _____ and I'm going to be leading you in the program. Each week I will teach you some rhymes your toddler will love to play with you and we'll repeat the rhymes every week so you will get a chance to learn them. I won't be handing out written words to the rhymes until the end of the ten-week program, but don't worry, you will all know them by heart by then so you won't need the written words. You'll learn the way your toddlers learn, through repetition. Everybody needs lots of repetition to learn new things.

The program will last for an hour and a half and each week we'll do the same thing. We'll play with our toddlers using rhymes for half an hour, then we'll have a little snack break, then we'll sing a lullaby and then I'll tell you a story at the end.

Don't worry if your toddlers seem a bit restless for the first few weeks. Let them explore and get used to the room and all the new people. They will settle in as the weeks go by.

Let's start by singing a hello song so that we can begin to get to know one another and remember everyone's names. We'll sing this song each week. This is how it goes. Say your name and then your toddler's name as we go around the circle.

3. Hello Song: Hickety Pickety Bumblebee

Talk:
Each week our pattern will be the same. I will teach you some rhymes to play with your toddler and we'll repeat them from week to week so that you will get to know them by heart and so you can play them often with your toddler at home. Toddlers love to do interactive rhymes with you and they love repetition.

This first rhyme is a bouncing rhyme called "Rickety Rickety Rocking Horse." Take your toddler on your knee facing you so that you can see how much your toddler is enjoying the rhyme, and so your toddler can see how much you are enjoying the rhyme too.

4. Bouncing Rhyme: Rickety Rickety Rocking Horse
(Repeat three times.)

Talk:
This is a nice rowing song you can do with your toddler. The rocking motion is very soothing. Take your toddler by the hands and rock back and forth while we sing.

5. Rowing Song: My Big Blue Boat
(Repeat two times as this is a longer song.)

Talk:
Here is a little tickle rhyme that is lots of fun to imagine. Sit facing your toddler. You start by drawing a circle in your toddler's hand, then you run up his arm for a little tickle in the end.

6. Rhyme: Chicken in the Barnyard
(Repeat three times.)

Talk:
Now that your toddlers have mastered some fine motor skills and can manipulate their little fingers, they love to play simple finger rhymes. Take baby's hand and point to each finger as you say this rhyme. Pretty soon your toddler will want to do it himself, and he will like to do it on you too.

7. Rhyme: Whoops Johnny
(Repeat three times.)

Talk:
Now let's say that rhyme again going round the circle and we'll say it for each child. Toddlers love it when we use their names in rhymes.

(Repeat "Whoops Johnny" as you go around the circle.)

Talk:
I see that many of the toddlers are standing up now because they need to stretch, so let's play some standing-up rhymes. *(The wonderful thing about toddlers is that they just do what they feel like doing! Follow their lead.)*

8. Stand-up Rhyme: Tick Tock
(Repeat three times.)

Talk:
Here is a nice and simple circle song that toddlers really enjoy doing. The different paces help them learn how to control their speed.

9. Circle Game: The Ponies Are Walking

Talk:
Now let's play Ring Around the Rosie, an all-time favourite.

10. Circle Game: Ring Around the Rosie
(Repeat three times.)

Talk:
It is just about time for our little snack break, so let's sit down and say a fun finger rhyme before we eat.

10. Rhyme: Here's a Cup
(Repeat three times.)

11. Snack Break
(Take the lead by showing parents what to do so that the toddlers are allowed to participate and help at their own speed.)

12. Clean-up Song: Let's all Clean up Together
(Encourage parents and toddlers to participate in the clean-up.)

13. Repeat rhyme: Tick Tock
(Repeat three times.)

Talk:
Each week we will sing a lullaby before we have a story. This will calm everyone and get them ready to listen. This is a lovely lullaby that your toddlers can do some actions with.

14. Lullaby: Bed Is Too Small
(First verse only this week. Repeat three times.)

Talk:
Now I'm going to tell you a story. This is a finger story and if you tell it again at home, your toddler will enjoy playing it with you. Here's how it goes.

15. Story: Mr. Wiggle and Mr. Waggle

Talk:
Now it's time to sing goodbye. Thank you for coming today. I enjoyed meeting all of you. Next week we will sing our songs again so don't worry if you can't remember them yet. And don't worry if your toddler didn't want to sit down during the program. The toddlers need to feel comfortable and familiar with the routine before they will sit for long. The goal of the program is that you will learn the rhymes and use them as you like with your toddler at home, so it doesn't matter if they are joining in all the time when they are here. I'll see you again next week!

And here is a box of toddler board books your toddler will enjoy. Take one home to read aloud and you will see a great response.

16. Goodbye Song: Goodbye Everyone

SOCIAL TIME

Your parents have now been exposed to thirteen new songs. Assure them that they will learn the rhymes as the weeks unfold and tell them you look forward to seeing them next week.

RECORD KEEPING

In week one I usually notice the parents are a little shy, and some of the toddlers are a little out of control. I know they will settle in by about week three. I will give them this time. I look forward to getting to know people so I can build on the skills I see developing. I keep attendance records. These help me remember who is learning a rhyme for the first time so that I can remember to teach it again and go slowly.

I make a note to remind parents that we will pause often so the toddlers have a chance to think and respond. Toddlers need more time than older children to get their thoughts organized and figure out how to express themselves. We want lots of patience.

Sample One-Hour Program for Parents and Toddlers, One to Two Years
Week Two: Welcome Back!

THE PLAN

1. Welcome Song: Up Down Turn Around
2. Introductions
3. Hello Song: Hickety Pickety Bumble Bee
4. Bounce: Rickety Rickety Rocking Horse
5. New Bounce: Mother and Father and Uncle John
6. Variation: Mother and Father and Uncle Jim
7. Rowing Song: My Big Blue Boat
8. Rhyme: Chicken in the Barnyard
9. Rhyme: Whoops Johnny
10. Stand-up Rhyme: Tick Tock
11. Circle Game: The Ponies Are Walking
12. Circle Game: Ring Around the Rosie
12. Rhyme: Here's a Cup
13. Snack Break
14. Clean-up Song: Let's all Clean up Together
15. Stand-up Rhyme: Tick Tock
16. Lullaby: Bed Is Too Small
17. Story: The Three Billy Goats Gruff
18. Goodbye Song: Goodbye Everyone

SETTING

The plan is ready and the snack has been prepared. All clutter and toys have been removed or hidden so the toddlers can stay focused on the program. Mats have been placed in a circle on the floor so parents know where to sit. A box of age-appropriate board books is ready. I welcome everyone by name as they come in the door.

SOCIAL TIME

The parents and toddlers are still getting used to the room, to one another, and to the program. They will settle in during the weeks ahead. Toddlers take a bit more time to settle in than babies or older preschoolers. They can be very shy, or very active.

THE PROGRAM

1. Welcome Song: Up Down Turn Around

2. Introductions:
Welcome back everyone!
(Introduce yourself and the program again for families who missed last week. Say you are going to repeat all the rhymes from last week and add a new one too.)

3. Hello Song: Hickety Pickety Bumblebee

Talk:
Turn your babies around now so that they are facing you, if you can, and let's play some bouncing rhymes. Your toddler may want to face out during the program, and that's okay. But play the games face to face when you are at home. Toddlers need to see your face to see how to make the word sounds.

4. Bounce: Rickety Rickety Rocking Horse
(Repeat three times.)

5. New Bouncing Rhyme: Mother and Father and Uncle John
(Repeat three times.)

Talk:
Toddlers love hearing rhymes with the names of people they know in them. You can make up rhymes and put your family's names in them. Let's say Uncle Jim instead of Uncle John.

6. Bouncing Rhyme: Mother and Father and Uncle Jim
(Repeat three times.)

Talk:
Now let's play our rowing song.

7. Rowing Song: My Big Blue Boat
(Repeat two times, as it's a longer song.)

Talk:
I see Michael really loves that rhyme! You must be playing that at home. Now let's play our little turkey rhyme.

8. Rhyme: Chicken in the Barnyard
(Repeat three times.)

Talk:
Finger rhymes are great fun to do as you wash your toddler's hands. The rhymes will help them stand still for you. Try this when you get home. It works like magic.

9. Rhyme: Whoops Johnny
(Repeat three times.)

Talk:
I see Aiden is ready to stand up now, so let's all stand up and play some stand-up rhymes.

10. Stand-up Rhyme: Tick Tock
(Repeat three times.)

Talk:
Oh-oh, someone is unhappy. Let's sing our lullaby to see if that makes Sam feel better.
(When a baby or toddler cries, show sympathy by singing a lullaby. When the toddlers' feelings are acknowledged in this way they learn they can trust us because we are showing that we care about their feelings. All the parents and toddlers will appreciate this approach and will stay with you as you carry on with the program.)

Lullaby: Bed Is Too Small

Talk:
Good. Sam feels better now. So let's play our pony game.

11. Circle Game: The Ponies Are Walking

12. Circle Game: Ring Around the Rosie

Talk:
It is just about time for our snack break, so let's say a fun finger rhyme before we eat. Remember this rhyme from last week?

12. Rhyme: Here's a Cup
(Repeat three times.)

13. Snack Break
(Again show parents what to do and encourage the toddlers to participate in the ritual at their own speed.)

Talk:
Everyone seems finished now, so let's clean up together.

14. Clean-up Song: Let's all Clean up Together
(Sing as you clean up, letting toddlers help, and then go and stand in the story circle again. Everyone will join you when you start to play.)

15. Repeat rhyme: Tick Tock
(Repeat three times.)

Talk:
And now it's time for our lullaby, so we can all snuggle in and get ready for a story.

16. Lullaby: Bed Is Too Small
(Sing the first verse, then teach the second verse. Repeat three times.)

Talk:
The story I'm going to tell you today is The Three Billy Goats Gruff. You can help me tell the story by making the sound of feet stomping over a bridge, like this, "Trip-trap, trip-trap, trip-trap. *(Slap your thighs as you say this and ask the parents and children to do it with you.)* Okay, now we're ready. Once upon a time . . .

17. Story: The Three Billy Goats Gruff

Talk:
Now it's time to sing goodbye. Thank you for coming today. Did you notice that your toddlers are settling in a bit more now? This will happen more and more as your toddler gets to know our routine.

18. Goodbye Song: Goodbye Everyone

SOCIAL TIME

I say goodbye to each parent and child. I usually notice in week two that families are chatting with one another as they walk out together. They are all getting to know one another a little more, and I notice some friendships forming. This is what I had hoped would happen.

RECORD KEEPING

I note that everyone is more relaxed this week. I note that the toddlers really love the finger rhymes so I will add "There Was a Little Mouse," which is one of my favourites, next week. I also notice that one of the children really needs a calming rhyme so I will teach "Slice Slice."

I must remember to watch the parents' lips next week, to see if they are learning the rhymes. I don't want to go too fast, or teach too many rhymes all at once. I want to remember, too, to notice if the parents are looking at me, or at their children. If they are still looking at me next week, that means they don't remember the rhymes. When they know them, they will look at their children while we are playing.

Five Easy Stories to Tell
in Parent-Toddler Programs

The Gunniwolf *196*
Mr. Wiggle and Mr. Waggle *198*
Ruth's Red Jacket *200*
Stone Soup *202*
The Three Billy Goats Gruff *204*

Bibliography of Stories to Tell *206*

Storytelling in a parent-toddler program involves engaging the parents and the children who are now active participants in listening to the stories. Stories with lots of expression and actions the listeners can join in on work best. Favourite folktales for young children are a good choice. They can be found in children's libraries in the 398.2 section, either in collections, or as single stories illustrated in picture book format. Longer rhymes, like "This is the Key to the Kingdom," and story songs, like "The Gingerbread Man," work well as little stories for young listeners too.

The Gunniwolf

Once there was a little girl who lived with her mother at the edge of a deep dark forest. The mother always told the little girl, "Whatever you do, don't go into that forest alone. Because if you do the Gunniwolf might get you!" The little girl always promised that she would never go into the forest alone.

One day the mother had to go away into town. Before she left she warned the little girl, "Remember what I told you. You can play outside, but don't even go near that deep dark forest. Because if you do, the Gunniwolf might get you!" The little girl promised that she would not go anywhere near the forest.

But as soon as her mother was gone the little girl started playing outside and she saw some pretty pink flowers blooming right at the edge of the forest. "Oh!" she said, "I must pick those little pink flowers for my mother."

And as she picked she sang: "Kum-kwa ... ki-wa ... kum-kwa ... ki-wa ... ."

Then the little girl saw ... deeper in the forest ... some pretty white flowers. They were so lacy and beautiful ... they would go so well with her pink flowers ... she just had to pick them too.

So the little girl went deeper into the forest and began to pick the white flowers.

And as she picked she sang: "Kum-kwa ... ki-wa ... kum-kwa ... ki-wa ... ."

Just then, deep, deep in the forest, she saw some bright red flowers! They were so beautiful she just had to pick them.

So the little girl went deep, deep into the forest and began to pick the red flowers.

And as she picked she sang:
"Kum-kwa ... ki-wa ... kum-kwa ... ki-wa... ."

When suddenly, UP sprang the GUNNIWOLF!

"Little Girl! You sing that GUTEN SWEETEN song AGAIN!" said the Gunniwolf in his big hoarse voice.

So the little girl sang in a timid little voice:

"Kum-kwa ... ki-wa ... kum-kwa ... ki-wa... ."

And while she sang, the old Gunniwolf fell fast asleep.

As soon as he was asleep off tiptoed the little girl.

Pit-pat ... pit-pat ... pit-pat ... .

Slap your hands on your knees in rhythm to the pit-pats.

But UP rose the GUNNIWOLF! And he chased after her!

HUNKER-CHA ... HUNKER-CHA ... HUNKER-CHA ... HUNKER-CHA ... .

And he caught the little girl.

"Little Girl. Why for you move?"

"I no move."

"Then you sing that GUTEN SWEETEN song AGAIN!"

So the little girl sang:
"Kum-kwa ... ki-wa ... kum-kwa ... ki-wa... ."

And as she sang, the Gunniwolf fell fast asleep.

Then off ran the little girl.
Pit-pat ... pit-pat ... pit-pat ... .

But UP sprang the GUNNIWOLF! And he chased after her!

HUNKER-CHA... HUNKER-CHA ... HUNKER-CHA ... HUNKER-CHA ...

And he caught her!

"Little Girl. Why for you move?

"I no move."

"Then you sing that GUTEN SWEETEN song AGAIN!"

So the little girl sang:
"Kum-kwa... ki-wa... kum-kwa... ki-wa..."

This time she sang a long, long time till she was sure the Gunniwolf was fast, fast asleep.

"Kum-kwa... ki-wa... kum-kwa... ki-wa..."

Then off ran the little girl.
Pit-pat ... pit-pat ... pit-pat ...
... past the red flowers ...
Pit-pat ... pit-pat ... pit-pat ...
... past the white flowers ...
Pit-pat ... pit-pat ... pit-pat ...
... past the pink flowers ...
... into her very own house ...
... and she SLAMMED THE DOOR!

And the little girl never went into that deep dark forest alone again.

Notes:
The picture book version of THE GUNNIWOLF, by Wilhelmina Harper (Dutton, 1967) is in most children's library collections. I learned this way of telling it from Margaret Read MacDonald. It is in her wonderful collection TWENTY TELLABLE TALES: AUDIENCE PARTICIPATION FOLKTALES FOR THE BEGINNING STORYTELLER.

I ask the adults to play the gunniwolf and the children to play the little girl in the story, but then they all seem to enjoy acting out both parts together. We rehearse picking flowers, the kumkwa song with a made-up tune, and pit-patting on our knees for the little girl's part, and we rehearse the hunker-cha chant for the gunniwolf's part. We all rest our heads on our hands as the gunniwolf falls asleep, and we all slam the door at the end. The parents "chase" their children and catch them for a hug when the gunniwolf catches the little girl. It is a really exciting game to play with little toddlers because you can make it just as scary or fun as they need it to be.

Mr. Wiggle and Mr. Waggle

Once there were two friends named Mr. Wiggle, and Mr. Waggle.

Hold up two thumbs, fists closed, and look at each thumb as you say their names.

They lived in identical houses.

The houses are your fists.

Mr. Wiggle went in his house like this:
he opened the door, went inside, and closed the door.

Open right palm, pull your thumb down onto your palm, and close fingers over thumb.

Mr. Waggle went into his house like this:
he opened his door, went inside, and closed the door.

Repeat actions with the left hand.

One day, Mr. Wiggle decided to visit Mr. Waggle. He opened his door, came outside and closed his door.

Open right palm, pop up your thumb, and close your fist.

Then he went up the hill and down the hill and up the hill and down the hill and up the hill and down the hill until he reached the home of Mr. Waggle.

Thumb points up, then down the hill, many hills, until the thumb meets the house (fist) of the other hand.

He knocked on the door, knock, knock, knock, and called out "Oh Mr. Waaaaguuuul."

Knock one fist on the other and call out.

But Mr. Waggle didn't answer, so Mr. Wiggle knocked louder and called out a little bit louder, "Oh Mr. Waaaguuul!"

Knock one fist on the other and call out.

But there was still no answer, so Mr. Wiggle knocked even louder, and called out,

Knock one fist on the other and call out.

"Oh Mr. Waaaaaguuuul!"

but there was no answer.

Knock fists together, and call out several times.

So Mr. Wiggle decided to go home.

He went ... up the hill and down the hill, and up the hill and down the hill and up the hill and down the hill until he reached his own house, where he opened the door, stepped inside, and closed the door.

Thumb travels up and down the hill, back to the home position. Fingers open, thumb pops down, fingers close in a fist.

Well, wouldn't you know it, the very next morning, Mr. Waggle decided to go visit Mr. Wiggle.

Do the whole thing over again with the other thumb.

He opened his door and stepped outside.

He went ... up the hill and down the hill and up the hill and down the hill and up the hill and down the hill until he reached the home of Mr. Wiggle.

He knocked on the door, knock, knock, knock, and called out, "Oh Mr. Wiggle!"

But there was no answer. So he knocked on the door again, knock, knock, knock, and called out a little bit louder, "Oh Mr. Wiiiggle!"

But still there was no answer. So Mr. Waggle knocked again, as loud as he could, knock, knock, knock, and called out as loud as he could,

"Oh Mr. Wiiiiiggle!"

But there was no answer.

So Mr. Waggle decided to go home.

He went ... up the hill and down the hill, and up the hill and down the hill and up the hill and down the hill until he reached his own house, where he opened the door, stepped inside, and closed the door.

Now repeat using both thumbs at once.

Well wouldn't you know it! The very next morning, Mr. Wiggle AND Mr. Waggle decided to go visit each other.

They both opened their doors, they both stepped outside, and they both closed their doors at the same time.

And they both went ... up the hill and down the hill, and up the hill and down the hill and uuuup!

THEY MET AT THE TOP OF THE HILL!!!!

They shared the news, they shared the gossip, they talked about hills, and doors and the ups and downs of life, and when they had said everything they had wanted to say, they said,

"Goodbye!"

"Goodbye!"

And they both went home.

They went ... down the hill and up the hill and down the hill and up the hill and down the hill and up the hill ... until they got to their own houses, where they opened their doors at the very same time, stepped inside at the very same time, and closed their doors at the very same time.

And the next time they wanted to talk, they used the TELEPHONE!

Notes:
This little thumb play story is fascinating to toddlers who will want to join in with the actions. It comes from the oral tradition, and I learned this way of telling it from a storyteller named Kevin MacKenzie.

You can use any names you like, Mr. Wibble and Mr. Wabble, Mr. White and Mr. Brown, etc. You can add all kinds of thumb actions. The two friends can slide down the hill, roll in the leaves, and they can embrace when they say goodbye. It's also great to adapt for the seasons. The two friends can exchange valentines, toys, and show off their costumes at Halloween.

Ruth's Red Jacket

One day Ruth came home from playschool and she saw a package sitting on the kitchen table. It was all wrapped up in pretty pink paper with a white ribbon around it and she knew it was for her because today was her birthday! And so she opened it right away and inside there was a beautiful red jacket. It was so soft and so pretty and red was her favourite colour. On the inside there was a little tag that said, "To Ruthie, Love Grandma." Her grandmother had made it, just for her! Ruth loved her new red jacket and she put it on.

Well Ruthie loved that jacket so much she wore it all the time. She wore it to school and she wore it to the park, and she wore it to grandma's house, and she wore it and she wore it until she wore it right out!

Her grandmother looked at that jacket. It now had frayed cuffs and a hole in one elbow and it looked all tattered and worn out. Her grandmother looked at it this way and she looked at it that way, and she thought and she thought and she thought until she had an idea. She got out her scissors and she cut and she cut and she cut. Then she took out her needle and thread and she sewed and she sewed and she sewed until from that worn-out jacket she made a beautiful red vest.

Ruth loved her new vest. It was even softer than her jacket had been. She loved it so much that she wore it everywhere. She wore it to school and she wore it to the park and she wore it to grandma's house and she wore it and she wore it until she wore it right out!

Her grandmother looked at that vest. It had a big stain on the front and one of the arms was torn a little bit. Her grandmother looked at it this way and she looked at it that way, and she thought and she thought and she thought until she had an idea. She got out her scissors and she cut and she cut and she cut. Then she took out her needle and thread and she sewed and she sewed and she sewed until from that worn-out vest she made a beautiful tie.

Now Ruth's mom said, "You're a girl and girls don't wear ties." But Ruth did. She loved her new tie! And grandma knew she would love it too. She wore it with everything. She wore it with dresses and with shirts. She loved that tie so much she wore it everywhere. She wore it to school, and she wore it to the park, and she wore it to grandma's house, and she wore it and she wore it until she wore it right out!

Her grandmother looked at that tie. It had fallen in many mud puddles and was quite stained. There wasn't a whole lot of fabric left but grandma was a clever woman. She looked at it this way and she looked at it that way, and she thought and she thought and she thought until she had an idea. She got out her scissors and she cut and she cut and she cut. Then she took out her needle and thread and she sewed and she sewed and she sewed until from that worn-out tie she made a beautiful headband.

Ruth loved her new headband. She wore it all the time and with every outfit. She wore it to school and she wore it to the park and she wore it to grandma's house and she wore it and she wore it until she wore it right out!

Grandma looked at that headband. There wasn't much left. But she thought and she thought and she thought until she had an idea. And she said, "Ruthie, come here and sit on my knee." And so Ruthie climbed up on her grandmother's knee, and her grandma said, "I can't really make anything more for you out of this headband but I can make up a story about Ruth's red jacket!" And that's just what she did. And grandma told that story to Ruthie for years. And now, I've told it to you too!

Notes:
Retold by Ginger Mullen. This story originally came from a Yiddish folk song. It was made into a story by Nancy Schimmel and published as "The Tailor" in JUST ENOUGH TO MAKE A STORY *(Berkeley: Sisters Choice Press, 1992). Versions of it also appear in the picture books* SOMETHING FROM NOTHING *by Phoebe Gilman (New York: Scholastic, 1993) and* JOSEPH HAD A LITTLE OVERCOAT *by Simms Taback (New York: Viking, 1999).*

I love this story. I like to tell the Nancy Schimmel version first, and then, the following week, tell Ginger's version. I like doing this to show parents how they can personalize stories for their own children, as grandma has done here.

When telling for your audiences, encourage the parents and children to cut with their imaginary scissors and sew with their imaginary needles and thread along with you. You can also make this a participation story by pausing for audience suggestions of garments to make. You can also extend or contract the story by adding or taking away garments.

Stone Soup

Once long ago there was a soldier named Jack who was coming back from fighting in a war. He had to walk a very long way to get home and this one particular day he'd been walking all day long and he hadn't had any food so he was very, very hungry. Well he happened to come to a village, and he thought surely somebody there would spare him some food. He walked up to the first house and knocked on the door,

Knock, knock, knock.
The door went EEEK ...
and an old woman answered.

"Hello, ma'am," said Jack. "I've been walking a long way today and I'm very hungry. Could you spare some food perhaps? A potato perhaps?"

And you know what the old woman said? She said "No!" and she SLAMMED the door right in his face.

So Jack went to the next house, and he knocked on the door,

Knock, knock, knock.
The door went EEEK ...
And this time an old man answered the door. "Yes, hello," he said.

And Jack said, "I've been walking a long way today and I've run out of food and I'm very hungry. Could you spare a few carrots?"

And you know what the old man said? He said, "No!" and he SLAMMED the door right in his face.

Well, Jack was still hungry so he went to the next house. He knocked on the door,

Knock, knock, knock.
The door went EEEK ...

And this time a young couple answered the door. Jack said, "I've been walking all day and I'm so very hungry. Do you have a little bit of meat to spare, just a little bit that I could have? Scraps from your dinner perhaps?"

And you know what that young couple said? They said, "No!" and they SLAMMED the door in his face.

Well, Jack thought, something is not working here. I need to think of a better idea because nobody wants to share with me. So he sat down at the side of the road and he thought and he thought and he thought, and then he saw an unusually shaped stone by the side of the road, and he had an idea. So he took that stone and he went right into the middle of the town, right where all the important meetings are held and he called out,

"STONE SOUP, STONE SOUP, I'm going to make some STONE SOUP. Would anyone like some STONE SOUP?"

Well, of course, nobody had ever heard of anyone making soup from a stone before. And this man didn't even have a pot! How could he make soup? So out of curiosity all the people came out of their houses and looked at him and they said, "You can't make soup from a stone."

And Jack said, "Oh yes I can. All I need is a pot of boiling water, a fire to keep it hot and a spoon to stir it with." Well, someone thought, no harm in giving him a pot and some water to put in it. Water from the river was free. So someone made a fire, someone else brought a pot filled with water, and someone else brought a spoon, and they waited 'til it boiled.

And he stirred and stirred and then he dropped the stone into the water. SPLASH!

And he stirred and he stirred and he stirred. He dipped in his spoon, blew on it, whoo, and tasted it and he said, "This soup is very good, very good. But maybe it could use a potato."

And remember that old woman who slammed the door in his face? She said, "Oh, I think I've got a potato or two I could put in." And she went home, pat-pat-pat, she got a potato and she came back, pat-pat-pat, and she gave the potato to that soldier and he chopped it up, chop-chop-chop, chop-chop-chop, and he took it and SPLASH! he put it in the boiling water and he began to stir.

And he stirred and he stirred and he stirred. He dipped in his spoon and blew on it, whooo, and he tasted it and he said, "Oh those potatoes just made it so delicious. But if only it had a few carrots, it would be perfect."

Now remember that old man who slammed the door in his face? He said, "Well I might have a few carrots. They're a little bit withered, but you can have those." So he went home, pat-pat-pat, got the carrots and came back, pat-pat-pat, and gave them to Jack. Jack took the carrots and chopped them up, chop-chop-chop, chop-chop-chop, and he threw them in the water, SPLASH!

And he stirred and he stirred and he stirred. He dipped in his spoon and blew on it, whooo, and he tasted it and he said, "Oh this is heavenly. It's so good. Oh, but if only it had ... what else could it use?" And the young couple said, "What about some meat?" And he said, "Yes! That would be great."

So the young couple went home, pat-pat-pat, got come meat, came back, pat-pat-pat, and gave the meat to the soldier. The soldier took the meat and chopped it up, chop-chop-chop, chop-chop-chop, and he put it in the water, SPLASH!

And he stirred and he stirred and he stirred. He dipped in his spoon and blew on it, whooo, and he tasted it and he said, "Oh," he said, "it's perfect. All I need is a little salt and some bowls so we can all share it." So someone went home and got salt, Jack added it and stirred it in, and he dipped in his spoon, blew on it, whooo, and said, "It's delicious!"

So they all ran home, pat-pat-pat, and they got their bowls, pat-pat-pat, and they held up their bowls. And Jack put soup in all their bowls. They all had a wonderful feast of stone soup.

And that night the mayor let Jack stay at his house overnight. The next morning before he left, Jack gave that stone to the mayor and he said, "Whenever you need to make stone soup you can use this stone to do it."

Notes:
Retold by Ginger Mullen. There are many picture book versions of this tale in children's libraries. Check out Marcia Brown's version Stone Soup *(Scribner, 1947).*

Children love to join in with the repetitive actions—opening the door with an "eeek," slamming the door with a big clap, chopping up the vegetables, stirring the pot, holding up their imaginary bowls, and tasting the soup. Children love it when the storyteller fills up each of their little bowls (cupped hands).

The Three Billy Goats Gruff

Once there were three billy goats, and all three billy goats were named Gruff. Now these billy goats lived on a bare piece of land. They had eaten every bush, every flower, and every blade of grass, so they were very hungry. Nearby there was a beautiful hillside, filled with flowers and trees and sweet green grass. But ... to get to the hillside, there was a bridge over which they had to cross. And under the bridge there lived a great, ugly troll, with eyes as big as saucers and a nose as long as a poker.

The Smallest Billy Goat Gruff was the first to cross the bridge.

TRIP TRAP, TRIP TRAP, TRIP TRAP went the bridge.

When the Smallest Billy Goat Gruff got to the centre of the bridge, up jumped the ugly troll!

"WHO'S THAT TRIPPING OVER MY BRIDGE?" roared the troll.

"Oh, it is just me, the Smallest Billy Goat Gruff, and I am on my way up the hillside to eat the green grass so I can get fat."

"OH NO YOU'RE NOT!" said the troll. "FOR I'M COMING TO GOBBLE YOU UP!"

"Oh, don't eat me! Wait for my brother. He's much bigger and fatter than I, and he'll make a better meal for you."

"Bigger, you say?" said the troll.

"Yes, much bigger," said the Smallest Billy Goat Gruff.

"All right. I'll wait. Be off with you!"

So the Smallest Billy Goat Gruff went on across the bridge and up onto the beautiful hillside where he began to eat the sweet green grass.

Then it was the turn of the Middle Size Billy Goat Gruff. When he crossed the bridge, the bridge went TRIP TRAP, TRIP TRAP, TRIP TRAP, a little bit louder.

"WHO'S THAT TRIPPING OVER MY BRIDGE?" roared the troll.

"Oh, it is just me, Middle Size Billy Goat Gruff, and I am on my way up the hillside to eat the green grass so I can get fat."

"OH NO YOU'RE NOT!" said the troll. "FOR I'M COMING TO GOBBLE YOU UP!"

"Oh, don't eat me! Wait for my brother. He's much bigger and fatter than I, and he'll make a better meal for you."

"Bigger, you say?" said the troll.

"Yes, much bigger," said the Middle Size Billy Goat Gruff.

"All right. I'll wait. Be off with you!"

So the Middle Size Billy Goat Gruff went on across the bridge and up onto the beautiful hillside where he began to eat the sweet green grass.

Then it was the turn of the Biggest Billy Goat Gruff. When he crossed the bridge, the bridge went

TRIP TRAP, TRIP TRAP, TRIP TRAP, and he was so big that the bridge creaked and groaned under his weight.

"WHO'S THAT TRIPPING OVER MY BRIDGE?" said the troll.

"IT IS I," said the Biggest Billy Goat Gruff, "AND I AM ON MY WAY UP THE HILLSIDE TO EAT THE GREEN GRASS AND GET FAT." And his voice was even bigger and louder than the troll's.

"OH NO YOU'RE NOT!" said the troll. "I'VE BEEN WAITING FOR YOU, AND I'M COMING TO GOBBLE YOU UP!"

"WELL COME AHEAD. I'M NOT AFRAID OF YOU," said the Biggest Billy Goat Gruff.

And so the Biggest Billy Goat flew at the troll. And the troll flew at the billy goat. They fought for a long time. At last the billy goat lifted the troll up on his horns and threw him into the river where he landed with a big SPLASH. And the troll floated away down the river and was never seen again.

As for the Biggest Billy Goat Gruff, he went on across the bridge and up onto the hillside to join his brothers in eating the sweet green grass. And as far as I know, they are still there eating grass and getting very fat.

Snip snap snout. This tale's told out.

Notes:
There are many wonderful picture book versions of this tale. Check out the classic by Peter Christen Asbjornsen and illustrated by Paul Galdone (Seabury Press, 1973), and the version retold and illustrated by Val Biro (Oxford University Press, 1992).

Your children will love to join you as you pat your knees for the trip traps across the bridge, and you can add this in as many times as you like.

Bibliography of Stories to Tell
in Parent - Toddler Programs

FOLKTALES IN COLLECTIONS

Lottridge, Celia Barker. TEN SMALL TALES. My favourite stories are: "The Big Old-Fashioned Bed," and "The Great Big Enormous Rock."

MacDonald, Margaret Read. TWENTY TELLABLE TALES: AUDIENCE PARTICIPATION FOLKTALES FOR THE BEGINNING STORYTELLER. H. W. Wilson, 1986. My favourites from this collection are: "The Gunny Wolf," "Jack and the Robbers," "The Little Rooster and the Turkish Sultan," "Old One-Eye" (for Halloween), "Parley Garfield and the Frogs," "Roly Poly Rice Ball," and "Sody Sallyrytus."

MacDonald, Margaret Read. LOOK BACK AND SEE. H. W. Wilson, 1993. My favourites from this collection are: "Grandfather Bear," and "A Penny and a Half."

MacDonald, Margaret Read. THE STORYTELLER'S START-UP BOOK: FINDING, LEARNING, PERFORMING AND USING FOLKTALES. H. W. Wilson, 1993. My favourites are: "The Little Old Woman Who Lived in a Vinegar Bottle," and "Ko Kongole."

Sierra, Judy. THE FLANNEL BOARD STORYTELLING BOOK. H. W. Wilson, 1997. There are many easy-to-tell versions of folktales in this useful collection. I especially like to use "The Strange Visitor" for toddlers at Halloween. They can identify their own body parts as you tell the story.

Sierra, Judy. MULTICULTURAL FOLKTALES: STORIES TO TELL YOUNG CHILDREN. Oryx, 1991. My favourites from this collection are: "Anansi and the Rock," "Drake's Tail," "The Goat in the Chili Patch," and "The Teeny Tiny Woman."

FOLKTALES IN PICTURE-BOOK FORMAT

THE BREMEN TOWN MUSICIANS, retold from the Brothers Grimm and illustrated by Janet Stevens. Holiday House, 1992.

CAPS FOR SALE, retold by Esphyr Slobodkina. Harper and Row, 1987.

THE FAT CAT, retold by Jack Kent. Parent's Magazine Press, 1971.

THE FUNNY LITTLE WOMAN, retold by Arlene Mosel. E. P. Dutton, 1992.

THE GINGERBREAD MAN, retold by Eric Kimmel. Holiday House, 1993. And, "The Gingerbread Man" song on Kathy Reid-Naiman's CD TICKLES AND TUNES.

GOLDILOCKS AND THE THREE BEARS, retold by Jim Aylesworth. Scholastic, 2003.

THE GREAT BIG ENORMOUS TURNIP, by Alexei Tolstoy: illustrated by Helen Oxenbury. F. Watts, 1968.

THE LITTLE OLD LADY WHO WAS NOT AFRAID OF ANYTHING, by Linda Williams. Harper and Row, 1986.

SODY SALLERATUS, retold by Aubrey Davis. Kids Can Press, 1995.

THE THREE LITTLE PIGS, retold and illustrated by Barry Moser. Little, Brown, 2001.

WE'RE GOING ON A BEAR HUNT, retold by Michael Rosen; illustrated by Helen Oxenbury. Walker Books, 1989.

Sample Half-Hour Programs

Introduction *208*

For Parents and Babies, Birth to One Year
Week One: Hello Everyone *211*
Week Two: Welcome Back *214*

For Parents and Toddlers, One to Two Years
Week One: Hello Everyone *217*
Week Two: Welcome Back *220*

Half-hour programs for families with young children are wonderful fun, and are the standard in most public libraries. These sample programs for both parents and infants, and parents and toddlers, include both my Plan (the list of things I intend to do), and my Program (the delivery, which sometimes requires changes). I have included both to show you how easy it is to change things in your delivery in response to what you observe in a half-hour program. I have included a Talk heading to show you how easy it is to incorporate communication with the parents in your delivery.

Introduction to Half-Hour Programs

HALF-HOUR PROGRAMS

The children's staff in public libraries are stretched in many directions providing services and programs for all ages of children and their families. With such busy schedules it is sometimes difficult to find the time required to deliver an hour-long baby program. Half-hour programs are fun to do, and they introduce families to the wide range of services and programs available at the public library and they are now considered a fundamental part of basic public library services.

MY GOALS FOR THE PROGRAM

1. To bring new families into the library.
2. To introduce parents to the free materials and services available at the public library.
3. To teach parents some rhymes and songs they will enjoy using at home with their babies.
4. To introduce parents to books their babies will enjoy.

DROP-IN OR REGISTRATION?

Depending on my neighbourhood and the demand for the program, I like to register families so I know how many children to expect and the children's ages. This helps me plan a program that is appropriate for everybody. However, I always take drop-ins too. I collect their names after the program.

Drop-in programs, advertised as drop-ins, are more suitable in some communities, and are more inviting to people who either cannot, or do not want to register for a whole series. The planning process is the same in both cases. The only drawback is that drop-in programs often attract large numbers. If this happens to you, the trick is to take a deep breath, and carry on in the calm way you would with a smaller group. Don't give in to panic. Keep your pace slow.

NUMBERS

I think fifteen families is an ideal number. Fewer is fun, too many more can be overwhelming.

I like to offer baby programs all year long in eight or ten-week segments. I think parents appreciate having the program accessible for long periods so their attendance can become a part of their routine, and they get a broader window of opportunity to attend.

COMMON PITFALLS

Many Baby Programs are offered as simplified Toddler Programs using the same puppets and felt stories and props as in Toddler Programs, with a few more bounces and lullabies mixed in. While this can be entertaining for the parents, this kind of program is usually beyond the comprehension and ability of babies under two who will wander and squirm and try to grab the props. Also, the rhymes are often too complex for babies to enjoy.

Therefore, I like to focus my programs on the rhymes and activities the parents and babies can enjoy and participate in together. My goal is to teach the parents the rhymes and songs so they can use them at home. I choose interactive rhymes, and I repeat them from week to week, adding new ones as the parents show they are remembering them.

PROPS

The only "props" I use regularly in my half-hour programs are the read-aloud books. I also sometimes use chimes or a tambourine to begin and end the program. I don't use more props because I don't want to tantalize the babies with things they can't touch, and I also want the parents to understand that they don't need these things to engage their children happily in play.

BABY BOARD BOOKS

I assemble a plastic tub full of baby board books to take to the program.

MY TEACHING METHODS

As in the hour-long programs, when I introduce a rhyme for the first time, I say it through once, then I ask the parents to repeat the lines back to me line by line. Then we all say it a second and third time together. When the parents know the rhymes, all of us, babies and parents alike, enjoy repeating the rhymes three times each time we do them.

When I teach a song, I use this same method. I also often separate the tune from the words. We sing la-la-la through the tune, then we sing the lines one line at a time, then we all sing it again with everybody joining in.

WRITTEN WORDS TO RHYMES

In half-hour programs, I hand out written words to the rhymes within the first few weeks so parents can learn them this way too. There is often not enough time in a half-hour program for parents to learn them well enough to remember them. This helps.

QUESTION FOR THE DAY

There is not enough time in a half-hour program to pass a question around to the parents. I try to create other opportunities for community building such as making the room available to the families before and after the program so they can meet and visit with one another.

TODDLER PROGRAMS

When babies start to walk, around one year of age, it is time to include stand-up rhymes so they can have a little stretch, and to include finger rhymes they will enjoy doing on their own.

Slow down for toddlers. It takes them time to understand what you are saying and what you want them to do. Because they are so active, people often speed up to keep them engaged. This has the opposite to the desired effect.

MY FORMULA

Greeting song
Name song
Five or six rhymes
Lullaby
Story
Two or three rhymes
Goodbye song

RHYME SELECTION

I choose my selection of rhymes by type. I always include at least one bouncing rhyme, a face rhyme, a tickling rhyme, a song and a lullaby. I also alternate between saying and singing rhymes.

PACING

I keep a relaxed pace. It is better for parents to learn a few rhymes they can use at home than it is to be exposed to so many that they can't remember them. You will know when they are remembering them when they sing along with you, and when they look at their babies instead of at you!

GETTING STARTED

I select about ten rhymes along with the opening and closing songs to get started. Then I teach new rhymes as the parents show they are ready to learn more. I build on the types of rhymes and activities they seem to enjoy the most.

REPETITION

I tell the parents we are going to repeat most rhymes three times on the spot so they will all get a chance to join in, and so they will find out how much their babies love repetition. I repeat all the songs and rhymes I teach in the succeeding weeks, and each week I add a new one or two as the parents seem to be remembering the rhymes and are ready to learn more.

SINGING

Whenever attention seems to stray, usually as a result of parents chatting, I draw attention back to the group activity by singing. If this doesn't work, I say that social time is before or after the program. For now we will play with the babies.

When a baby cries, and this will happen sometimes, I sing. This always calms the babies and their parents. I never ask a parent to leave during a baby program because the baby is crying. If a parent decides to take the baby home for a needed nap, this is a different matter.

ABOUT THE STORY

I choose books to read-aloud that are participation stories so the parents and babies can join in. These keep the babies engaged.

I choose participation stories to tell that will entertain the parents if their babies are sleeping, or they can participate in if their babies are awake. I also suggest ways the parents can use the stories at home.

RUNNING OUT OF TIME

A half-hour goes by very quickly. Plan more rhymes than you will need, then be prepared to drop some rhymes if you are running short of time rather than rushing to fit them all in.

Every group is different. You can fit in more rhymes with some groups than you can with others.

RECORD KEEPING

I keep a record of my activities, and of what worked and what didn't. I note anything special I want to do at the next session. I note participant responses, and any questions or comments they had. Some of these things may need follow up the next week.

HAVE FUN!

Everyone has his or her own style and way of delivering parent-baby programs. Please use my samples as a starting point and substitute the rhymes, stories and activities that you love best. The more rhymes you know, and the more flexible and responsive you are, the happier you will be with your program.

Sample Half-Hour Program for Parents and Babies, Birth to One
Week One: Welcome Everyone!

THE PLAN

1. Song: Bell Horses (with a tambourine)
2. Brief Introduction
3. Song: Come Along and Sing with Me (clap with me, stretch with me)
4. More introduction: repetition of rhymes.
5. Bounce: From Wibbleton to Wobbleton
6. Rhyme: Mix and Stir
7. Rhyme: Wiggle Waggle
8. Rhyme: Round and Round the Garden
9. Song: What'll I do with the Baby-o? *(chorus and one verse)*
10. Face Rhyme: The Moon is Round
11. Lullaby: Ho, Ho, Watanay
12. Read-aloud Story: Baby Knows Best
13. Repeat rhymes if time.
14. Bounce: Tick Tock
15. Song: Bell Horses (with a tambourine)
16. Goodbye Everyone

Conclusion: Show samples of age appropriate books for babies

SETTING

The room has been prepared. All clutter that will distract the babies has been removed. I've brought in a collection of baby board books and some great read-alouds the parents can take home with them after the program.

SOCIAL TIME

I greet parents and babies as they come in. I let them get to know me. There will be lots of questions: can I bring my husband, my mother, my three year old, how long is the program, etc. In the beginning, I just say yes to everything. I'll find out what doesn't work as I go along.

THE PROGRAM

1. Song: Bell Horses
(Bring out a tambourine, and shake as you sing the whole song.)

Talk:
You can sing that little song with your car keys if you like it. Babies love car keys.

2. Talk: (Brief Introductions)
Hello everybody, my name is _____ and I'm going to be teaching you some rhymes to play with your baby today. Our program is half an hour long and we will meet every week at this same time for ten weeks to play with our babies. Take your baby on your knee and we'll get started with a nice little welcome song you can do with them.

3. Welcome song: Come Along and Sing with Me (clap with me, stretch with me)

4. Talk: (More Introduction)
I'm going to be teaching you some rhymes and songs you can play with your babies at home, so it's fine if your baby is sleeping or crawling around. The program is for you with your babies joining in when they are ready. I will be repeating all the rhymes so you will have a chance to learn them.

Face-to-face interaction with your baby is very important, so take your baby on your knee facing you, and we'll play a great little bouncing rhyme.

5. Bounce: From Wibbleton to Wobbleton
(Repeat three times.)

Talk:
When you look at your baby, you can see how much your baby is enjoying the rhyme, and he can see how much you are enjoying it too! The more we repeat the rhymes, the more the babies will know what we are doing and the more they will enjoy them. Babies love and learn through repetition.

Now lay your baby down on his back and we'll sing a little peek-a-boo song. First we'll flutter our fingers down the baby's body to imitate the rain and then we'll let the sun peek out. Get up close to your baby's face so that he can see the connection between the sounds you make and the face muscle movements that go with them. This is how babies learn how to speak, by watching us.

6. Rhyme: Mix and Stir
(Repeat three times.)

Talk:
Here is a great diaper-changing rhyme. Diaper changing can be a fussy time, so it's good to use a rhyme that will distract and entertain the baby while you do it.

7. Rhyme: Wiggle Waggle
(Repeat three times.)

Talk:
Here is another nice rhyme to use at diaper-changing time or any time.

8. Rhyme: Round and Round the Garden
(Repeat three times.)

Talk:
Here is a great song you can use to bounce and dance with your baby. Stand up and dance if you need to jiggle the baby, or you can clap along with me. By the way, calico is a cotton cloth.

9. Song: What'll I do with the Baby-o?
(chorus and one verse: dress her up in calico)
(Repeat three times.)

Talk:
Now take your baby in your arms and we'll say a face-touching rhyme. Babies love to have their faces touched, don't they? And they learn the names for their facial features too.

10. Face Rhyme: The Moon is Round
(Repeat three times.)

Talk:
Now while you're holding your baby close we'll sing a soothing lullaby. Singing will calm your baby whenever you do it, not just at bedtime.

11. Lullaby: Ho, Ho, Watanay

Talk:
And now we're ready for a story. I love this one because it so perfectly describes what a baby is like.

12. Read-aloud Story: Baby Knows Best

Talk:
It's just about time for us to say goodbye now, so let's play "A Smooth Road" again. Would you like me to repeat any others? Don't worry if you can't remember them all when you go home. We will repeat them again next week, and add some new ones. By the end of our ten-week program, you will know them all.

13. Repeat rhyme: A Smooth Road
(Repeat three times.)

14. Song: The Wheels on the Bus
(I hadn't planned on singing this song, but a parent has asked for it as it is her child's favourite, so I will add this to my program for this session.)

Talk:
Here is another bouncing rhyme. Babies love the pause at the end.

15. Bounce: Tick Tock
(Repeat three times.)

Talk:
It's time for us to say goodbye. I look forward to seeing you all again next week at this same time. I've brought in some baby board books and some read-aloud books you can borrow if you like. Don't forget to get your baby her first library card!

16. Song: Bell Horses
(Bring out a tambourine, shake as you sing, ending at "time to go away.")

17. Goodbye Everyone

(Show samples of age-appropriate books for babies, and set your box of books on the floor so babies and parents can get easy access to them.)

SOCIAL TIME

I say goodbye to each parent and baby as they leave.

RECORD KEEPING

The half hour went by very quickly today. Next week there will be less talk and more play, and I plan to add one more bounce and a circle song if we have time. One of these days when I read a short read-aloud story I will also tell the "Wide-mouthed Frog" story. I think they'd like it.

Twenty parents and their babies came. They loved standing up to jiggle with "What'll I Do with the Baby-o?" Next week I will teach "Shoofly" so we can all get up and dance together some more.

One of the parents asked me to sing "The Wheels on the Bus" today, which is her baby's favourite song so I will add that next week and invite other parents to tell me their baby's favourites too.

A couple of the parents brought their preschoolers along, so I stood up to play "Tick Tock" with them. They liked doing the stop sign.

Sample Half-Hour Program for Parents and Babies, Birth to One
Week Two: Welcome Back!

THE PLAN

1. Song: Bell Horses(with a tambourine)
2. Brief Introduction
3. Song: Come Along and Sing with Me (clap with me, stretch with me)
4. More introduction: repetition of rhymes
5. Bounce: From Wibbleton to Wobbleton
6. New Bounce: Bouncy Bouncy Baby
7. Rhyme: Mix and Stir
8. Rhyme: Wiggle Waggle
9. Song: Wheels on the Bus
10. Rhyme: Round and Round the Garden
11. Song: What'll I do with the Baby-o? *(chorus and two verses)*
12. New Circle Song: Shoofly
13. Face Rhyme: The Moon is Round
14. Lullaby: Ho, Ho, Watanay
15. Read-aloud Story: Baby Goes Beep
16. Repeat rhymes if time.
17. Bounce: Tick Tock
18. Song: Bell Horses
19. Goodbye Everyone

Conclusion: Show samples of age-appropriate books for babies

SETTING

The room has been prepared. All clutter that will distract the babies has been removed. I've brought in a collection of baby board books and some great read-alouds the parents can take home with them after the program. I've also brought library card application forms for the babies, and some rhyme resources for the parents.

SOCIAL TIME

Social time is more like a happy reunion today. The parents say they only remembered a couple of the rhymes, and they are glad I will be repeating them, and that their baby loved "A Smooth Road," etc.

THE PROGRAM

1. Song: Bell Horses
(Bring out a tambourine, and shake as you sing the whole song.)

2. Talk: (Brief Introduction)
(Repeated for those who missed last week.)
Hello everybody, my name is _____ and I'm going to be teaching you some rhymes to play with your baby today. Our program is half an hour long and we will meet every week at this same time for ten weeks to play with our babies. Take your baby on your knee and we'll sing our welcome song.

3. Welcome song: Come Along and Sing with Me (clap with me, stretch with me)

4. Talk: (More Introduction)
Each week we will sing the same songs and add new ones as the weeks go by so you will learn them. Babies love it when we repeat things for them. They quickly get to know the routine and the more you do it, the more they love it. Remember, it's okay if your baby is sleeping or crawling around. The program is for you, with your babies joining in when they are ready.

Turn your baby around so you are facing one another, and let's play a bouncing rhyme.

5. Bounce: From Wibbleton to Wobbleton
(Repeat three times.)

Talk:
I can see your babies love that rhyme! Isn't it fun? Let's play another one!

6. New Bounce: Bouncy Bouncy Baby
(Repeat three times.)

Talk:
Now lay your baby down on her back and we'll play "Mix and Stir."

7. Rhyme: Mix and Stir
(Repeat three times.)

Talk:
Now take your baby's feet in your hands and we'll play our diaper-changing rhyme. By the way, this is also a great rhyme to use to move gas in the baby's tummy. Gently push baby's knees right up against her tummy.

8. Rhyme: Wiggle Waggle
(Repeat three times.)

Talk:
One of the moms asked for the Wheels on the Bus last week, so let's sing that again. Let me know if your baby has a favourite and we can do that one too.

9. Song: Wheels on the Bus
(Pause to let parents suggest verses they want to do.)

Talk:
Last week we played a fun tickling rhyme. Let's say it again and then I'll teach you a little tune that can go with it. Draw a circle on your baby's tummy or on his hand in the beginning then move in for a little tickle.

10. Rhyme: Round and Round the Garden
(Repeat three times.)

Talk:
Let's clap and sing "Baby-o." We'll sing two verses this week.

11. Song: What'll I do with the Baby-o?
(Two verses only.)

Talk:
Now everybody stand up and I'll show you a great circle song.

12. New Circle Song: Shoofly

Talk:
Didn't the babies like coming together with the other babies! You can sing this song in front of a mirror at home too. Now let's sit down and start to snuggle in for a story.

13. Face Rhyme: The Moon is Round
(Repeat three times.)

Talk:
Now let's sing our lullaby.

14. Lullaby: Ho, Ho, Watanay

Talk:
You can personalize that lullaby for your baby by putting your own baby's name in it, like this, "Ho, ho, Natalie, ho, ho, Natalie, ho, ho, Natalie, now go to sleep, now go to sleep."

Here's a story you can read along with me.

15. Read-aloud Story: Baby Goes Beep

16. Bounce: Tick Tock
(Repeat three times.)

Talk:
Now it's time for us to start saying goodbye.

17. Song: Bell Horses
(Bring out a tambourine, shake as you sing, ending at "time to go away.")

18. Goodbye Everyone

(Show samples of age-appropriate books for babies, rhyme resources for parents, and library card application forms for the babies. Set the box of baby books on the floor so babies and parents can get easy access to them.)

SOCIAL TIME

The parents wanted to stay and nurse their babies today so I told them they could stay, and that they could come early next week too if they wanted to relax and visit in the program room.

RECORD KEEPING

Eighteen parents and their babies came. Some were new.

Many of the parents said they don't read books with their babies because they put them in their mouths. I reassured them that this is perfectly normal and to let the babies taste the books. Some of the parents who tried them last week said they were amazed at how much their babies loved them. Lots more parents took home books for their babies this week. Next week I will add a little talk about the important concepts babies learn when we read aloud to them.

Next week, I will read a short pop-up I really love, CHARLIE THE CHICKEN, and I'll tell them THE WIDE-MOUTHED FROG story.

Sample Half-Hour Program for Parents and Toddlers, One to Two
Week One: Welcome Everyone!

THE PLAN

1. Welcome Song: Up Down Turn Around
2. Brief introduction
3. Hello song: Hello, My Friends, Hello
4. More introduction
5. Bounce: A Smooth Road
6. Bounce: Mother and Father and Uncle John
7. Song: Big Blue Boat
8. Rhyme: Chicken in the Barnyard
9. Rhyme: Come a' Look a' See
10. Stand-up Rhyme: Tick Tock
11. Stand-up Rhyme:The Ponies are Walking
12. Stand-up Rhyme: Ring Around the Rosie
13. Rhyme: Here's a Cup
14. Lullaby: Fuzzy Wuzzy Caterpillar
15. Read-aloud Story: Baby Goes Beep
16. Song: Tall Trees
17. Goodbye Song: Up Down, Turn Around

Conclusion: Show samples of age-appropriate books for the toddlers.

SETTING

The room has been prepared. All clutter that will distract the toddlers has been removed. I've brought in a collection of baby board books, rhyme resources and some great read-alouds the parents can take home with them after the program.

SOCIAL TIME

I greet parents and toddlers as they come in. There will be lots of questions. The toddlers will need a few weeks to settle in to the routine. I reassure the parents.

THE PROGRAM

1. Welcome Song: Up Down Turn Around
(Repeat two or three times.)

2. Talk: (Brief Introduction)
Hello everybody, my name is _____ and I'm going to be teaching you some rhymes to play with your baby today. Our program is half an hour long and we will meet every week at this same time for ten weeks to play with our babies. Take your baby on your knee and we'll get started with a nice little hello song.

3. Hello song: Hello, My Friends, Hello

4. Talk: (More Introduction)
I'm going to be teaching you some rhymes and songs you can play with your toddlers at home. Don't worry if your toddler is walking or crawling around, toddlers need a few weeks to get used to the place, the people, and the routine. The program is for you so you can do them at home with your toddlers joining in when they are ready. I will be repeating all the rhymes so you will have a chance to learn them.

We'll start with some bouncing and rowing songs your babies will enjoy. Hold your baby on your knee facing you so you can see how much he is enjoying the rhymes and so that he can see how much you are enjoying the rhymes too.

5. Bounce: A Smooth Road
(Repeat three times.)

Talk:
One of the reasons we play with our babies

face to face is so they can see how our face muscles move when we make word sounds. Your baby will use this information to make his own first word sounds. Make sure you have eye contact, and that the baby can see you when you talk to her so she can see the connection.

Here's another fun rhyme. Bounce your baby on your lap, then lean over to one side, and then the other.

6. Bounce: Mother and Father and Uncle John
(Repeat three times.)

Talk:
This next one is a rowing song. Take your toddler by the hands and row back and forth as we sing.

7. Song: Big Blue Boat
(Repeat two times as this is a longer song.)

Talk:
Here is a great little tickling rhyme. Take your toddler's hand and draw a circle, then creep up under his arm for a little tickle at the end.

8. Rhyme: Chicken in the Barnyard
(Repeat three times.)

Talk:
Now let's play a finger rhyme. Take your toddler's hands and touch each finger like this ...

9. Rhyme: Come a' Look a' See
(Repeat three times.)

Talk:
Once your toddler becomes familiar with that rhyme, it's wonderful to use at hand-washing time. Toddlers generally don't like having their hands washed, do they? And this rhyme will keep them happy while you do it.

Let's all stand up now and play some stand-up rhymes.

10. Stand-up Rhyme: Tick Tock
(Repeat three times.)

11. Stand-up Rhyme: The Ponies are Walking
(Repeat two times as this is a longer song.)

12. Stand-up Rhyme: Ring Around the Rosie
(Repeat two or three times.)

Talk:
Let's sit down now and pretend we're having some tea. Make a teacup with your fist like this.

13. Rhyme: Here's a Cup
(Repeat three times.)

Talk:
Didn't the babies love that little finger rhyme! Now let's sing a lullaby before we have a story.

14. Lullaby: Fuzzy Wuzzy Caterpillar
(Repeat three times.)

Talk:
The story I'm going to read today is full of noisy sounds. Please join in with me. You can do the actions and make the sounds.

15. Read-aloud Story: Baby Goes Beep

Talk:
Wasn't that fun! Now let's all stand up and sing our last song before we sing goodbye.

16. Song: Tall Trees
(Repeat three times.)

Talk:
It's time to say good-bye. Let's end the way we began. And I will see you all again next week! I have set aside some books here that you and your toddler will enjoy. You can take these home with you after the program.

17. Goodbye Song: Up Down Turn Around

(Show samples of age-appropriate books for toddlers, and set your box of books on the floor so toddlers and parents can get easy access to them.)

SOCIAL TIME

I say goodbye to each parent and child, and say I look forward to seeing them again next week.

RECORD KEEPING

Fifteen parents and their toddlers came today. It seemed like a lot at first, but they were all so calm that things went smoothly. I noticed they loved the finger plays and the stand-up rhymes the best. I will use more of those.

Sample Half-Hour Program for Parents and Toddlers, One to Two
Week Two: Welcome Back!

THE PLAN

1. Welcome Song: Up Down Turn Around
2. Brief introduction
3. Hello song: Hello Everyone
4. More introduction
5. Bounce: A Smooth Road
6. Bounce: Mother and Father and Uncle John
7. Song: Big Blue Boat
8. Rhyme: Chicken in the Barnyard
9. Rhyme: Come a' Look a' See
10. New Rhyme: Whoops Johnny
11. Stand-up Rhyme: Tick Tock
12. Stand-up Rhyme: The Ponies are Walking
13. Stand-up Rhyme: Ring Around the Rosie
14. Rhyme: Here's a Cup
15. New Rhyme: Let's Go to Sleep
16. Lullaby: Fuzzy Wuzzy Caterpillar
17. Told Story: Mr. Wiggle and Mr. Waggle
18. Song: Tall Trees
19. Goodbye Song: Up Down, Turn Around

Conclusion: Show samples of age-appropriate books for the toddlers.

SETTING

The room has been prepared. All clutter that will distract the toddlers has been removed. I've brought in a collection of baby board books, rhyme resources and some great read-alouds the parents can take home with them after the program.

SOCIAL TIME

I greet parents and toddlers as they come in. The toddlers will be more settled but will still need a week or two to settle in to the routine. I reassure parents.

I ask if they enjoyed using the rhymes they learned last week. This will tell me which ones they remembered and which ones need repeating more slowly.

THE PROGRAM

1. Welcome Song: Up Down Turn Around
(Repeat two or three times.)

2. Talk: (Brief Introduction)
(Repeated from last week.)
Hello everybody, my name is _____ and I'm going to be teaching you some rhymes to play with your baby today. Our program is half an hour long and we will meet every week at this same time for ten weeks to play with our babies. Take your baby on your knee and we'll sing our hello song.

3. Hello song: Hello Everyone

4. Talk: (More Introduction)
Don't worry if your toddler is walking or crawling around, toddlers need a few weeks to get settled in to the routine. The program is for you so you can do the rhymes at home with your toddlers joining in when they are ready. I will be repeating all the rhymes so you will have a chance to learn them.

Let's start with some bouncing rhymes. Hold your baby on your knee facing you so you can see how much she is enjoying the rhymes and so she can see how much you are enjoying the rhyme too.

5. Bounce: A Smooth Road
(Repeat three times.)

6. Bounce: Mother and Father and Uncle John
(Repeat three times.)

Talk:
Now take your toddler by the hands, and row back and forth as we sing.

7. Song: Big Blue Boat
(Repeat two times.)

Talk:
Are you ready for a little tickle? Take your toddler's hand and draw a circle, then creep up under her arm for a little tickle at the end. By the way, this is a great settling rhyme for little wrigglers on the change table. Then you can draw a circle on your baby's bare tummy.

8. Rhyme: Chicken in the Barnyard
(Repeat three times.)

Talk:
Now take your toddler's hands and touch each finger as we sing.

9. Rhyme: Come a' Look a' See
(Repeat three times.)

Talk:
Last week we played some finger rhymes and I noticed the babies really liked them. Did you try them as you washed your baby's hands? I will teach you another one. Hold your baby's hand, and point to all the fingers then slide down to the thumb and back up again, like this.

10. New Rhyme: Whoops Johnny
(Repeat three times.)

Talk:
Let's say that again, only this time, say your own baby's name instead of Johnny.

(If you have a large group, repeat "Whoops Johnny" once as parents say their own baby's names. If you have a small group, go around and say all the baby's names one at a time.)

Talk:
Let's all stand up now, and we'll play some stand-up rhymes.

11. Stand-up Rhyme: Tick Tock
(Repeat three times.)

12. Stand-up Rhyme: The Ponies are Walking
(Repeat two times.)

13. Stand-up Rhyme: Ring Around the Rosie
(Repeat two or three times.)

Talk:
Let's sit down now and pretend we're having some tea.

14. Rhyme: Here's a Cup
(Repeat three times.)

Talk:
Here is another beautiful little finger rhyme we will say before we sing our lullaby.

15. New Rhyme: Let's Go to Sleep
(Repeat three times.)

Talk:
That's a wonderful rhyme to say before naptime at home. Now let's sing our lullaby.

16. Lullaby: Fuzzy Wuzzy Caterpillar
(Repeat three times.)

Talk:
The story I'm going to tell today is actually a little finger rhyme you can tell when you get home. Toddlers love it when you tell stories to them over and over again.

17. Told Story: Mr. Wiggle and Mr. Waggle

Talk:
It's almost time to go. Let's stand up and sing "Tall Trees."

18. Song: Tall Trees
(Repeat three times.)

Talk:
Now it's time to say good-bye. I will see you all again next week! Don't forget to check out some books to read to your toddler.

17. Goodbye Song: Up Down, Turn Around

(Talk briefly about the kinds of books toddlers like, and set your box of books on the floor so toddlers and parents can get easy access to them.)

SOCIAL TIME

I say goodbye to each parent and child, and say I look forward to seeing them again next week.

RECORD KEEPING

Twelve parents and their toddlers came today. Two brought their partners. The toddlers are beginning to know what to expect and are settling in. The parents are remembering some of the rhymes, and they are beginning to make friends with one another. I'm glad they are making new friends. Lots of the parents are checking out books for their toddlers. Some of the parents are asking for the words to the rhymes, so I will bring those next week, but also reassure them that they will learn them just by coming to the program.

Sprinkles:
What to Say to Parents

Introduction *224*
Bonding, Attachment, and Emotional Development *224*
Early Brain Development *225*
Communication and Language Development *226*
Early Literacy *226*
Sharing Books with Babies *226*

Briefly explaining the rationale behind what we are doing helps us build relationships with parents, and it helps them understand the importance of what they are doing for their babies when they sing, and play, and talk to them. When we do this in a gentle and informal way, we encourage the parents, empower them, and make them feel proud of the important contribution they are making to their babies' development.

INTRODUCTION

These are some of the comments I make to parents as I am doing parent-baby programs. I say them very casually before I teach a rhyme, and I repeat myself as often as needed. I don't say too much at any one time, but I sprinkle these comments throughout my programs over the days and weeks we are together. I also say these things in response to what I observe the parents need to know, and in response to their questions, so this is an interactive process.

It's important to repeat these comments from week to week. Parents attending programs with their babies are often distracted by the baby's need for attention, or by a lack of sleep, or a desire to chat for a moment with a neighbour, so it may take several repetitions before the parents actually hear what you are saying.

I try to keep it simple so that every parent understands. If a particular parent or group wants a more academic explanation, I am ready to give that too.

I find that parents generally do not know these things about their baby's development and that they are very eager to learn.

When we intersperse these little comments with the laughter and fun of playing with a group of parents and infants, we offer encouragement and explanation in a professional, yet casual, way. Parents learn why they are doing what they are doing, why it's important for them and for their baby, and as a result are motivated to continue to respond to their infants in positive ways at home.

Most of these comments fall into the categories of bonding, early brain development, and early literacy development. It should be noted, however, that many of the outcomes for these suggestions are interrelated.

BONDING: ATTACHMENT AND EMOTIONAL DEVELOPMENT

1. Hold your baby on your knee facing you, so that you can see how much your baby is enjoying the rhyme and so that your baby can see how much you are enjoying the rhyme too. Face-to-face interaction is very important.

2. Your baby learns about a whole range of human emotion from studying your face. Let your baby see your face.

3. Babies' vision is blurry at birth and so for the first couple of months you have to move in to about twelve inches away, so your baby can see you. Let your baby see your beautiful face. It is the vision she loves best in the whole world.

4. Make eye contact with your baby. We know that eye contact stimulates synapses or connections in the baby's brain, and contributes to brain development, so we want to engage them in this way often. Your baby will look away when she's had enough stimulation for the moment, and then she'll come back for more.

5. When we respond consistently and lovingly to our babies, our babies learn that they can trust us and rely on us. Building trust at this stage in life is very important, and will last you a lifetime.

6. If you can remember to use a rhyme at a fussy or difficult time, this will help distract and soothe your baby. Diaper changing can be a difficult time, so let's pretend we're changing the baby as we say "Leg Over Leg."

7. The relationship you are forming with your baby now will create the pattern for all your baby's future relationships with people. Happiness later in life begins with a strong connection between you and your baby now.

8. When we see things from the baby's point of view, and respond to him accordingly, we are teaching him self-esteem. We are also teaching him by example how to have empathy with others. Babies naturally have empathy with others. Have you noticed that? When one cries, they all cry, or look sad. Isn't that remarkable? Let's help him keep that ability to empathize by showing empathy for him.

9. Your baby's hearing is very sensitive. Hearing is the baby's most highly developed sense at birth, in fact babies can hear you months before they are born when they are still in the womb. Maybe that's why they find the sound of your voice so comforting now.

10. Sing whenever you can, especially during troubled times. The singing voice calms and reassures your baby, and will certainly get his attention when other methods of soothing him have failed. (Follow up by singing a lullaby when one of the babies is crying or fussy in a program. Show the parents how this works. It's magic, and it's so easy.)

11. Remember to sing. And remember, your voice is the most important sound in your baby's world. It doesn't matter what you think it sounds like. Your voice is the voice your baby loves the best.

EARLY BRAIN DEVELOPMENT

1. Touch your baby gently but firmly. Stroking will comfort and calm your baby.

2. Physical touch releases chemicals in the baby's brain that will make her feel good. Physical touch is important for your baby's mental and physical development. Let's hold our babies close and rock them as we sing this lullaby.

3. Repeat the rhymes often at home. Even very young babies will understand the game you are playing with them with lots of repetition. Once the baby knows the game, he will let you know he knows it by moving his body in a particular way to let you know he understands. He will also move his body in a particular rhythm to let you know he wants you to play a particular rhyme. This happens long before he can speak. Repetition is the key to success.

4. (Baby's name) seems upset now, so let's say this calming rhyme together and see if it helps her. Let's say "Slice, Slice." (When you respond to a fussy child in a program in this way you are showing the parents how to be receptive to their babies' needs in the moment. This usually works and calms the baby. If it doesn't work, I ask the parent for the child's favourite rhyme and we all sing that together. It has to be a rhyme the baby is familiar with.)

5. I like this rhyme ("Tick Tock") because it teaches the baby how to gain some self-control. Self-regulation is something the baby needs to learn. So when we say 'stop' and hold still for a moment, the baby learns how to stop, and hold still for a moment too, and he enjoys it! Babies find this little game very amusing.

COMMUNICATION AND LANGUAGE DEVELOPMENT

1. Talking to your baby in that high-pitched cooing and babbling voice we all use when we talk to babies encourages your baby to communicate with you. Linguists call this "parentese" or "motherese." Imitate his sounds, and he will imitate you back. This way you can have a "chat" with him, long before he can say words. He is practicing the language sounds and the turn-taking of conversation.

2. Talking to your baby, and listening to your baby when she makes sounds, will encourage her to learn to talk.

3. When a baby is born, he is so sensitive and open to learning language that he is capable of hearing and learning to speak any speech patterns of any language spoken in the world! It is through constant practice, and the exchange of sounds with you, that your baby will learn your language.

4. Babies learn languages much more easily than adults do because their brains are so receptive to the sounds of language in the beginning. This is a skill we all lose as we get older.

5. If you speak a first language that is different from English at home, use that language to speak to your baby. Speak the language that you know best. It is better for children to have a good grasp of grammar and vocabulary in any language than it is for them to learn poor English. They will learn English later as they play with other children and families who speak English.

EARLY LITERACY

1. We know that literacy begins in infancy, and it begins with the communication between you and your child. The patterns of speech and language that you are using now will help your baby learn how to speak. Later on, when the time comes, these language activities will help him learn how to read too.

2. Rhyming words are important to say to your baby. We know that children who can hear and say words with rhyme sounds and alliteration sounds are the children who will find it easy to learn how to read later on. Use rhyming words with your baby.

3. Bounce your baby to the beat of the rhyme. When we use beat in this way, we are helping the baby absorb the rhythms of our language with her whole body.

4. Sing to your baby. Songs often have different notes for each syllable in a word, so children who are sung to hear these different sounds, and they find it easy to learn how to break words into sound groups later on when they come to reading.

5. The vocabulary we use in these rhymes will often be the first words your baby learns to say. What a rich vocabulary these babies will have! Knowing the meaning of many words will help your child learn how to read later on.

SHARING BOOKS WITH BABIES

1. Your baby puts everything in his mouth because that's the way he explores his world. The mouth is the baby's primary sense organ, so everything of interest to him must be tasted and tested in this way. Let him taste those books! Board books are created with this kind of use in mind.

2. When we share books with our babies, babies learn important things about literacy that will help them love books and reading for the rest of their lives. They learn that books are interesting toys; they learn that books are about people like them; they learn basic concepts like upside down and right side up, front and back, and they learn that pages in books are turned from right to left. These are all things the baby has to learn before she can learn how to read. Later on, as your child learns how to read, you can help her with this concept too by tracking the print or moving your finger under the words in the sentences to show her that print in our culture moves across the page from left to right—the opposite to the way we turn pages. Hey, this is complicated!

3. When we read aloud to babies, and talk about the pictures they see, babies learn all kinds of vocabulary, and they learn that there are many interesting things to talk about in any one book.

4. The very first books that babies love are books of baby faces like this one by Margaret Miller, and the high contrast black and white books like this one by Tana Hoban. There is so much to talk about when you look at the pictures together. Take these ones home to try, and see what happens. I think your baby will love them.

5. Children who are read to often are the children who will grow up reading. Try to make reading aloud to your baby a part of your daily routine. Now is the best time to start.

6. When reading aloud is a shared activity with a loving adult, reading is always remembered as a warm and loving experience.

Program Resources

Books About Babies for Older Brothers and Sisters *230*
Great Read-Alouds for Baby Programs *233*
Rhyme Resources *235*
Parenting Resources *237*
Sample Parent Response Form *239*

Books about Babies for Older Brothers and Sisters

A great way to introduce children to the various delights and responses that are possible with a new baby is to share books about new babies with the whole family before the baby arrives. Not only do these stories provide insights and comfort for very young children who will see themselves and their feelings represented in the stories, the books can also give parents insights about their children's feelings, and give them ideas for things they can say and do to help their older children adjust to the changes the new baby will bring to the family. Transitions are always easier for young children when they know what to expect.

FICTION

Anderson, Rachel. HELLO PEANUT! Illustrated by Debbie Harter. London: Hodder Children's Books, 2003.
A toddler watches her mother's tummy grow bigger and bigger until the birth day. Slight, but appropriate for toddlers.

Bloom, Valerie. NEW BABY. Illustrated by David Axtell. London: Macmillan, 2000.
A young Caribbean boy is fed up with his new baby sister and he wants his mama to take her back and buy a different one, until the baby smiles at him.

Henderson, Kathy. BABY KNOWS BEST. Illustrated by Brita Granstrom. Boston: Little, Brown and Co., 2001.
An excellent read-aloud. Special toys and books and clothes and food are offered to baby to make her happy, but baby has a mind of her own. Rhyming text is complemented by lively and fresh watercolours.

Cutler, Jane. DARCY AND GRAN DON'T LIKE BABIES. Illustrated by Susannah Ryan. New York: Scholastic Inc., 1993.
Darcy and Gran are not happy about the idea of a new baby coming, but they change their minds after the birth.

Gray, Kes. BABY ON BOARD. Illustrated by Sarah Nayler. New York: Simon and Schuster, 2003.
A light-hearted and humourous countdown through the nine months until the new baby arrives.

Harris, Robie H. HAPPY BIRTH DAY! Illustrated by Michael Emberley. Cambridge, MA: Candlewick, 1996.
Large full-page illustrations show children what it was like in the first moments on the day they were born, and how much they were loved, right from the start.

Harris, Robie H. HI NEW BABY! Illustrated by Michael Emberley. Cambridge, MA: Candlewick, 2000.
A father recalls his preschool daughter's first reactions to her new baby brother. She isn't so sure she likes him, at first.

Henderson, Kathy. NEW BORN. Illustrated by Caroline Binch. London: Frances Lincoln, 1999.
A family lovingly tells their new baby about all the sights and sounds in her new world. Lots of illustrations of everyone holding the baby.

Henkes, Kevin. JULIUS, THE BABY OF THE WORLD. New York: Greenwillow Books, 1990.
Lilly is convinced that the arrival of her new baby brother, Julius, is the worst thing that has happened in their house, until Cousin Garland comes to visit, and then we see Lilly at her big-sister finest.

Hiatt, Fred. BABY TALK. Illustrated by Mark Graham. Margaret K. McElderry Books, 1990.
Joey, a preschooler, finds out he can connect with his new baby brother by learning to speak his own special language (baby talk) and he becomes the baby's interpreter for the family. Good for very young siblings.

Leuck, Laura. MY BABY BROTHER HAS TEN TINY TOES. Illustrated by Clara Vulliamy. Morton Grove, Illinois: Alvert Whitman, 1997.
A simple counting story in rhyme in which a preschooler plays with her baby brother and his things.

Lund, Deb. Illustrated by Hidroe Nakata. TELL ME MY STORY, MAMA. New York: Harper Collins, 2004.
As they look forward to the arrival of a new baby, a mother tells her young daughter of the time when they waited for her to be born.

Rockwell, Lizzy. HELLO BABY! New York: Crown, 1999.
Just the right book to show young children what to expect when mom's expecting. Shows simple illustrations of the baby's development in the womb.

Scott, Ann Herbert. ON MOTHER'S LAP. Illustrated by Glo Coalson. New York: Clarion Books, 1992.
A classic. A small Inuit boy discovers that Mother's lap is a very special place with room for everyone.

NONFICTION

Cole, Joanna. THE NEW BABY AT YOUR HOUSE. Photographs by Margaret Miller. New York : Morrow Junior Books, 1998.
Describes the activities and changes involved in having a new baby in the house, and the feelings experienced by the older brothers and sisters.

Deveny, Catherine. Photographs by Mario Borg. OUR NEW BABY. Melbourne, Aust.: Lothian, 2004.
A five-year-old explains pregnancy, labour and the birth of his new baby brother.

Douglas, Ann. BABY SCIENCE: HOW BABIES REALLY WORK! Toronto: Greey de Pencier Books, 1998.
This is a simply wonderful book for older siblings on how babies work and what they can and can't do. Lots of colour photos. Just right for children in primary grades.

Harris, Robie H. HELLO BENNY! WHAT IT'S LIKE TO BE A BABY. Illustrated by Michael Emberley. New York: Margaret K. McElderry, 2002.
Covers all the things Benny or any baby learns in the first year of life. Includes information about infant development that older siblings will understand.

Lasky, Kathryn. LOVE THAT BABY!: A BOOK ABOUT BABIES FOR NEW BROTHERS, SISTER, COUSINS, AND FRIENDS.Illustrated by Jennifer Plecas. Cambridge, MS: Candlewick Press, 2004.
Lots of pictures of preschool children doing things with the new baby. Has enough detail to be interesting and instructive to young children.

Rogers, Fred. THE NEW BABY. Photographs by Jim Judkis. New York: Putnam, 1985.
Explains the needs of toddlers faced with a new baby in the family, and some of the changes and disruptions the baby can cause in the life of an older brother or sister. Very reassuring.
Sears, William. BABY ON THE WAY. Illustrated by Tenee Andriani. Boston: Little, Brown and Co, 2001.
An excellent book for preschoolers and young children. Describes pregnancy, and the family's preparations for the new baby, in a joyful and loving way. There is one illustration of a fetus in the uterus, but the focus is on family preparations.

Stein, Sara. OH, BABY! Photographs by Holly Anne Shelowitz. New York: Walker and Co., 1993.
A perfect introduction for toddlers. Lots of colour photographs of families with babies. Includes simple descriptions of baby's activities.

VIDEOS TO WATCH AND TALK ABOUT TOGETHER

The following two videos offer help for sibling rivalry.

HEY, WHAT ABOUT ME? Writers, Jane Murphy, Karen Tucker. Newton, MA : Kidvidz, 1987.
1 videocassette (VHS) 25 mins.
Shows older brothers and sisters what they might feel with a new baby at home by watching three children with their new babies. Demonstrates games, lullabies, and bouncing rhymes that children can play with their new babies.

OH BABY: A GUIDE FOR BIG BROTHERS AND BIG SISTERS. (THOSE BABY BLUES: A PARENTS' GUIDE TO HELPING YOUR CHILD ADJUST TO THE NEW BABY.) Producer, Lorrie Garcia-Cottrell. Skydance Productions, 1994. 2 videocassettes (VHS) 60 mins.
Offers guidance about how to help older siblings adjust to a new baby.

Great Read-Alouds for Baby Programs

Baker, Keith. BIG FAT HEN. San Diego: Harcourt Brace, 1994.
Big Fat Hen counts to ten with her friends, and all their chicks. Big, bold deep colours.

Blackstone, Stella. BEAR AT HOME. Illustrated by Debbie Harter. New York: Barefoot Books, 2001.

Brown, Margaret Wise. GOOD NIGHT MOON. Illustrated by Clement Hurd. New York: Harper, 1947.
A little bunny says good night to each of the objects in the great green room: good night chairs, good night comb, good night air. A classic.

Brown, Margaret Wise. THE GOOD NIGHT MOON ROOM. New York: Harper and Row, 1984.
Pop-up.

Campbell, Rod. THIS BABY! London: Campbell Books, 1997.
Lift-the-flap.

Carter, David A. IF YOU'RE HAPPY AND YOU KNOW IT, CLAP YOUR HANDS! New York: Scholastic, 1997.
A happy sing-along. Pop-up.

Cimarusti, Marie Torres. PEEK-A-BOOOO! Illustrated by Stephanie Peterson. New York: Dutton, 2005.
Halloween theme. Big bold illustrations, great sound effects. Pop-up.

Cimarusti, Marie Torres. PEEK-A-MOO! Illustrated by Stephanie Peterson. New York: Dutton, 1998.
Big bold illustrations, great sound effects. Pop-up. The first book in this series.

Cimarusti, Marie Torres. PEEK-A-PET! Illustrated by Stephanie Peterson. New York: Dutton, 2005.
Same format, pop-up, with familiar animals.

Cimarusti, Marie Torres. PEEK-A- ZOO! Illustrated by Stephanie Peterson. New York: Dutton Children's Books, 2003.
Pop-up.

Cooke, Trish. SO MUCH! Illustrated by Helen Oxenbury. Cambridge, MA: Candlewick Press, 1994
Relatives arriving in succession give in to their desire to squeeze, and kiss, and play with the baby.

Crews, Donald. FREIGHT TRAIN. New York: Greenwillow Books, 1978.
Brief text and illustrations trace the journey of a colourful train as it goes through tunnels, by cities, and over trestles. Add a rhythmic "chugga chugga chooo choo" as you turn the pages.

Denchfield, Nick and Ant Parker. CHARLIE THE CHICKEN: A POP-UP BOOK. London: Macmillan, 1997. Also San Diego, CA: Harcourt Brace, 1997.
Charlie the chicken eats lots of healthy food so he will grow big and strong. Pop-up.

Denchfield, Nick and Ant Parker. DESMOND THE DOG: A WAG-THE-TAIL POP-UP BOOK. London: Macmillan, 1997. Also San Diego, CA: Harcourt Brace, 1997.
Desmond is a good dog until someone teaches him that being bad can be fun. Pop-up.

Denchfield, Nick and Ant Parker. TWO LITTLE DICKY BIRDS: A POP-UP BOOK. London: Macmillan, 1999.
A pop-up of the popular rhyme.

Faulkner, Keith. THE WIDE-MOUTHED FROG: A POP-UP BOOK. Ills. by Jonathan Lambert. New York: Dial Books for Young Readers, 1996.
A wide-mouthed frog is interested in what other animals eat—until he meets a creature that eats only wide-mouthed frogs!

Henderson, Kathy. BABY KNOWS BEST. Illustrated by Brita Granstrom. Boston: Little, Brown and Co., 2001. Originally published: London: Transworld Publishers.
Baby is presented with food, and books, and toys the family thinks she will like, but baby wants what everybody else has! Hilarious and charming.

Intrater, Roberta Grobel. PEEK-A-BOO YOU! New York: Scholastic, 2002.

McDonnell, Flora. GIDDY UP, LET'S RIDE! Cambridge, MA: Candlewick Press, 2002.
Describes ways people ride horses and other animals, such as the show jumper on her trrrit-trrroting horse, the raja on his rumpetta-trumping elephant, and the nomad on his lolloppy-plodding camel.

McDonnell, Flora. I LOVE ANIMALS. Cambridge, MA: Candlewick Press, 1994.
A girl names all the animals she likes on her farm, from Jock the dog to the pig and her piglets.

McDonnell, Flora. I LOVE BOATS. Cambridge, MA: Candlewick Press, 1995.
A girl names all the boats she likes to play with in the bath.

McDonnell, Flora. SPLASH! Cambridge, MA: Candlewick Press, 1999.
When the jungle animals are hot, a baby elephant has a good solution involving the squirting and splashing of water at the water hole.

Martin, Bill. BROWN BEAR, BROWN BEAR,WHAT DO YOU SEE? Illustrated by Eric Carle. New York : H. Holt, 1992. Originally published: New York: Holt, Rinehart, and Winston, 1967.
Sing this one. Large illustrations of a variety of animals, each one a different colour.

O'Connell, Rebecca. THE BABY GOES BEEP. Illustrated by Ken Wilson-Max. Brookfield, CT: Roaring Brook Press, 2003.
A baby makes various sounds as he explores the world around him. A great participation story.

Price, Mathew and Jean Claverie. PEEKABOO! New York: Alfred A. Knopf, 1985.
This book may be out of print, but it's excellent for baby programs. Pop-up.

Rowe, Jeanette. WHOSE EARS? Boston: Little, Brown and Co., 1999.

Rowe, Jeanette. WHOSE NOSE? Sydney: ABC Books, 1998. Also: Boston: Little, Brown and Co.

Rowe, Jeanette. WHOSE FEET? Boston: Little, Brown and Co., 1998.

Shaw, Charles Green. IT LOOKED LIKE SPILT MILK. New York: Harper 1947.
A thoughtful and calming classic. Get parents to join in. Simple white shapes on a blue background.

Walsh, Melanie. MY BEAK, YOUR BEAK. Boston: Houghton Mifflin, 2002.
Looks at what pairs of animals have in common, despite their obvious differences, such as sharks swimming in the deep ocean, and goldfish swimming in a bowl, both blowing bubbles.

Zelinsky, Paul O. THE WHEELS ON THE BUS. New York: Dutton Children's Books, 1990.
The traditional song adapted and illustrated by Paul Zelinsky. Pop-up.

Rhyme Resources for Parents

BOOKS

Chorao, Kay. KNOCK AT THE DOOR: AND OTHER BABY ACTION RHYMES. New York: Dutton, 1999.

Cole, Joanna. PAT-A-CAKE AND OTHER PLAY RHYMES. New York: Morrow Junior Books, 1992.

Emerson, Sally, comp. THE NURSERY TREASURY: A COLLECTION OF BABY GAMES, RHYMES AND LULLABIES. Illustrated by Moira and Colin Maclean. New York: Doubleday, 1988.

McGee, Shelagh. I'M A LITTLE TEAPOT: GAMES, RHYMES, AND SONGS FOR THE FIRST THREE YEARS. New York: Doubleday, 1992.

Ra, Carol. TROT, TROT, TO BOSTON: PLAY RHYMES FOR BABY. Lothrop, 1987. (sadly out of print.)

Williams, Sarah. RIDE A COCK-HORSE: KNEE-JOGGING RHYMES, PATTING SONGS AND LULLABIES. Illustrated by Ian Beck. Oxford: Oxford University Press, 1986.

Williams, Sarah. ROUND AND ROUND THE GARDEN: PLAY RHYMES FOR YOUNG CHILDREN. Illustrated by Ian Beck. Oxford: Oxford University Press, 1984.

Wilner, Isabel. THE BABY'S GAME BOOK. Illustrated by Sam Williams. New York: Greenwillow Books, 2000.

CDS AND CASSETTES

McGrath, Bob and Katharine Smithrim. THE BABY RECORD. Toronto: Kids' Records, 2003. (CD)

McGrath, Bob and Katharine Smithrim. SONGS AND GAMES FOR TODDLERS. Toronto: Kids' Records, 1985. (cassette)

Reid-Naiman, Kathy. TICKLES AND TUNES. Aurora, ON: Merriweather Records, 1994.

Reid-Naiman, Kathy. MORE TICKLES & TUNES. Aurora, ON: Merriweather Records, 1997.

Reid-Naiman, Kathy. ON MY WAY TO DREAMLAND. Aurora, ON: Merriweather Records, 2002.

Reid-Naiman, Kathy. SAY HELLO TO THE MORNING. Aurora, ON: Merriweather Records, 1999.

Reid-Naiman, Kathy. A SMOOTH ROAD TO LONDON TOWN: SONGS FROM THE PARENT-CHILD MOTHER GOOSE PROGRAM. Aurora, ON: Merriweather Records, 2001.

Williams, Sarah. RIDE A COCK-HORSE: KNEE-JOGGING RHYMES, PATTING SONGS AND LULLABIES. Illustrated by Ian Beck. Oxford: Oxford University Press, 1986.

Williams, Sarah. ROUND AND ROUND THE GARDEN. Illustrated by Ian Beck. Oxford: Oxford University Press, 1987.

BOOKS WITH CDS OR CASSETTES

Beall, Pamela. WEE SING FOR BABY. Los Angeles, CA: Price, Stern, Sloan, 1996. (cassette)

Beall, Pamela Conn and Susan Hagen Nipp. WEE SING NURSERY RHYMES. Los Angeles: Price, Stern, Sloan, 1999. (cassette)

Williams, Sarah. RIDE A COCK-HORSE: KNEE-JOGGING RHYMES, PATTING SONGS AND LULLABIES. Illustrated by Ian Beck. Oxford: Oxford University Press, 1986. (cassette)

Williams, Sarah. ROUND AND ROUND THE GARDEN. Illustrated by Ian Beck. Oxford: Oxford University Press, 1987. (cassette)

Yolen, Jane. THIS LITTLE PIGGY: AND OTHER RHYMES TO SING AND PLAY. Illustrated by Will Hillenbrand. Cambridge, MA: Candlewick Press, 2005. (CD)

VIDEOS

Jaeger, Sally. FROM WIBBLETON TO WOBBLETON. Toronto: 49 North Productions, 1998.
(From birth to 24 months.)

Jaeger, Sally. MR. BEAR SAYS HELLO. Toronto : 49 North Productions, 2000.
(For parents of infants from 12 months to 4 years.)

MUSIC BOOKS

Cass-Beggs, Barbara. YOUR BABY NEEDS MUSIC. Vancouver: Douglas and McIntyre, 1978.

Emerson, Sally. THE KINGFISHER NURSERY RHYME SONGBOOK: WITH EASY MUSIC TO PLAY FOR PIANO AND GUITAR. New York: Kingfisher Books, 1992.

Glazer, Tom. THE MOTHER GOOSE SONG BOOK. Illustrated by David McPhail. New York: Doubleday, 1990.

Larrick, Nancy, comp. SONGS FROM MOTHER GOOSE: WITH THE TRADITIONAL MELODY FOR EACH. Illustrated by Nancy Larrick. New York: Harper and Row, 1989.

Matterson, Elizabeth. THIS LITTLE PUFFIN… NURSERY SONGS AND RHYMES. London, England: Penguin Books, 1969. (Revised editions offer slightly different collections.)

NURSERY RHYME COLLECTIONS

Childs, Sam. THE RAINBOW BOOK OF NURSERY RHYMES. London: Hutchinson, 2001.

Gliori, Debi. THE DORLING KINDERSLEY BOOK OF NURSERY RHYMES. New York: Dorling Kindersley, 2000.

Denton, Kady MacDonald. A CHILD'S TREASURY OF NURSERY RHYMES. Toronto: Kids Can Press, 1998.

Jaques, Faith. THE ORCHARD BOOK OF NURSERY RHYMES. New York: Orchard Books, 1990.

Long, Sylvia. SYLVIA LONG'S MOTHER GOOSE. San Francisco: Chronicle Books, 1999.

Wells, Rosemary. MY VERY FIRST MOTHER GOOSE. Edited by Iona Opie. Cambridge, MA: Candlewick Press, 1996.

Wells, Rosemary. HERE COMES MOTHER GOOSE. Edited by Iona Opie. Cambridge, MA: Candlewick Press, 1999.

Parenting Resources

Eliot, Lise. WHAT'S GOING ON IN THERE?: HOW THE BRAIN AND MIND DEVELOP IN THE FIRST FIVE YEARS OF LIFE. New York: Bantam Books, 1999. 533 pages.

Fenwick, Elizabeth. CANADIAN MEDICAL ASSOCIATION COMPLETE BOOK OF MOTHER and BABY CARE: A PARENTS' PRACTICAL HANDBOOK FROM CONCEPTION TO THREE YEARS. Medical editor Catherine Younger-Lewis. Toronto: Dorling Kindersley, 2002. 264 pages.

Gopnik, Alison, Andrew N. Meltzoff, Patricia K. Kuhl. THE SCIENTIST IN THE CRIB: MINDS, BRAINS, AND HOW CHILDREN LEARN. New York: W. Morrow and Co, 1999. 279 pages.

Hogg, Tracy. THE BABY WHISPERER SOLVES ALL YOUR PROBLEMS (BY TEACHING YOU HOW TO ASK THE RIGHT QUESTIONS): SLEEPING, FEEDING AND BEHAVIOR—BEYOND THE BASICS THROUGH INFANCY AND TODDLERHOOD. New York: Atria Books, 2005. 402 pages.

Kitzinger, Sheila. Photography by Marcia May. THE COMPLETE BOOK OF PREGNANCY and CHILDBIRTH. New York: Alfred A. Knopf, 2004. 448 pages. Beautiful colour photographs.

Leach, Penelope. BABYHOOD: STAGE BY STAGE, FROM BIRTH TO AGE TWO : HOW YOUR BABY DEVELOPS PHYSICALLY, EMOTIONALLY, MENTALLY. New York: Knopf: Distributed by Random House, 1983. 413 pages.

Linden, Dana Wechsler. PREEMIES: THE ESSENTIAL GUIDE FOR PARENTS OF PREMATURE BABIES. New York; Toronto: Pocket Books, 2000. 578 pages.

Murkoff, Heidi, Arlene Eisenberg and Sandee Hathaway. WHAT TO EXPECT WHEN YOU'RE EXPECTING. New York: Workman Pub, 2002. 597 pages.

Murkoff, Heidi, Arlene Eisenberg and Sandee Hathaway. WHAT TO EXPECT THE FIRST YEAR. New York: Workman Pub, 2003. 806 pages.

Murkoff, Heidi, Arlene Eisenberg and Sandee Hathaway. WHAT TO EXPECT THE TODDLER YEARS. New York: Workman Pub, 1994. 904 pages.

Ramey, Craig T. RIGHT FROM BIRTH: BUILDING YOUR CHILD'S FOUNDATION FOR LIFE: BIRTH TO 18 MONTHS. New York: Goddard Press, 1999. 261 pages.

Sears, William, M.D. and Martha Sears. THE BABY BOOK: EVERYTHING YOU NEED TO KNOW ABOUT YOUR BABY— FROM BIRTH TO AGE TWO. Boston: Little, Brown, 2003. 767 pages.

Sears, Robert W., M.D. and James M. Sears, M.D. FATHER'S FIRST STEPS: 25 THINGS EVERY NEW DAD SHOULD KNOW. Boston: Harvard Common Press, 2006.

Small, Meredith F. OUR BABIES, OURSELVES: HOW BIOLOGY AND CULTURE SHAPE THE WAY WE PARENT. New York: Anchor Books, 1998.

Spock, Benjamin. DR. SPOCK'S BABY AND CHILD CARE: A HANDBOOK FOR PARENTS OF DEVELOPING CHILDREN FROM BIRTH THROUGH ADOLESCENCE. New York: Pocket Books, 2004. 967 pages.

Spock, Benjamin. DR. SPOCK'S THE FIRST TWO YEARS: THE EMOTIONAL AND PHYSICAL NEEDS OF CHILDREN FROM BIRTH TO AGE TWO. New York: Pocket Books, 2001. 153 pages.

VIDEOS

Brazelton, T. Berry and Joseph Pipher. TOUCHPOINTS, THE BRAZELTON STUDY. VOLUME 1, PREGNANCY TO THE FIRST WEEKS. New York: Goodtimes Home Video, 1991. (VHS, 50 minutes.)

Brazelton, T. Berry and Joseph Pipher. TOUCHPOINTS, THE BRAZELTON STUDY. VOLUME 2, FIRST MONTHS TO ONE YEAR. Old Greenwich, CT: Pipher Films, Inc.; East Hampton, NY: ConsumerVision, Inc. (distributor), 1991. (VHS , 50 minutes.)

Brazelton, T. Berry and Joseph Pipher. TOUCHPOINTS, THE BRAZELTON STUDY. VOLUME 3, ONE YEAR TO TODDLERHOOD. Old Greenwich, CT: Pipher Films, Inc: ConsumerVision, Inc. (distributor), 1991. (VHS , 50 minutes.)

THE FIRST YEARS LAST FOREVER. I AM YOUR CHILD series. New Screen Concepts in association with the Reiner Foundation; Johnson & Johnson. Skillman, NJ: Johnson & Johnson, 1987. (VHS , 30 minutes.)
Covers bonding, attachment, communication, health and nutrition, discipline, self-esteem, child care and self-awareness. 30 mins. Order from Canadian Institute of Child Health, 885 Meadowlands Dr., Suite 512, Ottawa, ON K2C 3N2, Tel: 613-224-4144.

Giangreco, Kathy. TEN THINGS EVERY CHILD NEEDS/ produced by WTTW/Chicago and The Chicago Production Center for Robert R. McCormick Tribune Foundation ; written and produced by Kathy Giangreco. U.S.: Robert R. McCormick Tribune Foundation, 1997. (VHS 60 minutes.)
Describes what every child needs for optimal brain development: interaction; touch; a stable relationship with a loving adult; a safe, healthy environmnt; self-esteem; quality child care; communication; play; music; and reading. Each need is expressed clearly and sympathetically from the child's point of view.

Hogg, Tracy. THE BABY WHISPERER: HOW TO CALM, CONNECT AND COMMUNICATE WITH YOUR BABY. Beverly Hills, CA: Trinity Home Entertainment: Distributed by Twentieth Century Fox Home Entertainment, 2002. (VHS, 74 minutes.)

PRECIOUS MINDS: NURTURING LITERACY IN THE EARLY YEARS. Ottawa: Kiwanis Club of Ottawa (Canada), 2000. (VHS, 15 minutes.)
Shows caregivers why and how they should expose children to literacy during the first three years of life. Order from: Kiwanis Club of Ottawa (Canada), Suite 601, 63 Sparks St., Ottawa, ON Canada K1P 5Z6, Tel: 613-233-1900.

A SIMPLE GIFT: COMFORTING YOUR BABY. Toronto: The Hospital for Sick Children, 1998. (VHS , 11 minutes.)
Shows parents and caregivers how to respond to baby's cues of distress, and emphasizes the importance of providing comfort when baby is emotionally upset, hurt, or sick, to create healthy attachment between parent and child. Also shows how infants are likely to interpret the responses of caregivers. Order from: Centre for Health Information and Promotion, The Hospital for Sick Children, 555 University Ave., Toronto, ON Canada M5G 1X8, Tel: 416-813-5819.

Sample Parent Response Form

The Mission Hill Mother Goose Program
Fall 2006
Parent Response Form

Thank you for your participation in our program!

1. How did you find out about the program?

2. What has coming to the program done for you?

3. What changes would make the program better?

4. What will you miss most when the program is not running?

5. What other programs in the community do you attend with your baby?

6. What would you like us to say about the program when we are seeking funding and other support?

7. Any other suggestions?

If you want to, please give us your contact information so that we can contact you about future programs.

Name:____

Address:____

Postal Code: ______________ Telephone: _______________ Email: ____________________

______ Please check on this line if we may quote you when we are seeking funding for more programs and for our reports.

Selected Bibliography

Bibliographies for each of the topics discussed in this book are printed at the end of each relevant section. They are not repeated here.

LIBRARY PROGRAMS FOR INFANTS

Some of the books listed here are old but worth reading for an historical perspective on library programming for babies and their caregivers.

DeSalvo, Nancy. BEGINNING WITH BOOKS: LIBRARY PROGRAMMING FOR INFANTS, TODDLERS AND PRESCHOOLERS. Hamden, Conn: Shoestring Press, 1993.

Ernst, Linda L. LAPSIT SERVICES FOR THE VERY YOUNG: A HOW-TO-DO-IT MANUAL New York: Neal Schuman, 1995.

Ghoting, Saroj Nadkarni and Pamela Martin-Diaz. EARLY LITERACY STORYTIMES @YOUR LIBRARY: PARTNERING WITH CAREGIVERS FOR SUCCESS. Chicago: American Library Association, 2006.

Greene, Ellin. BOOKS, BABIES, AND LIBRARIES. Chicago: American Library Association, 1991.

Jeffery, Debby Ann. LITERATE BEGINNINGS: PROGRAMS FOR BABIES AND TODDLERS. Chicago, IL: American Library Association, 1995.

Marino, Jane, and Dorothy F. Houlihan. MOTHER GOOSE TIME: LIBRARY PROGRAMS FOR BABIES AND THEIR CAREGIVERS. New York: H.W. Wilson, 1992.

Nespeca, Sue McCleaf. LIBRARY PROGRAMS FOR FAMILIES WITH YOUNG CHILDREN. New York: Neal-Schuman Publishers, Inc., 1994.

INDISPENSABLE RECORDINGS FOR LEARNING SONGS TO SING TO BABIES

There are lots of good sound recordings you can listen to to learn baby songs and rhymes. This short list will get you off to a great start.

McGrath, Bob and Katharine Smithrim. THE BABY RECORD. Toronto: Kids' Records, 2003.

Reid-Naiman, Kathy. TICKLES AND TUNES. Aurora, ON: Merriweather Records, 1994.

Reid-Naiman, Kathy. MORE TICKLES & TUNES. Aurora, ON: Merriweather Records, 1997.

Reid-Naiman, Kathy. ON MY WAY TO DREAMLAND. Aurora, ON: Merriweather Records, 2002.

Reid-Naiman, Kathy. SAY HELLO TO THE MORNING. Aurora, ON: Merriweather Records, 1999.

Reid-Naiman, Kathy. A SMOOTH ROAD TO LONDON TOWN: SONGS FROM THE PARENT-CHILD MOTHER GOOSE PROGRAM. Aurora, ON: Merriweather Records, 2001.

Kathy Reid-Naiman's CDs are available at most public libraries and can be obtained at: www.merriweather.ca.

Acknowledgements

Every effort has been made to trace the ownership of all copyright material and to secure the necessary permissions to reprint the material. The publisher would like to express apologies for any inadvertent errors or omissions. If you notice an error or omission, please contact us at publisher@blacksheeppress.com.

The baby board book on the front cover was designed by Jeremy Syme using images from Microsoft Media Elements.

Grateful acknowledgement is made to the following for permission to reprint the copyrighted material listed below:

"All Little Ones are Sleeping" © Jean Ritchie Geordie Music Publishing Co. With permission of the author.

"The Baby Bear Waltz" © Sally Jaeger and Kathy Reid-Naiman. With permission of the authors.

"The Bear and the Bees" from DINOSAUR DINNER (WITH A SLICE OF ALLIGATOR PIE) by Dennis Lee, copyright Compilation © 1997 by Alfred A. Knopf, Inc. Text © 1974, 1977, 1983, 1991 by Dennis Lee. Illustrations © by Debbie Tilley. Used by permission of Alfred A. Knopf, an imprint of Random House Children's Books, a division of Random House. Copyright from DINOSAUR DINNER (WITH A SLICE OF ALLIGATOR PIE) by Dennis Lee, copyright Compilation © 1997 by Alfred A. Knopf, Inc. Text © 1974, 1977, 1983, 1991 by Dennis Lee. Illustrations © by Debbie Tilley. Used by permission of Alfred A. Knopf, an imprint of Random House Children's Books, a division of Random House. Also from Jelly Belly (Macmillan of Canada, 1983) © 1983 Dennis Lee. With permission of the author.

"Circle of the Sun," © 1980 Sally Rogers P. Thrushwood Press Publishing. With permission of the author.

"Come A'Look A' See" © Louise Cullen. With permission of the author.

"Boom, Boom" © Ferron. With permission of the author.

"Dickery Dean" from DINOSAUR DINNER (WITH A SLICE OF ALLIGATOR PIE) by Dennis Lee, copyright Compilation © 1997 by Alfred A. Knopf, Inc. Text © 1974, 1977, 1983, 1991 by Dennis Lee. Illustrations © by Debbie Tilley. Used by permission of Alfred A. Knopf, an imprint of Random House Children's Books, a division of Random House. Also from Jelly Belly (Macmillan of Canada, 1983) © 1983 Dennis Lee. With permission of the author.

"Dirty Bill from Vinegar Hill" © Aubrey Davis. With permission of the author.

"Hugh, Hugh" by Dennis Lee. From JELLY BELLY (Macmillan of Canada, 1983). Copyright © 1983 Dennis Lee. With permission of the author.

"I Saw a Snake" © Lois Simmie. With permission of the author.

"I See the Moon" by Meredith Willson © 1952, 1953 Plymouth Music Co., Inc. © Renewed 1980, 1981 Frank Music Corp. and Meredith Willson Music. This arrangement

© 2006 Frank Music Corp. and Meredith Willson Music. All rights reserved. Used by permission.

"Lullaby, Lullaby" from LULLABY BERCEUSE by Connie Kaldor © Word of Mouth Music. With permission of the author.

"The Moment I Saw You." Traditional tune—lyrics by Graham Nash. © Nash Notes (CMRRA). Used by permission.

"Nelly Go 'Cross the Ocean" © Kathy Reid-Naiman. With permission of the author.

"Pick It Up" by Woody Guthrie © Folkways Music Publishers, Inc. Used by permission.

"Ponies Are Walking" © Kathy Reid Naiman 1998. With permission of the author.

"Put Your Shoes On, Lucy" by Hank Fort © 1947 by Bourne Co. Copyright Renewed. All Rights Reserved. International Copyright Secured. Used by permission.

"Prairie Lullaby" from LULLABY BERCEUSE by Connie Kaldor © Word of Mouth Music. With permission of the author.

"Ride, Baby, Ride" © Louise Cullen. With permission of the author.

"Rock Me Easy" by Dennis Lee. From JELLY BELLY (Macmillan of Canada, 1983). Copyright © 1983 Dennis Lee. With permission of the author.

"Rock-a-Bye You" by Theresa Mckay. With permission of the author.

"Sittin' in a High Chair." Words and Music by Hap Palmer and Martha Cheney ©Hap-Pal Music, www.happalmer.com, www.babysong-shp.com. With permission of the author.

"Three Tickles" from DINOSAUR DINNER (WITH A SLICE OF ALLIGATOR PIE) by Dennis Lee, copyright Compilation © 1997 by Alfred A. Knopf, Inc. Text © 1974, 1977, 1983, 1991 by Dennis Lee. Illustrations © by Debbie Tilley. Used by permission of Alfred A. Knopf, an imprint of Random House Children's Books, a division of Random House. Also from JELLY BELLY (Macmillan of Canada, 1983) © 1983 Dennis Lee. With permission of the author.

"What'll I do with the Baby-o?" © Jean Ritchie Geordie Music Publishing Co. With permission of the author.

"When The Rain Comes Down," © 1986 Bob Devlin. With permission of Jessie Devlin.

"Wobbidobs," © Tom Pease, Tomorrow River Music, 1993. With permission of the author.

And thanks to all the Parents, Teachers, Children's Librarians, and Early Childhood Educators who keep these rhymes and songs alive by passing them on through the oral tradition.

Index
to Rhymes and Songs by TYPE

ACTION RHYMES

Acka Backa Soda Cracker, 58
The Bear and the Bees, 63
Chop Chop Choppity Chop, 58
Criss Cross Applesauce, 58
Hickory Dickory Dock, 58
I Saw A Snake Go By One Day, 58
I'm Toast in the Toaster, 59
Jack in the Box, 59
Jelly in the Bowl, 59
Leg over Leg, 59
The Little Boy Goes in the Tunnel, 59
Little Man in a Coal Pit, 60
Marching in Our Wellingtons, 60
Mix and Stir, 60
The North Wind Shall Blow, 60
Pat Your Head, 60
Popcorn, 60
Slice Slice, 61
There Was a Little Man, 61
These Are Baby's Fingers, 61
This Is the Key to the Kingdom, 61
Tony Chestnut, 62
The Turtle Went Up the Hill, 62
Up Up the Candlestick, 62
Way Up High in the Banana Tree, 63
Wiggle Waggle, 63
You Be the Ice Cream, 63

ACTION SONGS

Baby Put Your Pants On, 66
Big Blue Boat, 68
Clap Your Hands, Little Sally, 66
Come Along and Sing with Me, 66
The Cuckoo Clock, 72
Dirty Bill, 71
The Eensy Weensy Spider, 66
Everybody Knows I Love Your Toes, 67
The Grandfather Clock, 67
Grandma Mose, 67
Head and Shoulders, 67
I Love Bubblegum, 69
I'm a Little Teapot, 68
Jeremiah, 68
Let's Clap Our Hands Together, 68
Mmm-Ah Went the Little Green Frog, 68
Obidayah, 69
On My Foot There Is a Flea, 69
Peek-a-Boo, 69
Rain Is Falling Down, 70
Roly Poly, 70
Round and Round the Garden, 70
Row, Row, Row Your Boat, 70
A Rum Sum Sum, 71
She Didn't Dance, 72
Teddy Bear, Teddy Bear, 72
These Are the Toes of My Baby, 72
Tick Tock, Tick Tock, 72
Tommy Thumbs, 73
Up Down, Turn Around, 73
The Wheels on the Bus, 73
When the Rain Comes Down, 74
Zoom Zoom Zoom, 74

BOUNCING RHYMES

Baby Baby Dumpling, 76
Bangor Boats, 76
Bouncy Bouncy Baby, 76
Cha-Cha-Chabogin, 76
Dickery Dean, 82

Doctor Foster, 76
From Wibbleton To Wobbleton, 76
Giddyap, Horsie, to the Fair, 77
Grand Old Duke Of York, 77
Here We Go Up, Up, Up, 77
Humpty Dumpty, 77
I Want Someone to Buy Me a Pony, 77
Mother and Father and Uncle John, 78
Och a Na Nee, 78
One, Two, Three, 78
Our Dear Friend Mother Goose, 78
Pace Goes the Lady, 78
Pony Girl, 78
Rickety Rickety Rocking Horse, 79
Ride a Cock Horse, 79
Ride, Baby, Ride, 79
A Robin and a Robin's Son, 79
Seesaw, Margery Daw, 79
She Fell into the Bathtub, 79
A Smooth Road, 80
A Smooth Road to London Town, 80
Ten Galloping Horses, 80
This Is The Way The Farmer Rides, 80
This Is The Way The Ladies Ride, 81
To Market, To Market, 81
Tommy O'Flynn, 81
Trit, Trot to Boston, 82
Trot, Trot, Trot, 82

CIRCLE GAMES AND DANCES

The Baby Bear Waltz, 84
Can You Point Your Fingers and Do the Twist?, 84
Creeping, Creeping, Creeping, 84
Here is a Beehive, 84
Mama's Little Baby Loves Dancing Dancing, 85
Nelly Go 'Cross the Ocean, 85
The Ponies Are Walking, 85
Rig a Jig Jig, 86
Ring Around the Rosie, 86
Round and Round the Cobbler's Bench, 86
Round and Round the Haystack, 87
Sally Go Round the Sun, 87
See the Sleeping Bunnies, 87
See the Ponies, 87
Shoofly, 88

FACE RHYMES

Brow Bender, Eye Peeper, 90
A Butterfly Kiss, 90
Chop-a-Nose Day, 91
Earkin, Hearkin, 90
Eye Winker, Tom Tinker, 90
Eyes, Nose, Cheeky Cheeky Chin, 90
Hana, Hana, Hana, 90
Head Bumper, 91
Here Sits Farmer Giles, 91
Here Sits the Lord Mayor, 91
Knock at the Door, 91
The Moon Is Round, 91
Ring the Bell, 92
Two Little Eyes, 92

FINGER PLAY and HAND RHYMES

Baby's Nap, 99
Bunnies' Bedtime, 98
Chicken in the Barnyard, 94
Cobbler, Cobbler, 94
Come A' Look A' See, 94
Creeping, Creeping, Creeping, 94
The Dog Says, "Bow Wow," 94
Foxy's Hole, 98
Here Are my Lady's Knives and Forks, 94
Here Is a Beehive, 95
Here Is a Bunny, 95
Here Is a Nest for a Bluebird, 95
Here Is a Tree, 95
Here Is the Church, 95
Here's a Ball for Baby, 96
Here's a Cup, 97
Here's a Leaf, 97
Here's a Little Boy, 97
Let's Go to Sleep, 97
Mix the Bannock, 97

Once I Caught a Fish Alive, 98
Pat It, 98
Pat-a-Cake, 98
See My Ten Fingers Dance and Play, 98
Soft Kitty, Warm Kitty , 99
There Was a Little Mouse, 99
These Are Baby's Fingers, 99
This Is My Mother, 99
This Is the Boat, the Golden Boat, 100
This Little Cow, 100
This Little Girl Found an Egg, 100
This Little Train, 100
Tommy Thumbs, 101
Two Little Bluebirds, 101
Two Little Dicky Birds, 101
Under the Darkness, 101
What Do You Suppose?, 102
Where Is Thumbkin?, 102
Whoops! Johnny, 102
Wind the Bobbin Up, 102

FRENCH SONGS

Alouette, gentille alouette, 104
Au clair de la lune, 104
Bateau sur l'eau, 104
C'est le temps, 104
Do, do, l'enfant do, 105
Fais dodo, 105
Frère Jacques, 105
Il pleut, il mouille, 105
Maman, papa, et oncle Simon, 105
Les marionnettes, 104
Le petit coupeur de paille, 105
Les petits poissons, 105
Sur le pont d'Avignon, 106
Tape, tape, tape, 106
Trotte, trotte, 106
Vent frais, 106

GREETING SONGS

Bell Horses, 108
Come A' Look A' See, 108
Come Along and Sing with Me, 108
Hello Everyone, 108
Hello, My Friends, Hello, 109
Here Are, 109
Hickety Pickety Bumblebee, 109
I'm in the Mood, 110
Let's Clap Our Hands Together, 110
The More We Get Together, 110
Up Down, Turn Around, 110

GOODBYE SONGS

Bell Horses, 112
Down By the Station, 112
Goodbye Everyone, 112
Goodbye, My Friends, Goodbye, 112
Goodbye Train, 113
It's Time to Say Goodbye to Our Friends, 113
Now It's Time to Say Goodbye, 113
So Long, 113
Up Down, Turn Around, 114

LULLABIES

All Little Ones Are Sleeping, 116
All the Pretty Little Horses, 118
Autumn Lullaby, 117
Babushka Baio, 117
Baby's Boat, 116
Bed Is Too Small, 116
Brahms' Lullaby, 119
Bye, Baby, Bye, 117
Bye O Baby, Bye, 117
Canadian Lullaby, 116
Close Your Eyes, 120
The Cuckoo, 120
Douglas Mountain, 122
Fuzzy Wuzzy Caterpillar, 117
Ho, Ho, Watanay, 118
Hush, Little Baby, 118
I See the Moon, 118
I'll Love You Forever, 116

Kum ba yah, 119
Listen to the Tree Bear, 119
Lou, Lou, Lou, Pretty Baby, 119
Lullaby, and Good Night, 119
Lullaby, Lullaby, 120
Mister Moon, 120
The Moment I Saw You, 120
Once: a Lullaby, 121
Prairie Lullaby, 124
Raisins and Almonds, 123
Rock-a-Bye, Baby, 121
Rock-a-Bye You, 121
Rock Me Easy, 121
Rose, Rose, Rose, Red, 122
Sailing, 122
Sleep, Baby, Sleep, 122
Star Light, Star Bright, 122
Tall Trees, 123
Twinkle, Twinkle Little Star, 123
Watch the Stars, 124
Yo Te Amo, 124

RHYMES IN OTHER LANGUAGES

Cho Chi, 126
Das Ist Der Daumen, 126
Deem Chung Chung, 126
Frère Jacques, 126
Hana, Hana, Hana, 126
Ho, Ho, Watanay, 126
Liang Zhe Lao Hu, 127
De Maan Is Rond, 127
Norwegian Lullaby, 128
Roly Poly (Cantonese), 127
Roly Poly (Mandarin), 127
Tortillitas, 128
Yo Te Amo, 128

SONGS

Ally Bally, 130
As I Was Walking to Town One Day, 130
Baby Put Your Pants On, 130
Boom, Boom, Baby Goes Boom Boom, 131
Circle of the Sun, 131
Coulter's Candy, 130
Dance to your Daddy, 131
Down By the Bay, 131
Dropped My Hat, 133
Horsey, Horsey, 132
Hungry, Hungry, 132
Hurry, Hurry, 133
I Had a Rooster, 133
It's Time to Put Away, 134
Land of the Silver Birch, 134
Let's All Clean Up Together, 134
Lightly Row, 134
May There Always Be Sunshine, 134
My Dog Rags, 135
My Paddle, 135
Pick It Up, 133
Pretty Painted Butterfly, 135
Put Your Shoes On, Lucy, 135
Simple Gifts, 136
Sittin' in a High Chair, 135
What'll I Do with the Baby-o?, 136
Wiggly Woo, 136
Wobbidobs, 132
You Are My Sunshine, 136

SPANISH RHYMES

Arrullo, 138
Caballito blanco, 138
Canción de despedida, 138
Cinco calabacitas, 138
Cinco pollitos, 138
Hallando un huevo, 138
Hola a todos, 138
Las Lechusas, 139
Mi carita, 139
Mis cinco sentidos, 139
Mis manos amistosas, 139
Manzana, 139
Palmas, palmitas, 139
Los pollitos, 139
¡Que linda manita!, 140

¡Que llueva!, 140
La señora gorda, 140
Tortillitas para mamá, 140
Tres pecesitos, 140

STORY RHYMES

As I Was Going Down the Stair, 142
As I Was Standing in the Street, 142
Catch Her Crow, 142
Diddle, Diddle, Dumpling, 142
Grandma Mose, 142
Gregory Griggs, 142
Grey Goose and Gander, 142
Hannah Bantry in the Pantry, 142
Here Am I, 143
Hippity Hop, 143
How Many Miles to Babylon?, 143
Ladybug, Ladybug, 143
Let's Go to Bed, 143
Little Jumping Joan, 143
The Man in the Moon, 143
My Old Friend Jake, 143
Old John Muddlecombe, 143
On Saturday Night I Lost My Wife, 143
One Misty Moisty Morning, 143
There Was a Man Named Michael Finnegan, 143
There Was a Young Farmer from Leeds, 144
There Was an Old Woman Lived Under the Stairs, 144
There Was an Old Woman Tossed Up in a Basket, 144

TICKLING RHYMES

Bumblebee, Bumblebee, 146
A Butterfly Kiss, 146
Chicken in the Barnyard, 146
Creepy Mouse, 146
Here Is a Beehive, 146
I'm Going to Bore a Hole, 146
Jeremiah, 146
The Little Mice Go Creeping, 147
Pussy Cat, Pussy Cat , 147
Round About, Round About, 147
Round and Round the Garden, 147
Round and Round the Haystack, 147
Round the World, 147
See the Little Mousie, 148
Slowly, Slowly, 148
Teddy Bear, Teddy Bear, 148
There Was a Little Mouse, 148
Three Tickles (Pizza, Pickle), 147
What Shall We Do with a Lazy Katie?, 148

TOE-WIGGLING and FOOT-PATTING RHYMES

Cobbler, Cobbler, 150
Cock-a-Doodle-Doo, 150
Diddle, Diddle Dumpling, 150
Hob, Shoe, Hob, 150
Hugh, Hugh, 150
Let's Go to the Woods Today, 151
Pitty, Patty, Polt, 151
Put Your Shoes on, Lucy, 151
See-saw, Margery Daw, 151
See-saw, Sacradown, 151
Shoe the Colt, 151
Shoe the Little Horse, 152
There Is a Cobbler on our Street, 152
This Little Cow, 152
This Little Pig Had a Rub-a-Dub-Dub, 152
This Little Piggy Went to Market, 152
Wee Wiggy, Poke Piggy, 152

Index

to Rhymes and Songs by FIRST LINE

A

Acka backa soda cracker, 58
Adiós a todos, 138
All through the night, 116
Ally Bally, Ally Bally Bee, 130
Alouette, gentille alouette, 104
Another day's passed, 116
Ansi font, font, font, 104
As I was going down the stair, 142
As I was standing in the street, 142
As I was walking to town one day, 130
Au clair de la lune, 104

B

Babies are born in the circle of the sun, 131
Baby baby dumpling, 76
Baby put your pants on, 66, 130
Baby's boat's a silver moon, 116
Bangor boats away, 76
Bateau sur l'eau, 104
Bed is too small for my tired head, 116
Bell horses, 108, 112
Boom, boom, baby goes boom boom, 131
Bouncy bouncy baby, 76
Brow bender, eye peeper, 90
Bumblebee, bumblebee, 146
A butterfly kiss, 90, 146
Bye-o baby, bye, 117

C

C'est le temps, 104
Caballito blanco, sácame de aquí, 138
Can you point your fingers and do the twist, 84
Catch her crow, 142
Cha-cha-chabogin, 76
Chicken in the barnyard, 94, 146
Cho Chi, 126
Chop chop choppity chop, 58
Cinco calabacitas sentadas en un portón, 138
Cinco pollitos, 138
Clap your hands, little Sally, 66
Cobbler, cobbler, mend my shoe, 94, 150
Cock-a-doodle-doo, 150
Come a' look a' see, 94, 108
Come along and sing with me, 66, 108
Come, my bunnies, 98
Creeping, creeping, creeping, 84, 94
Creepy mouse, 146
Criss, cross, applesauce, 58
Cum by yah, 117

D

Dance to your daddy, 131
Das ist der daumen, 126
Deem chung chung, 126
Diddle, diddle, dumpling, my son John, 142, 150
Do, do, l'enfant do, 105
Doctor Foster went to Gloucester, 76
The dog says, "Bow wow," 94
Down at the bottom, where you reach the ground, 132
Down by the bay, 131
Down by the station, 112
Duérmete mi niña, 138

E

Earkin, hearkin, 90
The eensy weensy spider, 66
Éste niño halló un huevo, 138
Everybody knows I love your toes, 67
Eye winker, Tom Tinker, 90
Eyes, nose, cheeky cheeky chin, 90

F
Fais dodo, 105
Frère Jacques, 105, 126
From Wibbleton to Wobbleton, 76
Fuzzy wuzzy caterpillar, 117

G
Giddyap, horsie, to the fair, 77
Go to sleep my darling baby, 117
Goodbye everyone, 112
Goodbye train, 113
Goodbye, my friends, goodbye, 112
The grand old Duke of York, 77
The grandfather clock goes, 67
Grandma Mose was sick in bed, 67, 142
Gregory Griggs, Gregory Griggs, 142
Grey goose and gander, 142

H
Hola a todos, 138
Hana, hana, hana, 90, 126
Hannah Bantry in the pantry, 142
Head and shoulders, 67
Head bumper, 91
Hello everyone, 108
Hello, my friends, hello, 109
Here am I, 143
Here are my lady's knives and forks, 94
Here are, 109
Here is a beehive, 84, 95, 146
Here is a bunny, 95
Here is a nest for a bluebird, 95
Here is a tree, 95
Here is the church, 95
Here sits Farmer Giles, 91
Here sits the Lord Mayor, 91
Here we go up, up, up, 77
Here's a ball for Baby, 96
Here's a cup, 97
Here's a leaf, 97
Here's a little boy, 97
Hickety pickety bumblebee, 109
Hickory dickory dock, 58
Hippity hop, 143
Ho, ho, watanay, 118, 126
Hob, shoe, hob, 150
Hola a todos, 138
Horsey, horsey, 132
How many miles to Babylon?, 143
Hugh, Hugh at the age of two, 150
Humpty Dumpty, 77
Hungry, hungry, 132
Hurry, hurry, 133
Hush little baby, 118
Hush-a-bye, don't you cry, 118

I
I had a rooster, 133
I dropped my hat, 133
I love to row in my big blue boat, 68
I saw a snake go by one day, 58
I see the moon, 118
I want someone to buy me a pony, 77
I'm a little teapot, 68
I'm in the mood for singing, 110
I'm toast in the toaster, 59
Il pleut, il mouille, 105
I'm Dirty Bill from Vinegar Hill, 71
I'm going to bore a hole, 146
It's time to put away, 134
It's time to say goodbye to our friends, 113

J
Jack in the box, 59
Jelly in the bowl, 59
Jeremiah, blow the fire, 68, 146

K
Knock at the door, 91
Kum ba yah, my Lord, kum ba yah, 119

L

Ladybug, ladybug, 143
Land of the silver birch, 134
Las lechusas, las lechusas, 139
Leg over leg, 59
Let's all clean up together, 134
Let's clap our hands together, 68, 110
Let's go to bed, 143
Let's go to sleep, 97
Let's go to the woods today, 151
Liang zhe lao hu, 127
Lightly row, 134
Listen to the tree bear, 119
The little boy goes in the tunnel, 59
Little man in a coal pit, 60
The little mice go creeping, 147
Lou, lou, lou, pretty baby, 119
Lullaby, and good night, 119
Lullaby, lullaby, 120

M

De maan is rond, 127
Mama's little baby loves dancing dancing, 85
Maman, papa, et oncle Simon, 105
The man in the moon, 143
La manzana se pasea, 139
Marching in our Wellingtons, 60
May there always be sunshine, 134
Mi carita, recondita, tiene ojos y nariz, 139
Mister moon, mister moon, 120
Mix and stir, 60
Mix the bannock, 97
Mmm-ah went the little green frog, 68
The moment I saw you, 120
The moon is round, 91
The more we get together, 110
Mother and father and uncle John, 78
My dog, Rags, 135
My mother and your mother, 91
My mother gave me a nickel, 69
My old friend Jake was thin as a snake, 143
My paddle's keen and bright, 135

N

Nelly go cross the ocean, 85
The north wind shall blow, 60
Norwegian Lullaby, 128
Now it's time to say goodbye, 113
Now it's time to say good night, 120

O

Och a na nee, 78
Old John Muddlecombe lost his cap, 143
On my foot there is a flea, 69
On Saturday night I lost my wife, 143
Once I was a baby lamb, 121
One, two three, one, two three, waltzing with bears, 84
One misty moisty morning, 143
One, two, three, 78
One, two, three, four, five, 98
Our dear friend Mother Goose, 78

P

Pace goes the lady, 78
Palmas, palmitas, 139
Pat it, 98
Pat your head, 60
Pat-a-cake, 98
Peek-a-boo, 69
Le petit coupeur de paille, 105
Les petits poissons, 105
Pitty, patty, polt, 151
Pizza, pickle, pumpernickel, 147
Los pollitos dicen, pió, pió, pió, 139
The ponies are walking, 85
Pony girl, 78
Popcorn, 60
Pretty painted butterfly, 135
Pussy cat, pussy cat , 147
Put your finger in foxy's hole, 98
Put your shoes on, Lucy, 135, 151

Q

Que linda manita, 140
Que llueva, que llueva, 140

R

Rain is falling down, 70
Rickety rickety rocking horse, 79
Ride a cock horse, 79
Ride, baby, ride, 79
Rig a jig jig, 86
Ring around the rosie, 86
Ring the bell, 92
A robin and a robin's son, 79
Rock me easy, 121
Rock-a-bye, baby, 121
Rock-a-bye you high, 121
Roly poly (Cantonese), 127
Roly poly (Mandarin), 127
Roly poly, 70
Rose, Rose, Rose, Red, 122
Round about, round about, 147
Round and round the cobbler's bench, 86
Round and round the garden, 147
Round and round the haystack, 87, 147
Round the world, 147
Row, row, row your boat, 70
A rum sum sum, 71

S

Sailing, 122
Sally go round the sun, 87
Scrub, scrub, splash, splash, splash, 71
See my ten fingers dance and play, 98
See the little bunnies, 87
See the little mousie, 148
See the ponies, 87
Seesaw, Margery Daw, 79, 151
See-saw, Sacradown, 151
La señora gorda fue de paseo, 140
She didn't dance, dance, dance, 72
She fell into the bathtub, 79
Shoe the colt, 151
Shoe the little horse, 152
Shoofly, don't bother me, 88
Sittin' in a high chair, 135
Sleep, baby, sleep, 122
Slice, slice, 61
Slowly, slowly, 148
A smooth road, 80
A smooth road to London Town, 80
Snow is falling on Douglas Mountain, 122
So long, 113
Soft kitty, warm kitty, 99
Star light, star bright, 122
The sun has gone from the shining sky, 117
Sur le pont d'Avignon, 106
Swing me just a little bit higher, 69

T

Tall trees, 123
Tape, tape, tape, 106
Teddy bear, teddy bear, 72, 148
Ten galloping horses, 80
There is a cobbler on our street, 152
There was a little man, 61
There was a little mouse, 148
There was a little mouse who found a piece of cheese, 99
There was a man named Michael Finnegan, 143
There was a young farmer from Leeds, 144
There was an old woman lived under the stairs, 144
There was an old woman tossed up in a basket, 144
There's a worm at the bottom of my garden, 136
These are baby's fingers, 61, 99
These are the toes of my baby, 72
This is baby ready for a nap , 99
This is my mother, 99
This is the boat, the golden boat, 100
This is the key to the kingdom, 61
This is the way the farmer rides, 80
This is the way the ladies ride, 81
This little cow, 100, 152

This little girl found an egg, 100
This little pig had a rub-a-dub-dub, 152
This little piggy went to market, 152
This little train, 100
Tick tock, tick tock, 72
Tis the gift to be simple, 136
To market, to market, 81
To my little one's cradle in the night, 123
Tommy O'Flynn, 81
Tommy Thumbs, 73, 101
Tony Chestnut, 62
Tortillitas para mamá, 128, 140
Tres pecesitos se fueron a nadar, 140
Trit, trot to Boston, 82
Trot, trot, trot, 82
Trotte, trotte, 106
The turtle went up the hill, 62
'Twas on a summer's evening, 120
Twinkle, twinkle little star, 123
Two little bluebirds, 101
Two little dicky birds, 101
Two little eyes, 92

U

Una boquita para comer, 139
Under the darkness, 101
Up down, turn around (goodbye), 114
Up down, turn around (hello), 73, 110
Up up the candlestick, 62

V

Vent frais, 106

W

Watch the stars, 124
Way up high in the banana tree, 63
Wee Wiggy, Poke Piggy, 152
What do you suppose?, 102
What is the matter with Dickery Dean?, 82
What shall we do with a Lazy Katie?, 148
What'll I do with the baby-o?, 136
The wheels on the bus, 73
When the rain comes down, 74
When the sun on the prairie is going to bed, 124
Where is Thumbkin?, 102
Whoops! Johnny, 102
Wiggle waggle, went the bear, 63
Wind the bobbin up, 102

Y

Yo te amo, 124, 128
Yo tengo dos manos, 139
You are my sunshine, 136
You be the ice cream, 63

Z

Zoom zoom zoom, 74

Songs Recorded

on the Enclosed CD

1. Lou, Lou, Lou, Pretty Baby
2. The Moment I Saw You
3. Yo Te Amo
4. Peek-a-Boo
5. Rain Is Falling Down
6. Baby's Boat
7. Lightly Row
8. Big Blue Boat
9. Up Down, Turn Around
10. Round and Round the Garden
11. Babushka Baio
12. The Moon Is Round
13. Mr. Moon
14. I See the Moon
15. Tall Trees
16. Dance to Your Daddy
17. My Paddle
18. Obidayah
19. A Smooth Road
20. Bouncy Bouncy Baby
21. Ten Galloping Horses
22. What'll I Do with the Baby-o?
23. Trit, Trot to Boston
24. Boom, Boom
25. Shoofly
26. Little Man in the Coal Pit
27. Baby Put Your Pants On
28. Norwegian Lullaby
29. Let's Go to Sleep
30. Fuzzy Wuzzy Caterpillar
31. Canadian Lullaby
32. There Was a Little Mouse
33. Ho, Ho, Watanay
34. All Little Ones
35. Tick Tock
36. Up Down, Turn Around

Listening time: approximately 30 minutes.

Praise for *I'm a Little Teapot! Presenting Preschool Storytime* by Jane Cobb

"All of the children's librarians in my system love this book and would be lost without it. It is their "storytime bible." Jane Cobb has come up with the most helpful storytime resource I have seen in ages (and I have seen a lot). ... Future children's librarians should not be deprived of such a treasure." —M. Conway

"I run a public storytime that caters to a wide variety of ages and I rely on this book for help—every season and every session. Great ideas and a wonderful selection of topics and materials are just a part of the charm of this book."—Gwynne Nelson

"Children's librarian Cobb has organized the material into 63 themes, but her focus is on good stories and songs rather than on sticking rigidly to a particular subject. She includes valuable program planning and presentation tips and useful bibliographies, all of which show and tell of her commitment to helping adults bring children the pleasure of great stories." —BOOKLIST

"Children's Librarians, preschool teachers, daycare workers, students and individuals teaching Early Childhood Education or library storytelling courses will find this book to be an invaluable resource. Buy it, use it, treasure it!"—RESOURCE LINKS

"The strength of this resource is in its comprehensiveness and practicality. Cobb's experience in planning and presenting storytime programs for young children shows in the wealth of information here. The extensive bibliography and first line index to nursery rhymes, fingerplays and songs, is presented in a well-organized and easy-to-use arrangement. Highly recommended."—BCLA REPORTER

"A wonderful and useful collection ... a must for anyone who regularly does preschool storytimes!"—EMERGENCY LIBRARIAN

"Jane Cobb captures the interests of preschoolers with her selection of children's picture books and with her age-appropriate storytime ideas. It has helped to bring children's literature alive for my students."—Joan Turecki

"A must for any preschool!"—Wanda Andrade

"An inspiration no facility should be without!"—Joanne and Kids at Sunshine Family Daycare

Order Form

To order by mail, print this order form and mail it along with your check or money order payment. You can also order ONLINE with your CREDIT CARD. Go to www.blacksheeppress.com

In Canada mail to:
Black Sheep Press
P.O. Box 2392
349 West Georgia St.
Vancouver, BC V6B 3W7

In the US mail to:
Black Sheep Press
P.O. Box 2217
Point Roberts, WA 98218-2217

Order Information

Qty	Description	Price	Total
	I'm a Little Teapot! Presenting Preschool Storytime	$29.95	
	What'll I Do With the Baby-o? Nursery Rhymes, Songs, and Stories for Babies (CD included)	$39.95	
		Add Handling +	$9.00
	*Please make check or money order payable to **Black Sheep Press**.*	**Add Shipping ($2.00 per book)** +	
		Subtotal +	
		Add 6% GST in Canada +	
		Total Payment Enclosed	

Shipping Information

Name ________________________

Address ________________________

City ________________________

State/Province ________________________

Zip/Postal Code ________________________

Phone ________________________

Email (optional) ________________________

Your order will be shipped via the postal system within five business days from the date of receipt of your payment and order form. If you have a rush order or a special request, please contact us.

Libraries, wholesalers and bookstores, please send purchase order numbers to Black Sheep Press by phone, fax, or email.

Black Sheep Press Contact Information:

P.O. Box 2392
349 West Georgia St.
Vancouver, BC V6B 3W7
Canada

P.O. Box 2217
Point Roberts, WA 98218-2217
U.S.A

Tel/Fax: (604) 731-2653
orders@blacksheeppress.com